Also by Sharon Sala

SUNSET

SHARON SALA

sourcebooks
casablanca

Published by Sourcebooks Casablanca, an imprint of Sourcebooks
P.O. Box 4410, Naperville, Illinois 60567-4410
(630) 961-3900
sourcebooks.com

Printed and bound in the United States of America.
BVG 10 9 8 7 6 5 4 3 2 1

Chapter 1

Bluejacket Hollow, Oklahoma

SATURDAY MORNING BEGAN LIKE EVERY OTHER morning on Charlie Bluejacket's farm until his nine-year-old daughter, Julia, came running in from outside in hysterics.

"Daddy, Daddy! Butters isn't in his pen, and I can't find him anywhere!" The little black-and-white pygmy goat was Julia's shadow, and a family pet.

Her mother, Frances, turned off all the burners at the stove and took off her apron, as Charlie put down the cup of coffee he'd been drinking.

Sonny Bluejacket, Charlie's younger brother, had been living with the family ever since a bull ride at a rodeo ended his career and nearly his life. He jumped up from the table, followed the others as they went outside to the goat pen, expecting to see coyote or cougar tracks, and blood.

But there was nothing to tell them what had happened. Just little goat tracks in the pen, and then leading out through a gate left ajar.

Julia was sobbing. "I shut the gate good last night, Daddy! I always do."

Sonny was circling the pen looking for signs but saw nothing but Julia's sneaker tracks. "I'll get the ATV and head north toward the creek," he said.

Frannie took her daughter by the hand. "We'll go south," she said.

"I'll check the driveway to see if I see tracks there, and if not, I'll go west," Charlie said, and they scattered like quail.

Sonny took off on the ATV, slowly winding his way through the heavily wooded areas around the farm, looking for signs. About a half hour later he rode into a clearing, saw little goat tracks on a patch of bare ground, and got off the ATV.

"Butters Bluejacket, you can't hide from me. I smell you, and I'm not going to chase you down. Get your little self out here now. Julia thinks something ate you, and hurry up. I don't have all day."

Moments later, the little black-and-white goat trotted out of the brush right in front of Sonny, and head-butted one of the front tires.

Sonny laughed. "Look at you being all tough," and as he slipped a lightweight cotton rope around Butters's neck, the little goat began to jump about in protest. "Oh no you don't! You had a chance to ride like a big boy, but you thought you needed to be all tough."

Sonny grabbed him by the horns, rolled him over onto his side, and hogtied the little goat's legs, like a calf at a roping competition.

Butters began protesting loudly, bleating pitifully as Sonny called his brother. "Hey bro, I found Butters. The little squirt came out of the brush and head-butted the ATV. Yeah, that's him making all this noise. I've got him hogtied, and he's riding in my lap all the way back, so you can tell Julia that Uncle Sonny found her baby."

"Good job," Charlie said.

"See you soon," Sonny said, then hopped on the ATV with the little goat in his lap and started the ATV with Butters bleating objections. "Yeah, yeah, I know," Sonny said. "Sorry about all this, but you shouldn't have run away. Julia thought something ate you, but I think you're too onery to be tasty."

They rode all the way home with Butters steadily bleating his disapproval. Fifteen minutes later, Sonny arrived and pulled up into the backyard where the family was waiting.

"Come get this noisy critter," Sonny said, and handed him off to Charlie.

"Thank you, Uncle Sonny," Julia cried, and then hurried to catch up to her father, who was carrying the goat back to its pen. There would be some remodeling to the goat pen before nightfall.

Sonny rode the ATV back into the shed, parked and hung the keys up on a nail beside the door, then headed back to the house. From the aroma drifting out the kitchen window, he guessed Frannie had gone back to making breakfast, but now he smelled like goat.

He went inside, bypassed the kitchen to wash up and

change clothes before going back to the table. He was headed up the hall toward the kitchen when Frannie called out.

"Sonny! Mailman needs you to sign for something!"

"Coming," he said, and hastened his stride to the front door and went outside to meet him. "Hey Wilson."

Wilson nodded. "Hey, Sonny. I need you to sign for this registered packet."

As soon as Sonny signed, Wilson handed over a large, fat, manila envelope. "Have a good day."

"You, too," Sonny said, glanced at the return address, then went back inside.

"Breakfast is ready," Frannie said.

"Coming," Sonny said, and headed to the kitchen while there was still food left to eat. He laid the packet aside and sat down at the table.

Charlie looked up. "What was it?"

"I don't know. From some law firm in Texas," he said.

"Are you in trouble?" Frances asked, as she put his plate of food down in front of him.

Sonny laughed. "Not that I know of. I left plenty of blood in the dirt back in Texas, but it was mine."

"Open it," Charlie said.

Sonny shrugged. "I will, just as soon as I eat this good food while its hot."

Charlie frowned.

Frances smiled at her husband's impatience and curiosity, and pretended not to see Julia sneaking food into her pocket to take out to Butters's pen later.

The meal progressed until Sonny had taken his last sip of coffee, and then he got up and brought the envelope back to the table. They were all teasing him about everything from being sued for child support for a kid he didn't know he had, to a pillow he'd taken from a motel when he was still on the rodeo circuit. But none of them could have ever guessed the contents of what was inside.

Sonny read the cover letter, then looked up in shock.

"Emmit Cooper died."

George frowned. "Isn't that the bullfighter who nearly got you killed?"

Sonny frowned. "Don't say that. It wasn't Emmit's fault. He stumbled and fell before he could distract the bull. But the bull was mad at me, not Emmit."

"Okay, so he's dead. Why is some lawyer telling you this?" George muttered.

"Because Emmit left everything to me in his will, which includes a thousand-acre spread in West Texas, and a horse operation, including a dozen registered Quarter Horses. I guess you all are finally getting me out of your hair. This is something I never saw coming, but it's my chance to start over."

Frances frowned. "Please tell me you're not going back to the rodeo."

"No way. I'll still be riding and training horses like I've been working horses for the ranchers around here, but these will be mine. This is unexpected, but I wouldn't deny this gift. Emmit had his reasons, and I will honor them," Sonny said.

At that point, his family reluctantly celebrated his good fortune, while Sonny read the rest of the paperwork in detail, then got his laptop and began looking up bus schedules.

Two days later, Sonny and Charlie were getting ready to leave for the bus station in Tulsa. He was loading his suitcase and duffel bag in Charlie's truck when he heard the sound of an approaching vehicle.

At the same moment, Charlie came flying out of the house with a harried look on his face. "Auntie just called. She said Dad heard about your inheritance and has been bragging around town that he's going with you."

At that moment, a dark cloud passed over the house, momentarily hiding the sun. Sonny felt the warning but was not surprised by the man's audacity.

"Doesn't matter, Charlie. He isn't going anywhere with me. He left Mom and us when we were kids, and has done nothing but drink and chase women ever since. She wouldn't let him back in the house, and I haven't said three words to him in years."

"There he comes, just the same," Charlie said, pointing as the old red Ford pickup came rattling up the tree-lined driveway.

Sonny took a deep breath, watching as Walker Bluejacket came to a sliding halt behind Charlie's truck and jumped out.

It was obvious the man hadn't changed clothes in days. His long hair was threaded with gray now, and hanging in two braids on either side of his face. His old black Stetson was as ratty as the rundown boots on his feet, and his once muscular chest had turned into a beer belly. But he still had the same oversized turquoise buckle on his belt, something he'd taken to wearing after Sonny won his first Championship Bull Rider buckle.

"Sonny! Sonny! Long time no see," Walker said and tried to hug him.

Sonny blocked the gesture with both hands and gave Walker a stony glare, a sign Charlie knew all too well.

"Walks-Off Bluejacket, as I live and breathe. I haven't seen you in what…fifteen or twenty years…and now you show up?" Sonny drawled.

Walker glared. "Did your mother teach you to call me that?" and the moment the words came out of his mouth, Sonny was in his face.

"Shut your mouth, old man. Our mother has been gone ten years and you did not even have the decency to show up to honor her at her funeral. You do not speak her name in our presence."

Walker eyed the men warily. They might be his sons, but they were also two big, angry men.

"Yeah, I know, I know. I was out of town, I think," Walker mumbled.

"You lie again. You were shacking up with Melissa Peters," Sonny said. "We have someplace to be. You need to go now."

"No, son. Don't be like that. Listen… I heard you're leaving the state again, and I'll drive you wherever you need to go," Walker said.

"I don't need a driver, and you lost your right to call me son a long time ago. You're a leech trying to scam what you can, even from your own family. You go nowhere with me," Sonny said.

Walker exploded. He came at Sonny with his fists doubled, and the first swing he took was aimed at Sonny's chest. He knew Sonny died twice on the operating table. But he wouldn't stay dead, losing Walker's chance to inherit a third of everything Sonny owned. Now he just wanted to hurt him.

Sonny threw up an arm in time to block the first blow, but the second one hit him hard in the ribs.

Before Sonny could respond, Charlie hit Walker with a flying tackle, and had him on his back in seconds. Charlie was so angry his voice was shaking, and it wouldn't have taken much for him to choke the life out of the old man where he lay.

"You son of a bitch! You aimed for Sonny's chest. You know what happened. You know how he suffered. What kind of a devil tries to kill his own son?"

Walker kept struggling to get free. "Damn it, Charlie, don't be an ass. I didn't think, that's all."

"Let it go, Charlie," Sonny said, then pulled his

brother off and grabbed Walker by the collar and yanked him to his feet, and dragged him back to his truck. He threw him inside, then slammed the door. "You are a disgrace to the Bluejacket name. Get lost. Leave. Me. The. Hell. Alone. I don't ever want to see your face again."

Walker's rage rose again like smoke up a chimney. "You should be dead. I would be living off your money, and walking on your grave."

The shock of the words rolled through Sonny in waves as he braced both hands on either side of the driver's side window, and leaned in until he was only inches from his father's face.

"You are a blight upon this earth. You cause trouble for Charlie or me again, and you won't see another sunrise."

It was the look in his youngest son's eyes that put Walker's gut in a knot. He slammed the truck in reverse, backed up through Frances's flowerbed, and spun out as he drove away. When he got to the highway, he turned south on Highway 62 toward Henryetta.

Sonny was still reeling from his father's last words as Walker's taillights disappeared.

Charlie walked up behind him, and put a hand on Sonny's shoulder. He could see by the look on his face something terrible had passed between them.

"Sonny, what did he say to you?" Charlie asked.

"That I should have died. He would have been living off my money, and walking on my grave."

Charlie was in shock. "I knew he was rotten, but that's evil talk. He's messed up, Sonny. Messed up bad. Forget him. Get in the truck, brother. You have a future to meet."

They loaded up into the truck and left the farm. Less than an hour later, they were in Tulsa. Charlie parked on Greenwood Avenue and began unloading Sonny's bags on the sidewalk, and caught a glimpse of lingering anger in Sonny's expression.

"Don't worry about Dad, he tried you on. You didn't bite, and now he's on to his next scam, whatever it will be. We are happy for you. You lost a lot, little brother, but you didn't lose your life. You deserve this new start. Just remember the ancestors are always on your side, and we're only a phone call away."

Sonny hugged Charlie hard. "I'm going to miss you all, including my little niece," he said.

At the mention of his daughter, Charlie thrust his hand in his jacket pocket. "Dang, I almost forgot to give you this. Julia gave it to me when I took her to catch the school bus. She said it was so Uncle Sonny wouldn't forget her."

Sonny looked down at the little blue rock Charlie put in his hand and swallowed past the lump in his throat.

"We found it in the creek. I told her it was a piece of the sky. Tell Julia I love it, and could never forget my best girl. Tell her to take care of Butters, too."

Charlie rolled his eyes. "That dang goat is getting neutered tomorrow. I'm about to put an end to that head-butting. It's probably how he got out. He just butted the gate until it opened."

Sonny slipped the blue rock into the inner pocket of his jacket and zipped it shut. "Thanks for the ride, Charlie. Drive safe going home," he said, then picked up his bags and headed for the station.

Charlie stood watching until Sonny was inside, telling himself not to worry, and trying to be happy about the gift Sonny had been given. But there was no denying how much he was going to miss him. Then he got in his truck and headed home.

———

The bus was less than half full when the driver pulled out of the station. Sonny had chosen a seat at the back because he didn't like having strangers behind him, and from where he was sitting, he could see most of the passengers. A young couple sat head-to-head, whispering, stealing kisses, and holding hands all the way to their destination. Another couple sat in silence. The woman was crying. The man with her had his arm around her shoulders. A sad trip for them, Sonny thought.

People disembarked and others got on. Some slept. Some were on their phones. A few were reading magazines or books. To Sonny, they were symbolic of the microcosms of humanity. All colors. All ages. Some with the weight of the world on their shoulders. Others were looking toward rosy futures. Some were running away. Others were traveling to destinations unknown. He didn't know where he fit into the constantly changing crowd, but he felt hopeful. He'd been treading water for a long time now, and he'd finally been given the opportunity to swim.

But he was leaving behind the wooded land, the network of myriad creeks and rivers, and the rolling hills of home, and the farther he went, the flatter the land became, and it occurred to him as he rode that the geography was going to give him an unfettered view, no matter where he stood.

As a hunter, this was a negative. As the hunted, the enemy would be visible from any direction, and the moment that went through his mind, his father's face appeared before him. Sonny closed his eyes and the image disappeared, but he took it as a warning.

Walker wasn't done with him yet.

———————

A very long trip later, Sonny became the last westbound passenger in the bus, and when the driver began slowing down, he sat up straight and glanced out the window to read the sign at the city limits.

Crossroads, Texas: Population: 2,500

He had reached his destination.

The past was behind him.

There was nothing but opportunity before him, and he wasn't going to waste it.

Magnolia Brennen was scurrying around the dining area in the Yellow Rose Café, just as she did every day, waiting tables, sweeping up after messy customers, then wiping down the tables after they were cleared.

She liked her job and loved her boss, Pearl Fallon, who owned the café.

The day was finally drawing to an end, and they were getting ready to close. Maggie began sweeping, and Pearl was at the register counting out the day's take. Maggie had been thinking about the dream she'd had last night. She hadn't had a chance to talk to Pearl about it, but it had been so real she wanted to tell someone.

"Hey Pearl…"

Pearl kept counting. "Yeah?"

"Last night, I had the strangest dream. I was lying in the grass and covered in clouds of butterflies."

Pearl Fallon paused and looked up. "What does that mean?"

Maggie shrugged. "Probably nothing," she said, and kept sweeping, but she hadn't been able to get the dream out of her head. It had been magic. Her entire body had been covered in butterflies—so many that she could still feel the breeze from the flutter of those fragile wings as she was waking up.

She sighed. It had been so real, it had to mean something.

Pearl didn't know what was in Maggie's head right

now, but it was always in the clouds. Still, she paused at what she was doing and gave Maggie her full attention.

"Butterflies mean transformation, or change. Maybe something's coming your way," she said.

Maggie shrugged. "Maybe so, but I hope it's someone better than Jerry Lee. Like every man I've ever known, who makes promises he has no intention of keeping."

Pearl grimaced, remembering how she'd first seen Maggie—a pretty but skinny nineteen-year-old girl who had just been dumped on the steps of the Rose by a good-for-nothing man. Abandoned in the middle of nowhere with the clothes on her back and her worldly possessions in the duffel bag beside her. In thirty-degree weather, and with a dusting of snow on the ground, all she had against the cold was the zip-up sweatshirt she'd been wearing.

Pearl saw the drama playing out in her parking lot. Saw the man driving away, and the girl staggering to the steps of the Rose before she fell apart. It broke her heart.

She'd brought the girl inside and put a cup of hot coffee in her hands, but the girl couldn't stop crying long enough to take a sip. She just kept saying the same thing, over and over. "Why do people keep giving me away?"

Pearl didn't ask her what that meant. She just hired her on the spot.

As it turned out, Magnolia Brennen turned out to be

the best employee she'd ever had. Maggie's high cheek-bones, arched eyebrows, and thick black eyelashes shading the bluest of eyes, gave her an unusual beauty. Her lips were full and most often tilted in a smile. She'd come a long way from the young girl she'd been, to the woman she was today. Long legs, a lean body, and all the energy that comes with being young.

Pearl shook off the memory, waiting for Maggie to elaborate on the dream, but she'd stopped talking about butterflies. Pearl let it slide and began wiping down the tabletops while Maggie went outside to sweep the front porch and steps. Pearl started to tell her not to bother, then let her go. They were about to lock up anyway, and Maggie had a thing about sunsets.

The wind was flirting with the hem of Maggie's blue-and-white puff-sleeved dress as she went out onto the porch. The two-tiered skirt gathered at the waist stopped short just above her knees, and the shirred stretchy bodice with a square neckline was comfortable to work in. She owned three pairs of shoes, which were two more than what she had the day she was dumped at the Rose. A pair of blue-and-white sneakers, one good pair of black flats, and the pink Roper boots she often wore to work.

She gave the entryway a couple of swipes with the broom, and then walked to the west end of the porch to watch the sun slowly sliding below the horizon. The sky was already an explosion of purple and orange, with pink and yellow feathered in among the hues, just to make sure you were still paying attention. She considered sundown on the prairie as God's apology for every heartache she'd ever suffered.

On the days when Jerry Lee's face would flash before her, she would get angry all over again. But when she dreamed of him at night, it was always about the time before, when he was good to her and made her laugh, until she woke up remembering how deeply he'd betrayed her, and how gullible she'd been to ever believe a man like that.

She wrapped her arms around the porch post and leaned into it, watching the sky as the colors continued to bleed one into the other, and thought. *Lord, am I going to grow old alone because I trusted so blindly? I don't want that, but I can't bring myself to grieve my situation when You give me a daily masterpiece like this.*

Every day, like today, she sought solace in the kaleidoscope of colors as the sun made a run for the horizon, and here she was again, staring down Highway 86 as if desire alone would bring her a knight in shining armor. She might have stayed until dark had Pearl not yelled at her from inside the Yellow Rose.

"Maggie! Come in and help me finish so we can close up!"

Maggie pivoted on one heel and bolted. "Yes, ma'am! Comin'!" she yelled, and ran back into the diner.

"Lock the door and turn the Open sign to Closed. I've already shut down the kitchen," Pearl said.

"Yes, ma'am," Maggie said, and turned around to

flip the sign when she saw the Greyhound bus slowing down, then pulling into the parking lot.

One very tall man got out, retrieved his luggage, and then moved toward the Rose as the bus pulled away. From the stoop of his shoulders, and the suitcase and duffel bag he was carrying, it appeared that he'd also brought the weight of the world with him. He looked like he needed a hug.

"Wait, Pearl! One more customer."

Pearl sighed. "Is he drivin' or walkin'?"

"Walking...just got off the bus," Maggie said.

Pearl sighed. "We may be the only opportunity he's had all day to find food. I guess we're still open," and she headed for the kitchen to turn the grill back on.

Maggie watched the man come up the steps, pause to take off a black Stetson before coming inside, and as he did, she felt the air shifting around her again, like the butterflies from her dream.

Oh my God! He looks like the actor who played Sam in the 1883 series! The one who was in love with Elsa! But he's famous. He wouldn't be riding a bus to the middle of nowhere, or would he?

"Am I too late to order food?" he asked.

Still rattled by what she was feeling, Maggie managed a smile. "No sir, you are not."

"Then I'll take a cheeseburger with fries and the biggest glass of sweet tea you serve. Is there a place I can wash up?"

"Men's room is right down that hall to your left," she

said. He set his bags down by a table and walked away. As he did, she couldn't help but notice the long black ponytail hanging down his back, then she went to turn in the order.

"I heard," Pearl said. "Do you know who that is?"

Maggie blinked. "Well, he looks like the actor who played Sam in the series *1883*, but it's surely not. Do you know who he is?"

Pearl grinned. "I never thought of him like that, but now that you mention it, he sure does. However, that's Sonny Bluejacket. Used to be one hell of a bull rider on the circuit before he got stomped near to death. I haven't seen him in ages. I thought he went back to Oklahoma. It's where he was from."

"Bluejacket is a different name," Maggie said.

"It's a Shawnee name, but I think his tribal affiliation is Muscogee. Never was another rider like him."

Maggie shuddered at the thought of being stomped by one of those big rodeo bulls, and went to set a place for him at a table, along with the big glass of iced tea.

She was refilling salt and pepper shakers behind the counter when he came out from the men's room carrying his jacket. He hung the jacket and hat on another chair at his table and sat down.

The first thing Maggie noticed was how tall he stood without the weight on his back, and how striking he was. The tint of copper in his skin. Wide shoulders. Long arms and legs, that handsome face, and chocolate-brown eyes. He had a presence that demanded attention, but he was focused on the icy drink before him.

When he reached for the tea and drank the glass empty, the look of ecstasy on his face was like nothing she'd ever seen before. She hadn't seen a water bottle anywhere on the outside of his backpack, and the thought that he had been that thirsty hurt her heart. Without talking, she filled up a pitcher with tea and carried it to the table, along with another glass of ice. When she set it down before him, he looked up at her and smiled.

"Thank you."

A bell dinged in the kitchen and Pearl yelled, "Pickup!"

Maggie pivoted to get his food, unaware she was being observed.

Sonny kept watching her—the way she moved—those long legs beneath that short dress, pink cowboy boots, and the way her face lit up when she was talking. And her eyes—blue as the sky. He turned his head before she caught him staring.

"Enjoy," she said, as she set the food in front of him.

"Thank you, ma'am, I will."

Maggie smiled. "Not ma'am, just Maggie. Short for Magnolia."

"A most beautiful and delicate flower," he said.

Maggie watched his teeth flash white beneath a near-smile, and then he began eating as she walked away.

For Sonny, the food filled the long-empty spot

in his belly, and this place marked the end of his journey.

Maggie was still thinking about being named for a beautiful and delicate flower when Pearl came out of the kitchen and pulled up a chair beside Sonny.

"Long time, no see," she said.

He wiped his mouth and looked up. "Hello, Pearl. You still make the best cheeseburgers in Texas."

She smiled. "Where have you been?"

"Back home, living with my brother and his family. Helping out on the farm and training horses for ranchers."

"Good to have family," she said.

"They are good people, but I had long outstayed my welcome. I am here, because I got a letter from Emmit Cooper's lawyer, informing me that Emmit named me his heir."

"Oh, my lord! Congratulations! Are you selling or staying?" she asked.

Sonny popped a couple of fries in his mouth, then chewed and swallowed before he spoke again. "Planning to stay. Emmit wouldn't have given it to me, otherwise."

"Just be prepared to have to reclaim what's yours," Pearl said.

He frowned. "What do you mean?"

"Remember Wade Sutton?" she asked.

He frowned, thinking back, then shrugged. "No."

"Well, without a by your leave, Wade has moved

all of Emmit's horses onto his property, and is driving Emmit's truck around town like it was his own."

Sonny stilled. "The hell you say."

Maggie had been listening without comment. She knew nothing of the backstory except that Emmit had recently passed and she missed the old man, and who-ever Sonny Bluejacket was, he must have meant some-thing special to Emmit. But from the look on Sonny's face, Wade Sutton was in for more than he might be able to handle.

"I don't know where Emmit's place is, but I have directions. I do not know Wade Sutton or where his property is," Sonny said.

Before she knew it, Maggie heard herself offering him a ride.

"I know where Emmit's place is. I used to go out twice a month and clean his house for him. And I know where Wade Sutton's place is, too. Last I knew, the power was still on at your house, but I doubt there's any food. And if Wade didn't steal Emmit's furniture, too, it should still be fully furnished. We're about to close up shop. If you'll wait until I can help Pearl mop up, I'll take you, myself."

"I can mop," Pearl said, then got up and went behind the counter and pulled out a twelve-gauge shotgun. "It's loaded. You just aim and pull the trigger. It might be the incentive Wade needs to turn over stolen property without an argument."

"No gun," Sonny said. "I won't need it. Sheriff

Reddick already knows I inherited the property. We spoke while I was still in Oklahoma. Apparently, Emmit's lawyer notified him, too. And Matt Reddick is a friend from my rodeo days. Excuse me a moment," he said, and walked away to make a call. The phone rang three times before Sonny got an answer.

"Hello, this is Reddick."

"Matt, this is Sonny Bluejacket. I'm at the Yellow Rose. Pearl Fallon just told me that Wade Sutton has been driving Emmit Cooper's truck around town, and that he's moved all of Emmit's horses onto his place. Just want you to know, I'm about to go get my property back."

"Well shit, Sonny. Don't do something you can't take back. If he gives you a hard time, just tell him I'm on the way. Lucky for you I was on a call not too far from the Rose. I can be at the ranch in about half an hour. How are you getting there?"

"Magnolia Brennen is giving me a ride."

"Then go straight to Emmit's house. I'll pick you up there and you send Maggie home. I don't want her in the middle of this. It could get ugly."

Sonny looked across the room at the slender brunette with the pretty blue eyes and ready smile. The idea that she might come to harm because of him, made him cautious.

"Right. Thanks. I'll be waiting for you," he said.

"I'll be there as soon as I can," Reddick said.

Sonny walked back to where the women were talking.

"I'll take that ride out to the house. Sheriff Reddick is going to pick me up there and go with me to Sutton's."

Pearl nodded. "Good move. Maggie, I know you don't know Sonny, but I do, and you will always be safe with him."

"Yes, ma'am," Maggie said.

"Pearl, I appreciate the vote of confidence, and Miss Magnolia, I appreciate the ride," he said, left a handful of bills on the table, put his jacket and hat back on, and shouldered the backpack. "I'm ready when you are."

Maggie took a quick breath. "You can call me Maggie. Magnolia is a mouthful. I'm parked out back. We'll go this way," she said, and led them through the delivery entrance and across the parking area to her car—a gray 4x4 SUV.

Sundown had gone ahead and happened without Maggie tonight, but fortunately, the security lights surrounding the Yellow Rose were shining the way as she unlocked the trunk.

Sonny put his bags in it, then slid into the front seat and put his hat in his lap.

Maggie pointed to a lever beneath the seat. "Give yourself some leg room," she said, and then waited until he got settled and buckled up before she drove away.

Chapter 2

THE LIGHTS OF CROSSROADS WERE SCATTERED throughout the little town like fireflies, twinkling and blinking behind drawn curtains and shades that had been pulled. Sonny eyed them as they passed, wondering if people pulled curtains shut against the dark, or to trap the light within. Personally, he liked the night. It blurred the obvious and left everything to the imagination.

The residential area was a mixture of single-wide and double-wide trailers, simple houses with vinyl siding, and a few two-story houses, one of which had long since been turned into a hotel.

The small-town businesses consisted of a small branch of a bank that was based in Amarillo, a post office, a gas station with a mechanic on the premises, a small grocery store with a pharmacy inside, a feed store, a barber shop, and a vet clinic that was only open one day a week, compliments of a vet who drove down from Amarillo. There was a small urgent care with two nurses on staff, and a weekly visit from a doctor out of Silverton, and a small school that had a rattlesnake for a mascot.

The streets in town were blacktopped and potholed, and of the twenty streetlights in Crossroads, only eight lit up. It was said there were more dogs than people in residence, and better security than any Ring doorbell.

"Where do you live?" Sonny asked.

Maggie pointed to a little house just up ahead on the corner of the last paved street. "The one with the Christmas lights along the edge of the porch."

"Are those year-round or just up early?" he asked.

She grinned. "Year-round. I rent from Pearl. She used to live there and likes Christmas stuff. She lives above the Rose now. Right before I came to Crossroads, a couple of guys tried to break into the café. They didn't know she was still there in the back, and both of them got a butt load of buckshot for their troubles. Then she followed them out of the Rose as they ran, reloading as she went, and shot up their truck. They were lying on their bellies in the dirt, begging for mercy and an ambulance, when Emmit Cooper drove up. He called the sheriff and the ambulance, and then sat with Pearl until they came. After that, she remodeled the upstairs at the Rose and moved on-site, then made sure the world knew it."

Sonny nodded. "Pearl is typical of women who live out here. You either get tough, or you don't survive. I used to rodeo. When I was still on the circuit, I was in and out of this area all the time. She's always been good to me."

"And to me," Maggie said. "I was abandoned at the

Rose by a good-for-nothing man who had promised me the moon. But nineteen is a stupid age, and I made stupid mistakes. I don't know where I'd be if she hadn't given me a job on the spot."

Sonny frowned, but she didn't see it. Her gaze was on the dark road in front of her and the headlights shining the way.

"Lots of men are fools. Appears you ran across one. It's good you landed on your feet. Some don't have the grit to do that," he said.

Maggie spoke before she thought. "Are you a fool, Sonny?"

He chuckled softly, and the sound made the hair stand up on the back of her neck. Pearl said he was safe, but there was something about him that felt a little dangerous, yet well-contained.

"Oh, I've been a fool about a whole lot of things, but never about a woman. I was raised to honor the good ones, and stay shy of the wild ones," he said.

"How can you tell the difference?" she asked.

"Same way you can tell a good man from a bad one. There are givers and there are takers. You want a man who wants to give you the world, and even when he can't, just knowing that he wants to, is enough."

Maggie was speechless. That might be the most beautiful thing she'd ever heard come out of a man's mouth. She glanced at him quickly, got a glimpse of his silhouette from the dashboard light, and then focused her attention on driving. He was so still he looked like a statue, likely thinking about dealing with Wade Sutton. She felt bad for his situation and kept her eyes on the road.

———————

Sunset, the name Emmit Cooper had given his ranch, was three miles south of Crossroads. It had been little more than a shack when Emmit bought the place for the land and location, but the first thing he did when he moved in was clear out a lot of the yucca and sage on the north half of the property and seed it in several varieties of prairie grasses hardy to the climate, to create more grazing ground good for horses.

Rain was scarce up here, and every drop that fell was a blessing. Between the random rains and a good winter of heavy snow, it was enough to support his efforts.

Emmit had resisted the urge to buy livestock until the pasture had a whole years' worth of growth behind it, and the grass roots had taken hold, and during that time, he began remodeling the house.

He added a front porch that ran the length of the house, and a matching porch on the back, then remodeled and updated the entire interior. Even when he'd finished the remodeling project, the house itself was still small by rancher standards.

One bedroom, one bath, and a utility room on the back half, leaving the front half of the house as a kitchen/dining/living area. The appliances were all up-to-date, and the finishings and furniture inside the house were large, leather, and sturdy for the comfort of big men.

He lived there for ten years while bullfighting in rodeos, and in his off-times, trained horses for other people, all the while dreaming of owning his own horses to train and sell.

But the night they carried Sonny Bluejacket out of the arena on a stretcher, he went home, packed away his bull fighting gear, and never went back. He stayed on Sunset and did what he'd always wanted to do, then passed it on to the man who had cheated death.

Now that man was here, ready to reclaim Emmit's legacy.

═══════════

As Maggie and Sonny drove south, all there was to see was a sky full of stars, until they passed a single-wide trailer just off the road. There was no security light burning—just a dim light shining through slightly-parted curtains, and Sonny thought, *Whoever that is will be my neighbor.* Less than a mile later they came over a slight rise and Maggie pointed to a light in the distance.

"That is the security light in your front yard, which means power is still on."

Sonny sat up a little straighter. The light marked the beginning of a future he never thought he'd have, but he had not expected to deal with thieves before he even got in the front door. And then it occurred to him as they were approaching, that he didn't have keys to the house.

"Do you happen to know if Emmit kept a key hidden somewhere outside?" he asked.

"No, but you can have mine. He wasn't always home when I went to clean, so he gave me one."

"Thanks," Sonny said, and then the headlights swept across the fencing and the rather grand metal sign over the gateposts at the entrance. The headlights caught long enough for him to see the name on it.

"Sunset?"

"Oh…right, I guess I thought you knew. Emmit named his place Sunset Ranch. I'm sure you know his horses are registered Quarter Horses. They have lip tattoos with numbers that correspond with their papers. I know, because sometimes I helped him fill out the paperwork when a new one was born. His eyesight wasn't what it used to be, and he was always on the lookout for yearlings to buy and train, too, with bloodlines he liked."

A shiver went up Sonny's back as they passed through the entrance. Maybe it was Emmit still hanging around to welcome him home. The drive from the gate to the house was about the length of a football field, and the closer they got, the faster his heart began beating.

Anticipation of the unknown.

When they pulled up to the house, Maggie parked. Before they got out, she took the house key from her key ring and handed it to him.

"Welcome home, Sonny Bluejacket."

"Thanks for the ride," he said.

"Sure thing, but I'll go in with you. I'll know if anything is missing inside."

"I appreciate that," Sonny said.

She popped the trunk so he could get his bags, and as soon as he grabbed them, he followed her up the porch. Unlocking the door to his new home was yet another first, and then the door swung inward.

"Light switches just to your right," Maggie said, and moments later, the room was bathed in light. The house smelled a little musty, but it was clean. "Kitchen, dining area and living room in the front part. The TV is still here. He had internet service via the satellite dish on the roof of the house. You'll have to switch all that over. You can get the address of the company from a copy of his old bills," she said, and then began talking more to herself than to him as she began a quick walk-through. "Bed and bath are in the back, as well as a utility room with a washer and dryer, and a small chest-type deep freezer. Emmit liked to hunt. It kept him in meat through the winter."

Sonny was surprised by the simple beauty of the place, and kept absorbing her information as he followed her to the bedroom. He dumped his bags on the bed as Maggie opened the closet, then frowned.

"His clothes are still here. I didn't think about that," she said.

"I'll deal with it," Sonny said. "Is there a place around here that takes donations?"

"The Baptist Church in Crossroads has a charity closet. They'll be happy to get them," she said, and then went to see if the appliances were still in the utility room, and they were. She walked back into the front of the house and opened the first cabinet door next to the sink. There, hanging on a hook inside, were Emmit's keys. "That's Emmit's ring of keys, and looks like the extra set of keys to his truck."

Sonny pocketed both sets as Maggie opened the fridge. "Not much in here, and it's all out of date."

"What do you do about trash around here?" he asked.

"We don't burn it, ever. Don't want to set the prairie on fire. Drought and prairie fires play havoc with ranchers' winter feed. There's a trash bin off the back porch. Once a week you haul it to the road outside of the entrance. A local man has his own trash route. He charges forty dollars a month with a weekly pickup. You'll have to make sure he knows you're in residence, so he'll keep coming by." She grabbed her phone, pulled up the name and number, and wrote them down for Sonny. "This is his contact info, and this is mine, just in case."

Sonny glanced at the info on the little notepad. In other circumstances, he would be delaying her exit, but Matt Reddick was on the way, and he had to go talk to a thief about his horses.

"Thank you, Maggie. You have been more than kind to a stranger, but I hope we won't be strangers for long.

Sheriff Reddick will be here soon, so you can head home. I'll be seeing you and Pearl now and then. The Yellow Rose is hard to pass up."

Maggie was fidgeting with her car keys, wanting to talk more, but it wasn't the time. "I'm claiming you as a new friend, and now I'm going to worry until I know you got your stuff back without a fight."

Sonny stilled, letting that kindness settle within him. "Thank you, but I'll be fine."

She gave the room a long, lingering glance, then palmed the keys. "See you around," she said, and headed for the door.

She tried not to think of what might happen as she drove away, and kept telling herself this was none of her business. But she'd thought the world of Emmit, and Pearl seemed to think Sonny Bluejacket was all that and a box of crackers, and now Maggie had become a part of Emmit Cooper's last act, by aiding the man who'd become his heir.

She couldn't wait to get home and get out her paints. Drawing pictures had always been her hobby, but after having a solid job and a steady place to live, she branched out into experimenting with acrylic paints and small canvases, and painted sunsets, then painted pictures of patrons dining in the Rose, like the three old men in the corner who came every morning for coffee. And pictures of Pearl at the counter, ringing up a sale, and more sunsets.

Only tonight, for the first time, she wanted to sketch

Sonny Bluejacket's face while it was still fresh in her mind. There was something dark and beautiful about him that turned on the need to capture it on canvas.

Drawing and painting were the two things innate to who she was. It made being abandoned as a baby less of a tragedy. At least she'd been born with a gift. One that was hers alone.

———

Sonny didn't go back into the house until the taillights were out of sight, then he dug a flashlight out of his bag, and headed to the barn and stables.

Once he passed the security light in the backyard, the dark swallowed him. He turned on the flashlight as he went, thinking there should be feed and hay stored in the barn. He already knew the horses were gone, but he wanted to see what else Sutton stole.

Walking in unfamiliar territory in the dark should have felt strange, but it wasn't anything he hadn't done countless times before on the family farm back home. The only difference now was that everything ahead of him was unknown. Sonny wasn't afraid, but he was wary. He was not a man who acted upon impulse, and right now he was focused on what he could see and hear.

The stables were empty. He'd expected that. But when he turned on the light in the tack room and saw it was empty, too, as was the feed room, he realized Sutton had stripped the place clean. He went through

the stables into the attached barn, then climbed the
ladder up into the loft.

Remnants of straw were scattered across the floor,
but it was empty. He climbed down and walked out
into the attached corral, sweeping the surrounding field
with his flashlight, and as he did, caught a glimpse of
round bales fenced off from the pasture, and a tractor
with a hay spike parked inside next to the bales.

The large building off to the west between the stables and the house was just a looming shadow in the
dark, but he guessed it was likely the roping arena. He
would check that out in the daylight. At that point, he
turned off his flashlight and looked up at the starlit sky
as a wave of emotion washed through him.

"I'm here, Emmit. I've got this. Be at peace, my
friend."

He was walking back toward the house when he
saw headlights coming toward the house at a clip. He
started running. Sheriff Reddick had arrived.

———

Matt Reddick pulled up in front of the house just as
Sonny emerged from around the house, heading toward
him in long, hasty strides. He hadn't seen Sonny since
the night they carried him out of the rodeo arena covered in blood.

Sonny opened the door and slid into the passenger
seat. "Thanks for this."

Matt gave him a fist bump. "Good to see you again, my friend. It's what I do. You still single?" he asked.

"Yes," Sonny said, as he reached for the seat belt. "Are you?"

"I am now," he said, as he turned around and headed toward the main road. "Are you single by choice, or you can't find someone who would put up with you?"

"A little of both," Sonny said. "What do you know about Wade Sutton?"

"Without bad-mouthing him too much, he gambles, womanizes, and wouldn't know the truth if it kicked him in the ass. Did you know him from before?"

Sonny shrugged. "I don't think so."

"It's the trailer house just up ahead," Matt said.

Sonny frowned. "I saw an old trailer on the side of the road when Maggie drove me to the house."

"That's it, and we're almost there," Matt said.

Yvonne Sutton, Vonnie to all who knew her, was tacking up an old bedspread over the back door of their trailer house to cover up the window Wade had just broken after throwing his plate of food at the wall and hitting the window, instead. All because she'd cooked the meat too done for his taste. And after the window shattered, she'd gotten a backhand across the face for the error. Now she was sporting a bruised cheek, a nose still dripping blood, and busted lip throbbing with every heartbeat.

Their seven-year-old son, Randy, worshipped his father, and for the life of her Vonnie didn't know why. Wade was never home. He paid little attention to either of them. He left every night after sundown, and never came home until morning. She didn't know what he did, and she didn't want to know, but whatever it was, he came home with enough money to keep the rent paid and food on the table.

They were living on land that belonged to Emmit Cooper, in a trailer house they'd pulled onto the place when Randy was two. A man who'd worked for Emmit in the past had lived in a trailer house in that location, and the hookups were still in place, which led them to settle there. They paid Emmit five hundred dollars a month for rent and utilities, and for the privilege of living in the middle of a high-plains prairie.

Only Emmit was dead now, and Vonnie didn't quite get the connection between the old man's death and Wade acting like he'd won the lottery. He was driving Emmit's nice truck, and had moved all the horses onto their place. People were coming and going at the trailer, and Wade was flashing money. She didn't know what was going on, and never asked, but knowing Wade, she was waiting for the other shoe to drop.

She finally managed to get the bedspread tacked over the window when Randy came running through the house. "Mama, Mama, someone's coming!"

"Where's your daddy?" she asked.

"In the shitter."

Vonnie frowned. "Randall Wade, we don't talk like that."

"Daddy does," Randy said, and bounced off toward the living room.

Vonnie frowned and followed him, stopping him short from running out the door.

"No, sir! You do not just go running out of this house without knowing who drove up. Remember?"

The little boy stopped. "Yes, ma'am," and climbed up onto the sofa on his knees and looked out the window instead, as the car pulled up and parked.

When Vonnie saw the county sheriff emblem on the doors, and Sheriff Reddick and a stranger getting out, her gut knotted. Nervously, she swept the hair back from her face, careful not to touch the achy places, and stepped out onto the stoop. "Evening, Sheriff. You're out late."

"Evening, Mrs. Sutton. Is Wade here?"

"Yes, sir. I'll let him know you're…"

All of a sudden, the door opened behind her. Wade emerged, grabbed her by the arm and gave it a yank. "Get your ass back in the house."

Vonnie ducked as if to dodge another blow, and scooted back inside.

The hair stood up on the back of Sonny's neck as Sutton came down the steps and out in the yard with his head back and his chest thrust forward in a gesture of defiance. If he'd known him from before, he would have recognized him. He never forgot the assholes.

"Wade Sutton, you have something that belongs to me."

Wade frowned. "I ain't got nothin' of yours. I don't even know who the hell you are."

"I'm Sonny Bluejacket…Emmit Cooper's heir. You have property that belongs to me. My truck, my horses, and all the feed and tack. There was a list of his property that came with the will. I just came from his place, and a good amount of it is gone. According to the word in Crossroads, you've been driving Emmit's truck and flashing money, talking big about all kinds of things. So, I'm guessing there is a good amount of my things already in your possession, which makes you a thief."

Wade froze, looking wild-eyed from the sheriff to the stranger, and then back again.

"Damn it, Reddick. What's happening here? How can you take the word of a stranger like this?"

"Sonny Bluejacket is no stranger. And I received the same information from Emmit Cooper's lawyer that Sonny did. He is the legal owner of everything that belonged to Emmit. You took property that wasn't yours, and I am here as an officer of the law to make sure Mr. Bluejacket gets his property back."

Before Wade could speak, his son came out. "Are we selling some more horses, Daddy?"

Wade's knees went weak, and before he could think, Sonny was in his face. Wade's first instinct was to punch him, but the man was way bigger than him, and in the dark, damn scary, to boot. This day had just gone to hell, and was dragging him with it.

Sonny poked his finger hard in Wade's chest. "How many are gone, and who did you sell them to? I ask because they'll be charged with receiving stolen property, and I'm pressing charges against you for car theft, theft of a dozen horses, theft of animal feed and hay, theft of property, selling stolen property, and everything else on that list that's now missing. Last I heard, stealing horses in Texas is still highly frowned upon."

Wade's gaze went straight to Reddick. "Listen, Sheriff. This is all just a misunderstanding. I was making sure they were taken care of, is all."

"How many did you sell?" Reddick asked.

Wade ducked his head. "Four. I needed money to take care of them, didn't I?"

Matt shook his head. "That dog won't hunt, Sutton. They still had pasture and water. They didn't need anything, and you already had a vehicle. You took Emmit's because you thought you'd get away with it." The sheriff pulled out a set of handcuffs. "Wade Sutton, I'm arresting you for horse theft and property theft. Where are the keys to the truck?"

"In my pocket," Wade muttered, and handed them over as Reddick cuffed him. "I need to talk to my wife."

"I don't think much of men who beat women, and I doubt you two do much talking. From the looks of her face when she came out of the trailer, she's probably heard all she cares to hear from you," Sonny said.

Wade glared, but said nothing as Reddick put him in the back of the cruiser used for transporting prisoners.

Wade waited until Reddick buckled him in and closed the door before he began yelling and cursing.

The little boy was standing on the top step, big-eyed and crying. "Where you takin' my daddy?"

"To jail, son. Go get your mama for me, okay?" Reddick said.

Randy ran back into the house, and moments later, Vonnie came out with her son beside her.

"What did he do?" she asked. Then the fear on her bruised and bleeding face went from shock to horror when the sheriff told her about Sonny being the true owner now.

Embarrassed, it was all she could do to look Sonny in the face. "I'm really sorry about this, mister, but I never know what he's doing. All I know is that he said Emmit gave it to him. He cut the fence between us and ran the horses in here. You can probably move them back the same way. Emmit's horse trailer is behind some scrub brush out back, but you can't see it in the dark. Wade sold horses to a man named Delroy Kincaid. He drives a late-model black Dodge truck. I know that because I saw them together, and I saw the wad of money he gave Wade after he loaded up four horses. It was two thousand dollars. I watched him count it."

Sonny was still frowning, but he knew the woman was not to blame.

"Thank you for the information," Reddick said.

Vonnie nodded. "How long will you keep him?"

"He's going to jail, and he'll have to be arraigned

and charged, and he may or may not be let out on bail. He can plead innocent, but he already sold horses that didn't belong to him, so I doubt that plea will fly."

"Do I have to stay here?" she asked.

"What do you mean?" Reddick asked.

Vonnie was shaking. "This is my chance to get away from him before he comes back. My parents live in Bossier City, Louisiana. I want to go home."

"We're not charging you with anything. You are free to go where you choose," Reddick said.

Vonnie glanced at the police cruiser. She couldn't hear him, but she could see Wade shouting. She sighed.

"Sheriff, Wade has a gun, and probably some drugs too, likely under the seat of the truck. I don't want Mr. Bluejacket to get in trouble because of it, not knowing that it's there."

"My baseball cap and glove are in the truck," Randy cried.

"I'll get your things, son," Reddick said, and then popped the trunk of his cruiser to get some evidence bags.

As she'd warned, the sheriff found a semi-automatic handgun under the seat, along with a hefty bag of marijuana, and some shady-looking pills. He bagged and tagged them and dropped them back in his trunk, and then gave the cap and glove to the little boy.

Tears were still rolling down Randy's face as he clutched them up against his chest with both hands.

Vonnie frowned. "Son, what do you say to the sheriff?"

The little boy's expression was heartbreaking. He didn't say thank you, as Vonnie expected. Instead, he looked up at Matt Reddick, his eyes swimming in tears.

"Why did you 'rest my daddy?"

"Because he broke the law. He took things that didn't belong to him, and sold them. That's called stealing, and people go to jail for that, understand?" Reddick said.

Randy looked up at his mother for confirmation.

"Yes, it's true," Vonnie said. "It's not the first time, but he finally got caught, and we're leaving. Go to your room and start gathering up the things you want to take with you. I'll be in soon to help you pack."

"Where are we going?" the little boy whispered.

"To Louisiana, to Grammy and Pawpaw's house."

Sonny had been listening, but he doubted this woman had five dollars to her name. She was bruised and bloody, and starting out to Louisiana with a child.

He knew it was intrusive to ask this, but he couldn't, in good conscience, let her go without an offer to help. "Mrs. Sutton, do you have money to travel on?"

She lifted her chin. Her voice was trembling, but her gaze didn't waver. "I have our truck and enough to get me started."

Sonny took out his wallet, counted out five hundred dollars into her hand. "This will get you home. Do you have a cell phone in case you need to call your parents?"

She was staring at the money with tears running down her face. "Yes, sir, I do, but why are you helping me? My man stole from you."

"I do not believe in visiting the sins of the father upon the family," Sonny said. "You take your boy and raise him better than whoever raised your man."

Vonnie clutched the money to her chest as tightly as Randy was holding his cap and glove.

Sonny sighed as he turned away. The image of her battered face, and her son's tears would stay with him.

Reddick clapped a hand on Sonny's shoulder. He couldn't comment upon the monetary gift, but he was surprised, and eyed Sonny with new respect.

"Sonny, I've radioed for a deputy to stand guard at this property tonight to make sure no more horses disappear before you get them back home. He'll be here in an hour or so," Reddick said.

"I thank you," Sonny said.

He nodded, glancing back at the dilapidated trailer before he got in his cruiser and drove away while Vonnie stood on the stoop, watching them leave, knowing this was likely the last sight she'd have of the man she'd married.

"I'll be back in the morning to get the horses home," Sonny told her.

"I won't be here," Vonnie said. "As soon as I can get our things together, we're leaving, and when I get home, I'll get my daddy to find someone around here to pull the trailer off your property," she said.

Sonny frowned. "Emmit owned this land, too?"

She nodded. "Yes, sir, and if I were you, I'd take down all these hookups, or you'll just have some other loser like Wade Sutton begging you for the right to squat. God bless you, mister. I'm really sorry to have caused you all this trouble."

"Not your fault," he said, and as soon as she went back into the trailer, he headed for the truck.

But once he got in, he was immediately disgusted by the garbage and beer cans scattered all over the floorboards. He kicked them aside and started the engine. This was a job for tomorrow. He regretted leaving the horses, but trusted Matt's promise to send a guard.

He was exhausted from the long bus ride, and stressed from having to deal with all this. By the time he got back to the house and parked, all he wanted was a hot shower and a good bed.

He locked up, left a nightlight on, and porch lights on outside, and went to the bedroom. His bags were still on the bed, and Emmit's clothes were still in the closet. Another task for tomorrow.

He stripped, twisted his hair and fastened it to the top of his head, then turned on the shower. While he was waiting for the water to get warm, he glanced up at himself in the mirror, then down at his chest, tracing the thick ropy scars with his fingertips before putting the flat of his hand over the tattoo on his chest. Although the image was not traditional in shape, it was a geometric depiction of a butterfly.

Four turquoise-colored triangles outlined in black— two large ones, two smaller ones—joined together at their vertexes, like a pinwheel—an iron butterfly, forever in flight.

Because he had died twice on the operating table, he considered his recovery the same thing as a new life. Tribal elders declared he'd been transformed from the man he'd been, to one born anew, and the butterfly signified the transformation.

When the mirror began to fog up from the hot water, he grabbed a washcloth and stepped inside. The fading bruises on his arms and ribs were a memento of the fight he'd had with his father, but he ignored them, and took pleasure in the simple act of getting clean.

As he soaped and rinsed the long hours of travel from his body, he wondered if Walks-Off had disappeared again, or if he was bugging his brother, Charlie, for information as to where he'd gone, then let it go. He had no control over Walker's actions—only his own.

Chapter 3

DAYLIGHT DAWNED WITH WADE SUTTON SITTING IN a cell at the county jail. This wasn't his first time being arrested. He had a rap sheet that had begun before he was old enough to drive, and was pretty certain probation for this mess would be out of the question.

He knew horse stealing was a third-degree felony in the state of Texas, and highly frowned upon, especially if you're stealing pricey registered horses, rather than some kid's pony. Stealing a horse was worth two years in prison and a $10,000 fine. He didn't want to know how that stacked up when he was responsible for the theft of twelve high-priced horses and the illegal sale of four, plus auto theft and theft of personal property. What he didn't see coming was that ballistics was about to identify the gun they'd confiscated from his truck as the weapon used in a robbery/murder in Amarillo. The same gun he won in a poker game last month. But he did wonder what they would do about charges for possession of the drugs he'd had.

The charges were mounting by the hour, and he was due to be arraigned this afternoon. He was expecting bail to be set, but with his rap sheet and the multiple felony charges pending against him, bail was likely to be high, and he didn't have the money to pay a bondsman.

He couldn't afford a lawyer, and knew he'd have to depend upon a court-appointed one, but he still needed to talk to Vonnie. He had been booked and sitting in his cell for hours before he finally got to make a call, and then the phone just rang and rang before going to voicemail.

Even as he was leaving a message, he guessed she was pissed, but he didn't know she was already on a highway heading east, with their son asleep in the back seat of their extended cab truck, and her phone on Silent.

Yvonne Sutton had driven all night and up into the morning, stopping only for a potty break and to refuel. She bought snacks on the way out of the truck stop, and settled Randy in the back seat with food and a bottle of water.

Randy hadn't seen his grandparents in two years. He'd almost forgotten what they looked like, but he remembered they laughed a lot. He opened his bag of chips and shoved one in his mouth as his mama buckled herself back in and started the car. He chewed and swallowed, and as he was reaching into the bag for another one, he glanced up in the rearview mirror.

He could see from the dashboard light that his mama

was crying. It worried him. Daddy was in jail now, and he was supposed to be the man of the house, but he didn't know how.

"Mama, don't cry," he said.

Vonnie swiped the tears off her face and glanced up in time to see the worried look on Randy's face.

"Honey, I'm fine. I'm not sad. I'm just really, really mad at your daddy, and I'm crying to keep from screaming, understand?"

Randy's voice shook a little. He was coming to terms with the reality of their life.

"Cause Daddy is a stealer?" he asked.

"Yes, and a gambler, and a liar, and because he was always hitting me. I'm gonna tell you right now, jail is right where he belongs, and we're going to home to Bossier City, and Grammy and Pawpaw will help us start over. We're gonna be just fine. Don't be scared. I've got this. You just eat your snacks, and then try to get some more sleep."

"Yes, ma'am," Randy said, and leaned back as they drove away. He stuffed another chip in his mouth, chewed, then washed it down with a big drink of water, relieved that he didn't have to fix anything.

By the time Vonnie reached I-20 east, she put the car on cruise. Randy was asleep again in the back seat with the blanket pulled up beneath his chin, and snack wrappers in the floorboard.

For her, taking that on-ramp and feeding into the intermittent traffic was like getting a shot of adrenaline.

She'd been lost since the first time Wade gave her a black eye, but without the courage she needed to get away, and having a baby with him later was an even bigger anchor to the man she'd come to fear.

But no more. Wade Sutton's greed and stupidity had turned out to be their getaway ticket. Her face still hurt where he'd hit her, but he'd never hurt her again. She was tired between her shoulders from driving, but her focus was on the horizon, knowing that she was going to see the sunrise before she saw home again, and she couldn't wait. She didn't want to arrive in the dark. She needed her first sight of home to be in the bright light of day.

And she did just that. Without stopping to sleep.

————————

When Vonnie finally got her first glimpse of Shreveport from I-20, the sun was in her eyes and Randy was awake and eating a sausage biscuit from the last place they'd stopped to refuel. She had already eaten, but she felt like the food was stuck in her throat. She'd been strong for so long that the relief of knowing they were going to be safe was an emotional release she'd never allowed herself to feel. When she took the needed exit off into the city, a moment of déjà vu brought tears.

Thank you, God, we made it!

She swiped them away before Randy could see, and started winding her way through Shreveport to the

Texas Street Bridge spanning the Red River. Crossing it would take her into the suburb of Bossier City where she'd grown up, and where her parents still lived.

When she drove onto the bridge, Randy glanced up. "Are we almost there?" he asked.

"Yes, baby. We're almost there."

"Will Grammy and Pawpaw remember me?" he asked.

Vonnie sighed. "Of course. They send you birthday cards and money every year, don't they? And Christmas presents?"

"Oh yeah," Randy said, already mesmerized by the huge span of metal supports on the bridge they were on. There weren't many bridges where he grew up, and he'd never seen one like this.

Vonnie knew there was going to be a huge adjustment for both of them, but it was already happening. She'd sent her parents a text when they stopped for breakfast earlier. All she'd said was sorry for the short notice and that she and Randy were coming home. The reply she'd gotten from her mother was what she'd needed to see.

Praise God. Daddy and I can't wait. I'm getting
your rooms ready now.

———

Crossing the bridge was as good as already being there.

Bossier City was where she'd grown up. As she drove, she could tell some things were different, but the landmarks and the streets were the same, branded into her memories like the Sunset brand of Emmit Cooper's ranch. Sonny Bluejacket's ranch now. She thought of the money he'd given her to get here, and knew she'd say prayers for that man for the rest of her life, because he'd saved her.

When she stopped at an intersection for a red light, she glanced up in the rearview mirror. Randy looked anxious.

"It's gonna be okay, son. Even if you don't remember Grammy and Pawpaw, they remember you. And there are so many wonderful things to see and do here in this big city."

"I'll have to go to a new school. I won't know anyone," he said.

"They won't know you either, so you will have a chance to make new friends, and you know all those games you play by yourself at home? Well, you'll have kids to play with here. You'll see. I'm sorry about Daddy, but I'm not sorry he can't hurt me anymore, okay? He made the mistakes. Not us. It's not our fault. Just remember that."

Randy nodded. "Okay, Mama. I gotta pee."

She laughed. "Me, too, but we're almost there. Can you wait about five minutes?"

"Yep. I can wait."

"That's my boy," Vonnie said, then the light turned green, and they drove through.

Five blocks later, they turned down a street lined with Craftsman-style houses set on manicured lawns awash with colorful shrubs and flowers, and massive trees shading the yards and walkways.

When Vonnie spied the yellow house with gray shutters and the vehicles parked beneath the two-car portico, her eyes welled. As she began slowing down, Randy sat up straighter.

"Are we there?"

"Yes, honey, we're there," and pulled up into the drive.

Within seconds, the front door opened, and both of her parents came rushing out. The moment Vonnie and Randy stepped out of the truck, they were caught up in hugs and laughter, until her daddy, Mike Arnold, saw her face, and his eyes narrowed.

"Did he do that?"

Vonnie nodded.

Mike wrapped his arms around her. "Where is he?"

"In jail. It's a long story," Vonnie said, and then reached for Randy's hand. "Let's get our things and go inside, okay?"

"Not before I get me a hug," Ruth Arnold said, and hugged her girl. "You're still my baby girl. Welcome home," she whispered.

Mike put his hand on his grandson's head. "Randy's gonna be my helper, and show me which bags to take inside, aren't you, son? Your grammy's gonna take Mama on in the house," Mike said.

Randy puffed out his chest and nodded.

The moment the door closed behind them, Vonnie burst into tears.

"Mama, it's such a mess. Our old landlord passed away, and Wade just confiscated his truck and started driving it all over, then moved all of the old man's horses into the pasture behind our trailer. I didn't know what was going on. He told me he was just looking out for the stuff because Mr. Cooper had passed. Then he sold four of the horses illegally, and all of this without knowing that an heir to the property was arriving. Long story short, the heir brought the sheriff with him, and all of the ugly stuff came out in the wash. Wade was arrested for horse stealing, auto theft, illegal possession of a weapon, and possession of illegal drugs. He's going to prison for a long time. Randy is devastated and trying not to show it. And I wouldn't be here if the heir, a man named Sonny Bluejacket, hadn't taken pity on the two of us, and gave me five hundred dollars of his own money to get us home."

Ruth was horrified on her daughter's behalf. "I suppose Wade is responsible for that bruise on your face, too?"

Vonnie swiped at the tears on her face and shrugged. "Oh, that's nothing new."

Ruth was horrified. "Why did you stay? Why didn't you call us before? We would have come after the both of you."

"Because he would have come after us, and hurt

you and Daddy." Vonnie sighed. "Wade's arrest was the chance I'd been waiting for, and the money I was given made it possible for us to leave. I need to get that old trailer pulled off of the property, though. It's junk, but it's ours, and I'll have to get someone down in the area to haul it to a scrap yard for me. But that's something to deal with another day."

"Your daddy will help you figure all that out," Ruth said. "I have your old room ready, and the adjoining bedroom is Randy's. You two will share the Jack and Jill bathroom, okay?"

"Yes, and thank you, Mama. I'm ashamed to come home like this, but we didn't have anywhere else to go."

"No, baby, it's never a disgrace to come home. This is where you come to heal. Now, here come the boys. Wipe your eyes."

"Yes, ma'am," Vonnie said, and then got up and followed her son and her father down the hall.

———

Just before noon the next morning, Wade was standing before a judge as the charges against him were being read. He expected the horse, property, and auto theft charges, but he nearly passed out when he heard the gun charges. No way was he going down for murder. He'd won that gun in a poker game, and there were people he knew who could attest to that, but his claim of innocence there would mean nothing, so he stayed silent. After that, the judge set a bail so high Wade knew he'd never be able to bond out. He requested a court-appointed lawyer and went back to jail as dejected as he'd ever been, and waited for the lawyer to show.

The lawyer arrived a few hours later, and he was taken to an interrogation room, but when he walked in and saw a woman, he balked.

"I don't want no female lawyer," he muttered.

"Beggars can't be choosers," Jane Mallory said. "Sit down, Mr. Sutton. We have a lot to discuss and not a lot of time to do it in. Today is my son's eighth birthday, and I have to pick up his cake before I go home."

It was the comment about her son that shifted Wade's attitude enough to do what she said. The guard handcuffed Wade to the table.

"Mrs. Mallory, I'll be right outside the door when you're ready to leave," the guard said.

Jane nodded, then focused on her new client. "I'm Jane Mallory. I've read the charges against you, and they aren't a joke. They've already run ballistics on the gun. They have verbal testimony from the arresting officer, stating your son telling them you'd already sold four of the twelve horses you stole. They were registered animals, worth a minimum of $20,000 apiece, which puts the money value in the felony category."

Wade nearly passed out when he heard their sale value. He'd sold all four for two thousand bucks. Delroy Kincaid must have laughed his ass off all the way home. Then he realized the lawyer was still talking.

"The missing horse regalia belonging to Mr. Bluejacket was found in your possession. The pills they found in your truck were fentanyl. That's a felony charge. And the gun they found in your truck was used in a robbery/murder at a liquor store in Amarillo. That's another felony charge. So don't lie to me or I can't help you at all."

Wade was sweating. "Whoa! Whoa! Whoa! I didn't murder anybody! I did the horses and Emmit Cooper's property. I can't deny the pills were mine, but I wasn't selling, just using, and I won that gun in a poker game less than a month ago. There are three men I played poker with who can verify that."

"Then give me their names and contact info," she said, and wrote down what Wade told her. "What's your defense for taking the horses?" she asked.

Wade shrugged. "I rented from him. He died. Wasn't nobody around to take care of them. I thought I was doing the right thing. I didn't take them off his property. They were still on land he owned."

"But you didn't need bridles and saddles, yet you stripped the tack room. You didn't need the horse trailer, because you cut the fence and let them through, and yet you took the horse trailer to your property, too. Why?" she asked.

He couldn't look her in the eye and lie, so he focused on a spot just over the top of her head. "So someone wouldn't steal it."

"But someone did steal it. You stole it," Jane said.

He glared at her, but didn't respond.

"What made you think you had the right to sell property that didn't belong to you?" Jane asked.

Wade sighed. "I needed the money."

Jane checked her notes. "You're married, right?"

He nodded.

"Where's your wife? Would she have any testimony that would help you?"

"She isn't answering her phone. I don't know where she is. But she wouldn't testify for me," he said.

Jane looked up from her notes. "Why not?"

He shrugged. "We fight a lot. Sometimes I lose my temper."

"Do you get physical with her? Do you hit her?" Jane asked.

"I said, I lose my temper," Wade muttered.

"So, you abuse your wife. What about your son. You have a son, right?"

"I never laid a hand on my son," Wade shouted.

Jane arched an eyebrow. "Don't yell at me, Mr. Sutton. Unlike your wife, I will not tolerate that shit."

Wade's rage shifted to a mutter. "I don't hit my son."

"So, your wife is out of the question when it comes to testifying for you, and they can't make her testify against you, so we'll hope she chooses to stay out of this. I think this is enough for me to start with, and the first thing we need to do is get that gun charge dealt with. I'll be in touch."

She packed up her stuff and left him sitting. The officer let her out and Wade was taken back to his cell.

––––––––––––

Sonny had been dreaming that Walks-Off was scratching at the window screen beside his bed when he woke abruptly.

The first thing he heard was the wind, then realized it was already sunup. The scratching he'd heard now sounded more like something loose at the back of the house, but he wasn't one to ignore signs, and went through the utility room and out the back door to investigate.

Almost immediately, he found the source of the noise—a twist of baling wire hanging on a nail beneath the porch was swinging back and forth in the wind. Relieved that it wasn't Walks-Off, he pulled it off the nail, and tossed it in the corner of the porch before going back inside.

His first thought was of the horses, but it was just after six. A little early to deal with getting them home. The house felt chilly, so he turned up the thermostat on his way to the kitchen to make coffee, and went to get dressed. He thought about braiding his hair, then decided it would take too long and fastened it back in a ponytail at the nape of his neck, instead.

Two cups of coffee later, he headed to the truck with a garbage bag, and began cleaning out the mess Wade had left behind, then began going through the console and the glove box.

Emmit's proof of vehicle registration and insurance were in the console. He was going to have to find out how to transfer the title into his name since it was inherited, rather than purchased.

Once he had the trash removed, he dug through Emmit's cleaning supplies and went back to the truck and wiped it down with disinfectant. It smelled a little lemony by the time he was finished, but he'd removed the scent of Wade Sutton's presence. He went back into the house long enough to clean up, found an out-of-date box of Little Debbie cakes, and ate two as he finished his coffee before heading out.

He had two main items on his agenda today: get the horses and the stolen property back to Sunset, and get food in the house, which meant a trip to Crossroads.

Within moments of reaching the main road, he realized how close the Sutton trailer was to his home. At night, he'd had little concept of distance, but this morning he realized he could see it from the end of the driveway. Living on the prairie meant there was nothing between here and there but land and a horizon that went on forever, so spotting anything that rose above the horizon was easy.

In the bright light of day, the trailer looked even more rundown. The deputy was still parked at the residence when Sonny pulled up. He noticed the front door to the trailer was ajar. Likely from Vonnie Sutton's hasty exit. He pulled it shut and walked over to the deputy.

"I'm Sonny Bluejacket," he said and flashed his ID. "Thanks for standing guard. I came to get my horses."

"You're welcome," the deputy said. "Just part of the job," and then drove away.

Sonny was already in search mode as he circled the trailer, slipped through the rickety gate and out into the pasture to look for the horses. He didn't know how far back the property ran, but the fence between the trailer and the ranch proper was only a few yards away. As he drew closer, he could see the hastily repaired stretch of wire that Wade had cut to run the horses through, so the first thing he did was cut the wire again. But this time, he pulled it all the way back into the fence line on both sides so the horses wouldn't get tangled in it, then started walking toward a rise. The grass was still good, so they hadn't gone hungry, but he was sick about the four that had already been sold.

It was instinct that told him to stop and whistle, rather than hunt them down and try to herd them on foot. Horses were curious, and he knew Emmit would have worked with them constantly, so they shouldn't be spooked by another man. If they weren't far away, they might come to him.

He took a deep breath, and the sound that came out from between his teeth pierced the air and rode the wind all the way out of hearing. He whistled one more time, sent out the thought...*bring them to me*...then stood, watching the rise.

When the faint thunder of hoofbeats began to sound, it sent a shiver all the way up his spine. The ancestors had heard him. The horses were coming. He settled the Stetson a little tighter on his head, unaware he was holding his breath.

The first one topped the rise on the run—a roan with a black mane and tail, followed by a dun, a buckskin, a big gray, and two chestnuts with white blazes, and then one more bringing up the rear.

But the one in the back soon passed them all. That's when Sonny's heart skipped a beat. It was the biggest, most magnificent Appaloosa he'd ever seen, and for a split second, Sonny felt the horse's heartbeat.

This one, he'd never sell.

Even though they kept running, he didn't budge, and just when he thought this might be a bad idea, they came to a sliding halt around him instead. He held out his hand, then began moving among them, softly talking to each one as he went, stroking a nose, laying a hand on the side of a neck, scratching an ear, and all the while waiting for the Appaloosa to approach.

As he reached up to pick a burr out of the dun's mane, he felt a nudge at his waist, and then a velvety-soft nose on the back of his neck. He turned. The Appaloosa was before him—black head and neck, black legs, long black mane and tail, and the back half of the body, a white blanket with spots. He slid a hand up the side of the horse's jaw and softly blew in his nose.

The horse snorted and tossed its head.

"I see you," Sonny said. "Let's go home."

When he started walking back toward the break in the fence, he whistled again. They were trotting toward him when they saw the opening and took off running. The sight of the running herd made his heart soar.

They know the way home.

He pulled a pair of wire pliers out of his jacket pocket and quickly repaired the broken fence. It wasn't ideal, but it was good enough for the time being. As soon as he got back to his truck, he hooked up the horse trailer, pulled it up to a crumbling shed behind the mobile home, and began loading up the stolen tack and feed. When he finally got the last of it loaded up, he hauled it home.

The horses had all gathered around a hay ring out behind the barn, eating from the round bale inside of it when Sonny began unloading everything back into the tack room.

The windmill in the pasture was spinning, and he could see water coming out of a pipe into the tank. The horses were home. They had hay and water, and he hadn't seen a mark on any of them, but he grieved the four that were gone, and hoped Sheriff Reddick was able to track down the buyer and get them back.

Once the trailer was empty, he drove around behind the barn, unhooked the trailer, then went back to the house to search for the registration papers, but had no success, and now he was concerned. He needed this information.

The big gray was the only stallion. The rest were geldings or mares, so it stood to reason the mares would have been bred. He just had no idea when, or what the timeline was to watch for foaling.

Frustrated, he shifted focus and began making a list of things he needed for the house. By the time he headed into Crossroads, it was nearing noon, and he was hungry. Grocery shopping would have to wait. He was going to the Yellow Rose to eat, and if he was honest, he was hoping to see Magnolia Brennen again.

Chapter 4

THE MOMENT MAGGIE ARRIVED FOR WORK THE NEXT morning, Pearl started filling her in on the day.

"Morning, honey. We're likely to be busy today. This is delivery day for the bread truck and the wholesale house, so there'll be a lot of in and out in the kitchen for a while. The Dillon Ranch is having an open roping competition. All kinds of trucks pulling horse trailers have been going past the Rose since before daylight. I'm beginning to think I need to see about hiring a second waitress again, what with that Amber girl just up and leaving without a word to either of us. You don't have a single day to yourself anymore."

"I wouldn't mind having my day off again, but we're managing just fine for the moment. If all that's going on today, do we have enough pie on hand?"

"I think so, and I just put a big batch of fudge brownies in the oven. Even if we do run out, a scoop of ice cream on top of one of those and they won't even miss the pie. Did you get Sonny to Emmit's house okay last night?" Pearl asked.

"Yes," Maggie said, and turned away to hang up her coat and store her things in her little locker.

Pearl eyed her as she was putting on her apron and making sure she had her order pad and pen in the pocket. "Well? I need details, girl."

Maggie looked up. "Oh, right. There isn't much to tell. I got him to the house and went in with him to make sure Wade Sutton hadn't been inside taking things there, too, but everything inside was okay. Sonny sent me home. He was waiting on the sheriff when I left. I don't know what happened after that, but I did worry about it."

Pearl sighed. "Now I'm going to worry until I know the outcome."

Maggie shrugged. "We'll find out soon enough. I have a feeling we'll see him sometime today. There wasn't any food in the house, and what was in the refrigerator was spoiled or seriously out of date."

"Well then," Pearl said, and glanced at the clock. It was just past 6:00 a.m. "Better open up. The grill is hot and ready, and the first batch of biscuits is in the warmer. Check and see if there's toilet paper and paper towels in both bathrooms for me, will you?"

Maggie nodded and left the kitchen to flip the Closed sign to Open, turned on all the lights, while Pearl began frying up more bacon for the warmer. At that point, customers began trickling in, and by 7:00 a.m., the Rose was packed, and the parking lot was full of pickups pulling horse trailers, and people from the area stopping for breakfast before continuing to the Dillon Ranch.

Maggie was darting about the room delivering orders, taking new ones, and refilling drinks.

Carson Wright, a thirty-year-old high school dropout, and Pearl's dishwasher for years, was washing dishes as fast as he could get them off the tables, and Pearl was filling orders as fast as she could get them off the grill.

It was two straight hours of chaos and then the lull. Everybody took off for the roping contest, and Pearl, Maggie, and Carson finally had a moment to catch their breath and prepare for the locals who wandered in and out for food at noon.

Carson swept the dining room floor clear of breakfast crumbs. Maggie refilled the complimentary condiments on the tables, and Pearl took a box of hamburger patties from the freezer and began slicing tomatoes, onions, and shredding lettuce, and got the bin of dill pickles from the cooler. Buns were on the shelf, and Pearl began frying chicken in both of her deep fryers just before 11:00 a.m.

Maggie was looking out the window when she saw a white, older-model Mercury Cougar turning off the highway into the parking lot. It was rusted out and mud-splattered, and backfired after the driver parked.

Pearl shouted from the kitchen. "What was that?"

"Car backfire!" Maggie said, and patted her apron pocket to make sure she had her order pad and pen, and then pretended to be busy at the drink station when the driver walked in.

She heard the bell when the door opened, then turned. For a few seconds, she couldn't move, and then shock turned to cold-blooded rage.

Jerry Lee! The man who had abandoned her in the parking lot of the Yellow Rose all those years ago. That he'd had the audacity to return to the scene of his crime, was like a slap in the face. When he picked up the menu and started reading it, Maggie grabbed a pitcher of water, strode over to the table like she was going to war, snatched the menu out of his hands, and emptied the pitcher over his head.

"What the hell?" Jerry yelled, then looked up and gasped. "Uh...oh hell... Maggie, is that you? I didn't... uh...you're still..."

Her voice was somewhere between a whisper and a hiss.

"Get. Out."

"I just wanted to—"

"NOW!" she screamed.

Pearl came flying out of the kitchen with the shotgun, and Carson was right behind her with a baseball bat.

"What's happening out here?" Pearl shouted, and then she saw the man's face. "Holy shit, Magnolia! Is that—?"

"Yes," Maggie muttered, and snatched the bat out of Carson's hand.

Jerry Lee stood up to run, slipped in the water,

and hit the floor face down, cutting his lower lip with his own teeth. Blood was spurting, and he was on his hands and knees crawling toward the door when Sonny Bluejacket walked in.

Sonny saw a bloody man crawling like a whipped dog, Pearl holding the shotgun, and Maggie coming toward the man with a baseball bat, screaming something about "sorry, good-for nothing, lying…"

And that was all it took. He reached down, grabbed the man by the collar of his jacket, and dragged him the rest of the way out the door and dumped him in the dirt.

"Are you the sorry son of a bitch who abandoned Magnolia here?"

Jerry was spitting blood and dirt as he rolled over to get up. "That ain't none of your—"

Sonny yanked him to his feet with one hand. "If I ever see your face in Crossroads again, I will strip you naked and stake you on an ant hill. Do we understand each other?"

Jerry Lee's defiance ended. Pee was running down his leg and his heart was pounding. This big man was as scary as Maggie, and he wouldn't put it past either one of them to do him in.

He bolted for his car and leaped inside with tears rolling, locked the doors, then jammed the key in the ignition, desperate to make a quick getaway, but when he turned the key, the starter just clicked.

"Oh shit, oh shit…not now, not now," he cried.

He tried the starter again, afraid to look up for fear

he'd see the whole bunch of them coming for him. Then to his undying relief, the engine ground and started. Still bawling like a baby, Jerry revved it loud and long, put it in Drive, and took off out of the parking lot, slinging gravel as he went.

Sonny watched until the taillights disappeared, and then went back inside.

Carson was mopping up water.

Maggie was cleaning up the table and drying off the menu.

Pearl was sitting in a chair at one of the tables, laughing so hard she couldn't get up.

Sonny started grinning. Maggie's face was still flushed, and she was muttering beneath her breath as she worked.

"Was I too late, or too early?" he asked.

Maggie flinched. She didn't know Sonny had come back inside. "Are you asking about the fight or some food?"

"I haven't eaten since Pearl's burger and fries last night, so I suppose a little of both."

Pearl was wiping tears off her face as she dragged herself up from the table. "How about fried chicken, mashed potatoes with white gravy, and some creamed corn?"

"Add a side salad and you have a deal," Sonny said.

Pearl winked. "Done, and it's on the house for your part in exterminating a rat if you'll tell us what happened at the Suttons' last night."

"Yes, ma'am," Sonny said.

Pearl headed for the kitchen as Sonny walked over to Maggie. "Just for the record, Magnolia, I don't intend to ever make you mad, but I want you to know that you were nothing shy of magnificent."

"Thank you for your assistance," she mumbled.

"It was entirely my pleasure," he said, and found himself wanting to wrap his arms around her until she quit shaking from the rage, but since he was also of the male sex, and she was still looking real put out, he didn't have the guts to touch her.

"You yanked that dude up out of the dirt like a boss, but what did you say to him that made him run?" Carson asked.

"I told him that if I ever saw him in Crossroads again, or found out that he bothered Magnolia in any way, that I would strip him naked and stake him to an ant hill," Sonny said.

Maggie looked up. "Did you really say that?"

Sonny shrugged. "I said it, and from the look on his face, he obviously believed people did that. I always thought it was something Hollywood thought up for the old westerns," Sonny said.

The corner of her mouth twitched. "Thank you for saving me from myself."

He winked. "You are most welcome. I'll just go wash up."

As he walked away, Maggie glanced at her reflection on the shiny surface of a nearby window. Last night he'd also walked away from her when he'd gone to wash up. Maybe one of these days he wouldn't walk away. A few minutes later he was back, seated at the table, and waiting to eat.

Pearl brought out Sonny's plate of food herself, then sat down at the table with him, as Maggie brought his drink.

"I don't have much time for listening, so give me the highlights," Pearl said.

Sonny nodded as he chewed and swallowed the first bite he'd just taken.

"Reddick took me to the trailer. Sutton's wife answered the door with a bloody lip and big red mark on her face."

Pearl frowned. "I've seen her with a black eye, and she always has bruises. I said something once, but she just shrugged and said something about it was nothing to what he'd do to her if she left him, so I minded my business, after that."

"Figures," Sonny said. "At first Sutton denied stealing, and said he was only taking care of the stuff so nobody could steal it, and then Sutton's little boy came out, asking his daddy if they were going to sell some more horses. After that, he was caught. Four horses are gone, all to the same man. Mrs. Sutton gave us the man's name. Reddick is in the process of running him down, too. He'll likely be charged with receiving stolen property. I may or may not get those horses back."

Maggie frowned. "Oh no! I'm so sorry, Sonny."

"Yes, so am I, but after Wade was cuffed and in the sheriff's cruiser, the sheriff also confiscated a handgun and illegal drugs, which will add to the charges."

Pearl frowned. "I hope Vonnie is not in trouble."

"No, ma'am, she's not. Reddick knew she wasn't complicit in any way. She and the boy left last night. Said she was going home to Louisiana. I didn't know until she mentioned it, that Emmit had been their landlord, and that trailer is on his property."

"Your property now," Maggie said. "What about the horses? Please tell me the Appaloosa wasn't one that was sold. He is so pretty."

So, she has an affinity for the Appaloosa, too. "No, he's still there with the other seven horses. They're back on the property by the house," Sonny said.

At that moment, a car pulled up in the parking lot.

Maggie pointed. "Customers, Pearl."

Pearl nodded. "Thank you, Sonny. What you told us stays with us. If there's anything said about it in Crossroads, it will come from you."

"None of it is a secret," Sonny said. "If anybody asks, the thief is in jail and his wife and son left the state. That's all they need to know."

The bell over the door jingled as customers entered, with more beginning to arrive. Pearl disappeared into the kitchen, and Maggie went into waitress mode and began taking drink orders.

Sonny dug into his food with a careful eye on Maggie as people came and went. He was getting ready to leave when she came back to his table with a to-go box.

"Apple pie to go," she said. "Don't be a stranger."

"Thank you, Magnolia. I appreciate you and Pearl more than you know. See you soon."

It wasn't until she began to bus the table that she saw he'd left her a ten-dollar tip. But he'd also left her with more inspiration for the picture she was painting. His eyes weren't actually as dark as she'd first imagined. That must have happened because he was angry. In the bright light of day, they were the color of Hershey's kisses. She wondered if his kisses would be as sweet.

━━━━━━━━━

Sonny got his first good look at the town of Crossroads. A small school campus with a rattlesnake for a mascot. One pool hall. One really big gas station with eight lanes and sixteen pumps in the service areas, and one bay at the far end of the station to accommodate the big haulers and semis that wound up passing through Crossroads. There was one supermarket, and one bank, the post office, and the usual assortment of small-town businesses.

He made a quick sweep through Belker's Grocery to stock up on food and supplies, then headed home with the image of Magnolia Brennen wielding a baseball bat like a war club.

Two days later, Sonny had developed a routine with the horses, and on this morning, as soon as he was finished with morning chores, he gathered up all of the paperwork he'd been given by Emmit's lawyer, and headed into town.

Before cancer claimed him, Emmit Cooper had his lawyer go through all the legal steps needed to eliminate the need for probate, and upon his death, everything had immediately transferred to Sonny Bluejacket.

It was almost as if Emmit knew delay might jeopardize the safety of his home and animals, and he'd been right. In the short time between Sonny being notified and traveling to Crossroads, Wade Sutton did what he did.

But now that Sonny was in residence, he had things to finalize, and as soon as he got to Crossroads, he went to the bank. He needed to transfer his bank account in Oklahoma to a new account in this bank, and get the balance of the money in Emmit's account transferred there, as well. He knew the bank had been notified, and all he had to do was present the proper identification and a death certificate, and it would be done. He suspected Emmit had a safety deposit box, because there was a key on Emmit's keyring that looked like the key to a lockbox, and he needed to check that out. He still hadn't found the registration papers on the horses, and he needed them.

His appearance at the bank caused a great deal of curiosity, first because he was a stranger; second, because of his striking appearance; and lastly, when they realized he was Emmit Cooper's heir. After going through the legalities, Sonny asked about the deposit box, and showed the bank manager the key.

"Oh, yes, I believe he did," he said. "I'll get one of our people to let you into the vault. Just know that we can print you a few counter checks until your official checks and bank card arrive if you wish," the bank officer said.

Sonny nodded. "Yes, please, to the checks," and then followed a clerk who escorted him to the vault.

He signed his name on Emmit's card, and then followed the man into the vault and handed him his key. A couple of minutes later, Sonny was alone in the room with the box before him.

The moment he opened the lid, he breathed a sigh of relief. There were the missing registration papers. Reddick was waiting for tattoo numbers on the horses Wade sold. He took the papers out, then went through the contents. There was a personal letter to Sonny, a ledger with all of the breeding info, and a picture of Sonny on a bull. All four of the bull's feet were in the air and its back was twisted sideways, trying to buck him off.

Sonny had one arm up in the air, and he was "booting the bull" when the shot was taken, digging his spurs into the bull's hide. The bigger they bucked, the longer he stayed on, the better points he got, and such was a bull rider's life. The photo was obviously taken by a professional. Likely one of the media who covered the national finals. He hadn't expected this, and was unnerved by seeing an actual photo taken only seconds before the bull nearly killed him.

He sighed. "Damn it, Emmit. I wish you were here to hear me say, it's okay."

He took the 8x10 black-and-white glossy and put it with the rest of the stuff, then finished emptying the box, putting everything in the manilla envelope with the papers. Once he got the info he needed from the paperwork, he could come back and rent a lock box for himself.

He left the empty box and Emmit's key in the lock, and exited the vault. As he was passing by the clerk's desk, he paused.

"The box is empty. I left the key, so I'm turning it back. Also, is there an insurance agent in Crossroads?"

The clerk nodded. "Yes. The office is in a small metal building in the lot beside the post office. You can't miss it. Weston Insurance."

"Thanks," Sonny said, and as soon as he was through at the bank, he made a U-turn at the corner and drove to the post office to let them know he was in residence at Emmit's old house. Once he finished there, he went next door to the insurance agent.

Because Emmit had prepared for every contingency, and had signed the title over to his heir, all Sonny had to do was present a copy of the will proving his inheritance, and handed over a certified copy of Emmit's death certificate to finish the process. He left the office, relieved the truck was officially insured and registered to him.

After that, he gassed up the truck and went to Belker's. By the time he'd checked out, the cashier knew his name, knew that he'd inherited Emmit's place, and officially welcomed him to Crossroads.

He loaded the groceries in the back seat and was about to get in when he caught a glimpse of something beneath the front wheel. He squatted down to look, then smiled as he picked up a little turtle.

"Hey…little lòca…you picked a bad place to get out of the sun," he said, and carried it beyond the parking lot into the grass.

A teenage boy was sitting nearby on the tailgate of a shiny black-and-silver Dodge dually, and glanced at Sonny as he came back.

"Hey, mister, why did you say that turtle was loco?"

"Not loco. Lòca. It means turtle in the Muscogee language."

"My daddy is over there getting a haircut. He saw you go into the store. He said you are a famous bull rider."

Sonny shook his head. "Was… I don't rodeo anymore," Sonny said. "Who's your daddy?"

"Garrett Dillon. I'm Travis."

"Nice to meet you, Travis," Sonny said. He knew the name and the family. They raised mean-ass bulls for the rodeo. He'd ridden some in his day.

"Gotta get home and get my groceries put up. Say hello to your daddy for me."

"Yes sir, I will," Travis said. "Lòca, right?"

Sonny grinned. "Right," then got in and drove away.

He smiled to himself as he passed by Maggie's house with the Christmas lights, remembering her cursing a blue streak and coming at Jerry Lee with that ball bat. So much fire in her. The thought of seeing her again was enticing, but he needed to tend to business before pleasure.

He was a couple of miles from home when he drove up on a big truck pulled over at the side of the road. The driver was out checking a tire.

The trash truck!

Sonny braked and got out. It didn't take long to tell the driver about taking up residence at Emmit's place. He gave the man his name and phone number for billing, before hurrying home to get his trash up to the road for pickup and did it before taking his food inside.

He was inside and unloading groceries when he saw the trash truck pull up, then watched the man dump his trash and drive away and made a mental note to go get the bin.

After he finished putting up groceries, he went back up the road, pulled the bin back to the house, then headed inside.

The first thing on the agenda was to go through the registration papers. Emmit had a photograph of each horse attached to its registration certificate, so all he had to do was find the photos of the four missing horses. It was easy to figure out which ones were gone. He was missing a black with white socks and a solid black, both of which were mares, and two bays. He took photos of all four of the photographs, and sent the tattoo numbers along with them to Matt Reddick at the sheriff's office. At least now Matt would know what to look for. Then he picked up the letter Emmit had left for him, and took it to the sofa to read.

Sonny,

I knew when I got the cancer diagnosis that my time was limited. I thought about contacting you then to tell you how much I hated what happened to you, but I thought it was about five years too late for that. I will go to my grave blaming myself. But along with my diagnosis came another reality. I had no living relatives. I have worked long and hard building up this place, and the thought of my property and horses being sold at auction with all the proceeds going to the state, was a gut-wrench.

I worried about it for weeks, and then one night you were in my dream. I saw you standing on the banks of a shady creek, and you turned and looked straight at me. I woke abruptly, and knew I had my answer. You would love this place for me. And love the horses for me. And have the skills and knowledge to train them. And since my one stumble in the arena ended your career, I felt the need to give something back to you to set you on a new path. Everything you need to know about them is on these papers, or in my vault.

I have lived a good life, as far as cowboy life can go. I had a good woman once and didn't know what I had lost until she was gone.

Don't do life alone, Sonny Bluejacket.

Love what you're doing, but find yourself a life partner, too.

The Appaloosa is registered with the Appaloosa Horse Club, but don't sell him. He's yours for life. His name is Fancy Dancer, but I just called him Dancer. I bought him as a yearling. He was broke to ride on this property, but I didn't train him to sell. He's got magic in him.

Watch the sunsets for me.

Sunset was always the best part of my day.

Emmit

Sonny read the letter with a lump in his throat, and then folded it up and slipped it back in the envelope. This he would keep, but he was puzzled about the phrase "my vault." What did Emmit mean that this wasn't all of the info?

———

Nearly a week had passed since Sonny's arrival.

Waking up every morning and having the joy of walking out of the house and knowing all that he could see was his was like winning the lottery without buying a ticket. The regret was not being able to personally thank Emmit for the generosity, but he hoped to keep Sunset Ranch everything Emmit had built and keep it successful.

Sonny knew his rodeo roots would give him a level of authenticity with the horses he trained and sold, and the bloodlines in the horses he bred or bought would do the rest. He had the registration papers now, and the notes Emmit left on breeding and foaling, but there was a lot of information missing.

He'd walked through the covered roping arena where the old man worked the horses, but he was wondering if Emmit broke the horses born on the ranch, or if he hired a bronc buster. Sonny had ridden his last bucking animal for a reason, and inheriting this place presented him with a problem. He needed to know more about Emmit's trusted contacts for winter feed and the vets that he used, but didn't know who to ask. And then he thought of Maggie. She'd been to the house twice a month for years. Maybe she had answers.

Before he talked himself out of it, he sent her a text.

Miss Magnolia, I have questions about the ranch and Emmit. I hope you have answers. Would you please call me at your convenience?—Sonny

He dropped the phone in his jacket pocket, and then went back outside, tossed a sack of apple treats into the back seat of the truck, and drove into the pasture. He knew what Emmit owned was all fenced, but he wanted to see property boundaries, and began driving the fence line just to see how far his land really went. He knew it was a thousand acres, and that a narrow piece of it had been fenced off years ago to provide a small pasture for whoever was renting from him. As soon as the old Sutton trailer was removed, he was going to remove the separating fence and rework the fencing along the road, and get the power company to pull the meter. After that, there would be no more renters here.

Maggie was bussing a table when her phone signaled a text. Since Emmit's death, nobody but Pearl ever called her. Curious, she hurried to finish the table and as soon as she got the dirty dishes back to the kitchen, she checked the text. To her delight, it was from Sonny, and the moment she read the message, her heart skipped. He needed her!

She sent him a quick text back.

> We're swamped right now but I am happy to help if I can. How about I bring dinner out to your house after I get off work and you can bend my ear all you need? Meatloaf is on the menu today.

Sonny stopped the truck when he heard his phone ding. By the time he'd read her answer, he was smiling.

It's a deal. See you around sundown, and thank
you.

Maggie smiled, then paused beside the grill where Pearl was cooking.

"Save me two meatloaf dinners for tonight. Sonny asked me for help. I'm going over after we close."

Pearl arched an eyebrow. "Oh yeah?"

"Don't start," Maggie said. "I already offered my help if he needed answers that had to do with Emmit's business. He said he has questions, that's all."

Pearl nodded. "Oh…right. Two meatloaf dinners it is."

"Thank you," Maggie said, then heard the bell ring over the door and bolted toward the dining room.

———————

It was noon by the time Sonny got back to the house. The south half was still in its natural state. Shallow canyons and mesas, not a lot of grassland, but a lot of sage and yucca, and small arroyos lined with scrub brush, and not all of it fit to drive on.

The north half had better grassland, and three sturdy, three-sided shelters which provided shade out in the pastures and shelter in the winter, along with three other windmills and tanks, and a small creek that cut through the northwest corner. There were a few trees scattered along the creek, which reminded him of the heavily wooded area back home. He missed the trees, but this land had its own kind of beauty, even if some of it was a little ragged looking. At this altitude, and on the high plains, any kind of tree was a plus, and yucca grew at will.

He'd noticed early on that when he drove out into the pasture, the horses recognized the truck and stopped grazing long enough to see if he was going to stop. When he didn't, they ignored him. Now, as he was driving back to the house, they paused again, but this time he stopped and got out, then filled his jacket pockets with apple treats and whistled. Their heads came up, and then they began walking toward him. Moments later, he was encircled.

"You smell the good stuff, don't you?"

The distraction of feeding them treats gave him the opportunity to handle them. Becoming used to his voice and touch was imperative. The Appaloosa caught his eye again, as it waited behind the others before coming forward for a treat.

"Are you judging me, boy?" Sonny asked, and opened his fist.

The horse smelled the treat and took it, chewed, then nosed Sonny's pockets for more. He grinned. "You knew where they were, didn't you?" he said as he took out one more, loving the feel of the horse's velvety nose and lips against his palm as it gently picked up the treat.

He gave them all a second round before driving back to the house. He still had a lot of clean-ups to do around the trailer before he could redo the fencing. The last thing he wanted was for a horse to get cut from discarded wire or scrap metal from the old trailer skirting, most of which was in a pile behind the trailer, so that was next on the agenda.

He paused at the house long enough to make and eat a sandwich, then grabbed a pair of leather work gloves and a cold bottle of Coke as he headed back to the old trailer site.

Chapter 5

SONNY HAD BEEN ON-SITE FOR HOURS, AND THE truck bed was piled high with junk and bags of trash. As he tossed another garbage bag into the bed, he made a mental note to call the trashman to find out if he made special pickups.

He'd already uncovered a rattlesnake beneath some of the old trailer skirting that gave him pause. He'd been reaching down when the sound of the rattles warned him it was there, and by the time he saw it in the grass, it was coiled and ready to strike.

"You do not want to do that. It will get your head shot off. Get lost," he muttered, and stepped back a good distance without taking his eye off the snake. Moments later, it slithered off into the high grass.

He wondered how long that snake had been living under the pile of trash, and how close the little Sutton boy had come to being bitten, and hoped the woman and her son had made it to their destination.

He worked until the area around the trailer was finally devoid of trash, and was getting ready to leave when a man in a big 4x4 dually pulled off the road, then got out of the truck and walked up to Sonny.

"I'm Kevin from Hopkins Trailer Service. Is this where Wade Sutton lived?"

"Yes, it is," Sonny said.

"We have a work order from Yvonne Sutton to move it, and I need to disconnect the services and lock up the doors before we haul it out."

"I'm Sonny Bluejacket. The prior owner was their landlord. Go ahead and do what you need to do to disconnect."

"Excellent," Kevin said. "I'll get all this done now, and then we'll be back tomorrow morning around 9:00 to haul it off."

"I'll be here," Sonny said.

"You don't have to be," he said.

Sonny pointed to his truck. "See all that junk? That's what was outside the trailer. When you move it, I suspect there will be more of the same beneath."

Kevin nodded. "Understood. I'm not with the moving crew. I'm just the prep guy. Thanks for the info, Mr. Bluejacket. I'll let the crew know you'll be here."

Sonny went back to his truck, but instead of leaving, he waited, watching as the man went into the trailer with a bag full of ties and bungee cords. While he was waiting, he called the trash man about the added junk.

"Yeah, sure, Mr. Bluejacket. I can pick it up this evening around six after I finish my other route. It'll be sixty dollars extra for a junk pickup. I have to haul it to a junk yard rather than the garbage dump."

"No problem," Sonny said. "I'll Venmo you the money after you pick it up, okay?"

"Works for me," he said, and disconnected.

Now, all Sonny had to do was unload it by the gate. Satisfied he'd solved that problem, he sat back, waiting for Kevin to finish and leave.

A short while later, the man emerged and circled the trailer, then began removing the existing skirting to disconnect and cap off what was needed. By the time he was finished, the trailer was ready to roll.

Kevin gave Sonny a thumbs-up as he got in his truck and drove away. At that point, Sonny headed home. When he got to the entrance, he unloaded the scrap metal first, and then piled the trash bags on top before heading to the house. He was hot, tired, and hungry, and it was a while before sundown. Waiting for Magnolia Brennen's arrival was welcome anticipation.

He parked in the back, walked into the little utility room, and stripped where he stood, and this time untied his hair. A few minutes later, he was in the shower, washing the dust and leaves out of his hair, and the filth of Wade Sutton's trash off his body.

―――――――――

Maggie had never swept floors as fast as she did at closing. Pearl had the meatloaf dinners boxed and bagged, along with two containers of peach cobbler. She handed them over with a smile.

"Get on out of here. Say hello to Sonny for me, and take time to shower and change. We all smell like french fries."

Maggie laughed. "We always smell like french fries at the end of a day. Thank you, Pearl. You're the best." And out the door she went.

Once she reached her house, she jumped out of the car on the run. Moments later, she was inside, stripping as she went. She took a quick look at her painting in progress, eyeing the shadowing below his cheekbones and shivered. He was coming to life beneath her brush, but she would see the real man tonight. She took a quick shower, dressed in jeans and a pink T-shirt, brushed her hair until it was shining, then headed to Sunset.

The sun was hovering above the horizon as she drove, but she was less than three miles from Sonny's house. She wasn't going to miss that sunset, after all.

═══════════

Sonny was standing in his front yard with his hands in his pockets, watching the sky turning purple and pink. Emmit told him not to miss the sunsets, and now he understood why. He'd seen sunsets all of his life, but nothing to compare to the unfettered horizon of West Texas.

When he heard a car slowing down on the road, he turned to look and then took a quick breath.

She's here.

He wasn't going to admit, even to himself, how much he'd been looking forward to this.

———————

Maggie's heart skipped a beat when she saw him in the yard. The first thing she noticed was the wind teasing his hair, and it was the first time she'd seen him without it tied back. When the breeze caught it just right, it flared gracefully, like a crow's wings in flight, and it crossed her mind to wonder what his hair would feel like on her bare skin if they made love. But the moment she thought it, he abruptly turned.

Her heart skipped, imagining that he'd heard her thought, when in truth, he'd simply heard her car. But now he was motionless, his expression inscrutable, his hands stuffed into his pockets as he watched her driving toward him. Her heart was hammering, and she felt awkward until he smiled and lifted his hand in greeting.

Suddenly shy, it took everything within her not to turn around and drive away. She was so attracted to him, and getting out of the car would be crossing a threshold she didn't know if she was ready to face.

Come on, Maggie, quit acting like you're fourteen. This is no big deal.

But she was lying to herself, and she knew it. It was a big deal, because there was no one to buffer the space between them. Seconds after she parked, Sonny was at the car and helping her out.

"Magnolia, you are the best for coming out here after a hard day's work. Can I carry anything for you?"

She opened the trunk. "You can get that carry-out bag."

"My pleasure, and it does smell good," he said. He picked up the brown bag with both hands and carefully balanced it as she closed the trunk, then in true indigenous fashion, pointed with his chin. "A beautiful sunset for a beautiful woman. Just look at that!"

Maggie's gaze shifted from his face to the sky, and all of the tension of her day slipped away.

"Nothing more magnificent than a West Texas sunset," she said, unaware that Sonny was watching her and not the sky.

"Magnificent," he echoed, and then looked away before she caught him staring, and waited with her until the sunset began to fade. "Feels like we just got our food blessed. After you," he said, and let her lead the way into the house.

His words of the sunset blessing wrapped around her like a hug as they went inside. The house that had once been so familiar to her felt different. Sonny's energy had changed the feel of the place. She couldn't help but notice his housekeeping was far ahead of Emmit's, too. The floors had been swept. Everything was put away or in its place. And there was a bouquet of small yellow sunflowers and red butterfly weed on the table, with an empty pasta sauce jar serving as a vase. Emmit had been all about reusing and recycling, and she'd washed that same jar countless times when doing his dishes.

"Sonny! The flowers are beautiful!"

"They're in your honor. Not as beautiful as your namesake, but they're doing their best."

"I am unaccustomed to such an honor, and I thank you. I know you have questions, but can we eat as we talk? We were really busy today. I missed lunch and I'm starving."

"Absolutely!" he said, and pulled out a chair at the table that he'd already set. "You sit. I'll serve you."

She wasn't about to deny the offer. Within a couple of minutes, he had cold sweet tea in their glasses, and the food unpacked from the bag.

Sonny picked up his glass. "A toast to new friends, and to Pearl for the food."

Maggie smiled as their glasses clinked. "I'll drink to that," and then was the first with a question as they began to eat. "Are you settling in okay?"

He nodded. "Sutton's wife hired someone to haul off their trailer. They're moving it tomorrow."

She frowned, nodded, and took another bite, but Sonny could tell she was bothered about something.

"What?" he asked.

"What happens if Wade gets out of jail and comes back and finds it gone? Will he blame you?" she said.

"I don't know, but my first thought is that with his wife gone, that man won't have the money to bond out. There are so many charges against him that the bail is likely to be high, and unless he has a buddy some-where he can call to make bail for him, he isn't going anywhere."

"Oh, I didn't think of that," Maggie said. "I just know Emmit would be so bothered that all of this is happen-ing with your arrival."

"Magnolia, there is a reason Emmit trusted me with this place. I'm nobody's fool, and I'm not afraid of shit."

She paused, studying his calm demeanor. "I guess I should have known that when Pearl told me you rode bulls."

He shrugged. "That was all about trying to prove I was not my father's son. I should have focused on women more and bulls less, but here we are."

She laughed, and when she did, the sound of her joy rolled through him. He pinched off a tiny piece of his hot roll and threw it at her, which made her laugh even more. It was the best feeling he'd had in years.

They were down to the last bites of peach cobbler when Sonny started quizzing her.

"The reason I wanted to talk to you is that I found everything Emmit left for me in his safety deposit box, including a personal letter. He mentioned I would find everything I needed in the box, and the rest would be in his vault. I thought he meant the vault where the safety deposit boxes were kept, but they weren't in it, and I have looked this house over from top to bottom. Do you have any idea what that meant?"

Maggie rolled her eyes. "Oh my gosh! Yes! I

completely forgot to show that to you when we did our walk-through. Are you through eating?"

"Yes."

"Then follow me," she said, and got up and headed to the bedroom, talking all the way. "When Emmit bought the property, there was an old dug cellar behind the house, but when he added the addition, he had a stone mason remodel his cellar, and then he built the addition over it. The door to the vault is one of the panels of wood in your bedroom wall."

She bypassed his bed and went straight to the corner of the room nearest the foot of the bed and pushed on the panel. It popped open.

"I'll be damned," Sonny muttered, watching as she flipped a light switch on the wall at the top of a set of stairs, and then followed her down.

"As you can see, it's an actual room now. About a ten-by-ten-foot square. After the stone mason cemented the walls and painted them with some kind of water repellent stuff, Emmit didn't like the looks, and had it bricked over. The light fixtures are LED. They'll last a long time without burning out. He had shelves put on the walls for his keepsakes. His bullfighting outfit is in that little trunk. He showed it to me once. Those file cabinets are full of info about the horses he's raised and sold, and the two ledgers on his desk have extensive breeding and foaling dates in them."

Sonny saw tears in her eyes. "You really liked him, didn't you, and he obviously thought a lot of you. How long was he sick with cancer?" Sonny asked.

Maggie ran her hand down the sleeve of an old denim jacket hanging from a hook on the wall. It still smelled like Emmit's cigarettes, which ultimately caused the lung cancer that killed him.

"Longer than we knew. By the time he announced it, he said the doctors had given him two months. He refused to go to the hospital, and stayed on Sunset for the horses until the last day. He called for an ambulance just before sundown, but he was gone by the time they got here. I like to think he stayed for that last sunset."

Sonny handed her his handkerchief. She took it without looking at him and wiped her eyes.

"Thanks," she said, and handed it back. "Besides being the place where he kept his treasures, it's a really good storm shelter, too."

Sonny nodded. "I can see that. I have other questions. I've seen the roping arena. It's quite a setup. Did Emmit break his own horses?"

"No. There's a guy he used. I don't know the name but that green ledger was his Rolodex. He wasn't much for technology and there's a long list of contacts and what he uses them for in that ledger," she said.

"Did he train the cutting horses here, and if he did, what happened to the steers he would have used in training?" he asked.

She frowned. "He trained here, but I think he had a guy bring about a couple dozen or so half-grown steers to the ranch when he began training them for cutting or roping. I'm probably not using the right terminology, but you know what I mean. And when he had horses ready to go, he would hold a roping event, or take them to one, and compete to let people see them working and let them know they were for sale. If the horses did good, he got offers from buyers. But I think it all got too much for him after he was diagnosed." And then she looked up at Sonny. "I'm really glad you're here."

Sonny sighed. He could still see a faint shimmer of tears in them. "I'm glad I'm here, too. And thank you so much for all this. I know it's getting late. I've intruded into enough of your personal time and you must be exhausted. Next time you eat with me I will come get you, and you will not be driving about on your own in the dark."

"There's going to be a next time?" she said.

"I will ask. You have the option of refusing," he said softly.

"Well, that's unlikely. Now let's get out of here. I keep feeling like Emmit is watching us."

Sonny shook his head. "I've already sent Emmit on his way. Once I set foot here, he knew the place was safe."

Maggie frowned. "How do you know he's gone? What if—?"

Sonny shrugged. "I just know. Up you go, Magnolia. I'm right behind you."

Maggie climbed up quickly, well aware of Sonny's presence only two steps behind, and came out into his bedroom. She had one quick glance at the bed and then kept going all the way to the kitchen and began carrying dishes to the sink.

All of a sudden, Sonny was behind her, reaching around and taking a plate from her hand.

"No, ma'am. You were my guest. Will you please give Pearl my thanks for the food, and text me when you get home so I'll know you're safe?"

She had the strongest urge to turn and slide her arms around his neck. Instead, she nodded, relinquished the plate, and felt him step away to give her space.

"I'll walk you out," he said, as she slipped on her jacket and got the keys from her purse. When they reached her car, she opened the door, and then turned around. He was just a looming shadow now between her and the porch light. "Thank you for the visit and the sunset," she said.

He cupped the side of her face. "Thank you, pretty lady, for helping me. Remember, I will be waiting for that text."

"And I'll be waiting for another invitation," she said, then ducked into her car and closed the door. She didn't have to look to know he was still standing where she'd left him as she drove away. She could feel it.

———

Again, Sonny watched until he could no longer see the taillights of her car before he went back into the house, but this time, a piece of her had already settled in his heart. He wanted her. He wanted her to love him. But she still didn't quite trust him. Time would take care of that, and he was willing to wait as long as it took. He already knew she was worth it.

He began cleaning up the kitchen and gathering up the trash just to stay busy, but there weren't enough jobs left on earth to make him forget Magnolia Brennen. She was under his skin in an achy, yearning kind of way. For years, he'd had nothing to offer a woman. Emmit had given him more than a horse ranch. He'd given Sonny prospects, and the rest was up to him.

Maggie was running when she entered her house. She'd watched every expression on his face as they'd talked, until she knew exactly what had been missing that would bring his face to life. It was late, and she should have gone to bed, but she needed to fix this first, or she'd never sleep.

She took off everything but her underwear, and then sat down on her stool at the easel, uncovered her palette, and reached for a brush.

Once Matt Reddick received the pictures and tattoo numbers Sonny sent of the stolen horses, he applied for search warrants.

He'd already run a search on Delroy Kincaid days ago, but to his surprise he learned there were two men named Delroy Kincaid. A father and a son who did not live together, but both had horses and cattle on their properties.

Reddick's knee-jerk reaction to solving this problem was to go to talk to Sutton first. He went straight to the jail and had Wade Sutton brought into an interrogation room.

———

Wade was being removed from his cell and walked back to interrogation, and nobody would tell him why. He entered in cuffs with a jailer behind him, half-expecting it to be his lawyer, and saw the sheriff instead.

"What the hell do you want?" Wade muttered.

Matt Reddick didn't hesitate. "Information. But before I wade further into the mess you have made of your life, I'm hoping you'll be honest with me and save one family from more shame and embarrassment than is necessary."

Wade flushed, but said nothing.

Reddick felt the emotional wall between them, and was already wondering if this was a mistake, but he was here and so he asked.

"I'm here about the horses you sold. I'm going after them and returning them to their rightful owner. So, here's what I know for a fact, and I'd like your take on it.

It might help your cause for the judge to know that you assisted in this endeavor."

Wade was still glaring, but he was listening as Reddick continued.

"We know Delroy Kincaid is the man who bought the four horses. It is a given because Vonnie told us. We know he paid you cash. We know you did not give him a bill of sale. We also know that you sold four registered Quarter Horses already trained as cutting and roping horses, for five hundred dollars apiece, which means he conned you up one side and down the other, considering the going rate for animals of that caliber is eighteen to twenty-five thousand dollars apiece."

Wade grunted as if he'd just been punched.

"I'm guessing Delroy laughed all the way home. I'll bet he had a good laugh with his old man, too," Reddick said.

Wade had heard all he could take. "His old man doesn't approve of him or know the half of what his precious, lyin' son is all about."

Matt had struck the right nerve. He'd gotten everything he needed to know, and driven a wedge between Delroy and Wade, which might come in handy down the road, but he continued for more verification.

"I don't know. How would Delroy senior not know?" Reddick asked.

"They are estranged… I think that's the word Junior uses. I don't know the family secrets, but they haven't communicated in some years."

Matt began gathering up his things. "Okay, I'll take all that into consideration. I do appreciate your input, and I am truly sorry for the mess you have gotten yourself into, Wade."

"So, Vonnie snitched on me?" Wade muttered.

Matt frowned. "Snitched? Are you serious? You beat her to hell and back every day and kept her and your boy in that rotting piece of tin. You gambled and chased women all the way to Amarillo and back, and you expected loyalty? She honestly answered the questions I was asking to clear herself and your son. Would you have rather she wound up in jail for lying for you, and Randy wound up with no parents and a ward of the court?"

All the color washed out of Wade's face. "No. No, I wouldn't want that to happen," he muttered. "Is Vonnie okay? And Randy? She doesn't answer her phone when I call. I guess she's pretty mad at me."

"Mad doesn't even come close. She's gone, Wade. All I know is that she and your boy left the night you were arrested. I heard her apologizing to Mr. Bluejacket profusely, then saying she was leaving that night, and would see to having the trailer hauled off as soon as she could."

Wade blinked. "You mean they aren't even in the state anymore?"

Reddick shrugged. "I don't know where they are. She asked me if she was in trouble because of you, and when I told her that she was not, she cleared out. I'm sorry to be the one to give you this news, but you can't blame her. You put her in a terrible situation. There was no way she could hold her head up, and still stay in Crossroads knowing Randy would be laughed at in school. She did what any rational parent would do. She saved herself and her child."

"She's still my wife. He's my son, too," Wade said.

"But you broke every wedding vow twenty-times over, and let's be honest with each other. She ran when she got the chance to get away from you. You did this to her. And you can't fix it. You showed her time and again what you thought of her, and she has the scars and bruises to prove it. As for that trailer, I'll be surprised if it holds together when they try to move it. You failed your family. You failed yourself. Own it, mister, and do better."

Matt Reddick signaled to the jailer, and then walked out of the interrogation room, leaving Wade to consider the life choices he had made.

As for Matt, he had all he needed to know to get his search warrant.

———————

Delroy Kincaid's thirty-sixth birthday had just passed, and he was feeling good about himself. He was muscled up from years of hefting hay bales and roping cattle. He broke his own horses by riding them into the ground, wearing them down both physically and mentally, until they submitted to his commands.

He'd walked out to the barn this morning to feed and water his new horses, thinking what a deal he'd made. Wade Sutton didn't know squat about ranching, but he talked big because his old trailer was parked on a ranch, but likely not for long. Everybody knew old man Cooper had finally succumbed to cancer and the ranch was just sitting there, going downhill fast.

A horse nickered at him as he entered the stable. "I know you're there. You'll get your feed soon enough," he said, and went about scooping feed and filling water reservoirs inside each stall.

When he got down to the end of the stables where he'd put the new ones, he leaned over the door and looked in. They were fine-looking animals, especially that black, and the black with white stockings. He wanted to have the two mares pregnancy tested, but that would involve a vet knowing he had the animals, and that couldn't happen. He needed to get them sold and off his property. He had a man coming to get them in four days, and haul them to Amarillo. He had it all set up to sell at auction through a dealer, and would have fake Bills of Sale for all four ready to go with them.

He'd been careful not to leave a paper trail when he bought them off Wade Sutton, and considered himself in the clear. He didn't know Wade was already in jail, or he wouldn't have been so cocky. But the strut was just about to get kicked out of his step.

Matt Reddick was heading west with lights flashing and a deputy riding shotgun, and two more deputies in a second car behind him. They were on their way to Delroy Kincaid's property with a search warrant and an arrest warrant, and if the missing horses were still on Kincaid's property, he had copies of the registration papers and numbers of the lip tattoos to prove the man was in possession of stolen horses. When they finally reached the turnoff at the highway, they headed down the long drive to the house with lights flashing.

The single-story ranch house sprawled a half a football field in length across the land among a large scattering of outbuildings. As they drew nearer, they saw a man walk out of a barn and start toward the house.

Matt recognized him from his photo and accelerated as he grabbed his radio to notify the deputies in the car behind him. "Move it! That's our man in the yard!"

———————

In the five seconds it took for the flashing lights and the county sheriff logos on the approaching cars to sink into Delroy's reality, they were in his yard and then in his face, and Sheriff Reddick was coming toward him with handcuffs.

"Delroy Kincaid, you are under arrest for buying stolen property valued in excess of seventy thousand dollars. We have a search warrant for your entire property." Then Matt ordered his deputies to search the barns and stables. "You have photos of the stolen horses. Go see if they're there."

The moment Delroy felt the cuffs lock around his wrists, his shock turned to panic, but before he could say anything, his wife, Heather, came running out of the house with their baby daughter in her arms. The fear on her face tightened the knot in his gut.

"Del, Del, what's happening?" she cried.

Sheriff Reddick handed her a copy of the arrest warrant and the search warrant. "We have a warrant for your husband's arrest and a search warrant for the property."

Heather gasped. "Arrest for what?"

"Knowingly buying stolen property," Reddick said.

"I don't understand. If he did buy something, he would have had no way to know it was stolen," she cried.

"Eyewitness testimony named him, and the cash money he knowingly paid a thief for four stolen horses," Matt said.

At that point, the two-way radio clipped to the sheriff's belt crackled, and then a voice. "All four of them are here. Want us to check the tattoos, sir?"

"Yes, and photograph the horses as you found them, and also photograph the tattoos," Reddick said.

"On it, sir. Out."

Delroy started backtracking. "I didn't know they were stolen. I play poker with the guy. He just mentioned he had some horses to sell. I checked them out. They looked good, so I bought them."

"You bought four trained and registered Quarter

Horses for five hundred dollars apiece and left without a bill of sale for any of them. You knew they were Emmit Cooper's horses, and you knew Emmit Cooper was dead. You were trying to hide your tracks. Sutton's wife gave the both of you up, and his little boy, in his innocence, verified it without even knowing it. Delroy Kincaid, you are under arrest for..."

Delroy glanced at his wife. "Heather! Call the lawyer."

Heather was wild-eyed and motionless, staring at her husband as if he was a stranger, while the baby she'd made with him was fussing to be put down.

Before she left, Matt gave her a stern warning. "Ma'am, we will be removing these horses today. Do not interfere in any way during this process. Understood?"

She nodded, gave Del a last wild-eyed look, then turned and ran, unwilling to watch her husband being loaded into the back of a police car.

Matt buckled Kincaid in and shut the door, then got inside and drove to the barn to talk to his men.

"These cuffs are hurting my wrists," Kincaid whined.

"You're fine," Reddick said. "And while you're waiting on a lawyer, you might want to have a talk with your Maker, too," he said, and locked the doors on the cruiser before walking inside the barn. His deputies were coming out of the last stall as he approached. "Which stalls?" he asked.

A deputy pointed. "All the way to the end, last two on either side."

Once Reddick was satisfied that they had the right horses and the guilty man, they headed back to their cruisers.

Matt pointed out two of the deputies. "I need you two to stay here on guard. I'm going to try to get in touch with the owner, Sonny Bluejacket, to haul these horses back to the Sunset Ranch. I'll be in touch."

"Yes sir," they echoed, and proceeded to get in place as the sheriff drove away.

Matt glanced up in the rearview mirror as he drove toward the highway. Kincaid was pale and silent. Today, it sucked to be him. Satisfied that Kincaid was secure, he called Sonny as he drove, then listened to the rings as he waited for the call to be answered.

Chapter 6

REMOVING SUTTON'S TRAILER HAD BEEN DELAYED A couple of days, but Sonny finally received a text this morning that they were on the way and had gone down to the site to wait for their arrival. He was still thinking about his dinner with Maggie, and the three freckles he'd seen across her nose. He'd never noticed them before.

He smiled, remembering how she waved her fork in the air when she was making a point, and how easily she laughed, and how quickly the tears had come when she was down in the vault talking about Emmit. She was not afraid of emotion. Unlike Sonny, who kept everything inside.

Growing up, he'd had to fight his way through life, because people assumed, like father, like son. Walker Bluejacket was a con man, a ladies' man, and a liar. Neither Sonny nor his brother were any of those things—by choice.

The only times he'd been able to let true feelings go was when he would climb on the back of a kicking, snorting bull trying to bust out of the chute. And it was his fierce determination to go the full eight seconds of the ride every time, even when it didn't happen, just to prove to himself that there was something he could conquer.

He rarely let himself go there anymore, but as he looked out into the land that was now his, he was remembering the bull from his last ride, and knowing as he climbed into the chute and onto the back of that bull and began wrapping, then rewrapping, and tightening the rope around his gloved hand, that the bull's single intent was to destroy him.

He knew the crowd was screaming when he and the bull came out of the chute, but he didn't hear them. All he heard was his own heartbeat hammering in his ears, and the bone-shattering jolts as the bull bucked and twisted, the sound of its angry snorts, and the squeak of glove leather from the grip he had on the rope wrapped around the palm of his hand.

On the back of a bull, a second was a lifetime, and he was daring fate to waste eight of them. A ride was one bone-jarring jump after another, followed by the massive bull twisting in mid-air, then coming down headfirst trying to slide the rider over its head. A massive jerk from a huge horn-tipped head. Another bone-jarring leap and kick, and then suddenly Sonny was in the air.

He remembered coming down, hitting the dirt, seeing three bullfighters in the periphery of his vision coming to distract the bull to give him time to get up, then an explosion in the middle of his chest and not being able to breathe before everything went black.

The next thing he remembered was regaining consciousness in ICU and learning later that he'd died twice on the operating table, and had been unconscious in ICU for three days.

A horn honked. Sonny looked up, then shelved the memory for another time. The hauler had arrived. He and the driver traded greetings, then Sonny got back in his truck to watch the process. A short while later, the crew had it hooked up and tied down, and the driver pulled back onto the blacktop and headed toward the nearest junkyard with the old trailer wobbling along behind.

Sonny eyed their exit, doubting the trailer would hold together long enough to make it to its destination, then glanced at the mess that had been under the trailer and sighed. He was about to start cleanup when his phone rang.

When he realized it was the sheriff calling, he took a breath, preparing himself for the worst.

"This is Sonny."

"Sonny, this is Matt. We found your horses. Is Emmit's horse trailer roadworthy?"

His heart kicked. "Ah, man, that's great news, and yes, it appears to be. I hauled it from Sutton's place back to here with no issues, and the tires are all good," he said.

"Awesome. I left two deputies on guard at the ranch

where the horses were found. I'm sending you the address to go pick them up. They are in stalls, so bring some tack to lead them out. The ranch is nine miles west of Crossroads, just off the highway. The address is on the mailbox, and you can see the ranch house from the road. It's a long, white, single-story brick with wooden porch posts running the length of an equally long porch. Just drive straight up to the barn where the deputies are parked. They'll help."

"Thank you! You're the best," Sonny said.

"We can thank Vonnie Sutton for being honest with us, and you for giving me the photos and info I needed. All I did was wave my badge and arrest a thief," Matt said.

"Never belittle being able to wave that badge. I'm going to go hook up and head that way. I'll let you know when I have them back on the property," Sonny said.

"Sure thing, and FYI, looks like you have two mares who are going to foal. You're gonna be a horse daddy."

"Music to my ears," Sonny said, and disconnected. Even as he was heading to the house to get the truck keys, he heard his phone ding a text. That would be directions to the location.

———————

Pearl and Maggie were in the dining area of the Yellow Rose. The last customer had driven away moments earlier, and they were between customers and sitting at one of the front windows with their drinks of choice—Pearl with coffee black as coal, and Maggie with a Pepsi.

"Umm…hits the spot," Maggie said, as she took a sip.

Pearl nodded, then pointed out the window as two cars from the sheriff's office flew past with their lights flashing.

"Somebody's either in trouble, or about to be," Pearl said.

Maggie's eyes widened. "I wonder what's going on?"

Pearl shrugged. "No tellin', but I'll bet a double scoop of rocky road ice cream that we'll find out before sundown."

Maggie grinned. "I'm not betting against that, but I'll eat ice cream with you anytime."

"Deal," Pearl said, and took another sip of her coffee.

About an hour later, Maggie had just served customers at a table near the window when she looked out and saw a car from the sheriff's department driving back east with lights flashing.

A few minutes later, she saw Sonny in his truck, pulling the horse trailer. As soon as the traffic cleared, he turned west on the highway and drove away. At that point, she pivoted and made tracks to the kitchen.

"Pearl! I just saw the sheriff's car going back east, and then Sonny go westbound onto the highway pulling Emmit's big horse trailer. What if the sheriff found his stolen horses? What if Sonny's going after them?"

Pearl's eyes widened. "You might be right, girl. I sure hope it's so, and I pray those animals weren't harmed."

———————

The moment Heather got back inside the house, she put the baby in her playpen and then dropped onto the floor beside it, sobbing as she reached for the phone in her pocket. She was shaking so hard she couldn't get a grip, and dropped it twice before she was able to make a call. But it wasn't to the lawyer. It was to her father-in-law. The phone rang and rang, and she was still sobbing and afraid it would go to voicemail when she finally heard a voice.

"Hello?"

"Pop, it's me, Heather. Sheriff Reddick just arrested Del for buying stolen property. He told me to call the lawyer, but I can't deal with all this and the baby, too. Will you help me?"

"Well hell, darlin'. Sit tight. I'm comin' to you," Delroy said, then dropped the phone back in his pocket and turned to his foreman. "Manley, take over here for me. The vet will be out soon. Get the chutes ready. I have to leave for a bit. If you have any questions, you know how to reach me."

Manley nodded. "Yes sir, boss."

———————

Delroy Kincaid was nearing sixty, still the same good-looking man he'd always been, just a little older, and grayer. His stride was long and hurried as he crossed the barn lot to get to his truck. The moment he was inside, he started the engine and took off up the driveway.

And, as always, when he was bothered about anything, he started talking to his deceased wife, as if she was still riding in the seat beside him.

"Well, Arlene, he's done it again. You spoiled him and then went and died, leaving me to deal with his messes. You should have turned him over your knee and paddled his butt instead of 'making it all better' with hugs and kisses. He's made a big mess this time, and I'm telling you now… I'm not buying him out of it."

The minute he got to the highway, he stomped the accelerator, drove like a bat out of hell all the way to his son's place, and pulled up in the front yard in a skid and a cloud of dust. He saw a patrol car from the sheriff's office out at the stables as he got out and was coming up the steps on the run when Heather opened the door. He took one look at her red and swollen eyes and the tears rolling down her face, and opened his arms.

"Come here, little girl. Don't cry, honey. Don't cry. I've got you."

Heather fell against his chest, sobbing. "You and Del have been at odds for so long I didn't think you would come."

Delroy sighed. "I was ordered off his property. I

didn't quit any of you. All I needed was an invitation back. Now go wash your face, then we'll talk."

She nodded. "Okay, and thank you, Pop. You're the best father-in-law ever."

"It appears I could have done better in the parenting department," he muttered, as he went into the living room to sit down, then saw baby Carlie asleep in the playpen and paused, thinking...*my blood runs through her veins and I barely know her.* He tiptoed silently out of the living room and into the kitchen, so he and Heather could talk. When she returned, he pulled out a chair for her at the kitchen table.

"Sit, darlin', and tell me what you know," and so she did. When she finished, he was in shock. "From what you've said, I can tell you now that Del will likely do time, unless a judge decides a stiff probation would serve the same purpose, but that will be up to what his lawyer can do and what a judge decides. I can't tell him what to do, but there's no way he's going to get out of this. Not with eyewitness testimony, and the fact that four missing horses belonging to a dead man are in his stables."

Heather swiped a fresh set of tears from her cheeks. "Oh lord, Pop. I'll never be able to hold my head up in Crossroads again."

"Yes, you will. Nobody living in Crossroads was ever part of the social set. They're either running from something, or waiting for the last shoe to fall, so chin up. Today, life drop-kicked you and left you at your own crossroad. You have a lot to live for and a solid home that's paid for. I'll help you oversee running the ranch. Do you trust your foreman?"

She shrugged. "Del did, but I don't even trust him anymore, so I don't know what to think."

Delroy reached across the table and took her hand. "You just focus on yourself and Carlie. I'll handle the rest. I'll send my lawyer to talk to Del, and I'll talk to the hands. When family sticks together, they can weather just about anything."

"The sheriff said someone will be coming today to haul the horses back to the owner," Heather said.

Delroy frowned. "Owner? Did someone buy Emmit's place already?"

"I don't know. I don't think so. The sheriff said something about an heir," she said.

Delroy shrugged. "Okay then. So that explains the deputies I saw parked at the stables. No problem. We'll leave them alone to do their job, and be happy when the stolen horses are off the property, okay?"

"Yes, Pop, and thank you. Thank you forever."

He got up from the table and hugged her. "Give baby girl a hug from me. I've sure missed being around you two, but we're about to rectify that. I'm going to step out onto the porch to call the lawyer and then go talk to the crew and see what kind of workers Del has on the payroll."

Heather ran a shaky hand through her hair as she watched her father-in-law go out a side door. Del would be furious that she'd called him, but right now, she was so angry with Del, she didn't much care what he thought.

———————

The relief of knowing the missing horses had been found and unharmed was the best news Sonny could have had today, and every mile he passed brought him closer and closer to reclaiming them. He was coming up on the nine-mile location he'd been given, when he saw a mailbox on the side of the road. One glance at the house at the far end of the drive, and he knew he'd reached his destination. A quick check of the address confirmed it, so he turned off the highway onto the graveled drive.

Within moments, he spotted a car from the sheriff's office near what he assumed were stables, and drove all the way to the south end of the building and parked so that he could load up.

He got out carrying halters and lead ropes, and was met by the deputies.

"I'm Sonny Bluejacket. Sheriff Reddick called me to come pick up my horses," he said.

"Yes sir, right this way," they said, and walked him to the four stalls at the north end.

He paused at each stall, greeting each horse, and letting them smell him, but he could tell they'd caught familiar scents from the tack he was carrying.

"What do you want us to do?" the deputies asked.

Sonny eyed them with caution. "Either of you been around horses much?"

"We both grew up on cattle ranches," one of them said. "I'd say we've ridden our fair share."

"Good, then I want to lead them out two at a time, because this trailer loads from the side and the back. I'll get the halters and lead ropes on them, then I'll lead one while one of you brings the other one out with me. Okay?"

"Yes sir," they said, then watched as Sonny stepped into the stall with the black mare with stocking feet. He slipped a halter over her head, clipped a rope onto it to lead her out, then did the same for the other mare.

Sonny started up the aisle with the deputy beside him, both leading the horses walking at their sides. He didn't know he was being watched from the front windows of the house as they emerged.

———

Heather was in the house when she heard the approaching vehicle and the rumble of the horse trailer being pulled behind it. Delroy had already left the property, so she was hoping no one would come knocking on the door.

She quickly ran to the window, but when she saw the driver get out of the truck, then saw the long black hair tied back at the nape of his neck, she nearly fainted.

Sonny Bluejacket! She knew him, and like every other buckle bunny on the rodeo circuit, had chased after him back in the day, wanting to be the girl who stole his heart. But then she met Del, and he was interested, and so she went about making sure he didn't lose interest. Six months later, they were married. She'd heard through the grapevine about Sonny's near-fatal last ride, and then put him out of her mind for good.

Until now.

She watched as he came out leading one of the horses, with a deputy leading a second, and as he did, she got a clear look at his face. Age had refined the cut of his jaw. His shoulders were wider, but he still had that grace about him. He was a man well known in the cowboy world, and her own husband had stolen property belonging to him.

Her humiliation was complete.

She watched as they loaded the horses, before going back into the stables, and the thought crossed her mind that he walked like a man who made no sound. Like he was moving, but not quite in contact with the ground, and decided it had something to do with his height and stride.

Moments later, they came back out with two bays. When one of the geldings started dancing sideways, unwilling to load, she watched Sonny take hold of the halter, pull the horse's face toward him until they were looking eye to eye. She could see Sonny's lips moving, so she knew he was talking, and he kept talking and stroking the horse's head and neck until the big bay calmed down. At that point, Sonny led him into the trailer and then stepped back to get the last horse and led it inside.

A few moments later he came out, secured the door, then shook hands with both deputies, never once glancing toward the house. She watched him drive away, then turned away and checked her phone. She had a text from Delroy.

> Lawyer is on the way to the jail. Your foreman will do. He knows I'm running the show and to call me if there are problems. You are also to call me if you have questions, or something comes up that you need help with. Keep me in the loop. Love, Pop.

Heather sent him a quick thank you, telling him that the horses were gone, then dropped her phone in her pocket. She could hear Carlie fussing in her playpen. Time to get back to the cold, hard reality of her life, and the phone call she was going to have to make to her parents. But that would happen later. She didn't want to be crying in front of the baby.

———

Sonny's trip home was purposefully slower. His relief at being able to bring the horses back to the ranch was weighed down by the responsibility of first getting them there. They hadn't been gone long enough to come to harm, and since Delroy Kincaid had probably been planning to sell them, he would have made sure to protect the merchandise.

As he was driving, the patrol car with the deputies passed him heading east. He wondered if they were responding to a new call, or on their way back to headquarters, and was thinking about how easy he'd sleep tonight, knowing Wade Sutton's trailer house was gone, and the horses were back.

Then his phone signaled a text. He glanced down at the screen, and smiled.

Maggie.

But instead of reading the text while he was driving, he just hit Call, and waited for her to pick up.

———

Maggie was second-guessing her decision to meddle into Sonny's business by asking him if they'd found the horses, when her phone rang. She bolted for the kitchen to take the call, but she didn't answer with hello. She just blurted out what she was thinking.

"Are you mad at me?"

Sonny laughed, and that sound made her shiver with a sudden longing.

"No, Magnolia. Why would I be mad at you?"

"Because I butted into your business."

"Did you? I haven't read the text. I just saw it was from you and wanted to hear your voice."

She sighed. "We saw the cars from the sheriff's office go west past the Yellow Rose. Then later, we saw you at the highway with the horse trailer, waiting to turn. You also went west. We're just hoping your horses were found."

She could still hear laughter in his voice.

"So, the small-town grapevine is a real thing. I've always wondered," he said. "Yes, we found the horses, and I'm on my way home with them right now."

She could hear the delight in his voice. "Oh Sonny, that's wonderful. You must be so relieved."

"I am," Sonny said. "Can't wait to see what they do when I let them back out into the pasture with the herd. I expect a happy reunion."

"Are we allowed to know who had them?" she asked.

"It's not a secret. A man named Delroy Kincaid bought them off Wade Sutton, and yes, he knew they weren't Wade's to sell, but he bought them anyway for thousands less than what they were worth."

"Oh my God! We know the families, but are you talking about the son or the father? They're both named Delroy."

"I didn't know there were two, but it was nine miles west. Big white ranch house," Sonny said.

"That's the son. He goes by Del. Poor Heather. They have a little girl who's not quite two. At least Heather has her father-in-law to help her deal with all the mess."

Sonny was listening and thinking that once again, her empathy for others was uppermost. It was an admirable personality trait, and yet another thing that increased his admiration of her.

"I don't want to gossip, but is it okay to tell Pearl you got the horses back? She's almost as invested in you making a success of what you inherited as I am," she asked.

"I appreciate that, more than you know. I don't suppose you'd be up to coming out this evening after work to watch the sunset with me. If you're up for it, I will pick you up and I will feed you. It won't be as good as Pearl's cooking, but it would be my pleasure."

Maggie's heart skipped. "I would love to come watch the sunset with you, and eat your food, and celebrate the return of the horses. I'll call you when I get home. I need to change first. I always smell like french fries at the end of the day."

Sonny realized he'd just asked her out...like a date. It was a good feeling and a scary feeling. He knew what it felt like to take chances. It was like riding a bull and trying to hang on while hoping for the best outcome, and he was ready to take another chance.

"I like french fries, Magnolia. I'll be waiting for your call."

"I'm looking forward to it," she said.

The call ended, but his anticipation did not. He was feeling good by the time he reached Crossroads, and began slowing down to turn off the highway. As he did, he glanced up just in time to see Maggie come running out onto the porch of the Yellow Rose with two thumbs up.

He waved back and headed home, smiling all the way. As he passed the empty spot where the trailer house had been and saw the garbage, it was a reminder to get that picked up before it blew all the way to town.

When he drove through the gate, a horse nickered from the back of the trailer.

"You know you are home, don't you," he said, and drove straight to the barn, past the corral, then out into the pasture. He could see the other horses a distance away, but they were already moving toward him, and he didn't have time to waste. He began unloading horses, removing the halters one by one, and giving them a pat on the rump. All four were now out in the pasture with their heads up. The biggest gelding let out a whinny that brought the herd thundering toward them.

Sonny drove out of the pasture, leaving the horses to settle. As soon as he got back to the barn, he unhooked the horse trailer to clean it, then drove up to the house and got out, pausing a few moments to watch their reunion. They were at the water tank, drinking their fill.

"Look at that, Emmit. Your babies are back," Sonny said, and then went inside.

If he was going to feed Maggie tonight, he needed to get meat out of the freezer. After making sure he had spaghetti pasta and a jar of sauce, he chose hamburger meat, and set it out to thaw while he went back to the trailer site to pick up garbage.

Vonnie Sutton was sitting out on the front porch of her childhood home, watching Randy playing catch in the front yard with his Grandpa Mike when she received a text from the company who'd removed her trailer from Sonny Bluejacket's property. The trailer had already been sold and delivered to a metal scrap yard for five hundred dollars, and now that it had arrived, they were sending the money to her Dad's Venmo account today. She would add that to the balance of what Sonny had given her, and tomorrow, she was enrolling Randy in school. One more step to making a new life.

She'd didn't know what was going on with Wade, or the man who bought the horses, and didn't want to know. That part of her life was over. She was job-hunting and her parents kept telling her over and over how glad they were she'd come home, and they had her back, whatever she chose to do. The marks Wade had left on her face and body were fading, but Wade Sutton had scarred her soul. It was going to take longer to lose the bitterness than the bruises.

Randy made a flying leap to catch the baseball her dad, Mike, had just thrown, then fell backward with the ball firmly caught in his glove. He jumped up, grinning.

"Look, Mama! I caught it."

Vonnie smiled and clapped. "Way to go, son! Way to go!"

Chapter 7

WHILE VONNIE'S LIFE WAS EVOLVING FOR THE better, Wade was still mired with trouble, the worst of which was the gun charge linking him to a murder. He didn't know what his lawyer, Jane Mallory, was doing about that on his behalf, but he hoped that whatever it was she was gaining ground.

As it turned out, Wade's worries were for nothing.

Jane Mallory had a private investigator named Danny Brown, who she often used for running down reluctant witnesses for cases, and she'd taxed him with finding the poker players Wade Sutton claimed would testify to the fact that he had only recently won the gun in a poker game. And today, Jane received word that Danny had found two of the three poker players.

"I have video of their interviews, along with signed statements from both of them about the man Sonny won the gun from," Danny said. "They knew the guy wasn't a local, and that he'd been in the bar drinking when he joined their game. He called himself Rory. He was skinny. Long blond hair tied back in a ponytail.

Less than six feet tall. He had a tattoo of a bloody cross on his right hand, and a skull tattoo on the left."

"Thanks Danny, you rock," Jane said.

"Yes, I do," he said, and was laughing as he disconnected.

She shook her head at his audacity, but it was part of his personality that made his investigation skills so good. And the information was more than she'd known an hour ago. She scrolled through her contacts, found the name she was looking for, and made a call. It rang four times and then she got an answer.

"Amarillo PD. Detective Sheffler speaking."

"Hi Sheff, this is Jane. I need a favor."

"Of course you do. The only time I ever hear your voice is when you want something. We might as well be married."

She ignored that, and started reading off the description of the suspect who'd lost the gun in a poker game.

"I'm looking for a perp named Rory. Skinny, under six feet tall. Long blond hair worn in a ponytail. Tattoo of a bloody cross on his right hand, and a tattoo of a skull on his left. My client played poker with him and won a handgun in the pot. After my client's arrest, they tested that same gun he had in his vehicle, and found it to be a match to an open murder case in your city. My client is already facing felony charges for stealing and selling stolen property, but I seriously doubt he's the killer type. I have witness statements verifying they all played poker with the Rory dude, and that my client won it in one of the games."

Sheffler grunted. "I'll run the description through the database and see what pops. If I find anything, I'll let you know."

"As always, much appreciated," Jane said, and disconnected. She glanced at the time, then put away her case file and began gathering up her things. She'd had all of this day she could stand, and was ready to go home.

Moments later, she was out the door and headed to the elevator.

Pearl was also ready to call it a day at the Yellow Rose when a last-minute carload of customers pulled up.

Maggie groaned when she saw them. But to their relief, only one person came in and placed an order to go.

Pearl started cooking and Maggie kept wiping down the tables.

Carson, the dishwasher, waited until the order went out and the customer left, and then began sweeping the floor as Maggie turned the Open sign to Closed.

Pearl was extra tired today and had a headache of major proportions. She didn't have time to be tired, and she darn sure didn't have time to be sick. As soon as everyone cleared out, she was going to go upstairs, down a shot of whiskey, and take a long, hot bubble bath. And if she still needed a boost, there was that pint of rocky road ice cream with her name on it.

As soon as Maggie had everything ready to open up tomorrow, she blew a kiss at Pearl, waved at Carson, and shot out the back door.

Carson frowned. "Where's she going in such a hurry?"

Pearl sighed, remembering what it felt like to be young and falling in love.

"She's going to see a man about a sunset. Go on home, Carson. I'll lock up."

"Yes, ma'am. See you tomorrow," he said, and then he was gone.

Pearl stood for a moment in the empty room, looking around at all that was hers, and remembering how hard she'd worked to get it and keep it running. Then she winced at the shooting pain behind her eyes and began locking doors and turning out lights as she headed upstairs, thinking as she went that she needed to hire more wait staff. She and Maggie were running in circles every day without a single day off. Maybe she could hire a grill cook, and one more server. She wasn't picky about who, other than they needed to be good workers.

———

Maggie was a bundle of excitement all the way to her house. She was trying to decide what she should wear, then discarded that worry because they weren't going out, and she didn't want to overdress. The moment she got to the house she ran straight to the bathroom, stripped off her work clothes, and jumped in the shower, then impulsively washed her hair.

It was all over in less than five minutes, and she was stark-naked and standing at the mirror, blow-drying her hair. As soon as she finished, she sent Sonny a text to let him know she was home, then toweled off and ran to get dressed.

Without weighing the wisdom of the clothes she put on, she went for color and comfort instead of style. Stone-washed jeans. A long-sleeved turquoise T-shirt, and her pink Ropers. She was stomping her foot into the last boot when she heard him pulling up to the house.

Shivering with anticipation, she gave her dark hair a last brush, swiped a little lip gloss on her lips, and grabbed her purse and made sure her painting stuff was hidden. Seconds later, there was a knock at the door.

She flung it wide, unaware of the image she presented, framed in the doorway and backlit from the light behind her, or that the sight of her left Sonny momentarily speechless.

"I'm ready!" she said.

He blinked. "I don't know if I'm ready for you. You are a beautiful woman, Magnolia Brennen," and then he held out his hand.

She took it without question, locked the door, and

moments later she was in the passenger seat, watching him circling the truck to get in.

The last rays of sun flashed within the crow-black length of his hair, making it shine as if it had been polished. In her eyes, he was perfection, and when he sat behind the wheel, his shoulders spanned the width of the bucket seat.

He glanced at her and smiled, which melted her resolve to play it cool. At that point, she began fumbling for the seat belt, and Sonny was all business, backing up and pulling out onto the road leading to the ranch, then trying to miss the potholes in the road. She was grasping for a conversation starter, and went straight to the horses.

"Did you get the horses settled okay?" she asked.

His face lit up. "I did. I wish you could have seen their reunion. Within minutes, the race was on, and they were running across the prairie with their heads up and their tails and manes flowing. There's nothing more heart-stopping than a herd of running horses."

Maggie smiled. "You sound like Emmit. I guess most cowboys think alike when it comes to cattle and horses, except for the ones who aren't afraid to steal them. Thank goodness you found yours."

"I am definitely fortunate in that respect, although if it hadn't been for Wade Sutton's wife, it might never have happened," he said.

"When you got to the ranch, did you have to deal with any of the Kincaids?" she asked.

"No. If they were in the house, they were hiding their faces. I know this is the wrong time to ask, but I hope you like spaghetti with meat sauce, because it's what we're having for supper."

Maggie's eyes lit up. "I love it, and I haven't had it in ages."

"Me either, but it's something I know I can cook without messing up," he said.

After that, the tension between them lessened. When they drove past the place where Sutton's trailer used to sit, Maggie noted the absence.

"The trailer is gone!"

He nodded. "It was hauled off this morning. I kept expecting to see bits and pieces of it falling off as they went, but I guess it held together long enough to get wherever it was supposed to go."

"It looks different...but better," Maggie added.

"Still some fencing to repair, but I'm getting there," he said.

A couple of minutes later they drove through the main entrance to the property and headed toward the house.

"Looks like we're just in time to see the light show," Sonny said, pointing to the already changing sky.

He parked and then took her hand as they got out and walked out into the yard for a better view.

The sky was turning purple, and Maggie was already locked into the magic, wondering what colors were going to show up next when Sonny slid his arm across her shoulders and pulled her a little closer. As he did, she leaned against him, feeling sheltered and safe.

He glanced down. Her head was just below his shoulder, but he could see the changing expressions of wonder on her face, and knew one day he would take her to bed and put that same look on her face when they made love.

The sun was gone now, just below the horizon, but still showing off by flashing varying shades of pink and orange below the purple haze. Sonny could feel the weight of her hair on his arm as they watched the sky.

"There's nothing prettier than a sunset," Maggie said.

He glanced down. "Except you," he said, and then like flipping a switch, the sky was dark, and stars were coming out of hiding. "Let's go inside, Maggie. I still need to cook the spaghetti and then we can eat."

"I can help," she said.

"You've been waiting on people all day. Tonight is for you," he said, and led her in through the back door and into the light.

He set her down at the kitchen table with a cold drink, and then listened to her chatter while he put the water on to boil, then later, dropped the pasta in to cook. He set the meat sauce to warming, and put the garlic bread in the oven to toast. He was so preoccupied with getting everything right that he realized she'd gone quiet, and when he turned around, he caught her watching him. Before he could think what to say, Maggie leaned back in her chair, crossed her arms, still studying him.

"You are something of a Renaissance man, aren't you? A man wild and crazy enough to take on bull-riding, who knows his way around a kitchen as well as he does a rodeo arena. A man who has died and been resurrected by modern medicine. A man with a soft voice, but I suspect, an iron constitution. You hide your thoughts and feelings, and yet you are kind and have a subtle sense of humor."

He hesitated, then shrugged. "Yes, I guess I am all of those things. But I accept them. The question is, do you accept me as is?"

"I wouldn't be here if I didn't," she said, then blinked, as if shocked by what she'd said, and glanced at the steam rising from the pot of pasta. "I think it's time to test the pasta, don't you?"

A slow smile came and went as he turned to take the garlic bread out of the oven. He knew she'd scared herself by the revelation. And she'd been right. The pasta was ready. He drained it, poured the sauce over the hot pasta, and gave it a toss. After that came a sprinkle of parmesan cheese, and chopped basil leaves, then he made their plates and carried them to the table.

Maggie was seated beneath the light, giving him a clear view of those three freckles, when she looked up and smiled. "Smells wonderful and looks amazing!"

"Taste it before you get too excited," he warned.

"Too late, I'm already excited because I didn't have to cook," she said, twisting noodles on her fork before taking a bite, then rolling her eyes as she chewed and swallowed. "A sunset to die for. Delicious spaghetti, and someone to share it with. My heart is full, but my tummy is not. I'm going in for another bite," she said.

"Can't take credit for the sunset, but I'm glad you like the food," he said, and then joined her—happier than any time he could remember.

They talked as they ate, mostly asking questions about each other. It was the usual, getting-acquainted chatter, with undertones of the attraction between them politely unspoken.

"Tell me about Magnolia Brennen," Sonny said. "Family? Siblings? Where did you grow up? Witness Protection?"

The last question startled her and then she saw the twinkle in his eyes and laughed. "You have a sneaky sense of humor. You threw that last one in just to see if I was paying attention, didn't you?"

He grinned. "And clearly, you were. So?"

She sighed. "Not much to tell. There's no official record of my birth. They gave me a birthday on the day I was found on the doorstep of a fire station. They guessed I was about two weeks old. I don't know who my parents were. I don't know if I have relatives anywhere, but I know nobody wanted me, and no one came looking for me. I grew up in foster care. No horror stories, but no particular bonds ever made anywhere, or offers to adopt me, either. I learned to ride when I was twelve. Haven't been on a horse since I was sixteen. Nobody wanted me, but the state of Texas kept me alive.

I aged out of the system at eighteen, and have been on my own ever since. Just the one disastrous relationship with the loser you met at the Rose. After that, you had me at 'ant hill' and you will forever be my friend for life."

Sonny had a lump in his throat for the child she'd been, abandoned, never once feeling like she mattered, and shook his head in disbelief.

"That is a hard beginning for one small soul. For that, I am sorry."

She shrugged. "Don't be. You aren't responsible, and Pearl has changed my attitude and my life. I'm happy here, and even happier that you want me for a friend."

"And then some," he muttered, and got up to refill their glasses.

Maggie watched, knowing he had yet to say anything about his family. She didn't know whether that was off-limits, or if he was just waiting to be asked, but she knew one question would answer that for her. He'd either respond, or side-track her.

"Where did you grow up?"

He carried their glasses back to the table, then sat down. "Bluejacket Hollow, Oklahoma. It's in the blackjacks between Okmulgee and Henryetta, Oklahoma. Right in the heart of rodeo country."

She frowned. "What are blackjacks?"

He chuckled. "Scrawny excuses for great oak trees. They're actually a red oak variety. The biggest trunks won't be more than a foot in diameter, and they usually grow to about a twenty- to thirty-foot height. They are the shade down on our creek banks. The trees that cattle gather under in downpours. The scrub brush you have to ride through trying to find a lost calf, and hunting down a predator in those woods can get dicey, especially if it's a big cat you're looking for. Most likely it's laying on a tree branch above your head as you ride under."

"Oh my gosh. That's scary!"

"Would be, except our horses are sometimes smarter than we are. When they smell a big cat, they're not going a step farther. That's always a sign there's one around. If you're on an ATV, you're on your own."

"Do you have a lot of family there? I mean, since it's named after your family, I guess there must have been a lot of them living in the same area at one time."

He nodded. "There were a lot of them back in the day, before I was born. But the only elders left are my father and his sister. I'm Shawnee on my great-grandfather's side, and Muscogee on my great-grandmother's side. All of their children were enrolled into great-grandmother's tribe, and so it has been ever since. I have an older brother named Charlie. He has a wife named Frances and a daughter named Julia. She's nine. She has a pet pygmy goat named Butters, named so because it butts everything in front of it."

Maggie laughed. "I love that. Are you all close?"

"Very close with my brother and his family, and my auntie. Her name is Delores Bushy, which is also an indigenous name, but she is Auntie to all of us. After I was injured, they didn't think I would live, but the tribal elders said prayers, and they drummed for me. My heart stopped twice on the operating table, but I am told the elders were still singing, and the drums were still drumming, and so I lived. However, I had been rodeoing for so long that I had no permanent home, so when I survived and was finally well enough to be released, Charlie came to get me. I've lived with them ever since while working at nearby ranches."

"So, no more bull riding?" she asked.

He shook his head. "That man died. This man was still seeking a reason for what has been taken away, but I would never have imagined that Emmit Cooper would hold the answer."

Maggie was hypnotized. He spoke with a depth of wisdom she could only imagine, and in poetic analogies that made her ache. If she could paint pictures as beautiful as his words, she would die happy. She blinked away tears and leaned forward.

"What about your father? Where is he in your life?"

"Walker Bluejacket is nowhere in my life. He is the shame and scourge of all the family. I call him Walks-Off, because that's all he's ever done—walked away when he was needed. He walked away from my mother, leaving her to raise me and Charlie on her own. When she was dying, he was shacked up with yet another woman. He never came to her funeral. When I got hurt, he was nowhere to be seen. But the day word got around about what I had inherited, he showed up at the house wanting to come with me. Wanting his part of my gift."

"Oh, Sonny, I'm sorry. I didn't mean for—"

He reached across the table and clasped her hand. "No, don't apologize. These are simply facts of my life."

"So, what happened?" she asked.

He shrugged. "We exchanged words. He got angry and threw a punch. I blocked it, and he swung for the scars on my chest. I deflected the blow, but I thought Charlie was going to kill him. He ran him off. Then Charlie took me to catch the bus, and here I am. I didn't know there would be a second gift waiting for me at Crossroads until I got off the bus. I was guessing Pearl might still be around, but I wasn't prepared for a blue-eyed angel named Magnolia. You have helped me through all of this confusion more than you know, and while it appears all of my confusion with Emmit's world has been dealt with, I don't want to have to make up excuses anymore just to see you."

Maggie's heart skipped. *Oh God, please let this be real.* "You don't need excuses. And you've already seen me take a ball bat to the last man who betrayed me, so I'm assuming you have the good sense not to be stringing me along."

Sonny dropped his fork on the table and got up laughing as he swooped her up into a hug. "I swear on all that's holy, I've already tried dying, and it didn't set well with me. I don't ever want to face you and a baseball bat, and I'll never betray you or whatever grows between us, okay?"

She was trying not to give herself away too soon, but he was infectious. She couldn't help but laugh with him.

"Okay. Fine. I can live with that," she said.

She was still in his arms when the smile died on his face. He looked down just as she met his gaze. He could see the pulse of her heartbeat in a little vein along the side of her neck, and the long, dark lashes shading eyes the color of the sky. He watched her lips parting, as if she was trying to catch her breath, and then her arms were around his neck.

He lowered his head.

Maggie felt the warmth of his breath a moment before he kissed her, and then it was magic—like she'd always known this—and him.

Sonny was already in over his head, and he knew it. She abandoned herself to him like a wildling. Unabashed, and unafraid, and in that moment, vulnerable. She would have capitulated to whatever he wanted, and that left him the one in charge of making the decision. Now? Or later, when they had more than the few days that they'd known each other, to cross this bridge?

He paused, lingering for one last kiss, and then stopped, but didn't let her go.

"Ah, Magnolia…what you do to me. That was our first, but if I have any say in the matter, it won't be our last. As far as firsts go, that was skyrockets. I will spend a restless night tonight, dreaming of the angel I let go."

Maggie was trembling. Her heart was pounding, knowing how close they'd come to winding up on the floor in each other's arms. It was going to take longer for the ache she was feeling to ease. They were barely past the stranger stage, and she felt like she'd known him forever.

"Clearly, I have lost myself, or I would not have been this abandoned. I was about a zipper away from stripping. I want you, and that's a dangerous thought to have for a man I barely know."

Sonny stifled a groan. "If it's any consolation, I want you, too. I have since the first moment I saw you. The truth is, we strike sparks. Eventually, we'll set a fire, and when we do, there will be no turning back, okay?"

She nodded. "So, I guess you either take me home…"

He ran a finger down the side of her cheek. "Or take you to bed?"

She sighed. "Pretty much."

He hugged her again, but this time for reassurance. "I'm ready when you are."

"I need to get my purse. It's here somewhere."

He pointed to the sofa, then waited for her to get it, but when she came back, the first thing he did was reach for her hand and kiss it, then walk her out the door, locking it behind him as they went.

She climbed up into the seat and buckled up as he got in beside her.

"Do you ever have days off?" he asked, as he started the truck and backed up.

"I used to, but the other waitress quit and moved on, and Pearl hasn't hired anyone to replace her. There's not a lot of unemployment in Crossroads, mainly because there's also not a lot of businesses who need help."

"I might have to give her a hint about following through on that, since I'm hoping for more time with you," he said.

Maggie smiled to herself, wondering how Pearl would react to all that, then settled in for the short ride home.

They were nearing Crossroads when they caught sight of a little skunk waddling along the side of the road.

"Stay calm, little kùnu," Sonny said, as they drove past.

Maggie eyed him curiously. "Why did you call him that?" she asked.

"It's the Muscogee name for skunk. I was just honoring his presence."

Maggie absorbed the explanation. This man kept surprising her. "Do you think he heard you?"

"He did."

She frowned. "How do you know?"

"The same way I know your heart beats for me," he said.

"I pretty much told you that," she muttered.

He laughed, but didn't challenge her disbelief. Coming back from the dead had given him more than just a new chance at life, like knowing about things before they happen, and a heightened sensitivity to his surroundings. They were nearing Crossroads when

Sonny realized the town was dark. Not a light anywhere in sight.

He frowned. "The power is out in town. Does that happen often?"

Maggie looked nervous. "No. Not unless a storm comes through."

"My power comes from the same company yours does. I wonder if it's out now, too. At any rate, I'm not leaving you alone in your house until I find out what's going on," he said, and pulled over to the side of the road. "Who do we contact?"

Maggie quickly fumbled through her phone contacts until she came to Utilities, and found the number for the power company. She called and reported the outage, then moments later, she got a text back stating that they were aware of the problem, and had a crew on the way to check it out.

Sonny glanced out the side window while Maggie was reading the message to him, and once again, saw the little skunk waddling along, headed straight toward town. There must be a garbage dump behind some business that furnished his evening dining.

"I hope Pearl's okay," Maggie said.

"Phones still work. Call her," Sonny said, then headed toward town, but the closer he got, the more anxious he felt. Something was off. It was barely ten o'clock and he would have expected lights from within some of the houses. Lanterns, candles, something, anything. Instead, it was pitch black.

Maggie's call to Pearl went unanswered. She frowned. "Pearl isn't answering her phone," Maggie said.

"Do you have a key to the Rose?" Sonny asked.

"Yes."

"We'll drive by there, just in case, okay?" he said.

"Yes, and thank you," Maggie said, and the moment they drove up to the back of the café and parked, Sonny took a flashlight out of the console.

"Are we going to set off a security alarm?" he asked.

"Yes, it has battery backup for power failures, but I know the code," she said, and quickly unlocked the back door and disarmed the system.

Sonny closed the door behind them.

Maggie was already moving through the café, calling her name.

"Pearl! Pearl! It's me, Maggie. Are you okay?"

"I'm up here!" she cried.

They started up the stairs, found her phone on one of the steps, blood another step, and ran the rest of the way up in a panic.

Pearl was sitting on the sofa holding a dishtowel beneath her nose and an ice bag on her forehead.

"Honey! What happened?" Maggie cried, as she ran to her.

"Oh, I was on my way up the stairs when the power went out. It startled me. I missed the next step and did a header. Gave me a nosebleed, but it's stopped. I'm probably gonna have a bruise and a black eye. I lost my phone when I fell, but I was too rattled and hurt to go looking for it. I heard it ring, but that's why I didn't answer."

"Do you have any LED flashlights, or battery lanterns?" Sonny asked.

"One is on my bedside table, and another one on top of the refrigerator."

"I'll be right back," Sonny said, and used the flashlight feature on his phone to go get them, and left his flashlight with Maggie.

"Move the ice pack a second. I want to see what you've done," Maggie said.

Pearl sighed. "I could do with some painkillers. There are some in my medicine cabinet."

"In a minute," Maggie said, and began checking Pearl's forehead. There was a knot forming and bruising already apparent and spreading, and Pearl was right. She was going to have a black eye. "I'm so sorry, sweetie. I hurt for you."

Sonny came back with two LED lights and set them down around her, then handed Maggie a bottle of painkillers.

"I heard you ask for them," Sonny said.

Pearl winced as she glanced up. "You're not just pretty. You're handy as a pocket on a shirt."

He grinned. "I don't think I ever once set out to be pretty, so I don't know how to deal with that. Which cabinet has glasses? I'll bring you some water to down those pills."

"I'd rather have a shot of whiskey," she said, and then

saw the looks on their faces. "I know, I know, do not mix liquor and drugs. Glasses are in the cabinet to the left of the sink."

When he disappeared again, Pearl sighed. "If I was twenty-five years younger, I'd be fightin' you for that man."

Maggie smiled, but didn't comment. As soon as Sonny came back with the water, she shook out a couple of pain pills into Pearl's hand. Pearl downed the pills, chased them with a big drink, and then groaned.

"Crap, it even hurts to swallow."

"The Rose is going to be closed tomorrow," Maggie said. "There's no telling when the power will be back on, and I'm not leaving you alone tonight. I'm sleeping on your sofa, and don't argue."

Pearl got teary. "At least once a day, I say to myself that I don't know what I would do without you, and here you go again, proving yourself to be the daughter I never had."

Sonny laid a hand on Maggie's shoulder and gave it a quick squeeze. "She is special, for sure," he said. "Is there anything I can do? If there's a doctor in town, I'll bring him here, if you need treatment beyond an ice pack."

Pearl waved him off. "Thank you, Sonny, but I'll be fine."

He looked at Maggie for reassurance.

Maggie shrugged. "She has a knot on her head and

the beginnings of a black eye, but I think she's okay, and I'm going to be on hand. If I become concerned later, I know who to call here in town."

"Every piece of me says, 'don't leave you two alone,' but I bow to your judgment. I'm going to drive around a bit just to satisfy myself that all is well, and that it's just a simple power outage. I'll text to make sure you're okay before I leave town, but can I please help Maggie get you to bed?"

"Yes, of course," Pearl said. "I wanted to lie down, but I was afraid to stumble around again in the dark."

Between them, they got Pearl to bed, the ice pack back on her forehead, and her shoes off.

"Thank you," Pearl said, and closed her eyes.

Sonny left one LED lantern on the table beside her bed and gave the other one to Maggie.

"Pearl, I'm going to walk Sonny down so I can lock up behind him," Maggie said. "I'll be right back."

"Give him a kiss from me," Pearl muttered.

Sonny laughed. "You get one of your own," he said, and leaned over the bed to kiss her cheek. "Be good. Mind Maggie."

Pearl snorted softly, but she was secretly delighted.

Maggie walked Sonny down to the first floor and then back through the kitchen.

"Thank you for such a wonderful evening, and for being Pearl's hero. She thinks the world of you," Maggie said.

Sonny wrapped his arms around her. "The pleasure

of your company was mine. Stay safe, Magnolia. I'm going to scout out the situation before I leave."

She frowned. "What makes you think it's more than just a power outage, and don't deny it. I know you do."

"Just a feeling," he said, and kissed her. "Stay inside. Even if the power is restored. Stay inside until morning. Promise me."

She frowned, but agreed. "I promise. Just promise me you won't get yourself in harm's way."

He ran his thumb over the curve of her lower lip. "Lock the door." And then he was gone.

Maggie locked them in, reset the security alarm, and ran back upstairs.

Chapter 8

SONNY HATED TO LEAVE, BUT HE KNEW PEARL HAD A shotgun and Maggie swung a mean bat, and they were safer together than alone.

Something was off. He could feel it. It was the same way he always felt before getting on the wrong bull. There were bucking bulls that just wanted the rider off their backs, and killer bulls that wanted to destroy. He'd always known the moment he sat astride one, which one he was going to get. After that, it had been a matter of holding on tighter, riding smarter, clearing the fall safer. Only there were no bulls in sight and the hair was still standing up on his arms.

He began driving slowly through the business area, looking for something out of place. Some flash of light in a business supposed to be closed. Cars with out-of-state or out-of-county tags. He eased past the bank, the post office, and the quick stop—driving past alleys looking for a car that didn't belong. But it wasn't until he drove past Belker's supermarket and saw a flash of light in the back of the store that his senses went on alert. The only pharmacy in town was in the back of that store.

He parked in the shadows, got Emmit's hunting rifle from behind the back seat, and quietly walked to the alley at the back of the store. When he saw a car with out-of-state tags, and the back door to the pharmacy slightly ajar, he moved up to the door long enough to hear them talking, realized they were after opiates and narcotics, and moved back away from the building and made a quick call. A man answered.

"Briscoe County sheriff's office."

"This is Sonny Bluejacket calling to report a robbery in progress in the pharmacy at Belker's supermarket in Crossroads. The power is out in town."

"Dispatching officers to that location," he said. "Do you know how many there are?"

"I heard three different voices. All men. They're driving an old Dodge Charger. Red with a black racing stripe from front to back. Out-of-state tags."

"Did you get the number?"

"Yes, took a picture. Give me a sec," Sonny said, pulled up the photo and read off the numbers to the dispatcher.

"Where are you now?" the dispatcher asked.

"Parked on the other side of the street. Staying out of sight. I'm about to let the air out of all four tires. I'm putting my phone on Vibrate. Gotta go."

The dispatcher began relaying the information to the officers en route while Sonny slipped back up behind the car and quickly sliced the valve stems off of all four tires. They went flat within seconds. He was about to go back to his truck when he saw the little skunk come waddling out from behind the dumpster. There was a good fifteen feet between them, and Sonny saw no sign that the skunk was suddenly defensive. So, there they stood, looking at each other—judging their options.

Then Sonny saw a discarded paper bag with some garbage inside. He eased over and picked it up, noticed the partially eaten burger and leftover fries inside, then squatted down, so he would not be looming.

"Little Brother, I am asking for your help."

The skunk was still watching as Sonny carefully backed up, opened a door to the back seat, and emptied the contents of the bag into the floorboard, all except for one french fry, which he broke in two pieces. He tossed one close to the skunk, laid the next piece on the ground beside the open door, then stepped back.

The little skunk's nose came up, sniffing the air as it waddled toward the piece of potato and gobbled it down before following the scents, and found the other piece on the ground beside the car.

At that point, Sonny was a distance away, and holding his breath as he watched the skunk eat that, before sniffing the air for more.

"That's it, Little Brother. Just jump inside and dig in," he muttered.

The skunk's nose was in the air, sniffing, sniffing, then one leap and he was inside the car, digging through the garbage and nibbling away.

Sonny bolted toward the car, quietly pushed the

door shut without letting it latch, and then whispered, as if the skunk could actually hear and understand.

"Way to go, Little Brother. Be ready. You will know what to do." Then he ran back across the street into the shadows to wait.

Within minutes, the back door to the pharmacy opened, and three men came out heading for their car, each carrying bags stuffed with the stolen drugs. He could hear them laughing about the great haul they'd just made, and cutting off the power to a town with no police presence.

In the dark, they were moving fast as they jumped inside the car and slammed the doors, but when they started the engine and put it in Reverse, it was immediately obvious something was wrong with the tires and the driver yanked it back into Park just as the skunk fired away.

Sonny could see vague shadows of them waving their arms, and struggling to get out, then suddenly the doors flew open, and they were launching themselves out of the seats as if they'd been shot out of a cannon. They were screaming and gagging, cursing the skunk and each other.

He knew their eyes would be on fire and swelling with every heartbeat, and their noses were burning. He watched them gasping for air, only to take a breath and gag again. They began blindly running into each other and then falling and trying to get up and get away, even though they could barely see where they were going.

Sonny watched the little skunk hop out and run into the bushes, while the three men continued to stagger down the street, cursing and stumbling and falling.

Sonny drove all the way down to the main highway, then parked where he could still see them. One of them managed to get up and stagger blindly into a tree, promptly knocking himself out. Another ran into a parked car, fell onto the hood, then slid off into the street with a thud, and threw up all over himself. The third one had fallen in a ditch and was crying. He grinned. They were down for the count without a single shot fired.

It wasn't long before he began hearing sirens and then they grew louder as two patrol cars turned off the highway. He flashed his lights at them, then stepped out of his truck, making sure they could see he was unarmed.

When the sheriff saw it was Sonny, he braked and rolled down the window.

"Did they get away?" Matt Reddick asked.

"Naw, but they did get skunked. The stuff they stole is still in the car behind the supermarket, but you're not going to want to get too close to it for a while. One of the fools ran into a tree and knocked himself out. One's sitting up there by that parked car, throwing up all over himself, and the third one is in a ditch, crying for his mama."

Matt Reddick grinned. "How did you pull that off?" he asked.

"I let the air out of their tires, then put a skunk in the back seat. They did the rest when they got in and slammed the doors."

"I'm not even going to ask how you managed to get a skunk in a car without being sprayed, but now we have to drag their stinky asses back to the jail."

"They're pretty sick. Maybe you should call for an ambulance first," Sonny said.

"Hold that thought," Matt said, and immediately radioed for two ambulances to be dispatched to Crossroads, and to bring whatever they needed to offset the symptoms of direct skunk attacks.

At the same moment, Sonny saw a big bucket truck pulling up beneath the first power pole near the highway.

"That'll be the crew from the power company. The thieves are responsible for the blackout. A bunch of the residents called in the outage. If you don't need me anymore, I think I'll head home. Oh, tell your men if they see a skunk around, not to bother him. It's just Little Brother, and he's the actual hero in the story, okay?"

Matt stared. "You talk to a skunk?"

Sonny shrugged. "When the need arises."

Matt waved Sonny off, rolled the window back up, and dispatched one car to keep an eye on the thieves. He still had to notify the owner of the supermarket that his pharmacy had been robbed, and check in with the crew from the power company.

"We don't need weapons for this arrest, but we damn

sure could do with some gas masks," Matt mumbled, then called dispatch to get a phone number for the grocery store owner.

––––––––––––

Once Sonny got out of Crossroads, he stopped to call Maggie, then rolled down his windows to air out his truck. It didn't get any direct spray, but the scent of skunk was likely all over that side of town by now.

Maggie answered on the first ring. "I heard police sirens. What fresh hell did you start?"

He laughed. "Fresh isn't quite the right word. Skunky is more like it. Is Pearl okay?"

"Yes. I'm on the sofa in her living room. She finally got off to sleep and we will be closed for at least the next two days. What happened, seriously?"

"I saw a light in the back of the grocery store as I drove past and figured someone might be robbing the pharmacy, and they were. I called the sheriff, cut the valve stems off their tires, and waited. Along comes our little skunk friend. I tossed some garbage in the back floorboard of their car and left the door open. Long story short, he jumped in. I pushed the door shut, then went across the street to wait."

Maggie gasped. "You got a skunk to get into a car?"

"Pretty much. Then the thieves came out and jumped in their car and slammed the doors. That's when Little Brother went into action. They couldn't get out fast enough. They were blinded by the fumes, mostly screaming, and gagging, and running into each other. Right now, they're either unconscious or still puking, and the law has arrived."

Maggie burst out laughing. "This is legendary. You are going to be the talk of the town." And then a thought occurred. "Did the little skunk get away?"

Sonny smiled. There it was again—the concern for someone, or something else. "Yes, Magnolia, Little Brother hopped out during all the chaos and waddled off into the brush. He's fine."

"Good. I wouldn't like to think that they might have hurt him."

Sonny chuckled. "They only hurt themselves. I'm headed home now. Don't open your windows. If it gets stuffy, turn on the air conditioning. If Pearl doesn't need you and you get bored at home, come spend some time at the ranch. Oh, and call me if you need me."

Maggie sighed. "Ah, Sonny Bluejacket, I'm beginning to think I will always need you."

The words were still echoing in Sonny's ears when she disconnected. He drove home with a smile on his face, only to arrive at a house without lights. He stripped on the back porch, left his clothes where they fell, and stood naked, feeling the night air on his skin. The air was fresh and cool. The sky was littered with stars as he gazed across the land. And as he stood, the lights flickered inside and then came on. Power and order had obviously been restored. He gathered up his clothes and went inside, put them in to wash, then took a shower.

Much later, as he was finally getting into bed, he thought of the little kùnu and smiled.

———————

It was 3:00 a.m., the witching hour, when Sonny woke abruptly. His first instinct was to get up and run, but he didn't know why. He didn't know what had awakened him, so he laid there a few seconds, listening.

Within seconds, he heard a pack of coyotes yipping close by, and then he heard the horses and bailed out of bed. He yanked on a pair of jeans, stomped his feet into his boots and grabbed Emmit's rifle, making sure it was loaded as he pocketed a handful of shells and left the house on the run.

The moon was full, bathing the pasture in an eerie blue glow as he ran through the stable, through the corral, and out into the pasture. The herd was running, coming from the south, and behind them, a moving shadow on the ground.

Coyotes attacking a herd of full-grown horses wasn't normal unless they were running with foals, and he had none. He swung the rifle up into the air and fired two shots in rapid succession. The horses were still running, but at the sounds of gunfire, the shadow broke into pieces, and the distance between the coyotes and the horses lengthened.

Sonny swung the rifle down toward the shadows and fired shots in rapid succession. He heard one sharp yip—a sign he'd hit one of them, but their yipping and barking sounds were now moving back south, away from the ranch.

He stood in the pasture until the sounds had completely faded. He knew the horses would settle once they knew danger had passed. But come morning, he had some tracking to do, and needed daylight to see if any of the horses had been injured.

He went back inside the house to get a shirt, made some coffee, then took it to the back porch to drink, settling himself to a self-imposed guard duty with the rifle in his lap.

He was still sitting there when the sun came up, and the first thing he did was drive to the area where he'd first seen the shadow on the move. The horses were back near the ranch. He saw them up on a rise, but when he didn't drive toward them, they went back to grazing.

He found tracks almost immediately, got out and started walking on foot, backtracking south, looking for more signs. He was so focused on tracking, he didn't know that the Appaloosa had left the herd and was walking his way, likely thinking about apple treats.

He was still looking down when he saw a big shadow pass over the ground ahead of him, and looked up to see buzzards circling the sky. He thought of the pain-filled yip he'd heard when he shot into the pack, and wondered if one of them had crawled off and died. He started walking faster, curious to see what was down there.

It was buzzards on the ground that led him to the carcass. They flew off as he approached, giving him a clearer view, although they'd torn up the body enough that it was difficult to determine details. He squatted down, staying upwind of the carcass for a closer view, and was surprised by the size of it. It mostly looked like a coyote, but there were some differences in the features and the bigger bodies and longer legs. It was certainly bigger than normal, which made him think it might be a hybrid. A dog/coyote mating would explain it.

He straightened up, and as he did, heard a low, guttural growl behind him, and pivoted just as the pack began emerging from the brush. They stopped as he turned to face them, but the continuing growls were signs they weren't going to back down.

He was so focused on surviving this, that he didn't have time to be afraid. He swung the rifle up, guessing he could get about three of them before they attacked, and counting on the gunfire to scatter the rest. But before he could get off a shot, the thunder of hoofbeats was behind him, and then passing him.

It was Dancer, charging at the pack, kicking, and stomping, and screaming as only a horse can do in moments of pain or anger.

Sonny's shock was momentary, but now he couldn't get a shot for fear of hurting his horse, and he had to get Dancer out of that mess.

Without thinking, he ran into the fray, grabbed a fistful of Dancer's dark mane, and in a running leap, swung his leg up and over, landing on the horse's back. No reins. No halter, no saddle. All he could do was lock his legs around the horse's belly like he locked on to the back of the bull, and began firing at the pack.

The first shot scattered them, and when it did, Sonny kicked Dancer's flanks, urging him forward. The horse took off like a bullet. After that, Sonny began picking off the coyotes one by one as Dancer ran them down, racing them across the wide-open space like a guided missile locked on to a target.

Sonny's entire focus was on hitting coyotes and not falling off. He'd counted seven when they first appeared, but five were down, and now there were only two, still running ahead of him but veering west. He took aim and fired at the nearest one. It yelped and went down, and then there was one, still running at top speed.

Dancer needed no urging.

Sonny took aim and fired. The coyote yelped as it flipped in mid-air, then dropped. It was still kicking when Sonny rode up and fired one last shot, then leaned over Dancer's neck and hugged him.

"Good boy! Good boy! You are a warrior's horse, and magic isn't enough to describe what you just did. You saved my life. Now take me home."

The Appaloosa reacted to Sonny's urging, and turned north. When they reached the spot where he'd lost his hat, Sonny stopped Dancer and slid off. He laid his face against the horse's neck one last time to catch his breath, then gave him a pat on the rump, thinking the horse would rejoin the herd. But it wouldn't leave. Instead, it maintained a steady walk beside him all the way back to the truck. As soon as Sonny opened the door, he reached into the console and grabbed a couple of apple treats and gave them to Dancer one at a time.

Another shadow passed overhead. He looked up. Buzzards were already circling. They would clean up the carcasses, and the herd was safe.

As he got in the truck, Dancer kicked up his heels and took off running. By the time Sonny got back to the ranch house, the Appaloosa was at the water tank with the rest of the herd.

It wasn't until the rifle was back on the rack, and Sonny was standing within the silence of his house, that the reality of what just happened hit. His knees became weak, and his muscles began shaking from the adrenaline crash.

He'd taunted death every time he'd gotten onto the back of a bull. But that had been his choice. Today was a lesson. He couldn't walk on foot here and assume safety like he had back in Bluejacket Hollow. Existence out here came with a price.

———————

Walker Bluejacket woke up in jail. He didn't remember anything after downing his fifth beer, but his jaw hurt and his knuckles were swollen and bloody, so he assumed he'd gotten into a fight. He rolled over on the cot and sat up, glanced at the guy in the next holding cell who was glaring at him, and sighed. *Winston Billy. Oh yeah. Now I remember.* He stood up. "What are you looking at?" he muttered.

"An old drunk," Billy said.

"You're in the same place I am," Walker snapped.

"Because I punched the old drunk last night for insulting my wife," Billy countered.

Walker shrugged. "My tongue is loose when I am drunk."

Billy pointed at him. "You ever do that again, and you'll be picking up what's left of your teeth from the floor. Understand?"

"Yeah, whatever," Walker said, and sat down.

———

A short while later, Winston Billy's wife bailed him out of jail. When the jailer came to get Winston, Walker called out, "Ask your wife if she'll bail me out, too," and then laughed at him, but once Winston Billy was gone, there was no one to hassle. No one to laugh at.

Walker had burned too many bridges to hope anyone would even know he was missing. He would spend a couple of days in jail, pay a small fine, and be out with no one the wiser as to where he'd been.

He stretched back out on the cot, folded his hands

beneath his head for a pillow and stared up at the water-marks on the ceiling of the cell and realized something was leaking above him, and from the looks of it, it was an ongoing problem. Some of the spots were dark and rusty looking from age, while the spot beside it was gray and wet, and bulging like a loaded diaper.

He jumped up and began banging on the bars, yelling out until the jailer appeared.

"Damn it, Walker. It's not like you've never been here before. Keep it down," he said.

Walker pointed up to the ceiling above his cot.

"Something is leaking on the floor above. At least move me to another cell before all of that comes down on me."

The jailer looked up, groaned, and bolted out of the room.

"Hey! What about me?" Walker yelled, but he didn't get an answer. Frustrated, he pulled the worn mattress off the frame, dragged it to the other side of the narrow cell, then laid back down. At least the ceiling wouldn't fall on his face.

———

Charlie Bluejacket was on his way to work when his cell phone rang. He frowned at the caller's ID, then answered.

"Hello, this is Charlie."

"Charlie, it's Marcus down here at the bar. Your old

man got hauled off to jail last night for drunk and disorderly. His truck is still here and illegally parked. Does anyone want to come and get it?"

"Nope. Walker makes his own trouble. He cleans up his own messes," Charlie said, and hung up. On impulse, he called Sonny as he drove.

———

Sonny was outside on the back porch cleaning the rifle before hanging it back on the rack when Charlie's name popped up on caller ID. He smiled. They hadn't talked since parting at the bus station in Tulsa, and he quickly answered.

"Hey, brother, how's it going?" he said.

"Same old, same old," Charlie said. "Butters got neutered. Frannie wants a chicken house, and Julia is bugging me to take her to the daddy-daughter dance at her school. Walker is back in jail for D&D. Marcus from Dad's old hangout called asking me if I wanted to come get his truck before it gets towed. I told him to tow away."

Sonny ignored the update on their dad. "If you build that chicken house, remind Miss Frances that every hawk in Bluejacket Hollow will appreciate her offerings, unless you build a great big cage around the whole thing," Sonny said.

Charlie chuckled. "Good call. I'm going to price what it costs to build all that, what chicken feed and hen scratch are going to cost monthly, and see if she's still in the mood to raise chickens. So how are things going with you? What does a thousand acres of high prairie look like?"

"High mesas, a lot of sage and yucca and less grass. But it's beautiful in its way. My arrival got a bit hectic," Sonny said. "I arrived to discover the guy renting from Emmit just confiscated all the horses and equipment and his truck and had laid claim to it."

Charlie grunted. "Oh man. What happened?"

Sonny unrolled the story about the missing horses and truck. "Now they're in jail and I'm out here doing my thing."

"Awesome, little brother. I am happy for you. Any pretty girls out there in the middle of nowhere?" Charlie asked.

"Yes."

Charlie blinked. "I was teasing you, but you're serious, aren't you?"

"Yes."

Charlie grinned. "So, you're goin' all silent on me?"

"Yes," Sonny said, and then grinned to himself when he heard Charlie snort in frustration.

"Okay, fine. So, what's on your agenda today?" Charlie asked.

"Horse stuff. There is an Appaloosa in the herd named Fancy Dancer that I've taken a shine to. I will not be selling him, ever," Sonny said.

"Aah, an Appaloosa. I wish I could see you on that horse," Charlie said.

"Maybe I'll get that pretty girl to take a picture of me, and send it to you."

"Maybe take a picture of you and the pretty girl while you're at it?" Charlie suggested.

"Maybe," Sonny said. "Love to all. Tell Julia that Uncle Sonny loves her, and to send me a picture of you and her at the dance."

"Yeah, we can do that," Charlie said. "Stay safe, brother. Can't do without you."

"Doing my best, and thank you for always being there…for all of us," and then he disconnected.

Charlie always wanted to know everything. Sonny didn't mind. It was just Charlie being the big brother. He glanced at the time, wanting to call Maggie, but he hesitated. Without knowing what kind of a night she'd had with Pearl, he thought they may both be sleeping.

So, he sent her a text, instead.

You are on my mind. I wanted to call but didn't want to wake either of you if you were still asleep. Are you and Pearl okay? Let me know if you need help.

Then he hit Send, finished cleaning the rifle, and put it back on the rack.

It was Pearl's groan and then a string of muttered curses that woke Maggie.

Oh no! Pearl! The fall!

She flew off the sofa and ran into the bedroom to find Pearl teetering on the side of the bed, holding her head.

Maggie hurried to her side. "You headed to the bathroom?"

"I thought about it," Pearl mumbled.

Maggie slid her arm around Pearl's waist and helped her stand, then walked her into the bathroom before leaving her on her own. But her thoughts were already in plan mode. The Closed sign was staying on the door. She had to call Carson to tell him not to come to work, and get Pearl settled with food before she left.

As she sat down on Pearl's bed to make the call, she saw a text from Sonny. She read it and smiled. She'd answer after she got Pearl settled. She notified Carson, and was still sitting on the bed when the bathroom door opened. She jumped up to help Pearl, and saw the tears on Pearl's face.

"Do I need to get you to a doctor?" Maggie asked.

Pearl shook her head. "No, I'm just feeling sorry for myself."

"You go right ahead and do that," Maggie said. "Meanwhile, the Rose will be closed for at least the next two days, and depending on how you feel at that point, maybe more. The Closed sign is up. I called Carson not to come to work. And I'm going to the supermarket to get some food in for you that you don't have to cook. And don't argue with me."

Pearl threw her arms around Maggie's neck. "Thank you, baby. If you could make me some coffee and toast, I'll be good to go."

Maggie led her back to bed. "I'll do all of that and gladly, if you will stay up here, at least for today. No running up and down the stairs. Whatever you need up here, I'll bring it up before I leave. And if you need anything during the day, you will call me. Are we clear?"

Pearl sank into the pillows beneath her head. "Perfectly. Is the air conditioning on?"

"Yes," Maggie said.

"Why? I usually sleep with the windows open at night until later in the year."

Maggie shrugged. "Last night, Sonny said keep the windows closed. Something about a skunk."

"Ah, well, that makes sense. And it does feel good," Pearl said. "Thank Sonny for me, too. Did you ever find out what happened with the power last night?"

Maggie sat back down beside her. "Oh girl! Have I got a story for you!" And then she related the story Sonny told her, from seeing a light flash in the pharmacy, to the thieves, skunk-drunk and throwing up on Main Street.

Pearl was laughing and moaning all at the same time. "Oh, my lord! It hurts to laugh, but that's the best story I've heard in years. Did he get skunked, too?"

Maggie giggled. "No. I think he and animals are on

the same wavelength, but enough about all that. I'm getting your coffee and toast, then I'm going through your refrigerator. I can bring some stuff up from the kitchen downstairs, then I'm going to Belker's to get some food you don't have to cook."

At that point, she headed to Pearl's little kitchen to make coffee and toast. While the coffee was brewing, she sent a text back to Sonny.

> We're both okay. Pearl is sore and frustrated. I made the decision that the Rose will be closed for the next two days to give her time to recoup. I'm going home to get my car, run a few errands for her, and then I would love to come see you. Do you need anything from the store?

Chapter 9

SONNY WAS ON THE PHONE, OPENING AN ACCOUNT with the same feed store Emmit used to use, and putting in an order for bags of oats, and dry wood shavings for stall bedding. As soon as the call ended, he checked it off on his list of things to do. He'd already called the man Emmit ordered round bales and square bales from to put in an order when they began baling, and was looking up veterinarians in the area so he'd know who to call in an emergency, when his phone signaled a text.

It was Maggie! He read the message, and quickly replied.

I have food. All I want is you.

Moments later, he got his answer.

See you in a couple of hours or so.

After that, he forgot about vets, and horse feed and coyotes and put his breakfast dishes in the dishwasher, ran back to his bedroom to make the bed and then grabbed a dust mop and ran it over the floor in the front half of the house. He was wishing for some flowers to put into a vase to pretty up the place, when he realized Magnolia was the only flower needed to make his world perfect.

He'd just hung the dust mop back on the wall in the utility room when everything faded around him, and he was back in Bluejacket Hollow, standing on the creek-bank closest to Charlie's house, watching Julia wading in the water. He could see a man watching her from a distance, and it wasn't anyone he knew.

He was already reaching for his phone before the vision began to fade. His heart was pounding as he pulled up Charlie's number and called. It rang once, then twice, before he heard his brother's voice.

"Hey, Sonny, how's it going?" Charlie said.

"Where's Julia?" Sonny asked.

Charlie's heart skipped. "At home today. Some kind of teacher's workshop. Why?"

"I had a vision. She's wading water in the creek below your house, and there's a man watching her from a distance. I don't know if that's happening now, or in the future, but tell Frannie to call her home. For me. Then let me know if she's okay."

"Oh God," Charlie said. "There's an escaped inmate in the area."

The line went dead.

Sonny went numb—scared sick for his little niece. "The ancestors will keep her safe," he whispered, and then sat down. Unable to focus on anything until he heard from Charlie again.

Charlie yelled at his boss as he was running out the door. "Family emergency. Gotta go," and was calling Frances as he jumped in the truck and drove away. But to his horror, she didn't answer. He wasn't about to leave a message, so he disconnected, and the moment he slowed down to take a turn, he called her again. When she answered on the first ring, he breathed a quick sigh of relief.

"Hey honey."

"Frannie, where's Julia?"

"Playing outside. Why?"

"Can you see her?" he asked, as he took off out of the parking lot.

"Not this second. I'm in the laundry. I see I missed your first call. The dryer was making too much noise. What's wrong?"

"Go look, baby, go look. And if you can't see her, start calling her home. Hurry. Do it now!"

Frannie dropped the load of wet laundry back into the drum and stepped outside. Julia was nowhere in sight.

"I don't see her. You're scaring me, Charlie. What's wrong?"

Charlie's voice was shaking. "Sonny just called. He

had a vision of Julia wading in the creek and a stranger watching her from the woods."

Francine gasped. "Oh my God...the escaped prisoner!" she cried, and then started running toward the creek, screaming Julia's name as she went. As she passed the woodpile, she grabbed the hatchet they used for chopping kindling, and kept on going.

Charlie could hear the fear in her voice, as he flew through town.

―――――――――

Frannie couldn't see her daughter anywhere, but she kept shouting for her as she ran. She could feel the sun on the back of her head, and the thunder of her heartbeat as she ran. She had a death grip on the hatchet, and wasn't afraid to use it.

Just as she reached the tree line above the creek, she heard a scream. It was Julia! She stumbled, then caught herself from falling and started shouting, "I'm coming, baby! Mama's coming!"

Fear lent speed to her stride, and within moments, she was in the trees and running down the bank. She got a glimpse of Julia's little red sandals in the grass, and then heard her screaming for help.

One quick glance downstream and she saw Julia running in the water, with a full-grown man in pursuit. She let out a scream of pure rage and raced down the side of the creekbank after them.

The man saw her from the corner of his eye, running parallel with him at the creek bank with a hatchet in her hand. Startled by her sudden appearance, he pivoted in the water and started toward the far bank, thinking she would go after her kid, and he could get away.

But he was wrong. The moment he turned his back to her, she leaped from the bank, hit him in the back with her full body weight, and took him down in the water.

———

Charlie drove through the yard without stopping, driving all the way across the pasture until he reached the trees, then got out on the run. He could hear screaming in the distance as he took off running. Without them, his life meant nothing.

He knew it was Julia who was screaming, but he couldn't hear Frannie's voice at all, and Julia's voice was fading. Just as he reached the creek bank, he looked to his right and saw his wife running parallel with the man in the water, and his little girl still flying downstream.

Then as Charlie bolted forward, the man ceased his pursuit of Julia and turned to get to the other side of the creek. He was still running when he saw his wife leap off the creekbank and take the man down like a linebacker.

He didn't know she had the kindling hatchet until they both came up for air, but the moment Francine found her footing, she swung the flat side of that hatchet against the man's head like a baseball bat, dropping him back into the water, and he didn't get up.

Frannie staggered from the force of the blow that she'd swung, then reached down and grabbed him by the collar and began trying to drag him out of the creek, when all of a sudden, Charlie was there.

She staggered from the release of his body weight as Charlie yanked the man up by his arm and flung him onto the creekbank like he weighed nothing, then shouted down the creek, "Julia! Julia! You're safe, baby! You're safe."

The little girl heard her daddy's voice, then stopped and turned just as Charlie took his wife in his arms, hugging her and kissing her, and running his hands up and down her arms, checking for wounds.

"My God, Frannie, you ran him down and saved our girl. Are you all right? Did he hurt you?"

She shook her head. "No, no, get our baby. Get our baby," she kept saying.

He looked back downstream. Julia was standing in the water, too terrified to move.

"We need to call the police," he said.

"I dropped my phone somewhere on the bank."

Charlie handed her his phone. "This is Creek Nation land. Call the Lighthorse Police," he said, and took off downstream, while Frances climbed out of the water to make the call.

Charlie was focusing on the fact that his child was still alive, but terrified of what might have happened to her before they found her, and when he reached down to pick her up, she was shaking. Her skinny little legs were trembling. Her silky black hair was dripping wet, and her clothes were soaked and plastered to her body. He took off his shirt and wrapped her up in it, then picked her up like a baby, and when he did, she grabbed hold of the long braid in his hair like it was a life raft.

"I've got you, baby girl. Daddy's got you," he said, and carried her all the way back up the creek to where Frannie was waiting.

Francine had taken a seat beneath a tree with the hatchet across her lap. She knew that the unconscious man at her feet was still breathing steady. She hadn't drawn blood, so he wasn't in danger of bleeding to death, but she was afraid he would wake up.

Then Charlie came out of the creek and climbed the bank to where she was sitting. He put Julia in her lap and then dragged the unconscious man off to the side, took off his own belt, and used it to bind the man's hands behind his back as they waited for the police to arrive.

The moment Charlie laid Julia in her lap, Frannie let go of the hatchet and cradled her daughter to her. There were questions she had to ask, and like Charlie, she was fearful of the answers. Her hands were gentle as she pulled back the shirt Charlie had wrapped her in, to look for wounds.

"Julia, did he hurt you? Did he touch you?" she asked.

Julia was still shaking, but the fear was gone. Mama and Daddy saved her.

"No, Mama, but he tore my shirt when he grabbed at me. I remembered 'stranger danger' and ran."

"Thank God," she whispered, then hugged her close. "You are so smart, and so brave. Mama and Daddy are so proud of you."

Charlie sat down beside them, slid his arms around his wife and child, and knew if it hadn't been for Sonny's warning, this would have had a whole other ending.

"Did you get in touch with the Lighthorse Police?" he asked.

Frannie nodded. Tears were running down her face when she handed him his phone. "They should be here soon. You call Sonny now. You tell him that he just saved our baby's life."

———

Sonny was watching the clock, marking the timeline in his mind of how long it would take to get to the creek if they were running, and what they might find after they got there, and coming to terms with a scenario he didn't want to consider. The passing minutes felt like hours, then finally, his phone rang. When he saw his brother's name come up on caller ID, he answered.

"Tell me," Sonny said.

Charlie took a deep breath. "She's safe, and you were right. The escapee was chasing Julia through the creek when Frannie got there. You should have seen her, Sonny. She ran him down, tackled him in the water, then knocked him out with the flat side of a hatchet. Our ancestors would be proud. Julia only has a torn shirt. When he grabbed at her, all he got hold of was the sleeve. She tore out of his grasp and took off down the creek with him chasing her through the water. He's still unconscious and tied up, and both my girls are in my arms. Lighthorse Police are on the way. We are so grateful. Your vision saved our baby's life. Thank you. Thank you."

"Just as you saved mine when you took me into your family. Love you all. Tell Julia I keep her 'piece of sky' rock on the table by my bed. It's the last thing I see before I close my eyes, and the first thing I see each morning when I wake. We share blood, and distance doesn't change that," Sonny said. "Thank you for letting me know."

Charlie glanced up. "Lighthorse are here. Gotta go."

"Julia's going to have nightmares. Ask Auntie for healing," Sonny said.

"On it," Charlie said, and the call ended.

Sonny sat within the silence of the house with his brother's voice still echoing in his ears. *Your vision saved our baby's life.*

He got up and walked out of the house into the sunshine and glanced up the driveway. He didn't fully understand the visions. He couldn't turn them on or off. They just happened when they happened. Maggie could appear at any time, and he needed to pull it together before she arrived.

He had never told anyone about what had happened to him when he woke up in ICU to the ghostly figure of a medicine man dressed in ancient buckskin standing at the foot of his bed. The old man waved an eagle feather through the sage smoking in his hand, then waved it over the bandages on Sonny's chest and started speaking in their native tongue while Sonny watched. He could hear the drums and the singers, but he couldn't see them.

He tried to stay awake, but he was sliding back into the sleep shadows and thought he was dreaming. Then, between one blink and another, the medicine man was gone, and all he could remember was something about being brought back to life with gifts he must not waste.

It wasn't until after he'd healed and was living with Charlie and Frannie that he began having lucid dreams and realized he was spirit-walking, and participating in the dreams he was having.

After that, the dreams began happening in the daytime when he was fully awake. What he didn't know for sure was whether what he was seeing was something from the past, something that was happening at that moment, or would happen in the future. But today, what he'd seen had saved his niece's life, and he felt satisfied that he was following the path he'd been given.

He thought of all the things he could be doing, but

he was too amped up to start another project, and anxious to see Maggie. She was the calm within his storm.

―――――――――

While Sonny waited for Maggie, Jane Mallory was at the jail, waiting to see her client, Wade Sutton. Considering the mess he was in, she actually was bringing a bit of good news.

She heard footsteps in the hall outside, then the door opened, and a guard brought Wade to the table and sat him down, still handcuffed, then gave Wade a look.

"Thank you, officer. This won't take long."

"Yes, ma'am. I'll be just outside the door. Knock when you're ready to leave."

As soon as they were alone, she started talking.

"One piece of good news. The charges regarding the gun in your possession have been dropped. Your witnesses came through with enough details that the man you won it from has been identified and arrested. You still have all of the theft and fraud charges against you, and nothing is going to change that."

Wade's relief was visible. "Thanks for believing me," he said.

"I didn't necessarily believe you, Mr. Sutton. But I do believe the evidence that was uncovered. Now we have another decision to make. You pled not guilty at your arraignment. Do you now wish to change your plea, or go to trial?"

"What happens if I choose trial?" he asked.

"Since you weren't able to bond out, you'll await a court date, which a judge will have to set, and it could be anywhere from a number of weeks to months. I also want you to tell me how you think you could beat the rap. You were caught by the law with the stolen property, and the man you illegally sold horses to has also been arrested. So, he'll go to trial somewhere, and likely try to claim he didn't know the horses weren't yours, which won't hold water because everyone in a hundred-mile radius knew Emmit Cooper was dead, and Kincaid also knew you didn't own a pot to cook in when you were playing poker together, so neither of you will be able to clear yourselves or each other. That's pretty much where you stand. I'll do what you want, but no matter, neither of you will get off free of guilt."

"What am I looking at?" he asked.

"A third-degree felony. Years ranging from ten to maybe twenty-five in prison, and likely fines. It will be up to the judge's discretion. But you can't do what you did and expect to be excused because you needed the money. The court will ask you why you didn't just get a job. And if you say it's because of the location where you live, then they'll ask then why didn't you just move? What are you going to say? Because I didn't want to leave my drinking, poker-playing buddies, and I liked chasing women more than I cared about my own family?"

Wade glared at her. This was why he hadn't wanted a

damn woman for a lawyer. They always have an answer for everything. And then he remembered something.

"Did your kid have a good birthday?"

Jane blinked, surprised by the question. "Yes, he did, but he has an inoperable brain tumor, and we don't know how many more birthdays he's going to have, so we go a little overboard."

Wade thought about Randy, and his eyes suddenly welled as the wasted years washed over him. No matter what happened to his son from this day forward, he would never know, or be a part of.

"I'm sorry," he said, and for the first time, saw the shadows in her eyes, and the grim set to her jaw. "I'll plead guilty and take my sentence from the court."

"I'll be in touch," she said, and got up and walked out before he could see her cry. The unexpected empathy was her undoing.

———

Sonny was still waiting for Maggie when Dancer came up to the corral on his own. Sonny walked out to the barn, grabbed an apple treat from the bag, and the dandy brush from a shelf, then opened the gate to the corral.

Dancer tossed his head and sauntered in like he owned the place, nosing for the treat he could smell in Sonny's hand.

"Just because you saved my ass, you want another

treat?" Sonny said, smiling as the horse took the treat from his palm, then stood like a king waiting to be dressed.

Sonny scratched the spot between his ears, then began brushing the stiff bristles of the dandy brush through the tangled mane, then down the side of his neck, slowly working his way from head to tail on one side, before switching to the other side and repeating the process, lulling Dancer to the point that he'd dropped his head slightly in total relaxation.

By the time Sonny finished, he had grass seed and horsehair on his shirt and jeans from the ever-present wind blowing it all back in his face. He took off his shirt to shake it out, then tossed it over the fence into the grass and without giving Dancer an option, once again, grabbed him by the mane and in one smooth leap, landed on his back.

When Dancer tossed his head, Sonny laughed, then fisted his hands in the horse's long black mane and rode him out of the corral, and took off through the pasture, riding south at a lope, with the wind at their backs, and the sun beaming down on their heads.

———————

Maggie had to walk home to get her car before she could run errands. As soon as she got home, she changed clothes, then drove to Belker's.

The parking lot was fairly crowded, but she soon

found a parking spot, walked into the store, and immediately wrinkled her nose. The little skunk had certainly left his calling card. Despite the circulating air from the central cooling system, and air fresheners open and sitting about, the scent still lingered. It was enough impetus for her to begin shopping in haste.

The scent hadn't deterred shoppers, though. The store was busy with customers, and everybody there was talking about the power outage, the attempted robbery, and Sonny Bluejacket letting the air out of the thieves' tires, and getting a skunk into their getaway car without being sprayed. She'd predicted this story would become legend in this little community, and it was already well on its way.

After getting everything she'd come for, she checked out and hurried back to the Rose. Pearl had moved from her bed to the sofa, and was stretched out with an ice pack on her forehead, and an open beer at her elbow.

"I'm back," Maggie said, and began unloading what she'd purchased into the refrigerator and the pantry.

"Did you have enough money?" Pearl asked.

Maggie nodded, and pulled out the change, along with the grocery receipt. "I did, with some left over. I'm leaving it on your counter. Rocky Road ice cream is in your freezer. Cream for your coffee is in the fridge, and I got two kinds of barbeque from the deli, a rotisserie chicken, and two kinds of those salads you like."

Pearl was suddenly interested, and shifted her ice pack. "The tabouli and the pasta salad with peas?"

"Yes, ma'am, and smoked pork ribs and brisket and that spicy barbeque sauce to go with them. There's also a container of potato salad and a new box of cereal. I also brought up three pieces of pie from the Rose earlier. Chocolate, coconut cream, and a dish of peach cobbler."

"Thank you, baby girl. You are a lifesaver," Pearl said.

Maggie eyed the beer. "You're still taking pain meds."

Pearl snorted. "Don't make me choose. Pain meds bother my stomach. Beer does not."

Maggie frowned. "Fine, but I'm just saying…you already fell up the stairs when the lights went out. Too many of those beers and you'll fall down the stairs and put your own lights out."

Pearl laughed, and then groaned. "Still hurts to laugh, but whatever girl, I hear you. Now go on home. Get some rest. Go see that pretty man. Give him a hug for me."

Maggie grinned. "I'm not telling you where I'm going. I'll leave all that to your imagination. It'll give you something to think about besides how much you hurt. I love you. Promise you'll call if you need me."

"I promise," Pearl said. "Oh…go ahead and set the security alarm when you leave."

Maggie hurried downstairs, set the alarm, and then slipped out the back, anxious to be on her way to Sunset. The first mile came and went, and then the second passed without seeing anything but grass and the ever-present turkey buzzards high in the sky. She was coming up to the place where the Sutton trailer used to set when she saw a horse and rider in the pasture, coming toward her.

It was Sonny, riding bareback on the Appaloosa with the southern wind behind them, playing fast and loose with his hair and the horse's mane.

Seeing Sonny riding bareback at that speed was heart-stopping, and she couldn't decide whether she was scared for him, or in awe.

He waved when he saw her, then turned the horse around and started back to the ranch. That's when she realized there was no bridle or halter on the horse. All that kept him off the ground were those long legs locked around Dancer's belly, and a handful of horse's mane.

Maggie gasped. "Oh, my God. Oh, Emmit, if only you could see this! Just look at them go."

Delighted by the race back to the ranch, she accelerated and drove the rest of the way with Sonny and Dancer running parallel to her car.

The moment she pulled up in his yard she grabbed her phone and got out running, climbed up on the third rung of the corral and began filming him as he rode up.

He threw back his head and laughed at the sheer joy of the ride, let go of Dancer's mane and slid off.

Dancer snorted, then began grazing his way back to the herd.

"How did you do that?" she said, as he climbed over the corral and landed at her feet.

He bent down to pick up the shirt he'd tossed earlier. "He let me, so I did," Sonny said.

But she didn't hear his answer. She was staring at the scars on his chest and the tattoo on his chest. Turquoise-colored geometric triangles connected in such a way that made her think of a butterfly, an iron butterfly. She was remembering the way the air had shifted around her when she'd seen him walking into the Yellow Rose.

His heart sank when he saw her staring, and wondered if the scars would be a turnoff. "Sorry. I didn't think. I'm so used to the sight of them that I forget how others might react."

"Oh Sonny, it's not the scars. It's that tattoo." Her hand was shaking as she reached toward it, needing to touch, yet half-expecting it to fly away.

He caught her hand and held it to his chest. "My rendition of a butterfly. It's a reminder to me of my second chance at life."

She shook her head. "No, you don't understand. I had a dream the night before you showed up at the Yellow Rose. In the dream I was lying in the grass and covered in butterflies. All over my body. In my hair. On my face. There were so many I could feel the air shifting from the flutter of their wings. I was waiting for them to take flight, when I woke up, and for a moment, it felt like I'd taken flight with them. That evening, you got off the bus and walked into the Rose. When I saw you, I felt the same flutter of wings against my face. Now I see this, and I don't know what all this means."

A chill ran up Sonny's spine as he watched the changing expressions of awe and disbelief coming and going on her face. Now the instant connection he'd felt with her made sense. The ancestors led them to each other, and both of their lives were about to change.

"The Old Ones did it," he said.

Maggie's heart began to pound. "Old Ones?"

"My ancestors. Spirits who sometimes guide me to what I need to know."

"Like angels?"

He shrugged. "I think of them as ancestors from the thousands of years behind me. The people in whose steps we walk. Does all this frighten you?"

There were tears in her eyes. "I don't even know who I come from. I don't know anything about me. And here you are, loved by your family and aware and guided by centuries of people who came before you. I'm not scared, but I've never felt more alone."

He put his arms around her and pulled her close, rocking her in his arms where they stood.

"My beautiful Magnolia, I thought I came here for Emmit, when all along, it was you." He tilted her chin until their gazes locked. "I look into those blue eyes and see forever. If you can learn to love me, I swear on all I am that you will never be alone again."

She slid her arms around his neck, closed her eyes, and gave herself up to the kiss. As she did, the wind began to circle around them, bringing with it the scents of woodsmoke and sage.

Sonny heard the drums, and the distant sound of singers chanting to the drumbeat. Just like the vision he'd had in ICU.

Then he felt Maggie's hands in his hair, holding on to him in the same way he'd grasped Dancer's mane. The heat between them was rising with the wind, and it was only going to get hotter.

"In the house," he mumbled, then swung her off her feet and into his arms.

He put her down the moment they were inside. When he paused to lock the door, she disappeared. He was taking off his clothes as he followed her to the bedroom, and found her already barefoot with her jeans in a puddle around her feet. She was in the act of pulling her T-shirt over her head when he kicked off his boots and took off everything he was wearing.

The drums were louder in his head, the singers singing at a screaming pitch as she stood naked before him. The first step he took toward her, she dropped onto the bed behind her.

There was nothing in his head but being inside her, and when she reached for him, as if asking him to save her, he slid inside her and saved himself instead.

The drumming stopped the moment they became one. The singers were gone. The Old Ones were gone. They'd set them on the path. It was up to Sonny and Magnolia to follow it.

"Oh wait…protection," he muttered.

She whispered against his ear. "Already am. Don't stop."

So, he didn't. He just buried his face in the curve of her neck and took her on the wildest ride she'd ever known.

Seconds turned to minutes, coiling the imminent climax within them with every thrust, with every gasp, with every moan, until the blood rush came and swept them both away.

When Sonny could bring himself to breathe and think at the same time, he raised up on both elbows and looked down at her face.

"Mine," he said.

Her hand was on the butterfly, feeling the pounding heartbeat against her palm. "Mine," she whispered.

He grew hard inside her again.

She wrapped her legs around his waist, meeting him thrust for thrust until she lost her mind.

Chapter 10

THEY SHOWERED TOGETHER, THEN DRESSED IN silence. Without words, he sat down on the bed and pulled her into his lap. Both of her hands were crossed over her breasts, and she was shaking.

"Talk to me," he said softly.

Her eyes were wide with shock as she put a hand over her heart. "The hollow place. It's been there all my life. I don't feel it anymore."

He was already crazy mad in love, and she was breaking his heart. "What did it feel like before?"

Her eyebrows knitted. "It had no feeling. It always felt empty. I thought this was how everyone felt."

He hugged her closer as she tucked her head beneath his chin. "I can't imagine what it would be like to be as alone in the world as that, but that part of your life has ended as abruptly as mine once did. I'm not asking you for promises you're not ready to make, but can we please do the rest of our lives together...at your pace?"

"Yes, but I am asking you for promises, or I won't be back. I just got mad when Jerry Lee dumped me. Losing you will destroy me."

He cupped the back of her head and kissed her slowly, softly. It was her moan that made him stop.

"Magnolia, look at me. I understand why you don't trust. But I promise to love you forever. I promise to protect you, and honor you, and cherish the ground you walk on. And when enough time has passed for you to feel ready, I will marry you with great joy. It will be an honor to call you wife. I will give you babies to love, and share my family and my people, and we will grow old together."

"Is Sonny your given name?" she asked.

"No, it's John Wesley Bluejacket, but I only ever heard that from my mom when I was in trouble."

"It suits you. I don't have a second name. Just Magnolia."

He stared at her a few seconds, thinking, then slid her off his lap and onto the bed. "Give me a sec. Be right back," and strode out of the room. Moments later he was back carrying a little bowl half full of water. He took her by the hand and led her outside.

"What are you doing?" Maggie asked.

"When you were born, you were not presented to the world. Nobody heard an elder speak your name. Nobody blessed you, so I'm going to. Is that okay with you?"

She was so moved by what he was saying that she could only nod.

He ran his fingers through the water, then touched her forehead and said aloud. "See this woman. Her first breath gave her residence here, but no one came to claim her. She has not been named aloud, and so as she grew up, she has wandered, looking for her place to belong. Today she has found her place. Today, I speak aloud her name for all to hear. You will know her now as Magnolia Rae Brennen. See her. She is a woman of substance, and she is mine."

Then he poured the water out at her feet and put his arms around her.

Blind with her own tears, it was all Maggie could do to hold on.

"Say your name," he said.

She took a breath. "Magnolia Rae Brennen."

He wiped the tears from her face.

"Who loves you?" he asked.

She swallowed past a sob. "Sonny Bluejacket loves me!"

"Who does Magnolia love?" Sonny asked.

"She loves Sonny."

He smiled. "And who does Sonny love?"

"He loves me."

"Yes, I do," he said, then brushed a kiss across her lips. "You have been seen. You are no longer lost in the world. And since this is your naming day, I think we should celebrate. How about a picnic?"

She nodded. "I'll help."

He brushed a last kiss across her lips. "I was hoping you'd say that. And don't let me forget to grab a bunch of apple treats for the horses or they will be begging for bread."

She frowned. "Apple treats? Like real apples?"

"No, they look a little bit like big crunchy biscuits. The horses love them. You'll see."

They went inside, and about a half an hour later exited again, this time with two small ice chests. One with the food, and one with cans of soft drinks covered in ice to keep them cold. They climbed into the truck, drove down to the barn long enough for Sonny to get the apple treats, then drove into the pasture and headed north, holding hands as he drove.

"As long as I knew Emmit, I've never been farther than his house. I've never been on this land before," she said.

"It's all pretty new to me, too, but I have driven most of the boundary. Some of it isn't made for wheels. It's good to know what belongs to you and what does not," he said. "The trouble with picnics around here is lack of shade, but if the horses haven't taken up residence, I know where we can find some, and with a beautiful view back to the south."

"Oh look! There's the herd," she said, pointing. "And there's Dancer, eyeing the truck."

"He'll be the first to follow. You'll see."

"Why?"

"He loves apple treats. They all do," Sonny said.

"I think he's laid claim to you," Maggie said.

"Why do you say that?" he asked.

She shrugged. "I don't know. Emmit always said the horse was standoffish. Magnificent, but a horse who dealt with humans on his own terms, was how he put it."

Sonny was surprised. He thought from the way the horse was with him, that Emmit was responsible for his easy-going nature. Now he was wondering if the Old Ones had whispered in Dancer's ear before he came, and that the horse was expecting his arrival. This whole conversation was a revelation.

Then Maggie looked back, delighted by what she saw. "You were right, Dancer is coming at a lope, and the others are following."

Sonny laughed and kept on driving.

As they passed the first windmill and water tank, he pointed in the distance.

"There's our picnic pavilion! It's one of the weather sheds Emmit built," then glanced in the rearview mirror and accelerated. He wanted to get to the shed before the horses swarmed him for treats. The moment he drove inside and parked, he jumped out on the run.

Maggie was getting out when he grabbed her and swung her over the side of the truck bed.

She laughed at the unexpected journey.

"Gotta keep my girl safe," he said, then moved the ice chests into the truck bed beside her. He was lowering the tailgate when the horses arrived and swarmed him, and Maggie was soon on her knees, petting the horses gathered around the truck. Seeing her so comfortable among them made him happy. They were a huge part of his life, and knowing she was at ease with them was a relief.

"They just want attention, but they're getting a bit pushy. I'll get them out of the shed," he said, and walked out with the treats, knowing they would follow, and they did.

Maggie scooted onto the tailgate, letting her legs dangle as she watched him moving among them, giving each one attention, stroking them as he called each of them by name, then finally giving each one a treat as they stood quietly, waiting to be next.

Dancer was the last to come to him, and when Sonny put his arms around the big horse's neck, the Appaloosa laid his head on Sonny's shoulder, almost as if he was trying to hug him back.

Maggie couldn't take her eyes off them, and seeing him like this among the horses made her wonder what he was going to do with Sunset. Whatever it was, it had to be good.

When he finally came back to the truck, he got some hand-wipes from the cab and they both cleaned their hands before getting to the food.

"Now that the babies have been sent out to play, how about those sandwiches?" he said, and pulled the ice chests up between where they were sitting, then leaned over and brushed a kiss across her lips. "Happy name day, darlin."

Maggie was full of new delight. "Maggie Rae! I can't wait to tell Pearl. That way she can call me by both names now when she's having herself a fit."

Sonny laughed. "She always was a pistol, but she has a big heart."

"That I know," Maggie said.

They unwrapped the ham and cheese sandwiches, opened a can of pop apiece, then started eating. "The true meaning of tailgating, right, honey?" he said.

"As long as it's with you, I'll tailgate anywhere," Maggie said.

A few minutes later, they were finishing up the sandwiches and digging into the cookies he'd packed, when she noticed the number of buzzards in the sky south of the ranch house. "Looks like something might be dead out there," she said.

Sonny was licking mustard off his thumb. "That's because something is dead out there. Eight coyotes to be exact, and big ones, at that."

Maggie handed him a napkin. "Exactly how did they get themselves dead?"

"They messed with what's mine. Pretty sure they were dog/coyote hybrids. We had a full moon last night and they got after the herd."

She immediately began looking at the horses. "Oh no! Are they all okay?"

"Yes, but only because I woke up. It was around 3:00 a.m. when I heard the horses raising heck and running, and then the coyotes yipping. I fired into the pack, and they scattered."

"Did you get one of them?" she asked.

"Yes, I found the carcass of the one I'd hit in the early morning hours after daylight, when I went looking. It had crawled off and died. It was at the edge of the grazing area, near some scrub brush. I grabbed my rifle and left the truck on foot, looking for tracks in hopes of finding the rest of the pack. I didn't want them holed up somewhere on the ranch, and having to deal with them when the mares begin to foal."

"Did you find more tracks?"

"I found more than I bargained for. One moment I'm looking down at a set of huge pawprints, and the next thing I hear growling and look up to see seven of them spaced out in front of me. It wasn't the best situation, and I was guessing I could get at least two, maybe three before they scattered and came at me again, when I heard a horse coming up behind me in full gallop. All of a sudden, Dancer comes racing past me squealing in rage, and ran straight into the midst of coyotes, kicking and stomping, and now I couldn't get off a shot."

The image of that scene sent a chill up Maggie's spine. "Oh my God. What did you do?"

He finished the story while eating his second sandwich.

Her eyes were wide with shock. "Excuse my language, but how the hell did you stay on a running horse with no way to guide it?"

"The same way I did when you drove up on Dancer and me in the pasture."

But Maggie wasn't buying the blasé delivery of the story. She was horrified and it showed. He could have died.

"You made kill shots riding at breakneck speed

and did it bareback without falling off. That sounds impossible."

He kissed the back of her hand and then grinned. "Except that's how my ancestors hunted buffalo. Riding bareback beside a stampeding herd of buffalo, hunting with bows and arrows, then riding them down until they fell over and died. Then later when they had rifles, shooting from the back of their horses at a dead run."

"So, does that mean the herd is safe now?" she asked.

"For a while, at least."

She dug into the ice chest and pulled out a bag of cookies and handed one to him.

"You should celebrate the fact that you're still here in one piece," she muttered.

He took the cookie and laughed. "Are you mad at me?"

"No, but I am learning things about you I did not know before, and I'm trying to get adjusted to the fact that the man I am falling in love with doesn't have the good sense to be scared," she muttered.

He scooted the ice chests back into the truck bed and scooted up beside her, then took her hand.

"Sweetheart, you should have known when Pearl told you I used to ride bulls, that once upon a time, I didn't have a lick of good sense. However, dying changes perspective. I celebrate every day I am alive. I do not take unnecessary risks, but sometimes life hands us tasks we must complete, and I don't live life in fear. Understand?"

She nodded. "I know that in my head, but my heart is just coming to terms with being loved. Selfishly, I don't want to lose that. I don't want anything to happen to you."

He gave her shoulders a quick squeeze. "When I was riding bulls, I lived like every day could be my last. I didn't like how that turned out. After that I felt like I was just biding my time, waiting to be shown what came next. I didn't know it would be you, but you are the gold at the end of my rainbow, and I want to be everything to you that you need me to be." He slid off the tailgate and then stepped between her legs and hugged her, as he did, the wind caught in his hair. "Dang wind. I'm gonna have to start putting my hair in a braid again, like I did when I was still riding bulls."

Maggie's eyes widened. "If you want, I can braid it for you now."

"I usually have to do it for myself, but that would be great. You sure you don't mind?" he asked.

"Not a bit, but I need an elastic hair tie."

"I think I have a couple in the console," he said. "Let me look." He headed for the cab, and came back smiling. "The console in a truck is the man version of a woman's purse. A little bit of everything in there," he said, and gave it to her.

She was all business as she slipped it on her wrist. "Okay dude, turn to face the wind," she said.

Sonny grinned as he turned his back to her. *Dude. She was going to be the saving of him*. When she began combing her fingers through his hair, he closed his eyes.

As soon as she got the tangles out, she paused. "One braid, right?"

He nodded.

His hair was silk between her fingers as she separated it into three parts and began the braid at the nape of his neck, alternating sections until she got all the way to the end, slipped the elastic band onto the end of the thick rope of hair and wrapped it firmly in place.

"Done!" she said.

Sonny turned around, cupped her face in his hands and kissed her. "In our culture, it is a loving, bonding thing to brush and braid each other's hair. Thank you."

She beamed. "If I get to choose a bonding moment... other than making mad crazy love with you, I'll take a good foot rub."

Sonny laughed. "You got yourself a deal."

He made her heart skip. Slowly but surely, this man was putting all the broken pieces of her together.

"Are you ready to go back to the house?" he asked.

"I don't have an agenda other than you. I'll help, or if you're busy, I can take myself home."

He frowned. "I don't want you to leave."

"Then we go where you need to go next. If it's to Crossroads, we can make waves by showing up together. If it's something on the property, I know how to stay out of the way and watch. And if I can help, I'm your second pair of hands."

Sonny shook his head. "You're second to no one. You're my one and done, darlin'. Get your cute little butt in the truck."

Maggie took her cute little butt to the truck and climbed in, but the grin on her face was there for anyone to see. Being someone's one and done said it all.

After a stop-off at the house to wash up and get the rifle, they started out again, only this time driving south. The turkey buzzards were still circling the sky, which meant there were likely more of them on the ground. He'd done what he had to do, and would do it again. Only this time, he was following the road Emmit's trips had worn into the area, and not chasing off into the sage and yucca for an escaping coyote. After noticing the intent expression on Maggie's face as they went, he wanted to know what she was thinking.

"What do you think about all this?" Sonny asked.

"It's beautiful in its own way, but different from the land around the ranch itself. How does that happen?" she asked.

"Emmit made that happen. It would have all looked like this. He cleared land and sowed some grass varieties that would be hardy in places that don't get a lot of rain and endure in winter, as well."

She nodded, absorbing the explanation. "So, what are you going to do with this land? The same thing, or leave it in its natural state?"

"Not sure, honey, but I've been considering a couple of different options here. I'm thinking I might rather buy good-blooded three- or four-year-olds already broken to ride, and train them here to sell, instead of breeding and raising them here first."

"And keep the herd on the north end of the property?" she asked.

He grinned. "You're thinking like a rancher already. If I do that, then I'll be fencing off the south end so I can keep them closer. Anyway, it's a start."

As he was driving, his phone rang. He glanced down. "It's my brother," he said, and braked to a stop.

"Hey Charlie, how's it going?" he asked.

"Good enough."

Sonny frowned. "How is Julia since the attempted abduction?"

"Nightmares. Afraid to play outside. We're going to have a big family dinner soon in hopes that playing outside with her cousins will help."

"Is Frannie okay?"

Charlie sighed. "She isn't sleeping well. Wakes up off and on all night and has to go see that Julia is safe in her bed before she can go back to sleep."

"I'm sorry, brother. I wish I had an answer for you."

"You did your part. You saved her life. On another note, is that pretty lady still in your life?"

"She's sitting right beside me," Sonny said, and winked at Maggie. "We'll send some pictures later, okay?"

"Thank goodness. Frannie thinks she needs to see her face."

"Works both ways," Sonny said. "I want a picture of all of you to show her. And you tell my little sweetheart that Uncle Sonny wants a picture of her with a big smile on her face, and she has nothing to fear. She fought her enemy and won."

"Yes, I will, and thank you, Sonny. She idolizes you. Maybe that will help. Oh…hell, almost forgot the reason I called. I heard through the family grapevine that Walker packed up his clothes and gave up his apartment when he got out of jail. Nubby Zane is missing, too."

"Shit," Sonny muttered. "Do you think he's—"

"Going to try and find you?" Charlie said, finishing the question Sonny was about to ask. "Probably, and taking Nubby for backup. You know that man is mean. Don't trust him anymore than you do Walker. Just be prepared."

Sonny sighed. "Thanks for the heads up, but don't worry. If he finds me, I'll see him coming. There's no place for him to hide out here."

"Just the same, be careful, and send me those pictures," Charlie said, and disconnected.

Sonny put the phone in a cupholder in the console.

"Is everything okay?" Maggie asked. "Did something happen to your niece?"

"A couple of days ago I had a vision. I saw a stranger stalking her while she was playing in the creek below the house. Long story short, I called Charlie…he called his wife, Frances, as he was driving home, and she took off running to look for her. It was an escaped inmate from a nearby prison, and by the time Frannie got to the creek, Julia had twisted out of his grasp, and he was chasing her in the water. Frannie ran him down and knocked him out with a hatchet. Charlie got there for the clean-up."

Maggie's voice was trembling. "You saw all that?"

He nodded. "I saw the danger. I didn't know what was happening after I called. Worst feeling in the world to be so far away and not be able to help."

She reached across the console and clasped his hand. "You were given a second chance at life for a reason, weren't you?"

He shrugged. "It would seem so."

"What did you mean by, there's no place here for him to hide? Are you in danger?"

"He thinks my father and one of his drinking buddies are looking for me. Walker wants a piece of all this, but if he doesn't get it, he'll do his best to destroy it. He's evil walking. Him and that giant turquoise belt buckle and scraggly gray braids. He hasn't told the truth twice in his life and he broke our mother's heart when he abandoned her, leaving her to raise us on her own."

Her eyes narrowed angrily. "Everybody who comes to Crossroads, comes to the Rose. If he walks in the door, I'll let you know."

"Okay, but don't even pretend you know who I am. I wouldn't put it past him to use you to get to me."

She nodded. "I promise, but never worry about

me. Pearl has the shotgun and Carson has his base-ball bat."

"When you are out of my sight, I will always worry about you." He kissed her. Softly. Lingering on the shape and taste of her lips until he was aching to be inside her. But that was for another time and place.

Her eyes were still closed as he pulled back, but not for long. She blinked, and the first thing he thought of was "pieces of sky," like the little blue rock Julia gave him when he left. Maggie was his piece of sky, his good-luck charm, the woman who held his heart.

"Love you, Magnolia."

"Love you more," she said. "Did you promise Charlie pictures?"

"Oh, yeah, I did. They want to see you, and they want to see me on the Appaloosa."

"I have video of you riding up on Dancer. When we get back to the house, we can take one of us in front of your house, so they can see that, too."

"They will love that, and I'm taking you back now. Bringing you out without knowing if there's more of the pack is dangerous. I'll come back by myself later."

Maggie didn't argue, and as soon as they got back to the ranch, they went to the front yard. Sonny put one arm around her, and then held up her phone and took a selfie of them with his house in the background.

"There you go. Send the stuff to my phone, and I'll send it to them later," he said. "I need to find the coyote den and make sure they're all gone. I don't want you to leave, but I hate to leave you in the house alone."

"You go do what you need to do. I'll be here when you get back, okay?"

"Perfect," he said, then gave her a quick kiss, then unlocked the door. "Lock yourself in, okay?"

"You're worried about your dad. Don't be. I'm sure I'll be fine, but I will do that, just the same."

"Thank you, baby. Call me if you need me," he said, as he closed the door between them. As soon as he heard the lock turn, he headed to the truck.

Maggie turned to face the empty house. She couldn't just sit here doing nothing, and it felt like it did when Emmit was still alive—her in the house, and him off being a cowboy. So, she rolled up her sleeves and went to get a dust mop.

———

Pearl was in a mood. Inactivity was the worst. Damn those skunked-up thieves for cutting the power. If the lights hadn't gone out when they did, none of this would have happened.

It hurt to blink, and every time she looked in the mirror, she moaned at the sight. Her eye and cheek were one solid mass of black and purple. And the more time passed, the more bruises appeared. There was a little one under her chin, and she'd jammed a couple of fingers on her right hand when she fell, and now the middle knuckles on both of them were swollen and bruised.

Once upon a time she'd been a pretty little thing, with her curly hair and turned up nose. Now she was all saggy, and her blond hair was white.

The cars passing by the Rose made her miss the hustle and bustle of a workday, but she knew she wouldn't last an hour standing at the grill. The fall was a kind of wake-up call. If she had extra help, she wouldn't have had to close, which prompted her to follow through on advertising for more workers.

She dug through a closet, looking for that piece of poster board she'd kept and then got out an oversized marker and made a sign to put in the window that read:

JOB OPENINGS:
GRILL COOK
WAITRESS

Then she grabbed a roll of tape, took it downstairs and hung it at eye-level on the big window by the entrance.

Satisfied that she was taking control of her business again, she made herself a Mountain Dew from the fountain and went back upstairs, taking care to hold on to the handrail as she went.

Maggie was at peace in the house, dusting and mopping like before, and when she finished, she crawled up onto the sofa, tucked a throw pillow under her head and covered up with the blanket from the back of the sofa.

The blanket smelled like sage and Sonny. The room smelled like lemon. She could hear the wind whipping around the corner of the house and a horse whinny somewhere beyond, but inside it was calm and quiet. She sighed, then pulled the blanket up under her chin and closed her eyes.

———————

Sonny felt bad asking Maggie to come to the ranch, and then leaving her behind, but he didn't want to put her in danger, and he needed to find the coyotes' lair. He began his search at the place where he'd first been attacked. If they had been denned up nearby, he would find it.

As soon as he reached the area, he took the rifle and got out to begin his search, looking for crevices, or a rise in the earth that had been dug out for shelter. He didn't find anything obvious and widened his search, and then smelled it before he saw it. It was the musky scent of dog and urine that gave it away, and then the bleached-from-the-sun bones scattered around the opening beneath a pile of rocks and dirt. The entrance was all but hidden by the yucca plants around it. He paused and made a three-sixty turn of the area to make sure he was still alone, and then squatted down near the entrance and aimed a flashlight into the darkness.

It was empty, and no fresh tracks going in or out.

Relieved, he began kicking at the base of the mound of rocks until he disrupted the balance, then watched in satisfaction as the den collapsed. It was a small victory, but it was enough, and maybe the scattered bones of the dead pack would deter other coyotes from making this place their home.

At that point, he shouldered his rifle and began retracing his steps to get back to the truck. He checked his phone as he went, saw the text from Maggie, and then remembered she was going to send him their picture and the video she'd taken of him riding Dancer. As soon as he got into the truck, he started it up, turned on the air conditioner, then sat and watched the video of himself riding up on Dancer, then studied the picture he'd taken of them in front of the house. *Charlie will like these. He will see where I live, and he will know by the look on my face that she's the one.* He sent Charlie a text message and the attachments with it, and hit Send, then put the truck in gear and headed home.

As he was driving, he got a call about the dried wood shavings and straw bales he'd ordered. They were being delivered tomorrow afternoon. Another step to getting the place up and running. Now all he wanted was to get back to Maggie. A few minutes later, he pulled up to the back door and parked, dropped his phone in his pocket and went inside.

Charlie walked into the house with Julia bouncing behind him. He'd just picked her up from school and couldn't wait to show Julia and Frannie the picture and video Sonny sent him.

Frannie was breaking fresh green beans to cook for supper when Charlie walked into the kitchen. "Sonny sent pictures," he said.

Julia squealed. Frannie set the beans aside and sat down at the table with Charlie.

"The first one is a video of Sonny on the Appaloosa. He's riding the horse bareback, without a bridle of even a rope. Mom always said Sonny was a throwback to the ancestors, and I guess she was right. Just look at this."

He'd watched the video a dozen times already, but now he was seeing it anew. Sonny was minus a shirt. His hair was loose and flying, and the horse was running like the wind. He had the biggest smile on his face and when he rode up to the corral, he swung his leg over and slid off.

"Charlie, just look at him," Frannie said.

"Uncle Sonny has a really pretty horse," Julia said.

"There's one more picture," Charlie said. "This is Sonny and his girl. Her name is Magnolia Brennan, but he calls her Maggie."

Frannie took the phone out of his hands and studied it, then nodded.

"She loves him. I can see it on her face."

"Yeah, and he loves her. Anybody can see that," Charlie added.

Julia frowned. "I thought I was his best girl."

"You'll always be his best girl, and one day Maggie will be his wife. Those are two different things."

Julia thought about it, then nodded. "She's pretty."

"Yes, she is, and we're really happy for Uncle Sonny, aren't we?" Frannie said.

Julia grinned. "Yes, we're happy. What's for supper?"

"So much for the burst of jealousy," Charlie said. "I promised Sonny I'd send pictures of us."

"I'll send pictures of you and Julia all dressed up for the father-daughter dance, and I'll pick out a good one of us, too," Francine said. "Sonny's woman should know who her family is going to be."

Chapter 11

JUST KNOWING MAGGIE WAS WAITING FOR HIM MADE going home a whole new experience. But when he walked in the back door, the silence was unexpected. Then he smelled the scent of lemon and noticed the floors were shining. She'd cleaned.

He hung up his hat as he went through the house, and then saw her asleep on the sofa and stopped, drowning in a new wave of emotions.

She looked so small lying still beneath his blanket. So small, and yet he knew how fierce she could be, and what an indomitable spirit dwelled within her.

Mine, waiting all these years for me to find her.

He sat down in a chair across from where she was lying to remove his boots, then padded quietly into the kitchen to get a drink before returning to the big easy chair. He stretched his long legs out before him and leaned back, thinking what it was going to be like in the years to come, with her at his side.

Lovers. Partners. Husband and wife. And he remembered then, the passage from Emmit's letter about not living life alone.

I found my partner, Emmit, and she was worth the wait.

He took the phone out of his pocket and set it on the table beside him, then closed his eyes. He was in the halfway-world between sleep and awake, when he saw an old red pickup broken down on the shoulder of a highway. The hood was up, and two men were working on the engine underneath it. He couldn't see their faces, but he could see a highway sign a few feet away from where the truck had stopped. BOISE CITY—5 MILES. Then the vision shifted back to the truck. As the men lowered the hood, he saw their faces, watched them kicking tires in frustration, then getting back inside. But they weren't moving.

Walker and Nubby—broken down in the westbound lane of a highway in the panhandle of Oklahoma.

His eyes flew open—his heart was pounding. *Charlie was right. They're on the hunt. Taking the roundabout road, but westbound just the same.* His gaze went straight to Maggie.

Damn Walker straight to hell. What was wrong with that man? How was he going to deal with them and keep her safe? He needed a way to know where she was at all times when she wasn't with him. Maybe some kind of tracker.

And then it hit him.

The Life360 app that Charlie and Frannie had on their phones. All they had to do to find each other during workdays was to pull up that app and look at the map. Wherever they were, the map pinpointed their locations, and if they were moving, it showed where to and in what direction. If he loaded this app on their phones, as long as their phones were with them, they could see each other's locations.

He sat up in the chair and pulled up Google Play on his phone, downloaded the app and set it up. When Maggie woke, he would add her phone to his group and show her how it worked.

But now he was unsettled. Trouble was coming but he didn't know when, and tossing a skunk into the cab of their truck wasn't going to come close to stopping them. Walker wanted him dead.

He got up and walked over to where Maggie was sleeping, pulled the cover back up over her shoulder, and then slipped outside onto the front porch, eyeing the road that ran past the entrance to the ranch.

The road was nearly always devoid of traffic, and today was no exception. He didn't even know who his nearest neighbor east was. He'd never followed the road any farther south than to his property. He was three miles from Crossroads and in the middle of a high-plains prairie. He would see them coming, and he'd be waiting.

Tomorrow they'd deliver the straw and shavings he'd ordered for stall bedding. Maggie would likely go back to Crossroads to check on Pearl. He needed to get some extra groceries in now so he wouldn't have to show his face in town, then hole up and wait it out.

He wasn't afraid for himself. What would be, would

be. Maybe he would call Matt Reddick, then discarded the thought. What would he say? *I think my father's coming to kill me? I don't have proof, but I saw it in a vision? God, what a mess.*

He was still staring across the land when he heard the click of the latch behind him. She was awake. And then her arms were around his waist, hugging him, and he could feel her face pressed against the middle of his back.

He turned around and pulled her close. The urgency of keeping her safe was uppermost, and to do that, she had to know what was going on.

"My Magnolia, in this very short length of time, you have stolen my heart. To quote the lines from a song I've always loved…'they didn't have you where I come from,' and it has taken me all these years to find you. Now, the thought of life without you is impossible to consider."

She stilled within his embrace. "What's happened?"

"Walker and Nubby broke down in the Oklahoma panhandle near Boise City, and they're headed west. They're looking for me."

Maggie's heart skipped a beat, but she wasn't going to let him know that it scared her to know that.

"How do you know? Did you see it?"

He sighed. "Yes."

"Maybe he's just curious," she said.

"You don't know Walker. He does nothing on impulse. Since I refused to include him in this journey, he is changing tactics. He asked and I refused. Now he's going to take or destroy, because that's how he rolls."

"Take? Take what?" she asked.

"My life, I think. The fact that he brought Nubby Zane with him is why I know this. Nubby is what medical experts would call a psychopath. He has no conscience. He'll be the one with the gun."

Maggie hid her spurt of panic. "What can I do?"

"Stay out of it or you'll become collateral damage. But just in case, I want to add an app to your phone," and he began to explain what he meant, and how they would know where each other was at any given time. "Would you be okay with that?" he asked.

She nodded.

"Then let's go inside. I want to do that now, and then I need you to not be here until this is over."

She didn't flinch. She didn't cry. She didn't let on for even a second that she felt like she was dying inside as they entered the house. She watched him add her phone number and address to his phone, and then he showed her how it worked, and how they could tell each other's location.

"Okay," Maggie said. "You've done what you need to do, and I'm going to do what I need to do. I'll go check on Pearl, but I'm not going to hide. If I'm with you, I'm with you in good times and bad. You don't do this alone. Understand?"

She saw resignation on his face and the want in his eyes, then wrapped her arms around his neck.

Sonny swung her off her feet and carried her to the bedroom. She'd made up the bed while she was cleaning, but he wanted her on his sheets, and when he put her down, he pulled back the covers.

She began to undress, but then he stopped her. "Let me," he whispered. She dropped her arms as he began removing the garments, one by one.

First her shoes, then her shirt, then her jeans, leaving her standing in nothing but lingerie, which was soon on the floor at her feet.

He laid her down on the sheets, and then began removing his clothes as she watched. He was hard and aching when he stretched out on the bed beside her, but he rolled onto his side and propped himself up on one elbow to see her face more clearly.

The arches of her dark eyebrows were perfect frames for the blue eyes looking up at him. The three freckles on her nose were endearing. The delicate oval of her face and the natural pout of her lips were forever etched into his memory. He slid his hand down the softness of her belly to the flare of her hips, to the junction of her thighs. When he slipped his hand between them, she moaned and reached for him. He accepted the invitation, parting her legs with his knee, and kissing the hollow at the base of her throat, and then her lips.

Flashes of the butterfly on his chest kept flitting in and out of Maggie's line of sight. It was like her dream, but so much more.

The reality of imminent danger lent a depth to the

passion between them as he finally slid into the tight wet heat of her, and with every ensuing thrust, every kiss, every frantic catch of breath, they moved closer to the climax they were chasing and didn't stop until it hit in a shattering blood rush.

Maggie was still coming down from the sexual high when she felt Sonny's cheek against her face, and heard the whisper in her ear.

"Love you. Trust me."

There was steel in the tone of her voice when she responded. "I already trust you. I love you beyond reason. But I'm not going to stand back and watch you get killed."

"I promise not to poke the bear, but my people do not run from the enemy. We meet them head on," he said.

"Understood," Maggie said and then hugged him fiercely. "The Rose will reopen in a day or so, and I will be your eyes. If your father shows up, I will know it before you. I will call the moment I see him. I won't let you be caught off guard."

He kissed her again, and then rolled out of bed and began putting on his clothes. "I need to get to Crossroads for supplies, and back here before nightfall."

She got up and began gathering up her clothes, then putting them back on. "I'll watch the sunset without you tonight, but you will be in my heart, just the same."

Sonny walked her out to her car, waited while she tossed her things inside, then wrapped his arms around her.

"This is hard and ugly, Magnolia. I'm sorry that I am my father's son. He is nothing short of a monster."

Maggie put her hand on his chest. "You are also your mother's son, and Charlie's brother, and Julia's special Uncle Sonny. You are a good man. You are the man I love. Let that be enough. Okay?"

He forced himself to let her go, and opened the car door.

"Drive safe, darlin'. Call and text me as often as you want. If anything changes, I will let you know immediately," he said.

"I will, and if I see him in town, you will know it. Old red Dodge pickup. Old indigenous dude with funky gray braids. Big turquoise belt buckle. I've got this."

"Just be careful. I can't say that enough," he said.

She nodded and then got into the car, and blew him a kiss before she drove away.

At that point, he went in to get his Stetson and wallet, grabbed his keys and locked the house on his way out. He was giving himself a couple of hours to do what he needed to do, and then make himself scarce in Crossroads.

───────

Maggie drove back to town, bypassing her house and straight to the Yellow Rose to check on Pearl to tell her what was happening. But when she got to the Rose, there were three cars in the front parking lot, and she could see Pearl through the windows, sitting at a table with three people. Frowning, she parked in the back and used her key to get in.

The security alarm was off, but she called out as she closed the door behind her. "Pearl, it's just me," she said, and entered the dining room.

Pearl looked up and smiled. "Maggie! Glad you're here. I'm interviewing prospective waitresses and grill cooks."

Maggie smiled and nodded. "I didn't know you were busy. I'll come back in an hour or so, okay?"

"We're nearly done here," Pearl said. "Why don't you make yourself something to drink and give me a few minutes to finish up."

Maggie headed for the soda dispenser, filled a glass with ice and Pepsi, grabbed a straw, and sat down at the counter out of the way. It didn't take her long to figure out that the man was there because of the grill cook job. He looked to be in his early sixties, was average height, and had a full head of curly gray hair. She recognized the two women as residents of Crossroads. She knew the man lived in a room in Crossroads Lodge, an old two-story house that had become the local hotel/boarding house, then she keyed in on what Pearl was saying.

"We've already discussed pay. I would expect you to show up at 5:00 a.m. to help get things ready. We open at 6:00 a.m. every day, and close around sundown. Davey, I have the names and numbers of your last two employers. I'll call them later. Darla, you worked for me for a couple of years way back when, so I know you know the ropes. Cheryl, I'll call your past employers this evening, as well, and be in touch with all of you before the night is out. If you pan out, then all of you come in tomorrow morning around 8:00 a.m. We'll go through the routines, and I'll show you where everything is and what I expect from all of you. Davey will make us all breakfast, and we'll see how that goes. I only have one waitress opening, but if you are both willing to split the time, I would hire the both of you. One of you would work from five to noon, and the other from noon to close. Maggie would be your boss on the floor, but on her days off, both of you would work the whole day. I'll be in the kitchen with Davey. What do you think?"

The women looked at each other, then nodded. "Yes, that works even better for me," Darla said. "I'm an early riser."

"And, if I had a choice, I would take noon to close," Cheryl said.

"If your people give you good recommendations, then we'll give this a try, but know this. I'm the boss. I expect a lot out of my workers, but I'm working just as hard right beside all of you. Understood?" Pearl asked.

"Understood," they said.

Pearl stood. "I'll be in touch. Darla, see you in the morning. See yourselves out, please."

"Thank you for the opportunity," Davey said, and the women echoed his sentiment before leaving the Rose.

Pearl pointed at the window. "Maggie, honey, would you take that Help Wanted sign out of the window for me?"

"How did you make this happen so fast?" Maggie asked, as she removed the sign and locked the door.

Pearl sighed. "I made some calls, and I feel exactly how I look, but this too shall pass. Bring your drink and let's go upstairs. I want to kick back in my recliner a bit. My head's killing me." And then she saw the expression on Maggie's face and frowned. "Something's wrong, isn't it?"

Maggie nodded. "Yes, and Sonny is going to need our eyes and ears for a while. We'll talk upstairs."

By the time Maggie had explained in depth about what was happening in Sonny's life, Pearl had moved past shock to a slow burn.

"Does he really think his father is coming to kill him?" she asked.

Maggie nodded. "Yes, he does, but I don't know why. His brother called to warn him, and Sonny believes his father and another man were westbound in the Oklahoma panhandle when the truck broke down and they're waiting for a tow. That's a very long way from Okmulgee, Oklahoma, so they're not out for a leisurely drive."

Pearl nodded. "So, when we reopen, we'll be paying close attention to the people who walk in?"

"Yes, ma'am," Maggie said.

"You two are in love, aren't you?" Pearl said.

Maggie nodded.

"You don't think it's too soon?"

Maggie eyes welled. "He said he'd been looking for me all his life. I don't feel broken anymore. Be happy for us."

Pearl groaned, and then held out her arms. "Oh honey, come here to me. I told you I trusted him, and I still mean it. If that man has laid claim to you, then you are most blessed."

Maggie got up from where she'd been sitting, knelt beside Pearl's chair. "I am so scared for him," she said, then laid her head in Pearl's lap and cried.

Hours later, she was home, sitting at her easel with a paintbrush in her hand, putting the finishing touches on the portrait she'd done of Sonny. After adding a highlight here, and a faint shadow there, she laid down her brush and stepped back.

It was him. Looking at her. A moment caught in time. If God was good, this man would grow old along with her, but this would never fade or age. She'd just given him immortality. In this painting, he was forever young.

———

Del Kincaid had just been released from jail. He had a court date in three weeks, and as he walked out into the sunlight, he frowned. He expected Heather to be waiting, but her car was nowhere in sight. The battery on his cell phone needed charging, and he had no way to make any calls, so he went back into the station to the desk sergeant.

"Pardon me, but my cell phone is dead, and I don't have a way to charge it. I thought someone would be outside to pick me up. Who bonded me out?"

The sergeant shrugged. "I have no idea, but you can use the phone to call for a ride," he said, and pushed the landline phone close to where Del could reach.

He called Heather's number, but she didn't answer. He didn't remember any other numbers by heart except his dad's, and calling him would be the ultimate humiliation. But without being able to access phone numbers, it was the only other person he knew to call.

His gut was in knots as he punched in the numbers, then held his breath, hoping he would answer. Otherwise, it was going to be a hell of a long walk home.

It rang once, twice, and then picked up.

"Hello?"

"Dad, it's me. Do you know where Heather is? I called her to come pick me up at the jail, but she didn't answer."

"I'll come get you. Sit tight. It'll take a good half hour to get there," he said, and then he hung up.

Del blinked. At least he had a ride home, but where the hell was Heather? The fact that his dad had ignored the question made him uneasy.

"Did you get a ride?" the sergeant asked.

"Yes, thank you, but it'll be a while before they can get here."

The sergeant pointed to a row of chairs against the wall. "You're welcome to wait inside if you want," he said, and then went back to work.

Del considered his options. Standing outside the jail for a half hour, or waiting inside a while. He opted to sit, with an eye on the clock.

———————

Delroy had been expecting the call. He already knew Heather had taken money out of their savings to post Del's bond, but she wouldn't be there when Del was released. She and the baby were going to live with her parents, and she wouldn't be coming back.

Delroy had been in tears along with her when she said it. He wouldn't see his granddaughter, Carlie, grow up, but he would be witness to his son's impending downfall.

"I'm sorry, Pop," Heather said. "But Carlie is not going to grow up tainted by the sins of her father. I know all the vows I took when we married, but none of them had anything to do with standing by a liar and a thief. I am heartbroken, and humiliated, and you're the only person I'm going to miss. You will always be welcome wherever we are, but if I never see Del's face again, it will be too soon."

"I understand, honey. Trust me, I do. You have to do what's best for you and Carlie. Just promise you'll stay in touch. Call whenever you want. Send me pictures as she grows."

"I will," Heather said, and then they were gone, and Delroy had been going through the motions ever since, keeping both ranches running, and waiting for the call.

That was two days ago, and now Delroy was on his way to the Briscoe County Jail in Silverton, to get his son and bring him home.

―――――

Finally, Del saw his dad's truck drive past the jail, and when he did, he got up and walked out, waiting for him to swing around again. To say he was glad to see his father's face was putting it mildly. He hadn't spoken to him since before Carlie was born, and acknowledged that was all his own fault. He wanted a redo on the last two years, but that wasn't happening.

When his dad braked in front of the entrance, he jogged out between parked cars and jumped in. Del glanced at his dad, saw the disdain and disappointment, and looked away.

"Thanks for the ride," he muttered.

"I've been waiting for your call," Delroy said.

"Where's Heather?" Del asked.

"Gone."

Del's stomach rolled. "Gone? Gone where?"

"She's at her parents'. She said she left you a letter."

Del felt the gut-punch of the words. He turned his head away from his dad and let the tears fall.

Delroy knew his son was crying. He guessed he

should feel sorry for him, but he didn't. He was just disgusted with him as a man.

They drove in silence for a few minutes while Del went through a gamut of emotions, ending in anger.

"So, she bailed on me at the first bump in the road," Del muttered.

Delroy turned on him, his voice rising with every word he uttered.

"Shut up now, before you say something to me that you can't take back. What you did wasn't a bump in the road. You dug your own grave here, and don't you dare blame Heather for any of this shit. You shocked her. Hurt her. Humiliated her, and then you expected her to wait for your ass to get out of jail and go home like nothing happened? And she's not just thinking about herself. She's thinking about the child you both have. That baby will be judged by your sins off and on throughout her life. You don't have the right to be mad at anyone but yourself, because if you'd been thinking about them, you wouldn't have done what you did."

"But I didn't know—"

"I know better. Save that story for the judge. I don't want to hear another word come out of your mouth. I'm getting you home. The rest of what happens after that is on you."

Del was holding on to indignation to keep from crying again. His old man was hard as nails, but he was honest, and that's more than Del could say about himself.

"Fine," he muttered. "My lawyer thinks I'll get off with a fine and probation anyway."

Delroy didn't respond. He was heartsick and sick to his stomach, too. Heather had a bolt-hole to go to. Whether he liked it or not, he, too, would be judged by his son's mistakes.

By the time they went through Crossroads, the only sounds inside that cab were the rattle of a piece of sucker rod in the truck bed, and the hum of the tires upon the highway.

A short while later, Delroy took the turn down Del's drive and pulled up at the front of the house. He didn't even put the truck in Park. As soon as Del was out and the door was closed, he backed up and drove away.

There was a moment when Del felt the abandonment, and then he grabbed the keys from his pocket and went inside.

The house was silent—the rooms so empty. The baby's room was stripped of everything that mattered. Seeing the empty crib felt like a death. No more baby hands pulling his hair. No more little fingers trying to feed him her snacks. He wanted to cry, but the tears were frozen. The lump in his throat kept getting bigger and tighter, leaving no room for the scream in his head to come forth.

Heather's wedding rings were lying on top of a note. Her clothes were gone. And she'd left their wedding picture upside down on their bed.

He took the rings and the note and sat down on the bed to read it.

You broke our vows. You broke my heart. You destroyed your daughter's future. I bonded you out with money from our savings and took enough to get home. You love money so much you can have it all. Don't call. Don't beg. I don't want you anymore. You shamed us and you don't deserve us. You go do you, Delroy Kincaid, and leave us the hell alone.

Del wadded up the note and threw it in the trash and put the rings in his pocket. They'd cost him a fortune when he bought them. He didn't know what the going rate for used wedding rings was, but he'd find a buyer. And she need not worry about him trying to get her back. He didn't have the guts to face her again.

Then he heard a knock at the door, swallowed the tears and his pride and went to answer. It was his foreman.

"What?" Del asked.

"Sorry to bother you, boss. Just checking in to see if you want us to continue branding tomorrow?"

Del's head was spinning. They were branding? Who'd authorized that?

"You've been branding while I was gone?" he asked.

The foreman nodded. "Miss Heather asked your daddy to come help her, so he did. He's been working two ranches nonstop, but told us you'd be back today, and that he wouldn't be available. So, do we resume tomorrow?"

Del nodded, then closed the door. His humiliation

was complete. Without thinking, he headed straight for the liquor cabinet, opened it, only to find it empty of liquor and a note from Heather propped up inside.

I knew you'd head straight for the booze, so I dumped it. You'll have to go out in public to buy more, or maybe you could just rely on the backbone you're supposed to have and grow a pair.

Every word in that note was like the other one she'd left—filled with rage and disgust. He wanted to be angry with her, but he was too ashamed of himself to bother.

He left the note in the liquor cabinet and quietly closed the door.

The empty house was a mirror to his life. He needed to take the next step, but he was afraid of where it might lead. The judge had yet to rule on his sentence. He was praying for probation and a fine, but he also knew he could end up doing time.

———

Wade Sutton was on his way to jail. There wasn't a lot of bargaining for his lawyer to do on his behalf, because the facts of his crimes could not be denied. He'd chosen not to have a court trial. It wouldn't have made a difference, and the humiliation of having it all made public was more than he could handle. He was standing in the courtroom with his lawyer by his side when the judge handed down his sentence.

Six years, with the possibility of parole. For the crimes he'd committed, he'd gotten off easy, but to Wade, it felt like a death sentence.

When they led him out of the courtroom, he didn't look back.

━━━━━━

The same day Wade was being transported to the Briscoe County Jail, Sonny was on his way home from Crossroads with food supplies, ammunition, horse feed, and a fresh block of salt.

Everywhere Sonny went on foot, Dancer followed like a puppy. This should have been good times for Sonny, but Walker's imminent arrival was the storm, and Sonny felt like he was filling sandbags to prepare for a flood, knowing no matter how many bags were filled, the dam would still break, and the waters would come. All he could do was hope he didn't wash away.

And while the mares looked good, he noticed the roan was limping, so he put a rope around the horse's neck and led him into the corral and went to get the farrier tools.

It didn't take but a few seconds to see the problem. A rock had become lodged in the soft part of the sole. He got a pick from the tools, propped the foot between his knees and dug it out. After a closer examination, he was satisfied he'd gotten it out before it had time to do any real damage, poured some antiseptic on it and then turned him back out in the pasture.

He was gathering up the farrier equipment when he glanced up, and realized sundown was happening in all its glory, bursting across the sky in colors achingly pure.

He reached for his phone and called Maggie. She answered on the second ring.

"Hello? Is everything okay?" she asked.

"No, everything is not okay. The sun is going down without you by my side," he said.

"I know. But we're still seeing the same sunset, breathing the same air, and I'm right here."

He closed his eyes as her voice wrapped around him, hoping she was right. He might be able to see future happenings for others, but he couldn't see them for himself. It was still a strange thing to accept that he'd gone from bull riding to psychic. Then he realized Maggie was still talking.

"Sonny, are you still there?" she asked.

"Yes, darlin'. I was just listening to the sound of your voice. Is Pearl okay?"

"Well, she looks like she went all ten rounds with a bear, but she's already stirring things up. I think she's just hired a grill cook to help her in the kitchen, and two part-time waitresses to help me in the dining room, which means I will now have my days off again."

"That's awesome," Sonny said. "I hope they work out for her, because selfishly, I want my time with you, too.

I just have to remember that my wishes do not come at the expense of what you need."

"You. I will always need you," Maggie said. "We're having a trial run tomorrow morning at the Rose with just us and the new employees to see how it all goes, and then we'll be open day after. I'm going to miss seeing you there."

"Not as much as I'm going to miss coming to see you and eat Pearl's good cooking," he said, then he heard Maggie take a quick breath.

"Oh, look at the sky, Sonny. The pinks and oranges are melting into gold."

"I see it, darlin'. I see it," he said.

"Maybe it's a good sign. A promise of a good tomorrow," she said.

"Maybe so," he said, but right now he didn't trust ambiguous signs. What he needed was the strength of his ancestors behind him because the storm was still coming, and he couldn't turn it back.

Chapter 12

IT TOOK THREE HOURS FOR THE TOW TRUCK TO arrive, and all the while, Walker sat frustrated and fuming about his plans to get to Sonny, while Nubby emptied a fifth of whiskey and passed out.

By the time the driver hooked them up and pulled them the rest of the way into Boise City, all of the local garages were closing. He dropped them off at the closest one, and as soon as he was paid, he was gone, leaving Walker and Nubby on their own.

After some haggling, the mechanic on duty promised to look at the truck first thing tomorrow to see what was wrong, and what it would take to fix it, then got Walker's name and a contact number, and locked up the broken-down truck inside his garage.

"Hey, where's the cheapest motel?" Walker asked.

"The Longhorn Motel up on Main Street. I'm going past it on my way home. Want a ride?" the mechanic asked.

"Much appreciated," Walker said, and then they were gone.

An hour later, they were checked in with the suitcases

they'd brought with them, and a credit card so nearly maxed that when Walker pulled it out at check-in, he might have heard it whispering *uncle*.

Nubby was nursing a hangover and cursing Walker at the same time.

"I don't know why I even bother with you and your wild schemes," Nubby muttered. "I could be home eating my sister's posole and fry bread about now."

"You can have your damn hominy stew any day. This is a big payoff for the both of us," Walker muttered.

"No, it's your big payday, but only if I pull the trigger," Nubby said.

Walker frowned. "You'll get your money."

Nubby shrugged. "I will, or you won't live to collect yours," he said, then kicked back on one of the beds. "I'm hungry. Where are we going to eat?"

Walker pulled a sack out of his suitcase and dumped the contents onto his bed. Cans of Vienna sausage and sleeves of saltine crackers fell out, along with bags of chips and candy bars.

"Well, shit. I'm gonna need a beer to wash down that crap," Nubby muttered.

"Then go out and buy your own," Walker said. "I'm not your concierge."

Nubby glared, rolled off the bed, picked up his key card and stomped out of the room.

Walker got the ice bucket from the room, went down the hall to fill it up, then went back to the room and pulled a can of Coke out of his bag. He divided up the cans and crackers and left the rest of the snacks in a pile in the middle of the table, got a clean glass from a shelf and iced down his drink.

———————

Nubby asked the clerk at the front desk where the nearest grocery store was, then started walking. It was seven blocks down from the motel before he got there, but once inside, he grabbed a shopping cart and started looking for the cooler with six-packs. He was still half-drunk from all the whiskey he drank, and needed something to smooth out the edges.

He was mad at himself for ever getting in the truck with Walker, and worried about getting stranded out here in the middle of nowhere. He didn't think Walker had any extra cash, so he decided to take matters into his own hands.

He began walking the aisles as if casually shopping, while checking out where all the security cameras were located and saw one aimed up at the ceiling and another that had been pulled partially out of the wall and was hanging down by its wiring. Satisfied that he wouldn't get caught, he meandered past shoppers, looking for the women with the giant purses on the baby seats, left wide open and unzipped. Some even left their carts unattended as they walked up an aisle looking for something in particular, or walking off to visit with a friend.

Small towns took safety for granted until someone

took it away from them, and Nubby was about to teach them a lesson. By the time he went to check out with his two six-packs of beer, he was over six hundred dollars to the good. Once he was outside, he was certain he was in the clear, but headed straight back to the motel.

He walked the seven blocks like he was sightseeing, pausing to look at window displays, once to help an old woman carry a box to her car, then sauntered on up the street like he had all day. It was only after he got to the motel that he glanced over his shoulder and saw a police car flying down Main Street with lights flashing. He was bracing himself for the confrontation when they went past without stopping. He watched to see where they were going, and when the cruiser pulled into the parking lot of the grocery store, he entered the motel with his grocery bag propped against his belly as he went.

Walker looked up from the table where he was eating and frowned as Nubby walked in with a weird expression on his face.

"What's wrong?"

"Nothing, I hope," Nubby said.

Walker stood up and tossed his garbage into a trash can. "What the fuck did you do?"

Nubby set the beer on the table, then dug out the wad of money he'd pickpocketed and tossed it on the table. "I know you don't have money to fix that truck or pay the motel bill, and if we don't fix that truck, we aren't getting out of here, and if we don't get out of here, your big plan to hit it rich is going to shit."

Walker was furious. "I have money, and my social security check will be in my bank account by tomorrow. You went to get beer and come back with a wad of money. What did you do, rob a liquor store? What the hell's wrong with you?"

"Six hundred dollars and change, and I got it from a bunch of purses in the grocery store."

Walker was stunned. "Damn it, Nubby. Security cameras will have you nailed within the hour."

"I scoped it out first. Two cameras. One aimed up at the ceiling. One hanging from a wire. Pretty sure neither of them work," Nubby said.

Walker shrugged. "Pretty sure is a risk. You better hope you were right. And you also better hope you stayed under their radar. If there are security cameras outside other nearby buildings, they'll be looking at strangers first."

Nubby shrugged and popped the tab on one of his beers and put the rest in the mini-fridge.

"Them Vienna sausages mine?" he asked.

Walker nodded. "Crackers, too. The rest we share," and then he sat back at the table and peeled the paper off a candy bar to top off his dinner. But he couldn't shake the feeling that bad luck had come with them. It had cost him money to pay a fine and get out of jail. Then the truck broke down almost halfway to their destination, and now Nubby had gone and pickpocketed a bunch of ladies in a town too small to get lost in. He didn't want to think about what came next, and kept listening for the thunder of too many footsteps coming down the hall toward their room.

Nubby ate, grumbling all the way about still wanting posole and fry bread until Walker picked up an empty beer can and threw it at Nubby's head.

"What the hell?" Nubby said.

"Sick of you whining about your damn fry bread. You can eat your fill when we get home," Walker said.

Nubby's eyes narrowed to the point of almost disappearing in the roundness of his face. The only thing that kept him from cutting Walker's throat where he sat was that he had no getaway car.

"I'm going to take a shower and give you time to readjust your attitude, or I'll do it for you and to hell with consequences," Nubby said, then stripped where he stood and walked naked across the room and into the bathroom, closing and locking the door behind him.

Walker's gut knotted. He needed to find a way to make sure that Sonny wasn't the only one dead when he left Texas. Someone needed to take the fall for Sonny's death. It might as well be the man who did the deed. He just needed to figure out how to explain away traveling with the man who killed his son. Maybe he could make himself look like a victim, too. Right now, there were too many pieces of the puzzle that didn't fit, but he still had time to figure it all out.

He was just about to turn on the television when he glanced out the window and saw two police cars pulling into the motel parking lot. His heart sank. He picked up the wad of money with a napkin and ran to Nubby's suitcase, grabbed a sock and stuffed the money inside, shoved it beneath the clothes, and tossed the napkin back into the trash.

As he'd feared, the footsteps he'd dreaded were nearing their door.

Let them pass. Let them pass, Walker thought, but they didn't.

Suddenly there was hammering on their door, and a man shouted from the hallway, "Boise City Police. Open up!"

Nubby was still in the shower when Walker went to the door.

"What the hell, man?" he said.

The police looked startled. This old Indian with gray braids wasn't the man from the security footage, and then they saw two suitcases, instead of one, and heard water running.

"Who's in the shower?" they asked.

"A friend from back home. I'm on my way to Crossroads, Texas, to visit my son. He's just traveling with me for company. Why?" Walker said.

The police walked into the room. "I'm Officer Denton. Ask him to step out of the shower now. We need to speak with him."

Walker shrugged and went over to the door and knocked, but Nubby didn't answer.

Denton pushed past Walker and began pounding on the door.

"Police! Open up!" he shouted, then tried the door, only to discover that it was locked.

The water went off. A few seconds later, Nubby opened the door. His graying hair was dripping wet and stuck to his neck and back, and he was making no attempt to hide his nudity.

"What the hell's going on?" he asked.

"Get dressed," Denton said. "You've been identified as the man who just pickpocketed his way through Moore's Food."

Nubby said nothing, but the look he gave Walker was a warning.

Denton eyed two of the officers with him, then pointed at the suitcases. "Search their bags," he said.

Walker frowned. "I haven't left this room since we checked in."

"You're traveling together. You're sleeping in the same room together. Until I know different, whatever happened, you're in it together," Denton said.

When the two officers began going through the baggage, Walker's came up clean, which shocked the hell out of Nubby. He'd watched Walker put the money in his suitcase.

"Found it," the other said, holding up the sock from Nubby's luggage.

Nubby let out a roar and lunged at the nearest cop, only to be taken down with a taser. He dropped to the floor, moaning and shaking. It was enough to take the fight out of him.

Walker was handcuffed while Nubby was allowed to get dressed, then they walked both men out of the motel in handcuffs, put them in separate cars, and drove both of them to jail.

Walker said nothing because there was nothing to say. He'd made the mistake of bringing Nubby when he should have just hired someone to take Sonny out and stayed in his apartment. But he'd wanted to watch the look on his son's face when he died. Even as a boy, Sonny had shown him no honor. Then when Sonny got famous, he refused to acknowledge his father's existence. He should have died when the bull stomped him. Walker could have claimed his third from Sonny's estate then, but by the time Sonny recovered, it was all gone to pay hospital bills.

Jealousy ate at Walker like a sickness. Never had he hated a man as much as he hated his own son, and he wasn't sure why. Maybe it was because Sonny had become everything Walker had failed at, and now Nubby's stupidity had derailed all of his plans.

He was still mute as the officers led him into the PD. Nubby was taken directly to booking, but Officer Denton still needed to hear Walker's side of the story, and took him into a room to question, started a tape recorder, and then began asking questions. When they got past the basic information, Denton began to question him, and Walker answered without hesitation.

"I told you before. We were only in your city because we broke down a few miles outside of town. We waited three hours before the tow truck arrived, and during that time, Nubby drank an entire fifth of whiskey on his own and passed out. By the time the tow truck pulled us into town, the mechanic was already locking up. He stored our truck inside his garage, and pointed us to the nearest motel, which is where we were. Nubby was still nursing a headache and wanted a beer. I had food and pop in my travel bag, and not a lot of money to waste, but he was still intent on beer. I told him this wasn't no five-star hotel, and I wasn't his concierge. It made him mad, and he left. I sit down to eat and a while later he comes back with beer, and a wad of money. I asked him what the hell did you do, and he said it was to make sure we could pay to get my truck fixed, because he didn't want to get stranded in the middle of nowhere."

At this point, Walker sighed, playing the hard-luck card for all it was worth.

"I told Nubby he was a fool. I told him he was going to mess up my trip to see my son. He said the security cameras were broken in the store and nobody saw him. At that point, I quit talking to him because I already knew I was going to be sleeping in the same room with him tonight and I didn't want my throat cut. He sat down and ate the food I brought and drank his beers, then went to take a shower and then you all showed up."

Officer Denton blinked. "So, you're saying your friend is dangerous?"

"I'm just saying, I don't want to make him mad, and what I've just told you isn't good for my health. I did not know he was going to steal anything. We did not plan anything but a trip to see my son. My son and I have been at odds for years, and my intention to visit was in hopes of making peace. Now, I feel like this incident was the ancestors telling me this is not the time, but I don't want to go to jail for something I did not participate in."

"But you didn't turn him in for theft," Denton said. "You could be looked at as an accessory after the fact."

Walker's shoulders slumped. "I am guilty of a poor choice in traveling partners, but I have not committed a crime in your town."

Denton ended the recording and got up. "I'm going to talk to your friend now, and see what he has to say."

Walker watched the cop walk out of the room, heard the lock click and then got up from the chair, went to the back of the room and curled up in the corner and closed his eyes. He was tired to the bone. Whatever happened next was out of his control. All he knew was that Nubby would kill anything for fun, and took money for requests. At the present moment, Walker could have fallen into either category. It didn't look good for him.

———

Nubby Zane already knew he was going to jail for this. They'd caught him on cameras he'd never seen, and Walker must have seen the cops drive up and put the money in his suitcase. He wanted to be pissed about that, but the weird part of his brain also saw that as logic. He would have done the same thing if the situation had been reversed. He'd done the deed. Walker had been mad about it, and he knew Oklahoma laws. This would fall under misdemeanors because it was less than a thousand dollars. He could get up to 180 days in jail and a fine, or be released on probation, but with his rap sheet, probation wasn't going to be an option. The way he looked at it, at least he knew where he'd be sleeping for the next six months, and made up his mind to absolve Walker, no matter what he said about him in his statement. That way, when he got out, Walker would owe him.

After talking to Walker Bluejacket, Officer Denton was expecting Zane to be combative, but it was just the opposite as he sat down to question him.

"Mr. Zane, please state your full name for the recording."

"Nestor Lee Zane."

"In your own words, what prompted you to rob all those ladies in full view of security cameras?"

"Well, first off, I only saw two broken cameras. And I was still mostly drunk when we got towed to Boise City, pissed off by the three-hour wait, and needing a drink. Me and Walker argued when we got to the motel, and then I left to find a grocery store to get some beers. Taking the money was just an impulse. Nothing I planned. There were too many big purses in the shopping carts left open and unattended. And, I wasn't sure Walker had the money to pay for getting the truck fixed and I didn't want to be stranded out in the middle of nowhere."

"But Walker saw the money when you came back, right?" Denton asked.

Nubby shrugged. "I showed it to him. It made him mad. We had an argument. He threw an empty beer can at my head. Instead of fighting with him, I went to shower. I acted on impulse. It was a bad decision. And I'm not gonna throw the old man under the bus for any of it. Tell him I'm sorry." Nubby said.

"But he knew you'd done it and said nothing," Denton said, and then watched a strange expression spread across Nubby's face.

"People who know me well, know enough not to piss me off."

The skin crawled on the back of Denton's neck, but he didn't let on that Zane had creeped him out.

"You'll be arraigned sometime tomorrow," Denton said.

"I'm not arguing the charges," Nubby said. "I know it's a misdemeanor. I reckon I'm looking at few months of jail time, but this ain't my first rodeo."

Denton felt something was off, but he couldn't put his finger on it, and it was charges for pickpocketing and nothing more. He motioned for the guard to take Zane back to jail, then returned to the interrogation room where he'd left Walker.

He walked in the room to an empty table, then saw the old man curled up asleep on the floor.

"Walker...wake up!" Denton said.

Walker jerked, then got up slowly. "It's been a long day," he said, and started back to the table.

"Don't sit down," Denton said. "We're releasing you. Mr. Zane confirmed your story and absolved you of abetting. He blamed it on still being drunk. Said to tell you he was sorry."

Now Walker was seriously worried, but he pretended to be relieved. Nubby didn't have an ounce of empathy for anyone. There had to be a catch.

"So, I am free to go?" Walker asked.

"Yes, sir. I'll have one of my officers drop you back off at your motel."

"Thank you," Walker said. "Hopefully my truck will be an easy fix and I'll be headed home."

"What about that visit to your son? Won't he be disappointed?" Denton asked.

"He didn't know I was coming, remember? This was to be a peace-making visit, but as I said, I think the ancestors are telling me this is not the time," Walker said.

"Right," Denton said. "I'll walk you out. One of my officers will pick you up out front."

Walker followed the cop to the lobby, and then went outside to wait. A couple of minutes later, a cruiser pulled up. He got in the back seat and rode in silence to the motel, then went back to their room.

His suitcase was still on the bed with the contents strewn about. He packed everything back inside, then took a quick shower and crawled into bed. He'd just dodged a bullet, and he'd told a cop a lie to set up an alibi. His intent hadn't changed. He had one more chance to get this right, and he'd be set for life.

Walker, being the heartless asshole that he was, pulled up the covers and slept like a baby. He was up by daylight and waiting at the garage when the mechanic opened up.

"Morning, Mr. Bluejacket. I need to get everything up and running before I check out your truck. You can wait inside if you want. I'm gonna start a pot of coffee."

Walker followed the man inside, already thinking about that coffee.

"I didn't get your name yesterday," Walker said.

"Oh…my name is Aaron Hershey, but everybody calls me Sonny."

The hair crawled on the back of Walker's neck as he sat down in a chair near the little coffee station. He didn't know what this meant, but he didn't see it as a coincidence. He found a Sonny, but it wasn't the right one. Was this a sign that he needed to end his search now? Doubt began to creep into his thoughts as he waited.

About an hour later, Sonny came back into the waiting area. "Your alternator is kaput. I can get a new one for three hundred dollars plus labor. Or I can get a rebuilt one for a hundred bucks, maybe less."

"Has to be the rebuilt one, and I'm holding my breath that I'll have enough to cover that and the labor," Walker said. "All I want to do is go home to Henryetta."

Sonny's head came up. "I got family in Henryetta."

"Small world," Walker said.

"Listen, if you have the bucks to pay for the part, I'll do the labor pro bono."

"Deal," Walker said.

Sonny Hershey grinned. "I'll call over to the parts store. They'll bring a rebuilt over for me. Shouldn't take more than an hour or so. Help yourself to coffee."

About an hour later Walker was back in his truck and headed to the motel to get his things. Now he'd told two people in Boise City that he was going home. It was like adding another layer of glue to the lie.

He checked out, went looking for a drive-in to get some breakfast to go, then headed west.

The delivery truck with Sonny's order arrived. He took them to the barn to unload and as soon as they were gone, he loaded up some fencing equipment and drove down to where the old trailer house had been, removed the broken-down gate, pounded a T-post into the gap and then strung high tensile wire across the five-wire opening to solidify the fence line. As he did, he noticed insulators and frowned. They weren't hot, and they should have been. Damn Wade Sutton anyway. When he'd cut the wire to let the horses into the pasture, he must have found where to disable the power. Something else Sonny would have to find and get fixed.

He'd just finished tying off the last wire and was gathering up his tools when he felt the wind changing. He'd been so intent on work that he'd hadn't paid attention to the weather, and was startled by the dark clouds rolling in. He wasted no time loading up his equipment and headed for the house. He could see the horses moving toward the shed where he and Maggie had picnicked, obviously to take shelter. He swerved to miss a trio of giant tumbleweeds rolling across the road in front of him, and continued to dodge tumbleweeds the rest of the way home.

The first raindrops were beginning to fall as he reached the back porch. He was fumbling for his keys to unlock the door as the first shaft of lighting flashed through the sky, then finally he was inside and out of the wind.

The first thing he did was turn on the television to check the weather. The weather station was running a crawl at the bottom of the screen, naming the counties under thunderstorm warnings, and when he saw Briscoe County in the warning area, he reached for his phone, pulled up the app to check on Maggie's location and saw her driving toward her house.

He watched her reach her destination, then gave her a few minutes to get inside. The weather alerts were coming steady now, warning of strong winds, rain, and possible hail and he needed to know she was safe.

Maggie flew into her house on the run, chastising the weather gods with every step that she took. She kicked off her wet shoes at the door, threw her purse and phone on the bed, and stomped off to the washing machine and started stripping where she stood.

"Mother Nature on the rampage and just look at me!" she muttered, and pulled her T-shirt over her head. "Soaked to the skin. Hair glued to my head," she added, and unzipped the red slacks she was wearing. "And I'm pretty sure these pants aren't color-safe. If my granny panties come out tie-dyed, we're gonna have a conversation! Some mother you are. My first mother gave me away and now you're trying to drown me."

She threw the red pants aside, tossed everything else in the washing machine, grimacing at the red dye streaks on her white panties. "Stupid pants. Stupid weather," she said, then threw in a sheet of color-catcher, added laundry detergent, and started the washer. She glared at the red pants before hurrying to the bathroom to get bath towels. One for her hair, and one for her as she ran to turn the heat up on her thermostat, then back to her bedroom to dry off and get dressed. She was almost finished when her phone began to ring. She reached behind her to get the phone and then answered.

"Hello."

"It's me, darlin'. Just checking to make sure you're okay."

"I'm fine. Just in a snit. Pearl closed the Rose and told all of us to go home. Got soaked getting into the car at the Rose. Got a second dose getting out of the car at my house. There was water in my shoes by the time I got inside. I look like someone gave me a swirly...you remember swirlies, right? When some jerk kid at your school shoves your head in the toilet and then flushes it? Oh...maybe you missed that. Anyway... I am naked as the day I was born trying to get dry enough to get dressed again. I have cursed Mother Nature up one side and down the other. You have to be a woman to understand the effort it takes to pull lingerie up over a wet butt."

Sonny was grinning through the whole soliloquy, thinking what a spitfire he'd fallen for when she got to "wet butt." At that point, he started laughing.

"Magnolia, my sweet, southern woman...you can bring down the wrath of God faster than anyone I've ever known. I'm sorry you got soaked. I'm even sorrier I'm not there to dry you off and set a fire in your belly that would reset your body clock."

She shivered with sudden longing. "I would so take you up on the offer," she said. "Are you okay?"

"As wet as you. As naked as you. But no longer worried about you. The weather is nasty, but the rain is good for the land, so I can't complain."

Maggie took a deep breath and then sighed. "I forget the world doesn't revolve around cheeseburgers and fries," she said. "I assume the horses are okay?"

"Last time I saw them, they were headed to our picnic spot. They have better sense than most people when it comes to weather."

"Good, but with the Rose being closed until tomorrow, I've had no way to keep an eye out for strangers coming into Crossroads. Do you know if they're still en route?"

"I don't know more than I did, but don't worry about me. Remember what I said to you. I'm not scared of anything, or at least I wasn't until you. Your welfare is important to me. Your safety is important to me. I love you like crazy."

Tears welled. "I've never been that important to anyone before, but I'm tougher than I look. I will always find a way to float…even if it's Mother Nature herself, trying to drown me. Love you more. Get dressed and get warm, and don't forget the vault if you need it."

"Yes, ma'am."

She heard the tease in his voice. "And stop smirking. I can feel it from here." He was still laughing when she disconnected, but her bad mood was over, and she had air-dried enough to get dressed.

She was on her way to the kitchen, trying to ignore the wind slamming rain against the windows, but there was a high-pitched whine within the storm that gave her goose bumps. It sounded a little like a woman screaming and she told herself it was just her imagination, and not a warning of things to come.

She glanced at the painting of Sonny still on the easel

and then covered it with a cloth and moved it away from the windows. If a twister was coming, she had that old cellar in the backyard. She might have to share it with a snake or two, but she had no intention of blowing away.

———————

Walker was already in the Texas panhandle when he drove straight into a thunderstorm. The rain was coming down so hard he could barely see the highway, so he pulled over onto the shoulder and stopped to wait for it to blow over.

He wasn't sure how far away he was from where he needed to go. He didn't know how to use the Maps feature on his phone and was relying on the directions he'd written down from a map in an old Atlas to get him there. Chances were, some of those highways no longer existed, or had been absorbed into interstates, or bypasses, but he knew he was going in the general direction before he had to go south, and if he was lucky, he should get there before dark.

He glanced down at his phone, frowned at the low battery, and attached the phone charger and plugged it into the dash.

While he was waiting for the storm to pass, he googled hotels in Crossroads, Texas, and got one hit. If there was only one, he wanted to make sure he could get a room. He hated sleeping in his truck, and this was no kind of weather for sleeping in the truck bed.

He made a quick call. A man answered. After a brief conversation, Walker was assured there would be a room waiting upon his arrival. It never occurred to him that he'd used his real name until it was too late. He was a man full of deceit and yet he was messing it up at every turn.

———

Like Maggie, Pearl's new grill cook, Davey Lewis, was still at the Yellow Rose going through the kitchen routine with Pearl when the storm warnings began. Pearl sent everyone home, with orders they were opening up tomorrow and everyone was hired. For the first time in months, Davey felt hopeful about his future. He hadn't meant to stay in Crossroads, but it happened, and now, over eight months later, he was finally going to be employed again.

He was standing at the front desk telling his friend, Ralph, the good news when the phone rang.

"Hang on a sec, Davey," Ralph said, and answered. "Crossroads Lodge, Ralph speaking. How can I help you?"

"Do you have a vacancy? I need a room for a few days."

"Yes, we do. Do you have an arrival date?" Ralph asked.

"I'm a couple of hours out, I think, but I've pulled over to wait for this storm to pass. If I don't get lost, I'll be there before dark."

"That's fine," Ralph said. "This is a hotel and a boarding house, so people come and go at all hours. I'll need your name and a deposit to hold the room for you," Ralph said.

"My name is Walker Bluejacket. Got a pen? I'll give you the credit card details."

"Go ahead," Ralph said, and took down the info. "Okay, Mr. Bluejacket. Your room is reserved. Safe travels, and we'll see you later."

Ralph hung up. "Sorry, Davey. Where were we?"

"Did you say that man's name was Bluejacket?" Davey asked.

Ralph nodded. "Walker Bluejacket. Do you know him?"

"I wonder if he's related to Sonny. You know…the guy who put a skunk in those drug thieves' car."

"Oh, yeah! The rodeo guy!" Ralph said. "Maybe he's coming to visit his son."

"Maybe so," Davey said. "Anyway…as I was saying, I got a job working for Pearl at the Yellow Rose. I'm her new grill cook."

Chapter 13

THE RAIN WAS LETTING UP WHEN WALKER GOT BACK on the highway, but while he'd been waiting, he'd also messed with his phone long enough to get driving directions to Crossroads Lodge.

His old truck was a gas guzzler and an oil burner. He kept glancing at the fuel gauge, measuring it against the distance he had yet to drive, and gambled that it was going to be okay.

It was just after sundown when he reached the little town of Crossroads, but with very few streetlights burning he wasn't sure of where he was going. Fortunately, the Crossroads Lodge was lit up like a church, and he'd seen on the website that it was a two-story building, so it was easy to find.

He found a parking place off to the side, got his bag and locked the truck. The motel in Boise City could have taken a few cues from this place. It was as close to looking like home as a hotel/boarding house could look, and the man behind the desk smiled as he walked in.

"Mr. Bluejacket?"

Walker nodded.

"Welcome to Crossroads Lodge. I'm Ralph. If you'll sign in for me, I'll get your key and walk you to your room."

Walker felt every bit of his sixty-eight years as they walked up the stairs to the second floor, with Ralph carrying his bag. They stopped at the third door down on the right. The clerk opened the door and stepped inside, put Walker's bag on the bed, and then handed him the key.

"There will be coffee in the lobby in the morning. There's a meal in the dining room here at night, but you'll have to find your food elsewhere during the day. The Yellow Rose is the café on the highway. It's the best place to eat, although there is also a deli in Belker's Grocery store, and they sell burritos and wings in the gas station. There is a no-cooking rule for all the rooms, and no mini-bar. You're welcome to bring food to the room, but be sure to get all your garbage gathered up and in the trash each night. The rooms are cleaned every morning, and the trash will be picked up then."

Walker nodded. "I guess it's too late for food tonight?"

"We only have one service a day and it's at six, but I'll get cook to make you a sandwich and a cold drink. I'll bring them to you myself," Ralph said.

"Appreciate that," Walker said, and was already opening his suitcase as the door closed behind him.

He began to unpack a few things and then set his

suitcase aside. A short while later, there was a knock at the door. It was Ralph with a tray. He carried it in and set it on the little table.

"Enjoy your food and sleep well. You can set your tray out in the hall when you've finished. I'll pick it up when I make my rounds."

Walker nodded, and then locked the door after Ralph left. He sat down at the table, eyed the cold sandwich, the bag of chips, a piece of pie and two cans of Mountain Dew. He didn't like Mountain Dew. But he popped the tab, poured it over his glass of ice anyway, then began to eat.

———

Long after he'd set the tray in the hall and crawled into bed, his heartbeat was pounding like a drum. He was in Crossroads and Sonny didn't know it. The downside was that he didn't know where the ranch was, and if he asked around, it would alert his son that he was here.

What he needed was a lure. Something to get Sonny to come after him. But it couldn't be here in front of a townful of witnesses. The storm he'd driven through to get here had passed, but the wind had yet to subside. Even within the walls of his room, and with the abstract noises of other residents within the house, Walker could still hear it blowing as he rolled over and closed his eyes.

He'd think of something. He always did.

Even though the storm was over, Sonny couldn't settle. He eaten leftovers, cleaned up the kitchen, and taken a shower to get ready for bed, then pulled on a pair of sweatpants and paced the dark rooms, periodically looking out the windows past the halo of the security light, half expecting to see his father lurking in the shadows.

He hated this—the uncertainty of the vision. He'd been so sure the men would be here by now. Maybe the storm slowed them down. It wasn't the first time this knowing he'd been given had frustrated him. Sometimes what he saw was an analogy for something else, and sometimes it was a mirror to past, present, or future. If the Old Ones had given him this gift, it should have come with instructions.

Then he got a text from Maggie.

Dude, I can hear you pacing. You are, aren't you? You're worried that they'll come when you're asleep. So, take that coyote-huntin' rifle and a box of ammo to bed with you and get some rest. I finally got dried off and warm. Don't make me have to come down there.

He burst out laughing and texted her back.

You're a little bit scary. How did you know this?

Within a couple of minutes, she answered.

Maybe the butterflies told me. Maybe it's just
me needing to believe nothing is going to take
you away from me. Love you forever, Sonny
Bluejacket. Meet you in my dreams.

Sonny read it through unshed tears.

Thank you for this. Now get some sleep. You have
to be at work early, and so do I. Love you more.

————————

Water was still dripping from the eaves of houses the
next morning, and the tumbleweeds that hadn't blown
away with the storm were stuck against fences, and up
against houses in people's backyards.

Pearl looked like hell and was functioning at about
seventy-five percent, but with Davey helping in the
kitchen, and Darla and Cheryl on half-day duty to help
Maggie, they could do it. She was intent on re-opening
the Rose, and already in the kitchen by five making biscuit dough when her employees began to arrive.

Maggie showed up first, with Davey right behind
her, and a couple of minutes later, Darla entered the
back door.

"Morning, everyone," Pearl said. "Let's do this."

After the run-through yesterday, they all knew the

drill, and began scattering to their respective duties. It wasn't long before Davey was taking bacon strips and sausage patties off the grill, filling up the warming trays so when orders came in, the meat portion of breakfasts were already done.

Pearl had pancake batter ready, biscuits in a warmer, and a stack of egg flats beside the grill, ready to go.

Darla glanced at Maggie as she flipped the Closed sign to Open, and unlocked the front door.

The first two cars pulling into the parking lot made Darla nervous. It had been a while since she'd done this.

"Darla, don't let them see you sweat. You've got this. You take the first table. I'll catch the second."

Darla gave Maggie a thumbs-up and picked up a couple of menus as the first customers walked in and sat down.

Three locals came in behind them, and chose a table in the back corner. Maggie knew them well. Three old cowboys who lived alone in their little trailers, and didn't like to cook.

Every time Maggie went to pick up an order, she could hear Pearl and Davey, and once even heard Pearl laugh. She smiled. This was a good thing.

There was a bit of a lull after the first early rush and Maggie had just bussed her last table, and was rolling a cart full of dirty dishes into the kitchen for Carson to wash, when she heard Davey talking, relating a story about a latecomer who'd showed up at the lodge just as the storm was passing, and keyed in on the story.

"He was an older guy...maybe late sixties. Looked like he'd been rode hard and put up wet. Gray hair braided in two braids that hung down the front of his chest and biggest damn belt buckle beneath his belly. Solid chunk of turquoise, it was. He seemed polite enough, but he had the coldest eyes I've ever seen, and I thought, glad he's just passing through. I wouldn't want to live under the same roof with him."

Maggie's heart skipped a beat. Before she could react, the bell over the front door jingled. Another customer had just come in, and Darla was in the bathroom.

She wiped her hands and went to get the order, and then she was going to call Sonny. But when she walked out into the dining area and saw the customer, her heart slammed against her chest.

It was him! Walker Bluejacket!

She carried the coffeepot with her as she put a menu on his table. "Coffee, sir?"

He looked up, first at her face, and then undressed her with a look that made her sick.

"Sir?"

"Oh, yeah, coffee," he said, and shoved the menu aside. "Sausage and two eggs over easy, with a side of biscuits and gravy," he said.

Maggie was writing as he spoke, and when he stopped, she nodded. "Comin' right up," she said, and started to walk away when he grabbed her wrist.

"What's your name, pretty lady?" he asked.

"Let me go," she said.

He laughed. "That's a funny name for such a pretty thing," but he turned her loose, then watched her walk out, thinking to himself if she was a little older, or he was a little younger, she wouldn't be playing so hard to get.

Maggie turned in the order, and was about to step outside to make the call when a trio of men walked in, and Darla still wasn't back.

Maggie picked up the coffeepot again and moved to the next table of men, all locals, and began filling up cups.

Bill Belker, the owner of Belker's Grocery, was the first to strike up a conversation. "You tell Pearl we're really sorry about her black eye, but we sure did miss her cookin' while the Rose was shut down."

Maggie grinned. "Yes, I will. And I don't suppose you need menus?"

They shook their heads and gave their orders, and then Maggie picked up Walker's order and carried it back to his table.

He gave her the side-eye, but said no more as he dug into the food.

Maggie refilled his coffee and then started to walk away when Bill Belker called out to Maggie from across the room.

"Hey, Maggie, you tell Sonny next time you see him that the back of the pharmacy still smells a little skunky."

Her heart sank. She wouldn't look at Walker for fear of seeing recognition dawning.

"I'll do that," she said, and when she saw Darla back on the floor, she bolted toward the kitchen.

Pearl looked up as Maggie entered the kitchen, saw the look on her face, and frowned. "What's wrong?"

"Walker Bluejacket. He's out there, eating in our dining room. He's alone, and Mr. Belker just made a very loud remark about me giving Sonny a message, which tells that man I know his son. And that I likely know where he lives, as well. I have to call Sonny. I'm just going to step outside to make the call. I won't be a minute," she said.

Pearl nodded, then walked away from the counter to look out into the dining room. She spotted the man immediately, then saw him throwing down some money on the table and walking out the door.

"Oh lordy," Pearl muttered. This didn't feel right.

———

Sonny was in the barn, putting down wood shavings in two of the stalls, getting them ready for the mares, when a gust of wind came through the open doors and blew an empty bucket off a hook.

Startled by the sound, he looked up, and in seconds the world around him vanished, and he was watching Maggie walk out the back door of the Rose and then turn away from the wind, unaware of the truck pulling into the employee parking lot, or the driver getting out. Sonny was watching Walker grab her, shove her up against the wall, and run his hands up her leg. Twice, he watched Maggie try to push him away, but when he put his hands on her breasts, she raked her nails down the side of his face. Quick as a rattlesnake strike, Walker's hands were around her throat.

For Sonny, watching this unfold was a waking paralysis, witnessing the woman he loved kicking, and scratching, fighting the man who'd accosted her. When he saw her go limp in Walker's arms, he felt actual pain. Something he'd never experienced in a vision before. Not knowing if she was just unconscious, or already dead—still watching his own father dragging her to his truck, throwing her body into the back seat, was horrifying, then seeing him tying her feet and hands before jumping into the truck and speeding away ended the vision, and he was back in the stall with a rake in his hand.

Rage rolled through him in waves. He dropped the rake and reached for his phone, praying that her phone was still on her, because if it was not, she was lost.

But when he pulled up the app and saw her on the move, all he could think was "thank God," and ran for the house to get the rifle and a box of ammo, then jumped in the truck. This was his worst nightmare come true.

Maggie stepped out of the Rose to call Sonny, but the

wind blasted her in the face, so she turned her back to make the call. She was about to reach for her phone when all of a sudden, there was a voice behind her.

"Hey, Maggie…that's your name, right? Maggie. You know my son."

She turned abruptly, and shoved him backward. "Get out of my face! I don't have a freaking clue who you are, so how would I know who your son might be," she snapped.

He blinked. He hadn't thought that through. "Sonny Bluejacket. You know him?"

Before she could react, he took another step toward her and shoved his hand up her skirt. She shoved him back again.

"Get your hands off me! What is wrong with you?"

Walker didn't move, and now there was an ugly, warning tone in his voice that made her gut knot. "I asked you a question. I want an answer,"

"I know everybody who lives here, and I know you're not one of them," Maggie said.

He sneered. "So, what are you doing out here?"

She gave him the same look he'd given her inside the café, looking him up and down like merchandise. "Throwing away garbage…but it appears I missed some."

Before she could react, he grabbed her breasts. She raked his face with her nails and saw his eyes turn black. Suddenly he had her by the throat, choking off her ability to breathe.

Maggie went into survival mode and began kicking and scratching, fighting him with every ounce of strength, even as he was choking the breath from her body. She was on the verge of passing out when he shoved a wad of napkins in her mouth, then began dragging her to his truck, and threw her in the back seat.

She was conscious enough to know he was tying her hands and feet. Then he slammed the door shut and jumped into the front seat, made a U-turn in the back parking lot, and sped out, heading toward the highway.

The speedometer on Sonny's truck was tipping eighty as he flew through town, sliding sideways when he reached the highway before straightening out the wheels and headed west, following Maggie's trail. At best guess, Walker was at least five or more miles ahead, and Sonny was driving ninety miles an hour now, and hearing drums and war cries. He needed to call the sheriff's department, but he also needed both hands on the wheel, and then his phone rang.

It was a good five minutes before Pearl realized Maggie hadn't come back inside. She opened the back door to check on her, but she wasn't anywhere in sight. Only the muddy tracks of a vehicle making a U-turn in the employee parking lot, and all of the cars belonging to her employees were right where they'd been parked.

Then she remembered seeing Walker throwing down money and hurrying out of the Rose, and in a panic, she called Sonny.

He answered in the middle of the first ring. "Hello."

"Sonny, Maggie's gone. I don't know where—"

"Walker has her. Call the sheriff's office. Tell them what happened. I'm tracking her on an app on my phone right now. I can see where they're going. Tell Matt Reddick to get a GPS location on my phone number, because I'm only a few miles behind them."

"Oh my God…yes, yes, I will. Oh Sonny, be safe, and bring my girl back safe, too."

"Yes, ma'am," Sonny said, disconnected, and tapped the map again to bring it back up. Walker was going west, there was nothing but dirt, yucca, and highway all the way to New Mexico, and the drumbeats were louder now, matching the beat of his heart.

Maggie finally spit the last of the paper napkins out of her mouth, but instead of screaming, she stayed silent, and began trying to loosen the ties around her wrists.

At first, she couldn't figure out what they were and then she realized there was a slight give to them…a kind of elasticity. She kept fumbling and fumbling, until she felt a hook, and realized he'd wrapped a bungee cord around her wrists and then hooked the ends together to keep it taut.

Knowing now what it was, she needed a way to dislodge the hooks. It took a few seconds for her to realize the thing poking in her hip was actually the lock end of a seat belt. It was hard metal and plastic, and in somewhat of a fixed position. If she could just force that buckle beneath the hooks, it might be enough to shift one hook enough to come undone.

Her other saving grace was believing Pearl would call Sonny as soon as she realized that Maggie had gone missing, and knew the first thing he'd do was check that tracking app. She was scared, but all was not lost. As long as she drew breath, there was hope.

———

Walker was congratulating himself on making such a slick move, but he hadn't thought past it. He'd taken her to draw Sonny out, but now that he had her, what next? He hadn't taken the time to search her person, and couldn't kill her now because he'd need Sonny's phone number, and he knew she knew it.

Showing up at Crossroads under his real name had nixed the secret part of his plot and eliminated the possibility that he could kill his son and get away with it. And by kidnapping the girl, he'd also made a big target of himself in the eyes of the law. He couldn't get away with this and ever go home. But he could do it, then cross the border into Mexico and get lost, and it would be worth it just knowing he'd wiped that smug look off his son's face for good.

He glanced up in the rearview mirror at his back-seat passenger. She wasn't moving and her eyes were closed. A part of him wondered if she was already dead. He'd choked her good before stuffing the napkins in her mouth. He didn't see the napkins anymore. Maybe she'd sucked them down her throat and choked herself to death. That wasn't good. He needed her to be able to call Sonny. She was his lure. Sonny had to hear her voice to know Walker had her.

At that point, he glanced down at the mileage, checking how many miles he'd covered since leaving Crossroads. More than twenty miles and counting. Now that he was this far gone, he slowed his old truck down to sixty-five. He didn't need another breakdown in this godforsaken place with a kidnapped woman in the back seat.

———

The moment Sheriff Reddick received Pearl's call, he made a call to the Muscogee/Creek Nation Tax Commission to get a number for the tribal tag on Walker Bluejacket's truck, then dispatched the message to the Texas Highway Patrol, along with Sonny Bluejacket's phone number, and his instructions to locate him via the GPS on his phone.

Reddick knew if they were headed west, they would drive out of Briscoe County, which was where his authority ended, so he stirred up a hornet's nest with the Texas Highway Patrol. Within moments of dispatch, they were en route from every direction, looking for an old red Ford pickup with a tribal tag from the Muscogee Nation in Oklahoma, and following the GPS location of Sonny's phone.

———————

Maggie was trying not to cry, but her feeble attempt to free herself was going nowhere and her hands were getting numb. The bungee cord had been wrapped so tightly she was losing circulation.

Then she glanced up in the rearview mirror and saw him watching her.

"So, you didn't die yet," Walker said.

The cold glare in her eyes surprised him. She wasn't scared. She was mad.

"Sonny is going to kill you," she said.

It felt like a prediction, not a warning, which startled him even more. Then he looked back up, panicked as the truck began to fishtail, before getting back on the highway. He'd nearly run himself off the road.

He glared back at her again.

"He'll have to find me first," Walker said, eyeing her swollen and bloody lips. But when she smiled again, his heart skipped. She knew something he didn't.

He gripped the steering wheel a little tighter and focused his attention on the stretch of highway before him, and then readjusted his rearview mirror away from her face to the road behind him, and for a second, thought he could see a vehicle in the distance.

He told himself it meant nothing. It was a highway. People used it. He'd already met eastbound traffic earlier, and had seen one vehicle behind him that eventually turned off the highway onto a private road. It was nothing to worry about, and he kept driving. But every time he glanced up, the vehicle was a little closer than it had been before.

Walker glanced at the speedometer. He was still sitting on sixty-five, so out of caution, he sped up a little. Within minutes he realized had hadn't gained any ground. The pickup truck was still behind him and coming closer.

He didn't know what Sonny would be driving, but if that was him, then he was starting to panic. How the hell did he find them so fast?

The whine of the tires had become a song in Sonny's ears, and the closer he got to Maggie, the louder the whine. He was doing ninety when he got his first glimpse of the truck. He still didn't know if Maggie was alive or dead, but he knew Walker Bluejacket was behind the wheel, and was debating with himself as to how he could stop him without causing a wreck.

When he realized Walker was putting distance between them, he stomped the accelerator and shot forward. For a heartbeat, it felt like coming out of a chute on the back of a bull, gripping the steering wheel as tight as he'd held on to the bull rope.

He glanced in the rearview mirror and in the distance, thought he could see a line of flashing lights coming up behind him. *Thank God.* And then high in the sky before him, a black-and-white chopper flying east.

Texas Highway Patrol chopper in the air and patrol cars behind me. Matt Reddick came through. All I need is Maggie…alive and in my arms.

He just kept driving.

———

Walker was so focused on the truck coming up behind him that he didn't see the patrol chopper flying straight toward him, low enough that the skids would come straight through his windshield, until it was too late.

"Oh hell," he shouted, and hit the brakes. Within seconds, he was rammed from behind just hard enough to jam the steering wheel into his belly. He was grabbing for the gun in the seat beside him when the driver's side door came open.

"You son of a bitch!" Sonny said, and yanked him out of the truck, threw him off his feet and into the air, where he landed on his back on the highway, then Sonny reached into the truck and killed the engine.

His first glance in the back seat was to look for Maggie, then locked into her beautiful blue eyes. *She's alive!*

"Oh my God…Maggie, sweetheart…"

"I'm okay. I'm okay! Don't let him get away."

Sonny looked down, saw the gun, pulled the clip and tossed them both in the floorboard as Walker was scrambling to his feet.

Sonny grabbed him again, this time by the back of the collar, slammed Walker up against the hood of his own truck and punched him in the face.

"You put your hands on my woman," he said, and hit him square in the nose. "I saw you. I saw you choke her into unconsciousness." He hit him again, this time in the mouth. "I saw you stuff napkins in her mouth and tie her up in the back seat of your truck." Then he hit him again—once in the ribs, and then in his belly.

Walker was spitting blood and teeth and absolutely certain he was going to die where he stood, and still trying to get free. "You lie…you couldn't see anything. You weren't there," he shouted.

Sonny yanked him so close that Walker could feel the heat of his son's breath.

"I can see, old man. I saw everything you did to her, and what she did to you. I came back from the dead with a gift. I see the past, the present, and the future.

You can't lie. You can't hide. I can find you anywhere," and then he pulled a hunting knife out of his boot.

Walker looked like he'd seen a ghost. "Don't kill me. Don't kill me," he begged.

Sonny grabbed one of Walker's braids, and with one quick slash, cut it off at the scalp, then grabbed the other one and sliced again, then threw them toward the ditch.

Walker shrieked. Losing his hair was the execution of his soul. He felt the pain as if the knife had actually pierced his flesh.

Just as Sonny tossed the braids, the patrol chopper was landing, churning the wind about them. The downdraft caught the braids and blew them out into the grassland beyond.

Highway patrolmen were pulling up in their patrol cars, and running toward them with their weapons drawn as Sonny picked Walker up by the shoulders and dropped him at their feet, then he ran back to Maggie and yanked the back door open.

The sight of her bruised face and the darkening imprints of Walker's fingers on her neck, and on her bare arms and legs crushed him to the core. This had happened to her because of him. Because of the evil of the man who was his blood.

Maggie was crying. "I knew you'd find me. I knew you'd find me," she kept saying, as Sonny began unfastening the bungee cords and then lifting her out of the truck.

He couldn't talk. All he could do was hold her. Tears

were rolling down his face. The guilt of what happened to her was killing him.

Then someone walked up behind him.

"Mr. Bluejacket, I'm Officer Landon. We can get an ambulance for Miss Brennen, but it will take a good hour for them to arrive, or we can chopper her to the nearest ER."

"No, I don't need an ambulance. There's an ER in Crossroads," Maggie said. "Sonny can take me there. I just want to go home."

"Yes, ma'am, but we'll need your statement about what happened...for the record."

"What are you going to do with him?" Sonny asked, pointing at Walker.

"We're taking what's left of him to an ER, and then straight to jail," Landon said. "We'll also need your statement, too, and smart move...having the tracker app on your phones."

Sonny nodded, then started toward his truck with Maggie in his arms. He put her down to open the door, then eased her into the passenger seat. When she fumbled with the seat belt, he took it out of her hands and fastened it for her.

"My hands...they're still a little numb," she said.

Sonny looked down at his own hands, blood-stained and knuckles already bruising, and grabbed hand wipes and began wiping his fingers and his palms, trying to remove every vestige of Walker from his person. When they were clean, he reached for Maggie's hands and began rubbing and massaging them, helping the blood to circulate, before turning them palms up and kissing them.

"Sonny, really, I'm okay," Maggie said.

He shook his head. "But I'm not. I knew Walker had you, but I didn't know if you were still alive."

He heard footsteps behind him and turned around. It was Officer Landon again.

"Sir, do you have any idea why your father did this?"

"He wants me dead. He used Maggie as a lure."

Landon had seen and heard a lot in his police career, but this was a first.

"Wants you dead? Why?"

Sonny shrugged. "Because he is a monster? Because of envy? Because his heart is black? I don't know. I used to rodeo. I rode bulls. I was good. Then five years ago I came off a bull and got stomped in the chest before I could get up. I died twice on the operating table. Against all odds, I survived. Right before I moved out here, we got into a fight, and he told me I should have stayed dead. I guess he came out here to finish the job. You have my phone number. Will someone come out to take our statements?"

"Just get your lady home and checked out. Someone will be in touch. We can take it via Zoom and record it if need be."

"Thank you," Sonny said, then got in his truck, backed up enough to turn around. As he did, he caught Walker watching him from the back of a highway patrol car and stared until Walker was the first to look away.

Then he got a blanket from the back seat and covered Maggie up, opened a bottle of water for her then held it so she could drink, and as soon as he was satisfied that she was settled, they drove away.

Chapter 14

SONNY KEPT LOOKING OVER AT MAGGIE AS HE DROVE. Every time she took a drink of water, she winced as she swallowed, and she was still shaking. All he wanted to do was hold her, but he needed to get her to the ER.

"Maggie...sweetheart...talk to me."

"I thought I might die before you found me. I didn't know how long it would be before Pearl would raise an alarm. I still had my phone in my pocket. I knew you could track the phone, but I was afraid he'd find it and throw it out of the window. How did you find me so fast?"

"I saw it happening," Sonny said. "I was already on my way to Crossroads when he drove out of the parking lot at the Rose."

Maggie blinked. "You had a vision about me?"

He nodded. "I've never been so scared."

Tears were rolling down her cheeks. "It was a scary thing that happened, but it was also the first time in my life I knew someone had my back. I don't know why you ever bothered to love me, but I will be grateful to the day I die that you do."

He couldn't look her in the eyes. "That happened to you because of me."

The despair in his voice broke her heart. "No, Sonny, no! Look at me!"

He shifted his gaze.

"Why would you think it was your place to accept the blame for his actions?" Maggie asked. "It happened because of him. And because of you, I am still alive. Understood?"

"Understood," he said, and as the word left his mouth, the horrible feeling within him began to fade. "Can you reach your phone?"

She nodded.

"Then call Pearl. Let her know you're still in the world. She was in a panic when she called me. She's also the one who called in the cavalry for us by notifying Sheriff Reddick, and she needs to hear your voice."

———

The Yellow Rose was full of customers, but nobody was eating or ordering. When the news spread through town that Maggie had been abducted, people began gathering, waiting for news. Pearl understood their concern, but it felt like a wake, and she couldn't let herself go there.

It had been over two hours since she'd talked to Sonny. She'd done everything he asked, but had no way of knowing if the messages were received in time, or if the authorities had even found them yet.

A car pulled off the highway, tried to find a place to park, and then drove off. Pearl didn't care. Right now, she couldn't have fried an egg and done it right.

Darla and Cheryl were both on-site, and Davey was hovering over them all like an old rooster minding his hens, when Pearl's cell phone rang.

She snatched it from her apron pocket, saw Maggie's name come up on caller ID, and started shaking. "Hello?"

"Pearl, honey, it's me. Sonny found me, beat Walker Bluejacket to hell and back and saved my life. We're on the way back to Crossroads. We'll take a little side trip to the ER, but it's all minor."

"Oh, thank God, thank God," Pearl said, and started crying. "The Rose is full of people all waiting and praying that you were found."

"Really?" Maggie said.

"Yes, really. Honey. Everybody in Crossroads loves you, didn't you know that?"

"No," Maggie whispered, and then she was crying, too.

"Well, you are loved here, and you tell that man of yours that he has forever won a place in our hearts. I'll talk to you soon. Love you."

Then Pearl turned to the gathered crowd and shouted. "Sonny found her, rescued her from her abductor, and they're on the way back to Crossroads now."

The room erupted in cheers and applause, while Pearl sat down and cried.

As soon as the call ended, Maggie put the phone in her lap and pulled the blanket back around her shoulders.

"You okay?" Sonny asked.

"Pearl said the Yellow Rose is packed, but not with customers. Just people waiting to get an update on me. She says to tell you that you have earned a place in their hearts forever."

He glanced at her again. "I beat him all the way to hell and back?"

"I heard the fight. I saw the end results. I could have been wrong about you beating him all the way back, though. He was missing body parts when you dumped him at the feet of the highway patrol and got me out of the truck."

Sonny was quiet a few moments, letting the words sink in, and then he nodded. "Missing some parts. That is very intuitive, and an accurate way to describe the totality of that man. It is my personal opinion that somewhere along the road of his life, someone poked a hole in his soul and all the good leaked out."

He knew she was physically and emotionally exhausted, and had to be hurting. "Recline the seat and close your eyes, Magnolia. You've seen enough ugliness today. When you open them again, we'll be home."

Walker was still bleeding from a cut over his eye. He was pretty sure Sonny broke his nose. He thought he'd heard a rib crack and now it hurt to breathe, and he was missing three teeth. The rage and power of his son's wrath had shocked him. When Sonny pulled out that knife, Walker thought he was about to die. Instead, his son cut off his braids.

It was the ultimate insult. A visual and public shaming, and it had scared Walker like he'd never been scared before. He had seriously underestimated his youngest son. If Sonny was to be believed, the ancestors *had* given him magic.

Walker wanted to deny the possibility, but there was no way in hell he could have described the abduction that way, unless he had seen it. If he'd known all that, he would never have messed with him, but it was too late for caution. He was, quite likely, going to spend the rest of his life in a Texas state prison. Kidnapping might not have been his best move.

Sonny was finally approaching Crossroads when Maggie sensed the truck slowing down and woke.

"Hey darlin', we're home," he said.

She reached down to put the seat up, then groaned. "I fell off a horse once when I was thirteen. He was running at a full gallop, and I swear I bounced when I hit the ground. I was sore for a week, and that's kind of how I feel right now."

He frowned. The fact that she was in any kind of pain hurt his heart. "We'll get you fixed up soon. I'm not sure where the ER clinic is located, though."

"It's on the same street as the post office, at the end of the block, but can we stop at the Yellow Rose, first? My purse is still in my locker, and I'll need insurance cards and stuff when I check in."

"Absolutely," Sonny said, and drove into the parking lot and parked. "Sit tight, honey. Pearl can get it for me, right?"

"Yes."

He leaned over and gave her a quick kiss on the forehead. "I'll be right back."

Maggie watched him go inside, then leaned back and closed her eyes. It hurt to swallow. Her wrists and ankles were bruised and bloody from the bungee cords, and she had the headache from hell.

———

Sonny came into the dining area in long, hurried strides. The moment the customers saw him, the room erupted in congratulations and questions.

Pearl heard the raised voices and came out of the kitchen, then saw Sonny and froze.

"Sonny! Oh my God, are you hurt?"

He frowned. "What?"

She pointed to his clothes. They were covered in blood.

"That's his blood, not mine," he said. "We're on the way to ER and Maggie needs her purse."

"I'll get it," Darla said, and hurried into the little storage room where they kept their personal property.

Pearl's eyes widened. "Maggie said you beat him to hell and back. I thought that was just a figure of speech, but now I'm thinking she meant it."

"It would have been worse for him if the Texas Highway Patrol hadn't found us when they did. I would hug you for getting all that information to the sheriff's office, but I'd contaminate your whole kitchen," he said.

"All I did was to make a phone call," Pearl said.

"Yes, but it resulted in the arrival of a Texas Highway Patrol chopper and four patrol cars just in time to keep me from killing him," he muttered.

Darla came back with the purse. "Here you go," she said. "Tell Maggie we were praying."

"Yes, ma'am," Sonny said.

"I hate to ask, but how bad is she hurt?" Pearl asked.

"Everything is superficial, but he had her arms and feet bound with bungee cords so tight that she lost feeling in them. She has bruises on her neck where he choked her, so she's hurting in a half-dozen places. You can call her later, and if you start looking for her, she'll be at the ranch with me."

He walked out with the purse and then they were gone.

Customers began plying Pearl with questions, until she held up her hands.

"Maggie's injuries are superficial. None of the blood on Sonny's clothes belongs to him or her. That's what he did to the man who took her. The highway patrol has her abductor in custody."

———————

Sonny pulled up in front of the small clinic and parked.

"Sit tight, Magnolia. I'm coming around to help you out."

The adrenaline crash was happening. All she wanted to do was lie in Sonny's arms and cry. She went limp when he picked her up and carried her inside.

Joan and Peggy, the two nurses on duty, had been alerted that they were en route, met them at the door, and led the way into the first exam room.

Sonny eased her down on the exam table. "Maggie, honey, I'll step out, but I'll be in the waiting room when you're ready to go," then he leaned over and kissed her forehead.

Maggie saw the shimmer of tears in his eyes. "You saved me. Remember that and let everything else go."

He brushed away a strand of hair caught in her lashes, then caught the nurses eyeing his bloody clothes.

"I'm fine. That's not my blood," he said, ran the back of his finger down the side of Maggie's cheek and left them to it.

He could hear them asking Maggie questions as they

began to remove her clothing. She was crying. It was a knife to the heart.

The moment he got back to the waiting room, he sat down and called Charlie. There was too much to tell to send a text.

———————

Charlie had just made a delivery for his boss and was on his way back when his phone rang. He saw Sonny's name on caller ID and pulled over to take the call.

"Hey, Sonny, how's it going?" he asked.

"Walks-Off kidnapped Maggie this morning. I followed them using that Life360 app like the one you and Frannie have. Ran him down about thirty miles away from Crossroads. She's okay. I've got her in ER. Texas Highway Patrol have him in custody."

Charlie gasped. "Sonny. Oh my God, man. Why?"

"To hurt me? Who the hell knows?"

"What did you say to him?" Charlie asked.

"We didn't talk much. He's got a broken nose, three teeth less than what he woke up with this morning. I think I heard a rib snap. I wanted to cut his throat. I cut off his braids instead. His eyes were swelling shut when I dumped him at the feet of the arriving highway patrol. I guess it's good they came when they did. I would have killed him."

Charlie was still processing the information about the braids, but he wanted to know more. "How did you get him stopped?"

"The highway patrol dispatched four chase cars and one of their choppers. Chopper came from the west. The rest of us came from the east. He stopped because the chopper was on the highway in front of him."

"Is Maggie okay? What did he do to her? Please tell me she's going to be okay."

"He choked her unconscious, threw her in the back of his truck and bound her feet and hands with bungee cords so tight it cut off circulation. She has a busted lip, bruises all over, but physically, she'll be okay. I, however, am never going to get over being the reason this happened to her."

"Damn it all to hell," Charlie muttered. "When did you know she'd gone missing?"

"You know how I saw Julia at the creek? So, I saw Maggie's abduction happening the same way. I was already in my truck and heading to Crossroads when he pulled out of the parking lot with her. Everyone else thinks I found them so fast because of the tracking app, but Maggie knows the truth...and so does Walker. I don't know why he hates me so much, but he does, and today, I told him what happened to me after I survived, that the ancestors who saved me gave me visions. That he can never run far enough, or lie enough, to hide what he does from me, because I will know. Scared the crap out of him. He wanted me dead. Now the feeling is mutual."

"What about Nubby Zane? Where was he?" Charlie asked.

"I don't know. He was with Walker near Boise City, but he wasn't with him today," Sonny said.

"What can I do?" Charlie asked. "If you need me, I will come."

The well of tears broke and rolled down Sonny's face. "Thank you, but we're good and we're safe now... Maggie and me. I called because you needed to know what he'd done, and you will need to tell Auntie. She will be ashamed of him, but he is still her brother."

"Yes, but I'm telling this at council. Our people deserve to know when there's a monster among us."

Sonny sighed. "There's no way to keep his dirt from rubbing off on us. People will think to themselves...are we like him?"

"No, Sonny. Good dogs can go mad, but he was never a good dog. He was the cur in the streets. The one in the alley going through garbage. The one who ran with a killing pack. He was just the bad one in a good family. We'll be fine, and he's finally where he needs to be...penned up away from society. You give your girl our love and prayers. We love you, little brother. You are the gift in our family that makes up for him. Remember that and call to talk any time."

"Thank you, Charlie. Love to all," Sonny said, and disconnected.

He sat within the silence, his elbows on his knees, just staring at the floor. Maggie wasn't crying now, but he was. This was a lot for both of them to deal with, but she was his to love, and he'd nearly lost her.

Both nurses brought Maggie out in a wheelchair. Her wrists and ankles were wrapped in gauze, and she was holding her sneakers in her lap. The bruises on her face and neck were getting darker by the hour, but she was smiling.

"I'm good to go," she said.

"With some caution," Peggy said. "She's going to be uncomfortable with swallowing for a while, but there are no internal injuries to her throat. She has no signs of concussion and the abrasions on her wrists and ankles should heal without issue."

Joan added to that. "We contacted the doctor in charge of this clinic. He comes from Amarillo one day a week, and will be here tomorrow if you have further questions. He's also called in some anti-inflammatory meds, and an antiseptic cream for her wrists and ankles, but they do not need to stay wrapped. They're putting a rush on the stuff at the pharmacy, so by the time you get there, they should be ready."

"You will mail the bill for this visit to me," Sonny said, and gave them his mailing address.

Maggie started to get up when Peggy stopped her.

"Sit tight, Maggie. You were carried in, so we're giving you a ride out," and took her to Sonny's truck.

He had the door open, waiting. As she stood, the nurses moved the wheelchair back to give her room, and before she could take a step, Sonny picked her up and eased her into the passenger seat. But instead of reaching for the seat belt to buckle her in, he wrapped his arms around her and held her where she sat.

He didn't talk, but she could feel the warmth of his breath against her cheek, and then moments later, his tears on her face.

"Sonny...darling...I'm really going to be okay. No drastic injuries. Just discomfort."

He finally let her go. "During that long frantic race to catch up with Walker I didn't know if you were alive or dead. The last sight I had of you in the vision, Walker threw your limp and lifeless body in the back seat. I did not know until I yanked him out of the truck and saw your big blue eyes looking back at me, that you still drew breath. It's gonna take a bit for me to let go of that gut-wrenching fear." Then he wrapped her up in the blanket again and buckled her in.

He started the engine, felt her watching him, and winked. "You're still the prettiest girl I've ever seen."

She sighed. "Dude, I saw myself already."

"And I saw what you did to Walker's face. That will scar, and for the rest of his miserable life, every time he looks in a mirror, he's going to remember how you fought back. Using you to get to me was the biggest mistake he ever made, and that's saying a lot, because he was always five minutes away from a new disaster. Now, let's go get your meds. You're coming home with me until you're back on your feet, and tomorrow I'll either bring you back to your house to pack up some stuff, or I'll do it for you if you're too sore to move. If I had my way, you'd already be living under my roof, but that's your call."

Maggie hugged herself, savoring the love in his eyes and the promises in his words as he backed up and drove away. He had to circle the block to get back to Belker's Grocery, then find a place to park.

"I won't be long, darlin'. I'm going to grab a few things that are easy to swallow. Want anything special?"

"No. I trust your choices."

He got out on the run, and then he was gone.

Maggie settled back in the seat, pulled the blanket up beneath her chin, and closed her eyes.

———

The moment Sonny entered Belker's, the conversation among the shoppers ended. They saw the blood on his clothes, the bruised knuckles on his hands, and the look in his eyes. Then someone clapped, and someone else joined in, and they swarmed him, asking about Maggie, and praising him for saving her.

Sonny could tell by the way some of them were talking that they didn't yet know her abductor's identity, and taking their praise seemed false without telling his side of the truth.

"Thank you, but just so you know, it was my own father who took her to get to me. He has not been in my life since I was five. But he's always been the dark blot on our family. He hates me and I don't know why, and Maggie suffered because she loves me, and he knew it. He'll die in prison for what he did. And I will spend the rest of my life trying to make it up to her." He took a deep breath, and then exhaled. "Just so you know. Thank you again for all the prayers for my girl, but I've got to get her meds, and get her home. She's had the day from hell."

Mr. Belker had been listening without comments, but felt compelled to speak up.

"Sonny, we all have someone in our families that we're ashamed of, or we regret the paths that they have chosen. But none of their actions came from anything we did, and none of that is your fault. You saved her life. That is what we see. That is what we think. The fact that you found her so fast is a miracle."

"Oh…you can all thank a tracking app I loaded on to our phones. As long as we had our phones on us, we knew where each other was. If we were at work, or if we were driving somewhere, or if we were home. My brother had it for him and his wife. Maggie worried about me being alone on the ranch, so I did that for us…for her. It was in her pocket when he knocked her out and tied her up. It wound up saving her life."

"I'll be danged," Belker said. "I didn't know there was such a thing. I'm going to check into that."

Sonny moved through the crowd and hurried to the pharmacy, picked up her meds, and then made a quick sweep through the store, getting things easy for her to swallow, then left the store and found her asleep again.

He slipped the bags in the back seat, but when he started the engine, she woke up. He handed her a to-go cup of Pepsi he'd gotten from the soda fountain at the deli.

"Cold drink for my baby. We're going home."

"Yumm," she said as she took a small sip. "Just what I needed."

———————

Sonny had Maggie settled on the sofa watching TV. She kept dropping off to sleep and then waking abruptly. He guessed she was dreaming, and there was nothing he could do to make the bad dreams go away. After she'd taken herself to the bathroom and back, he got her settled again.

"Sweetheart, you're locked in the house right now, and I need to make a quick head count on the herd before it gets dark. I'll whistle them up to the barn, so I won't be far. Are you okay with that?"

"It will cost you one kiss, then you go do what you have to do."

He leaned down, and very gently kissed her lips, then laid her phone in her lap.

"I have my phone. Call if you need me. I won't be long."

She snuggled back under the blanket that today,

smelled like sage and sunshine, and watched him walk out the back door.

———————

Sonny was in a place in his head he'd never been before. In the last few hours, he'd experienced the deepest of fears and the hottest of rages. There was no name for the level of devastation he'd felt, fearing Maggie was no longer alive. But the rage he'd felt against his father was beyond explanation. He would have killed him without an ounce of regret.

He kept remembering picking up the gun from the floorboard of Walker's truck and the urge he'd had to turn it on Walker, and Maggie screaming at him, "don't let him get away." At that moment, pulling the ammo clip and tossing the gun had been the better choice, but the blood rush of hate he'd felt at that moment was not something he ever wanted to feel again.

He walked all the way out toward the feeding troughs just outside the corral carrying a sack of sweet feed under each arm. Dumped them, and went back for two more, then emptied them out into the feeders and tossed the empty sacks into the corral to pick up later.

"Equine smorgasbord," he said, then turned to the north and whistled, waited a few seconds, then whistled again.

He heard a horse whinny, like an answer to his call. To his surprise, they came from the south, and as usual, they were running. The sight of them lifted his spirits as he knew they would, and they smelled the sweet feed.

They quickly found a place in the lineup to get a couple of mouthfuls, but not too much, just enough for them to get a good taste. And as they ate, he moved in and out among them, always checking for a wound needing to be doctored, or one with a loose shoe, then special attention to the mares close to foaling.

When he was satisfied all was well and they were already moving toward the round bale and water tank, he stepped away.

When he did, Dancer followed. But instead of nosing for a treat, he laid his head across Sonny's shoulder.

"You feel it in me, don't you, big boy? Don't worry. None of it is directed at you," Sonny said, and wrapped his arms around Dancer's neck and held on until the world stopped spinning, and the ground beneath his feet was firm once more before turning him loose. He climbed into the corral to get the empty feed sacks, took them to the feed room, and was on his way out of the barn when his cell phone rang. It was Sheriff Reddick.

"Hello."

"Sonny, I'm calling to check on your girl. I know what went down, but I didn't have any confirmation on her condition other than you were taking her to the Crossroads ER."

"Her injuries are superficial. Emotions, not so much. He choked her unconscious. Her neck looks a little like someone tried to hang her. Thank you a thousand times for getting the highway patrol on my trail. Their chopper landing on the highway in front of him was what stopped him, and the patrolmen coming up behind me is what stopped me from killing him."

"Timing was everything," Matt said. "If you hadn't been on to the abduction so quickly, it could have easily gone wrong. And, another reason I'm calling, considering the distance and law enforcement divisions involved, is to give you a heads up. Someone will be in contact with the both of you to take your statements."

"You have my contact information and Maggie is staying with me for the present time, so we're in the same place," Sonny said.

"I'll let them know," Matt said. "Listen... I'm sorry about what happened. I can't imagine how you must be feeling. But that old son of a bitch has never been a father to you, so don't take on any guilt for what he did. He was always a stranger to your family. He's still just a stranger who tried to hurt someone you love, and you dealt with it, like any man would."

"There's still one unknown about this whole thing," Sonny said.

"What's that?" Matt asked.

"I know that Walker was traveling with a friend when they started this way. A man named Nubby Zane from back home. He is as mean and worthless as Walker. I would have pointed him out as the trigger man. They were together as far as Boise City, Oklahoma. I don't know what happened after that, but Walker showed up alone and did the deed on his own. I would hate to think Zane is still out there somewhere, waiting to finish the job."

"Damn," Matt muttered. "Let me make a few calls. If anything happened in Boise City, I might be able to find out. If I learn anything, I'll let you know."

"I really appreciate that. I don't want to think I'm still a target and involve Maggie again."

"Understood," Matt said, and hung up.

Sonny slipped his phone back into his hip pocket, and when he looked up, Maggie was still wrapped up in her blanket, and sitting on the back porch.

He hastened his steps to get to her. "Did you get tired waiting for me?" he asked.

She stood as came up the steps. "No, I just like watching you with the horses."

He wrapped his arms around her, blanket and all. "Come inside with me, Maggie Rae. We can talk."

"About what?"

"For starters, the future of Sunset, the choice of a long engagement, or a shotgun wedding, and now inside, please. The nurses said for you to take it easy and rest, and I've got to get rid of these bloody clothes. I need to wash today out of them, and shower the rest of it off of me."

Sonny made Maggie a cold drink and warmed up a bowl of soup, settled her at the kitchen table, then kissed the top of her head.

"Just eat what you want of this. I'll make us some supper later, okay?"

She picked up the soup spoon as he turned to leave. "Sonny?"

He paused. "Yeah?"

"Today taught me one thing. That tomorrows aren't promised. I'd marry you in a heartbeat. I don't need to wait for anything. I just want to belong to you."

The look on his face said it all.

"As soon as you get well, we can make that happen, but just so you know, in my heart you're already mine. Eat your soup and stop worrying. We're good, okay?"

She picked up her spoon, then saw he was stripping as he went. By the time he walked out of sight, he was barefoot, shirtless, and all that long black hair hanging down his back. It was enough to make her forget about every pain in her body until she took a breath.

All that and him is for another day, she thought, and went back to her soup.

Chapter 15

While Sonny was at the barn, Maggie was on the phone talking to Pearl, reassuring her over and over that she was okay.

"I just need a few days to get healed up and I'll be back at the Rose, I promise," Maggie said.

"Darla and Cheryl have picked up the slack, and Davey is a big help. I'm not worried about the Yellow Rose. I'm just worried about you."

"Well don't," Maggie said. "Sonny's already on that job."

"I know, but you're my girl, and today I thought I'd lost you," Pearl said.

Maggie was silent a moment before she answered. "I know, Pearl, but Sonny went through the same thing you did. Even as he was tracking me, he didn't know if I was alive or dead. He's still dealing with the same thing you are. I knew I was alive, and I knew Sonny would be using that tracker he put on our phones. I just trusted he'd get to me in time."

Pearl sighed. "I didn't think about that. He really loves you, doesn't he?"

"To the moon and back," Maggie said. "Gotta go. Sonny is stalling the mares now, because he wants to keep an eye on them until they foal and then he's coming to get me."

"Where are you going?" Pearl asked.

"Outside to watch the sunset. It's our thing."

Pearl chuckled. "You and your sunsets. Then is there anything I can make for you two to eat?"

"I can't swallow much of anything right now without a lot of pain, so he's stocked up on soups and ice cream and soft stuff. Don't worry about us and food. He's a pretty good cook."

"Okay, but call if you need anything. I love you, girl," Pearl said.

"Love you, too. Take care," Maggie said, then got up to put her shoes on just as Sonny came in the back door.

He paused to grab one of his jackets. "The wind has laid, but it's a little chilly. Put this on, darlin', and we'll get more of your own clothes tomorrow."

She slipped her arms into his jacket, then he turned her around and fastened the snaps for her, because he knew her hands were still sore.

"Ready to watch the light show?" he asked.

"I'm ready for anything with you," Maggie said.

He led her out into the front yard then stood behind her, holding her close. The utter trust and faith she had in him was inspiring and humbling. Her presence in his life was the anchor to a stability he'd never known. He would die to keep her safe, and today, he'd come close to killing a man to get her back.

They stood in solemn wonder, like two people at a graveside, watching the sun's last performance of the day, and then watched for the first star of the night to appear.

"There it is!" Sonny said, pointing west and low to the horizon.

"So bright, and so very far away," Maggie said, then she turned within his arms, and laid her cheek on his chest. "With you is my heaven on earth."

"Ah, Magnolia, you are my healer, and so easy to love. You're shivering. I need to get you inside."

———

Later, as Sonny was tucking her into his bed, he realized that while they'd made love here, they'd never spent a night together, but this would soon be their normal routine. The thought of lying beside this woman, with her little feet against the backs of his legs, or her head pillowed on his chest made him ache to be with her.

"Are you comfortable, honey?" he asked.

"Yes, just so tired."

"I'm going to lock up. Be right back," he said, then smiled. Her eyes were already closing.

He went back to the front of the house to check the locks and turn out the lights, then stood for a few moments at a window, looking for more than the night shadows. Satisfied that all was well, he hurried back and eased into bed, then turned onto his side to face her, just watching her sleep.

Her sleep was restless, but he understood why. When she suddenly jerked and rolled over onto her side, he reached out and pulled her close against him, and as he did, he heard her sigh.

As she relaxed, curling up within his embrace, he whispered in her ear. "Love you forever."

Then he closed his eyes.

———

It was past daybreak when Maggie opened her eyes and saw Sonny watching her.

He smiled. "You sleep like a baby, curled up with the covers pulled tight beneath your chin. Your eyelashes flutter when you dream. You smiled once in your sleep. And you cried once, too."

Her eyes widened. "Did you even bother to close your eyes last night?" she asked.

He slid his arm beneath her neck and pulled her close. She could hear his heartbeat, and the rumble of his voice against her ear.

"I tried. Emotionally, I think I'm still on guard duty."

She raised up on one elbow, then kissed him. "Make love to me, Sonny."

He groaned. "I want to, but I'm afraid I'll hurt you."

"I already hurt. Only you can make me fly."

They made love in the quiet of the morning. With all the passion of young love and intention until they both lost control and the blood-rush rolled through them. It was like flying, but without a parachute, and knowing when they landed, it would be in each other's arms.

———————

Sonny went to tend to the mares, leaving Maggie with a bowl of oatmeal and a cup of coffee. It tasted good, but she was having to swallow it in small bites. The muscles in her neck were so sore, and the bruises looked awful. They would fade, and her throat would heal, and life would move on. She poured a little more milk on her cereal to thin it, after that it went down easier, and as she ate, remembered Emmit in this kitchen, and thought he would be overjoyed, knowing they were together.

She finally finished her cereal, rinsed the dishes, and put them in the dishwasher, then went to find her shoes. They were going to her house to pack some clothes, and see Pearl.

Maggie missed being at the Rose. It wasn't just her job, it was also like a social club, where she saw people she knew every day, and the ones she didn't know kept it fresh, and they became new faces to paint. The thought of coming home to Sonny every evening, instead of to her little house alone, seemed too good to be true. Then she heard his footsteps on the back porch, finished tying her shoes, and got up.

He came in smiling, bringing fresh air and an energy that permeated the room.

"Are the mares okay?" she asked.

"Doing good, and apparently pleased to be in their stalls. I think they have a ways to go, but I know I don't want them foaling in the pasture and me worrying about more coyotes."

Maggie stood up and pointed to the chair she'd just vacated, then picked up the hairbrush she'd brought into the kitchen.

"Sit. One braid or two?"

He grinned. "Yes, ma'am, and one. I could get used to this."

She stood behind him and began brushing out the tangles, then separating his hair into three parts before beginning the braid. Her wrists were still sore, but her fingers were quick and nimble, weaving the three strands together in no time, then fastening the end with an elastic hair tie.

"So, my beautiful man, I am done. Let that West Texas wind blow for all it's worth, but it's not going to mess with that braid."

He stood up, smiling at her audacity to challenge the wind. "Are you ready to go to your house now?" he asked.

She nodded.

"Do you have a suitcase?" he asked.

She frowned. "Only a duffel bag. I have collected more clothing since than what I first brought with me."

"I'll get mine," he said, and went to his bedroom to pull it out from beneath the bed, then they headed out the door, locking it as they went.

The drive into town was short. He pulled up to her house and helped her out, then grabbed the suitcases as she led the way inside.

Maggie pointed at her bed. "If you will put your suitcase there and open it for me, I'll start packing."

"Where's your bag?" he asked.

"Top shelf of the closet."

"I'll get it down for you and then I'm going to get out of your way so you can pack. Take all the time you need. I'm not going any farther than your living room, okay?" Sonny said.

Her heart skipped. If he ventured anywhere near the spare bedroom, he would find the paintings. All of them, even the one of him.

But when she didn't move, he saw the look on her face. "Anything wrong?"

"No, but there's something you don't know about me. Something nobody knows, and you're going to see it…all of it."

"Are you ashamed of it?" he asked.

"No! God no! But it's been the only part of me that I was ever proud of, and I was always afraid to share for fear someone would pull the veil off my eyes and reveal them as junk."

"Then you will show me, or I won't see them at all."

She sighed, then took him by the hand and walked

him back through the living room and down the hall to the other bedroom. The door was ajar. She pushed it open and walked in.

But Sonny hadn't moved. He was standing in the doorway with a look of awe on his face. "You painted these."

"Yes."

"My God, Magnolia. They are magnificent! The sunsets! The scenes from the Rose. The three old cowboys in the corner. Pearl with that look on her face. The little boy scooting that toy horse back and forth across a table. That old woman...alone."

Then she pulled the cloth from a canvas still on the easel, and saw Sonny's expression lose all emotion.

"This is how you see me?"

She shrugged. "I paint what I see. This is who you are. A beautiful man with a soul in shadows. Please don't be upset with me."

He just shook his head and wrapped her in his arms. "Your work is magnificent, but you have given me a gift beyond anything you could have known. I do not see even the smallest trace of my father in that face. Because of this, I no longer have to live my life believing that's how people see me."

Maggie didn't talk. She just held him until his world stopped spinning. Then when he finally let her go, he began sifting through the canvases stacked against the walls, exclaiming over one, and then another, and another.

"There are dozens and dozens of art galleries in Arizona. I know someone there. Please let me contact him for you. Let me take a few photos of your work and email them to him. If he reacts like I think he will, would you be willing to talk to him?"

She was in shock. "You mean…as in sell? I never thought them good enough to show anyone, let alone imagine money being spent to own one."

"Just let me try. Will you let me do that for you?" he asked.

She shrugged. "Sure, but don't be disappointed when you get rejected."

He kissed her. "Go pack. I'll be in here taking pictures. Let me know when you're finished, and I'll carry them out."

Maggie left in a daze, trying to take in all of what Sonny had said, and then chastised herself for daring to hope.

But Sonny was hoping enough for both of them, and taking pictures right and left, even the one of him. When he finally stepped out and went back to the living room, he could hear Maggie in the other room, banging drawers and doors as she packed up her clothes.

Knowing she'd do better without him hovering, he sat down on the sofa, then started looking at the photos he'd taken, still marveling at the skill of her art.

Later, he was about to go in and check on Maggie when his phone rang. One glance and his heart skipped. It was Matt Reddick.

"Hello?"

"Sonny, this is Matt. I have some info on Zane. The reason he didn't show up with your father is because he got himself arrested in Boise City. He's serving a six-month sentence in their jail for pickpocketing. You're good to go."

"Thank you for this. It takes a load off my mind."

"Of course. Have you heard anything from the Texas state police about giving statements?"

"Not yet," Sonny said.

"Well, I know for a fact they're coming because they have to collect the DNA evidence the nurses took for them when you brought Maggie to the ER. Mostly, the scrapings they took from beneath her fingernails. I mean, we all know he did it, and there were about eight officers who witnessed you taking Maggie out of his truck, but they're just covering the bases."

"We're here whenever they show," he said. "And thank you again."

"Any time," Matt said, and hung up.

As Sonny leaned back in the easy chair, he heard Maggie talking. At first, he thought she was on the phone, and then he realized she was talking to herself.

"What's the matter with you, Magnolia? Keeping these raggedy drawers. You know you're not going to wear them again. Might as well go buck-naked."

He burst out laughing, and Maggie's conversation came to an abrupt halt.

"Sonny?"

He was still chuckling. "Yeah?"

"Are you laughing at me?"

"Yes."

"Okay, just checking," she muttered.

He was instantly on his feet and back in her room. "Don't be mad. You are my joy, but your sense of humor is one of the best things about you…that and how freakin' beautiful you are."

She grinned. "Okay then," and threw the pair of panties at him that she'd been fussing about.

He caught a glimpse of pink as the wisps of nylon fell to the floor. He picked them up and started grinning again. "Looks like you failed to outrun a bobcat."

Maggie sighed. "Ruined a good pair of slacks in the process, too."

"If it's not too personal, what were you doing?" he asked.

"Reliving my youth. There's an old storm cellar out back with a piece of tin nailed over the door to protect the wood. It looked like a good place to slide. But it wasn't. I sacrificed more than underwear and pants to that slide. Had scratches on my butt cheeks, too. I ate standing up for a week."

Sonny was laughing again. "No more rusty slides for you, pretty lady. I'll buy you a slide if you'll promise not to go the rusty route again."

"Dude… I've given up slides for sunsets, and I'm ready to go, except for the paintings. Pearl doesn't know about them, but I'll just say I still have some things in the house and will get them out later."

"That issue is quite likely going to be dealt with for you, so I've got your bags. Now we go see Pearl."

———————

The Yellow Rose was in the lull between breakfast customers and customers who came for lunch. The last two diners were on their way out the door when Maggie and Sonny walked in.

Pearl was sitting at a table with her coffee, and Darla and Cheryl were sweeping up crumbs and Davey was banging something in the kitchen when Sonny and Maggie walked in.

"Maggie!" Pearl cried, and ran to meet her. "Oh honey! I'm so sorry for what happened. Sonny Bluejacket, you are a wonder," and then she hugged them both. "Come sit. Can I get either of you something to drink?"

Sonny shook his head. "Not for me, thanks."

"My usual," Maggie said, and sat in the chair Sonny pulled out for her. Pearl put the glass of Pepsi in front of her, lovingly stroking the back of Maggie's head before she sat back down.

Maggie took a sip of the cold drink and winced as it slid down her throat. But the taste was just what she'd wanted. As soon as they were settled, Pearl had to inspect all of Maggie's injuries, from the cut on her lip where Walker had jammed the handful of napkins in her mouth, to the purple bruises on her neck, wrists, and ankles.

"Were you so scared?" Pearl asked.

Maggie sighed. "At first, I was just mad. It was scary afterward. But I was awake and knew that as long as he kept driving, I'd stay alive. And time was all Sonny needed to find me."

"Lord," Pearl said, and glanced at Sonny, then down at the raw and swollen knuckles on his hands. "I would have given anything to have seen that fight. You saved my girl."

Sonny looked at Maggie, at the tears welling in her eyes. "I love her, Pearl…with every breath I take."

Pearl patted his hands. "I know and I'm happy for the both of you. So, what happens next?"

"We both have yet to give statements, and then I think we're done. There's no way for Walker to plead not guilty and waste a court trial on the obvious. but I know he's going to be charged with aggravated kidnapping, which is a class A felony, and at his age, will most likely spend the rest of his life in a Texas prison."

"Pearl, some of my things are still at the house. I have to figure out where to put them at the ranch, but I should be ready to get back to work in a few days. For sure as soon as my ankles and wrists aren't so sore," Maggie said.

Pearl nodded. "Your things are fine where they are. Move at your leisure, and we're ready for you when you're ready for us."

"Customers," Darla said, pointing to two cars pulling off the highway and into the parking lot.

Pearl got up, reluctant to go back to work. "Chicken and dumplings are on the special today. How about I send some home with you? The dumplings are soft and warm, and the chicken is tender. Shouldn't be too hard to swallow."

"We'll gratefully take some with us," Sonny said. "I can cook, but not at that level of goodness."

Pearl beamed. "I'll get some ready for you right now."

Maggie took another sip of her drink, then set it aside. She was hurting and just wanted to go back to the ranch and lie down.

Sonny saw the misery on her face. "This was too much, too soon. Home we go," he said.

Maggie nodded. Home was Sonny. Her iron butterfly man.

The next four days became the time of settling in.

On the first day, two people from the prosecutor's office arrived. One officer to film the statements being made, and another one for questioning. They took the statements separately and began with Maggie, so Sonny went outside to the back porch, then meandered farther to the corral. When they went out to get him, they saw him riding bareback in the corral.

"He can't sit still for long," Maggie said. "That's Fancy Dancer, his Appaloosa."

One officer pointed. "He's riding without a saddle."

"He's also riding without a bridle," Maggie said, and waved at him.

He pulled Dancer to a stop with a tug on his mane, and then slid off and gave him a pat on the backside and headed to the house.

Unconcerned with the police presence, Sonny was all about Maggie.

"Are you okay, darlin'?"

"I'm fine, but I'm going to lie down for a while, okay?"

"I've got you," he said, picked her up and carried her to the bedroom, put a pillow under her feet, then covered her with a blanket, with both officers following.

"What's the pillow for?" one asked.

Sonny saw the man frowning, so he pulled the covers up from her feet and pushed up the legs of her sweats. The raw places on her ankles were clearly visible.

"Did she not tell you he tied her up?"

"Well, yes, but…"

He sighed. "Honey, push the sleeves of your sweat-shirt up a bit, too," so she did.

Her wrists were even worse.

"He used bungee cords. Wrapped them so tight she lost feeling in her feet and hands, and rode that way for nearly two hours. The covers rub her ankles. I put a pillow under them because it's soft, and because I thought for two hours she was dead, and because…"

He stopped and took a breath, remembering Walker beating him and Charlie just because he was hung over and mean, then beating them for crying. Big boys don't cry, was always his excuse.

Maggie knew in those moments he was a lifetime away, and took his hand.

"Sonny, it's okay. I'm okay. Go do your thing so they can finish and go home." She pointed at the man who'd filmed her statement. "Today is his wife's birthday. This is probably the last place he wants to be."

Sonny tucked her into bed and closed the bedroom door, then led the way back into the living room, answered their questions, laid all of his good luck in knowing she'd been kidnapped onto the tracker app on his phone, explained how Pearl had called him, worried about Maggie disappearing, and how she became his go-between, notifying the Briscoe County sheriff to track the GPS on his phone, because he was using it to track Maggie, and when they found him, they would find her and her abductor, too.

And they asked a question he was expecting, knowing he would still have no answer.

"Why is there so much bad blood between you and your father? What happened?"

"I never knew, and I barely know him. I was five years old when he walked out on us. I had no bond to him, or with him. He was a shadow in our lives. He beat my older brother and me all the time before. We were glad to see him go. We grew up, learning of his escapades from time to time, but they weren't part of our lives because neither was he. It was only after I started rodeoing...riding bulls, that he showed up and began hassling me. Showing up dead drunk at events and wanting someone to take his picture like they were taking mine, telling them that I got my skills from him. But people knew different. He'd never sat a bronc or a bull in his life. I was a top gun on the circuit for years until I got stomped getting off. Died twice on the operating table, and yet I'm here. The last thing he said to me before I left Oklahoma was that I should have died in the arena, so you tell me. I think he's just plain evil."

As they were finishing up and going through their notes, the officer doing the questioning paused.

"Out of curiosity, why, after you had pounded him to a pulp, did you cut off his braids and throw them away?"

"In our culture, if a person loses a limb, or has something removed from their body, it is kept in some way, to be buried with them when they finally pass, so that they are whole again. Cutting off his braids, then throwing them away was the ultimate insult. He will not be whole when he is laid to rest."

Both men looked at Sonny with a different level of respect, then packed up and drove away, leaving Sonny trying not to dwell on the past as he went to check on Maggie.

Seeing her in his bed still felt like a gift he didn't deserve. He thought of what he could be doing, then discarded it all and eased down on the bed beside her, closed his eyes, and fell asleep to the soft sounds of her breathing.

Days passed as Maggie healed. She was getting antsy to go back to work and Sonny knew it, but it wasn't until he got a call from the art dealer in Santa Fe that he knew her world was about to change.

Maggie had gone to town, promising she was only going to see Pearl, and pick up a couple of things in the pharmacy. It was her first trip on her own since the attack, but it felt good to be in her own car, making decisions and taking care of business without bothering Sonny to do for her, and she'd left Sonny in the arena with the big bay, putting him through the paces of competition reining. He was fast. He was powerful, and Sonny said that horse could come to a sliding halt in a shorter span of time than any other horse he'd ridden.

Sonny had just taken the big bay through all of the stops, turns and pivots, and was riding him back to the stable to unsaddle and brush down when his cell phone rang.

He glanced at it, thinking he'd let it go to voicemail until he saw who it was, and pulled the bay to a halt to answer.

"Hello."

"Sonny, this is Max Andros. I was on a little buying trip, and just returned to find this email from you. All I have to say is, oh my God, to the photos you sent."

Sonny wanted to shout with joy. Instead, he played it cool.

"I know! Right? There's a whole room full of them in the little house where she'd been living. First time I walked into that room, I couldn't find the breath to speak."

"That portrait of you. Did you sit for that?"

"No. I didn't even know she'd done it."

"Those sunsets...those paintings in that little café... are those places real?"

"Yes. In the panhandle of West Texas, those sunsets happen daily. I've seen a few of them myself, having recently moved here. And that café and those diners in those paintings are real as it gets. Your twenty-six-year-old artist is a waitress there, and those are customers. Some regulars. Some just passing through."

"Twenty-six? Jesus, Sonny! What's her name?"

"Magnolia Brennen, soon to be Bluejacket."

Max laughed. "You're marrying her? Good move! She's going to put you in the money and herself on the map in the art world. Have you shown these to any other dealers yet?"

"No. She didn't think they were any good. Nobody knows she paints, except me, and now you."

"Where did she train?" Max asked.

"She's self-taught, is all I know," Sonny said.

"I have to see these. If they're as good as they look, will she let me take some? I want to splash her and her work all over the art world and be the first to do it. She's going to be as famous as Andrew Wyeth became. Her work has more motion and color than Wyeth, but the same empathy and solitude, the same kind of emotion. How do I get to where she's at?"

"Crossroads, where we live, and where the Yellow Rose exists, is about an hour south of Amarillo, and you already know it's a straight shot from Santa Fe to Amarillo. If you want to meet her, and see her work, let me know. I'll break it to her gently."

Max chuckled. "She's really that naïve about her work?"

"When you grow up in foster care, being bounced from one family to another, there will be few people in that life bragging on you, or cheering you on. What she's accomplished, she's done on her own."

"I'll check my schedule and then I'll text you to confirm, but let your little lady know that I'm going to make her famous. And if you don't have a studio on that ranch for her to paint in, then start building one. And thank you for the opportunity. She's going to be a feather in my cap, as well."

"So, if I tell her all this and get her hopes up, and then you back out, be prepared to see me on your doorstep."

Max laughed. "It's for real, and I don't make enemies of friends. I still have photos of you riding bulls in the Western art section of my gallery, and you know it because you get your share of every sale by direct deposit."

"Just making sure. She means the world to me, and I don't want her hurt."

"Of course, of course. I'll be in touch. Now go tell your Magnolia that I said she's amazing."

"Thanks, Max. Talk to you soon," Sonny said, then rode the bay on into the stable, unsaddled him, then took him out into the corral for fresh water and a brush down, before turning him out in the pasture.

Chapter 16

THE DUST WAS FLYING BEHIND MAGGIE'S CAR AS SHE came down the driveway. Sonny heard her coming, got up from the table where he'd been paying bills, and headed for the back porch to carry in her purchases.

She parked and got out with a smile on her face. "I'm going back to work tomorrow," she said.

He kissed the top of her head and then walked her into the house. "Think you're ready, do you?"

"Yes. I told Pearl. She's so excited, and so am I. And I wouldn't mind seeing you walk in now and then, too."

He winked. "I'll try not to make a pest of myself."

"You may get fed up with me leaving for work at 5:00 a.m. I'm starting off at a half day, and if I don't give out, it's back on the regular schedule."

"I have something I need your opinion on. Would you walk out to the front with me?"

"Sure," she said, and took his hand as they went down the steps and out into the yard.

Then Sonny stopped, and they turned around to face the house.

"The north end of the house is also the driveway to

the back, so if we built your art studio on to the south end, and added an extra bedroom and bath while we were at it for company, would that be giving you good light?"

She frowned. "Why would you be doing all that? It's just a hobby."

"Not any more it's not. Max Andros called me while you were in town. He's lost his mind over how good your work is. Can't believe you're only twenty-six. Is stunned that you've had no formal training. Says you paint in the style that reminds him of Andrew Wyeth, whoever the hell that is, and that you have more color and movement in your work, but he sees the same solitude and empathy and emotion. He wants to come meet you and see the stuff in person. He wants to take some of it back to get framed and ready for an art show to introduce you and your work to the art world. He says he's going to make you rich and famous."

Maggie's legs went out from under her. Had Sonny not been standing so close she would have hit the ground on her butt. He caught her inches shy of the landing.

"Honey, are you okay?"

Her heart was pounding. "Is this a joke?"

He frowned. "No. I would never make a joke about that. He's for real. I know him. He has some photos of me riding bulls in his studio in the Western section of his gallery. He was elated to find out you hadn't shown

them to anyone else. He wants the exclusive to introduce you to the art world, as he puts it."

She took a quick breath, then looked up at him. "Oh.
My. God."

He grinned, and kissed the tip of her nose. "Is now
the time when I can say, I told you so?"

"Sonny, I don't know what to think, or what to say,
or what to do."

"Don't worry about it for now. Wait until you meet
him in person and let him explain it all to you. You have
a gift, Magnolia. A rare and amazing gift given to few.
You won't just be Sonny Bluejacket's wife, and I will be
known as Magnolia Brennen's husband."

Tears were rolling down her face.

"Don't cry, darlin', this is wonderful news," Sonny said.

"I was always drawing, and getting yelled at for wasting paper where I was living, and remembering all of
the times when a teacher would snatch a drawing from
my desk and gave me detention for playing in class,
even though I'd already finished my work."

The stricken look on her face killed him. "I'm sorry
that happened. But look at the payback you're going to
dish out when your name becomes known in such a
distinguished portion of society. The art world, baby…
you're already in and you have yet to experience the
rush of seeing your work hanging on gallery walls. I'm
so proud of you I could bust. Now look at this house
again. Emmit did what he wanted to it. Now it's our
turn to add what we need."

She wiped the tears from her face and looked back at the house again.

"Big windows facing the east for light," she said.

"And more windows facing the west for the sunsets," he added.

A slow smile spread across her face. "Yes, for the sunsets."

Sonny nodded. "And real wooden shutters that can be closed when it hails."

Then she frowned. "What about Pearl? What about the Yellow Rose?"

"What was she doing with it before you got dumped on her steps?" he asked.

She smiled. "Taking care of business."

"You're not going to stop being her girl. You'll still see her, and she'll still be the mother you never had, and the grandmother to our kids, whether she likes it or not," Sonny said. "She's going to celebrate your success as much as you will. I can hear her now, pointing to one of your originals hanging on the wall at the Rose. 'That's a Magnolia Brennen original. She's my girl.'"

Maggie sighed. "You're right. I'm just having a hard time picturing myself as an artist."

"Well, how about you just remember you are Magnolia, and you know what you're doing. Titles don't mean a thing. It's what's inside you that counts. I know you just came from town, but I need to go back and pick up some horse feed. Do you want to come with, or would you rather rest?"

"I'm too hyped to close my eyes. I'll come with you. I just need to wash up first."

They'd already been to the feed store and had several sacks of oats loaded into the back of Sonny's truck, then gone straight into Belker's Grocery. They had just moved from the deli section into the bread aisle when another shopper appeared in the aisle, moving toward them.

Sonny barely gave him a glance, but Maggie saw the man's face flush a bright red as he made a U-turn in the aisle, and disappear.

"That's called a guilty conscience," Maggie said.

Sonny looked up. "What did I miss?"

"The guy who just started down this aisle saw you and booked it," she said.

"Why? Who was it?"

"Del Kincaid. The man who bought the stolen horses off of Wade Sutton."

Sonny shrugged. "He's suffering the consequences of his actions. Nothing to do with me. And he's either out on bail, or got off with a fine and probation, likely the latter. For men like him, money talks. I got my horses back, anyway. Which bread do you want?" he asked.

"Which is your favorite?" she asked.

"Auntie's fry bread," he said, and then grinned. "You pick. I'll eat anything."

"Fry bread… I have not had the pleasure," she said.

"Think indigenous version of a Mexican tortilla, but with flour not cornmeal. And deep fried."

"Yum. You had me at deep-fried," Maggie said.

He laughed, and the joy in the sound carried across the store, bringing smiles to other people's faces. Except for Del Kincaid. He paid for his things and slunk out.

Sonny and Maggie finally got to the checkout.

Lana, the clerk, greeted them with a smile. "Maggie, good to see you up and about," she said, and then winked at Sonny. "I heard they're thinking about putting a statue up in town in your honor, but they can't decide if there should be a skunk at your feet or just honor the cool dude that you are."

Sonny grinned. "They might want to nix the skunk. The scent has finally faded from the store. I doubt your boss would want to go through that again."

She giggled, finished checking them out, then stood watching as they went out the door.

The next shopper showed up. A fifty-something redhead named Rona started emptying her shopping cart on the conveyor.

"Who are you looking at?" she asked.

Lana sighed. "Sonny Bluejacket. I swear, he's the prettiest man I ever saw. And all that long black hair. I always did like a man with long hair."

"That's because you're an old hippie," Rona said, then grinned. "But you're right about one thing. He's seriously hot. Lucky Maggie."

Unaware they were the topic of conversation, they drove home with a back seat full of groceries, and a truck bed full of horse feed. He was listening to her talk as he drove, and wondering how he'd ever existed without her. They were nearing the entrance to the ranch when a large colorful bird with a long tail ran across the road in front of them.

"Look, Sonny!"

"Ring-neck pheasant," he said.

She watched it disappear into the pasture and decided she'd rather see it on the ground than on the table.

As soon as they got home, he carried in the groceries, then left her to put them away while he unloaded the sacks of feed and checked on the mares.

The sun was priming for the big show, hanging above the horizon like a high diver priming for the big plunge when Maggie came out the back door. Sonny was standing in the doorway to the barn and looking west. But the moment she came off the porch, he turned around.

Seriously dude? I know you didn't hear me. How did you know I was here?

Sonny was shaking inside, watching as she came toward him, and seeing three tall young men walking beside her. Their hair was long, and dark, and they were flanking her like a pack following their leader. And in that moment, he knew he was seeing the future.

Those were his sons.

A lump rose in his throat as the light around Maggie grew brighter, and then they were gone, and she was standing before him.

"Sonny, what's wrong?"

"Absolutely nothing," he said, then gave her a quick hug before they turned to face the west.

"I'm going to build you a gazebo in the front yard when you start building your studio, so you will always have a place to sit and watch the sunsets."

She smiled. "I would love that."

"I love you, Magnolia." Then he kissed the top of her head and held her closer.

———

Sunrise had yet to happen when Maggie downed the last of her coffee and turned around to kiss Sonny goodbye.

"Don't frown," she said. "I'm looking forward to going back to work. It's only half a day today. I'll keep working until life tells me otherwise."

"I know, love. Tell Pearl I said hello, and have yourself a good day, okay? I'm going to be in the arena working horses today, but I'll have my phone on me. You call if you need me, promise?"

"I promise. I gotta go. Pearl's probably already making biscuits. Love you," she said.

"Love you more. See you later. Drive safe."

She waved goodbye as she drove away, while he went back inside, locked the front door so he wouldn't forget later when he left the house, and began putting their breakfast dishes in the dishwasher, then went into the bedroom to make the bed and saw she'd already done it.

Little Miss "I'll do it myself," he thought, as he went back to get another cup of coffee, then sat down in the living room to watch the morning show and get an update on the local weather. About the only thing that changed daily with weather was the velocity of the wind.

He was thinking about the day ahead when his phone signaled a text. It was from Charlie.

Are you awake? If you are, call me.

He frowned, and immediately made the call. Charlie answered on the first ring.

"Sonny, I hope I didn't wake you?" he said.

"No, Maggie and I get up early. Her morning at the Yellow Rose starts at 5:00 a.m. I'm finishing off a cup of coffee before I head to the roping arena. What's up?"

"I told Auntie about what Walker did. She was shocked, and then she got so angry with him. She went to the council to let them know what he'd done. They dealt their own brand of tribal justice, and it isn't pretty. Whether he ever gets out of prison or not, he's lost all voting privileges with the tribe, and he's been shunned. If this was the old days, they would have put him on a horse with his belongings and sent him into the wild on his own. He would never be welcome among his people again."

"Is Auntie okay?" Sonny asked.

"Well, she will be. She's taken down the family pictures from the wall that he was in, even the ones when he was a kid. She said he has shamed the family name, and has burned enough sage in her house to smoke a turkey, and she cries because she thinks you will hate her for being his sister."

Sonny groaned. "No, no. That's grief talking. You tell her she's still my best Auntie and I miss her hugs and her fry bread. You remind her that you're his son and I don't hate you, and I don't hate myself, so why would I hate her? We all share the blood. But we don't share the guilt. Okay?"

"Yes, I will tell her," Charlie said. "Did you ever find out what happened to Nubby?"

"Yes. He got arrested for pickpocketing in Boise City. He's in the Cimarron County Jail for the next six months. The cops know that Nubby was initially with Walker, so when they release him, they'll be watching to see what he does next. If he knows what's good for him, he better make tracks for home and change his stripes."

"I know his sister, Retha. She's been worried about him. Nobody knows where he went. I didn't want to say anything to her before, but I will now. She's like Auntie. Related to a low life whether she likes it or not," Charlie said.

"Right, and thanks for calling, Charlie. I miss you guys."

"You gonna marry that girl?" Charlie asked.

"Yes."

"Then you better invite us to the wedding," Charlie said.

"I don't have a room for you to stay, but there's a decent little hotel called the Crossroads Lodge only three miles from my place," Sonny said.

"We'll make it work. Take care, little brother."

"You, too," Sonny said.

Chapter 17

THE SUN HAD YET TO COME UP WHEN MAGGIE PARKED and walked in the back door of the Yellow Rose.

"Something sure smells good in here," she said.

Pearl turned around, beaming. "Girl, I am so glad to see you. Welcome back, honey."

"Looking good," Davey added.

"Thanks. Glad to be back," Maggie said, then put on an apron, slipped an order pad in the pocket, and went to work. She wasn't saying anything to Pearl about her news until all was confirmed and her paintings were on their way to Santa Fe. Pearl was making biscuits, and Davey was frying bacon and sausage for the warmer. Darla arrived soon after, and the day began.

Sonny was back at the trailer house site watching the power company pull the electric meter from the pole. A fence crew from Silverton was just getting started on taking down the old fence that had run east to west behind Sutton's trailer. They had their orders and knew what to do, so as soon as the power company left, Sonny got Emmit's weed-eater out of the truck and began to clean up the area along the fence row, pausing every now and then to stop and check his phone. Rationally, he knew Magnolia was safe, but he would have nightmares of her kidnapping for the rest of his life.

He glanced up to see how the fence crew was doing, loaded up his equipment, then went into the pasture to help them roll up the wire they were taking down.

As soon as Cheryl showed up for her shift, Maggie headed home. In the short time she'd been living with Sonny, knowing she was loved and cherished had made all the difference in her life.

Magnolia Brennen was finally blooming into the woman she was meant to be, and Sonny had just cracked the wall behind which she'd been sheltering. As she drove by the trailer site, she saw men along the fence line, and Sonny's truck farther west. Whatever was going on, he was in the middle of it.

When she got home, she found a note on the table telling her where he was working, and to call if she needed him.

A quick check of the refrigerator assured her there was a package of thawed hamburger meat, so she dug around to see what else was in the pantry. After finding the needed ingredients, she mixed up a meatloaf, poured barbeque sauce over it just before she put it in the oven, covered it with foil, set the timer, and put it in to bake. Then she wrapped two baking potatoes in foil and put them in the oven with the meatloaf.

The house was neat, the floors were clean, so she changed out of her work clothes into sweatpants and a T-shirt. The sofa beckoned. Exhausted from the busy morning at the Rose, she took the blanket from the back of the sofa, covered herself up, then rolled over and closed her eyes.

She slept until the timer went off, took the meatloaf out, turned the potatoes, and reset the timer to finish them off, then sat down at the kitchen table. All of her things were now out of Pearl's house, and she had one last round of utility bills to pay before everything went back into Pearl's name. Once she had finished paying bills, she glanced at the time. Almost five. Sonny would soon be coming home.

––––––––

Sonny had hired a double crew to remove the old fencing. Six of them were rolling up old wire, while six more were pulling fence posts as they went. It was getting late by the time they loaded up the last of the refuse and drove away, leaving Sonny with a pickup load of T-posts and another couple of truck loads neatly stacked on the far side of some bushes, out of sight of anyone looking for something to steal.

He was tired and dirty, but satisfied with the day as he got back in the truck and drove home through the pasture. The horses watched him, but when the truck didn't slow down, they went back to grazing.

Once he got back to the house, he pulled around behind the roping arena and began unloading the T-posts. After the truck was empty, he fed and watered the mares before heading to the house.

His girl was there. All was right with his world.

He walked in the back door then stopped. "Dang, woman! Something sure smells good in here!"

Maggie came running and threw her arms around his neck. "It might be me, but I'm betting it's the meat-loaf you smell."

He groaned, picked her up off her feet and lowered his head. Her lips were soft and warm, and she smelled so damn good, he didn't know what smelled better— the lingering scent of lilac shampoo in her hair, or that meatloaf.

"Can you give me about ten minutes to clean up?" he said.

She brushed a kiss across his lips. "I already gave you my heart. I think I can spare ten minutes, too."

He gave her backside a quick pat. "If I wasn't so hungry, I'd go back outside and come in the house again just for this greeting."

"You're worth waiting for. Go do your thing."

Sonny was still smiling when he got in the shower.

Charlie Bluejacket's workday was over, but he had a stop to make before he went home, and called Frannie to let her know he'd be a little late.

"Hey, handsome. What's up?" she asked.

"Hi, honey. I'm going to stop by Retha's house to let her know where Nubby is. No need leaving her to worry he's lying dead somewhere, you know?"

"Nubby is a creep, but Retha is a good woman. She doesn't deserve that stress and worry. Drive safe," Frannie said.

"I will. See you soon, and tell Julia to feed Butters one scoop, not two. He's getting fat."

She laughed. "I will."

He was still smiling when he hung up, but the smile slipped once he headed for Retha Borders's house on the other side of Okmulgee.

He was pulling into her driveway when she came around the corner of the house pushing a wheelbarrow full of bedding plants. He knew she was in her fifties, but by the stoop of her shoulders, and the wobble of the wheelbarrow, she looked like an old woman. Life had been hard on Retha and his news wasn't going to make it better. Still, he got out and ran to help her.

"Here, Retha, I've got it. Lead the way," he said.

"Charlie! Thank you! If you'll get it to the far side of the porch, I can take it from there."

Charlie pushed the wheelbarrow where she wanted it to go, and then stopped.

"Before you start digging in the dirt, do you have a minute? We all know you've been worried about Nubby going off with Walker like that. I have some news. Come sit on the porch with me a bit out of the sun, okay?"

All the color faded from Retha's face. "Is it bad?"

"Oh, they're alive and kicking, but they both got themselves in trouble," Charlie said, then helped her up the steps and onto the porch swing, while he took a seat in a chair.

"What have they done?" Retha asked.

Charlie sighed. "They started out together for a really bad reason. Walker set out to find Sonny at the ranch he'd just inherited. He wanted payback because Sonny wouldn't take Walker with him. Walker told Sonny he should have died that night at the rodeo arena. That he should already be dead and buried, so when we found out they were headed in Sonny's direction, we both knew his intentions were to hurt Sonny in some way. I don't know what their specific plans were, but Nubby wasn't just along for the ride. They got as far as Boise City, out in the Oklahoma panhandle, before Walker's old truck broke down. Long story short, Nubby pickpocketed money from a bunch of women in a grocery store, and got caught. He's in the Cimarron County Jail serving a six-month sentence."

"Oh lord," Retha muttered. "He's been nothing but trouble his whole adult life."

"Well, he's not in as much trouble as Walker is, though. He went on and found the town near Sonny's ranch, then didn't know how to get to him without being seen, so he kidnapped Sonny's girlfriend to try and lure Sonny out of town and get him alone. He had a gun in the front seat of the truck when he was caught, and the young woman tied up in the back seat. Sonny beat the crap out of him before the Texas Highway Patrol caught up with them. Walker's facing years he doesn't have to give in a Texas state prison."

Retha gasped. "That's terrible!"

"Yes, ma'am, it is. He's never been a good man, or a good husband, or even pretended to be a father figure. I was told you were worrying about Nubby's where-abouts, and wanted to put your mind at rest. At least you know where he is, and why. I expect when it comes time for his release, he'll be expecting Walker to bring him home. So, if you call your brother, you might want to tell him to start making other plans."

"Can I call Nubby?" Retha asked.

"Not sure how it all works there, but you can call the Cimarron County Jail and ask. They'll give you the information you need."

"Yes, I will, and I sure thank you for letting me know," Retha said.

Charlie shrugged. "It's not good news for either of our families, but you're welcome. I'd better get home. I want to get my chores done before dark."

He went back to his truck as Retha went back to her

bedding plants, both of them thinking, life happens, and life goes on.

———————

Supper at Sunset had come and gone, and so had the sunset.

Sonny was stretched out on the sofa with Maggie lying between his legs, her head pillowed on his chest as she chattered away.

"Darla had a big spill at the Rose today. A whole order. Little kid rolled his Hot Wheels so fast it slid off the table and rolled right under Darla's foot. She caught herself from falling, but the tray of food went everywhere. The parents were horrified and were apologizing profusely. Paid for the wasted food and then gave Darla a huge tip. Dad put the toy car in his pocket and the kid spent a good five minutes crying about it."

"What a mess. Good thing she wasn't hurt, though," he said.

"Oh, I know. All those years at the Rose, and we've slipped and skidded, and dumped food and dirty dishes all over the place."

He frowned. "Did you ever get hurt?"

"Only my dignity," she said. "It's hard to get up and walk out of a room with mashed potatoes and gravy on your butt."

He grinned, then kissed the top of her head just because she was so damn cute. "My poor sweetheart."

She giggled. "Oh, you get over it or you never have the guts to go back to work the next day."

"Changing the subject for a minute," Sonny said.

She sat up and turned to face him. "Okay. What's up?"

"We still need to decide about our wedding. My timeline is yesterday, but we have all this excitement about your budding career, so it's your call. I have this terrible, male desire to make sure the world can see you're taken. There's no jewelry store in Crossroads to pick out rings, but it's not far to Amarillo. You google shops that carry wedding dresses and then we'll pick out the rings together. My brother and family want to come to our wedding, and I need you to meet the good people in my family. Maybe it will take away the nightmare Walker put you through."

"Saturday and Sunday are my next days off," she said.

"Then we'll make it happen," Sonny said.

———

After Charlie Bluejacket's visit, Retha couldn't quit thinking about Nubby, and when morning dawned, she dressed slowly, still thinking about wanting to call him. As soon as she'd finished her breakfast, she sat down with a pad and pen, googled the phone number for the Cimarron County Jail, and after being transferred to a couple of different extensions, she bought minutes on a calling card, and money in Nubby's name for the commissary.

She was assured they would notify her brother, and now she had to wait and hope he would call when he was allowed.

———————

It was later that afternoon before Nubby was notified that his sister had set up a calling card and money in his account for the commissary. The first chance he was given, he made a call. It rang and rang, and he was right at the point of thinking she wouldn't answer when he heard her voice.

"Hello!"

"Hey Retha, it's me. Thanks for setting up the accounts here. I appreciate it."

She sighed. "Well, Nestor Lee, once I found out you were still alive in the world, I thought about just letting you stew. But I guess I'm not mean enough."

Nubby didn't give a flip about another person in the world, except for Retha. "Yeah, well, I got enough mean for the both of us," he said. "Sorry about this, but I won't be here long. I got six months, and Walker will come get me and bring me home when I'm released."

"No. That's part of why I wanted to talk to you. Walker is in a Texas state prison, likely for the rest of his mortal life, for aggravated kidnapping."

Nubby was in shock. "What the hell? Who did he kidnap?"

"Sonny's girlfriend, in hopes of luring him out of town. Apparently, your friend had plans to kill his own son, which I'm sure you knew about, and it backfired. Sonny caught up to Walker on a highway somewhere between Crossroads and the New Mexico border. He beat him to a pulp and cut off his braids, and if the Texas Highway Patrol hadn't arrived when they did, he would have beaten Walker to death."

The skin crawled on the back of Nubby's neck. "Cut off his braids? Whoa! That's harsh!"

Retha snorted. "And what he did to that poor girl wasn't worse? My God, Nubby. What's wrong with you?"

"Sorry, but that was shocking. What happened to the girl?" Nubby asked.

"She's going to be okay, no thanks to Walker. And here at home, the tribal council has taken away Walker's voting privileges and shunned him. Even if he gets out some day, he will not be welcomed back in the tribe. There are devils inside him. And this is a reminder to you. The police know you were meant to be with him on this trip."

Nubby got defensive all over again. "How do they know that? Did Walker tell them?"

"No. Sonny has visions. Remember when that escaped inmate was trying to catch Charlie and Frances's daughter Julia? Sonny had a vision that it was happening, and called his brother. What he did saved her life. So, Sonny also saw you two broke down on the side of the road. He knew ahead of time that you were coming after him, and now the authorities have you in their sights. When you get out, you better get yourself home and stay on the straight and narrow, because they have you pegged as some kind of hit man. Do you understand what I'm saying?"

Nubby's skin crawled again. Sonny turned into some psychic, and Nubby's six months in jail felt like a prize. It sure beat the hell out of a life sentence in a state prison.

"Yeah, okay Retha. I hear you."

"Good. I'll keep money in your accounts. Call whenever you need. And when you're going to be released, let me know. I'll come get you."

"You don't have to do that," Nubby said.

"If you want to come home, then yes, I do. You've burned all the bridges you ever had with the people who know you."

His sister's words were like a knife in the back. He hadn't seen that coming. "Gotta go. Time's up," Nubby said. "Thanks again for this."

The line went dead in Retha's ear. She was swallowing back tears as she got up and went outside to water her new plants. Staying busy was the only thing that kept her from going mad.

Chapter 18

Max Andros called Sonny just after 9:00 a.m. to update him.

"It's me," Max said. "I have two dates. Both of them next week. Either this coming Monday, or Wednesday. It's taken this long to organize the trip. I and another driver will fly to Amarillo, which takes less than an hour, pick up the two vans I've rented, and drive them to Crossroads. We'll load up and head back home, which will turn into about a six-hour drive to get there. If Miss Brennen is agreeable, I want to take all of what she has finished, thus the reason for two vans. We'll need to sign a contract for the showing, and a receipt for moving the number of paintings, all of which I will catalog with a photo and a number before receiving them. I want to take that painting of you, too."

"You can take it, but it won't be for sale," Sonny said. "Not that one."

Jules chuckled. "I figured, but it will be a huge draw for the show, just the same."

"She's still waiting tables at the Rose, which is good, because all of her work is in the house in town that she's still renting. You won't be driving out to the ranch to pick them up, but I will come to town to meet you. I'm just going to make the decision as to when you come for her. Come Monday, text me when you are leaving Amarillo and I'll head to the Rose and meet you there."

"Great," Max said. "It will be good to see you again."

Sonny disconnected, thought about calling Maggie, then decided to wait until she came home. No need getting her all flustered and bothered at work.

————

It was just past noon and Sonny was mucking out the mares' stalls, cleaning the stall mats, then putting down clean bedding, and talking to them as he worked.

Every now and then one of them would knicker at him, or nose his back searching for a treat, and he would stop and rub their bellies, and talk to the babies they were carrying, because he knew that when that foal was born, it would already know the sound of his voice.

He had just finished up when he heard a vehicle coming toward the house. He stored the wheelbarrow, washed up at the sink in the tack room, and was walking up from the barn, when he saw a late-model silver-and-black pickup approaching, then noticed the Dillon Ranch logo on the doors.

When the pickup pulled up at the house, he recognized Garrett Dillon and his son, Travis, who Sonny had met outside Belker's Grocery. As soon as Garrett parked, he and his son got out and met Sonny in the yard.

"Sonny, don't know if you remember me. I'm—"

Sonny smiled. Garrett Dillon was hard to forget. A red-headed man with a temper to match. Average height. A little bit bowlegged and built like a weight-lifter from bulldogging in his youth before he went to raising rodeo stock instead of riding them.

"Welcome to Sunset, Garrett. I remember you, but I remember your bulls more. You had some good ones." Then he glanced at the teen. "Travis, right?"

Travis grinned, pleased the famous Sonny Bluejacket had remembered his name.

"Yes sir," Travis said.

"Where did you get off to after you quit bull riding?" Garrett asked.

"Home, back to Bluejacket Hollow, near Okmulgee. I've been training horses for ranchers there for the past five years, but looking forward to taking it to the next level here."

Garrett nodded. "I'm here looking for new blood in my herd, and Emmit always had good stock. I kept wanting to talk to him about it, but when we all found out how sick he was, I backed off. Didn't feel like it was the right time."

"Understood," Sonny said. "As you know, I haven't been here long, but when I arrived, Emmit's truck was missing, there wasn't a horse on the place and the horse trailer and tack were all gone."

"The hell you say! What happened?" Garrett asked.

"Wade Sutton, Emmit's renter, helped himself to all of it after Emmit passed. He moved the horses onto his pasture, sold four before I got here and was driving the truck all over town like he hit the lottery. I called Sheriff Reddick. He came the night I arrived, and we confronted Sutton. He'd already sold four horses. I finally got all of them back, but haven't had a lot of time with them, or pick up some steers to see them work. Mostly just trying to put the pieces of Emmit's world back together."

Garrett frowned. "Damn, what a mess. I know the man by name, but never had any dealings with him. What happened to the four he sold?"

"I got them back, too. Sutton's wife told us who'd bought them, and the sheriff found him and my horses. He got arrested for knowingly buying stolen property, and now I have all of the horses back that Emmit had left when he passed."

Garrett's eyes narrowed. "Can I ask who bought the four?"

Sonny shrugged. "Delroy Kincaid...the son, not the father."

"Son of a gun! I have to admit, I am shocked. I thought better of Del. After all that, were the horses okay?"

"Yes, just happy to be back with the herd. Did you talk to Emmit about horses in particular?"

"I've been looking for mares and maybe another

stud. I need new blood in the herd. I knew Emmit had two mares for sale. Do you still have them?"

"Yes, and both due to foal within the next few weeks," Sonny said.

"Really? Out of Emmit's big gray?"

Sonny nodded. "The mares are already stalled. They're in the stables. Do you want to see the rest of the herd? I can get them here within a couple of minutes. All I have to do is whistle."

"This I gotta see," Garrett said.

"Walk with me," Sonny said, and headed for the feed room to fill a little bag with apple treats. They took a good look at both mares, then followed Sonny out to the big corral attached to the stables.

Garrett glanced at the covered arena as they passed, then stopped outside the corral.

"This won't take long," Sonny said.

He climbed the corral fence and jumped inside, then opened the gate before walking out into the pasture.

"What's he doing, Dad?" Travis asked.

"We're about to find out," Garrett said, and couldn't help but admire Bluejacket's stature. He certainly didn't look like a man who'd died twice and lived to tell the tale.

They saw Sonny stop, then heard a shrill, high-pitched whistle. A few seconds later Sonny whistled again and then pointed to the north.

They began to watch the horizon.

All of a sudden, the horses appeared, coming

toward him on the run. Heads up. Tails flying out behind them.

Garrett's heart skipped. The magnificence of horses never failed to make his heart skip.

"Wow, Dad. Look at them!" Travis said, and then he gasped. "Look! Look at the one coming up from behind. It's an Appaloosa. Oh, Dad! Look at him run! He's passing all of them!"

Garrett's heart was in his throat. He'd never coveted a horse before, but he did now. To own a magnificent animal like that would be a dream come true.

"They're gonna run over him," Travis said.

But then they didn't. Instead, they surrounded him, milling and pushing to get to him and the treats they knew he had. Garrett could hear Sonny talking to them, speaking words he didn't understand, and realized Sonny was talking to them in his native language, walking through the herd, stroking necks, scratching the spot between their ears.

When Sonny had the herd's attention, he turned and walked back inside the corral, with every one of them following. As soon as the last one was in, he shut the gate and began moving among them, giving each of them an apple treat, before walking back to where Garrett and his son were standing just outside the rails.

"What do you think? Want to see any of them closer?" he asked.

"They look good, Sonny. Real good. I like that big bay."

"The one beside it is a full brother." Sonny said.

"Which ones have you ridden?" Garret asked.

"At first, only the Appaloosa, and that was unplanned, but I've ridden all of them now except for the mares. I don't distress the mamas to be."

"What do you mean, riding the Appaloosa was unplanned?" Garrett asked.

"I had a pack of coyotes get after the herd in the middle of the night. It was right after I got here. I shot into the pack that night and knew I hit one, but I had to wait for daylight to do any tracking."

Garrett frowned. "I've heard rumors about a big pack running in the southern hills, but they don't usually mess with a herd unless there are babies," he said.

"Right, which was why I had concerns," and then he began telling them the story. "All of a sudden, I'm facing seven of the biggest, strangest-looking coyotes I've ever seen. Some kind of hybrids, I think. They had a lot of big dog in them, I think. But I had walked too far away from the truck, there I stood, wondering how many I could shoot before they attacked, when the Appaloosa came flying past me and tore through the pack, kicking and stomping. Now I can't get off a shot for fear of hitting him, and I'm afraid they'll tear up his legs, and did the only thing I could think to do. I ran into the middle of the mess, grabbed him by the mane and leaped. Made a bareback landing and started shooting. He ran them down and I shot them. He pretty much saved my life."

Garrett's mouth dropped. "You shot coyotes from

a running horse without a bridle, or a saddle, and you didn't fall off?"

"I had a really good incentive not to," Sonny said.

"No wonder you were so good at riding bulls," Garrett muttered.

"Are there any horses you'd like to ride? I can saddle some up and take them into the roping arena for you," Sonny asked.

"Do you mind if I call a couple of guys?" Garrett asked.

Sonny shrugged. "I don't mind. Tell them we'll be in the roping arena."

"The big gray is Emmit's only stud?" Garrett asked.

"Yes, and the only one not for sale is the Appaloosa. He's mine for life."

"I agree with not working mares that close to delivery, but I'd like to see their papers, and saddle up the gray and the biggest bay. I don't want to sit a horse and feel like my feet are about to drag the ground."

Sonny grinned. "I can identify with that. Just so you know, he's damn good at reining, like competition good if you're into that thing. I've been working with him on that a lot. How about I bring them into the arena? The door is unlocked. You two can go on in and take a seat in the bleachers. I think there's still some cold cans of pop in that old refrigerator just inside the door. Help yourself," Sonny said, and walked off.

He stopped by the tack room to get bridles for the bay and the gray stud and led them into the stables to saddle up. He heard a couple of other vehicles arrive while he was inside, and assumed it was whoever Garrett had called.

As soon as they were saddled, he mounted the gray and grabbed the reins on the big bay, then headed for the arena, riding one and leading the other.

Within moments of riding into the arena, he heard a whoop, and then someone shout "Bluejacket." He looked up, saw three men standing up waving their hats at him, and grinned.

Three bull riders he used to compete with. Where the hell had they come from? He rode over to the stands, dismounted, and tied the horses to the railing.

"Garrett, you know you're running with a wild bunch," Sonny said, then pointed at the trio. "Thumper. Colorado. Garza. I thought you three would have rattled your brains by now and be sitting in some of those rocking chairs out in front of the Cracker Barrel."

They started razzing him back. "You're still as ugly as ever, Bluejacket. I guess that's why you still ain't got a woman."

Garrett laughed at their camaraderie. "I knew they were at the Yellow Rose. People still talk about you, Sonny. You have been missed. Take that gray around the ring a few times for me."

Sonny got back in the saddle and began putting the stud through the paces, going from a walk to a lope, mimicking all the moves a horse would make cutting a steer out of a herd. Starting at one end and letting him run at full speed to the other end, knowing Garrett was timing it, then rode up to a sliding halt in front of the men.

Without saying a word, he tied up the gray and grabbed the reins on the bay. The horse was already moving when Sonny grabbed the saddle horn and swung into the saddle on the run.

Garrett's son Travis was so hyped he jumped up, shouting. "Dang, Dad! Teach me to ride like that!"

Garrett laughed. "That's not happening. Did you ever see me do anything like that?"

Travis turned to the men sitting beside them. "Can you do that?" he asked.

"We ride bulls, son, not rockets. That man is a legend for a reason," Colorado said.

Sonny put the bay through a whole training set for reining, before bringing the ride to an end.

"Damn, Sonny. You're right. I was timing that bay. His stops are spectacular. He's built like a tank, but light on his feet."

"Any other horses you want to see?" Sonny asked.

"I know he's not for sale, but would you ride the Appaloosa?" Travis asked.

Garrett frowned. "Now, Trav, we don't want to bother him—"

"His name is Fancy Dancer. I call him Dancer. You want to see him do his thing?" Sonny asked.

Travis nodded. "Like you did when you killed the coyotes?"

Sonny laughed. "Sure kid, but only if I don't have to chase coyotes down again. Let me get these two back to the stables and I'll bring Dancer back."

He leaned over and untied the gray's reins and this time rode out on the bay, and leading the gray.

Thumper got his nickname because of a nervous habit. Every time he sat down, his knee started bouncing, which made the heel of his boot repeatedly thump on the floor. It was bouncing up a storm as Sonny rode out.

"What does he mean, chasing down coyotes?" Thumper asked.

Garrett began repeating the story Sonny told them. "He said the horse saved his life."

Garza was a short, stocky man in his early thirties, who had a scar on the underside of his jaw, and a nose that had been broken so many times it no longer healed straight. He was quiet through the whole story, trying to imagine what it would take to run into a pack of wild coyotes, never mind holding a rifle and trying to mount a kicking, stomping horse with one hand, and without a saddle or bridle. He wanted to deny the truth of it, but it was Sonny Bluejacket. He'd seen his last ride. He'd heard about Sonny's heart stopping twice during surgery. In Garza's world, living through that was nothing short of supernatural. Hell, maybe it wasn't the horse. Maybe Sonny was the one with the magic.

And then they saw Sonny entering the arena with the Appaloosa walking beside him. No lead rope. No bridle. No saddle.

Travis scooted all the way to the edge of his seat and leaned forward.

Then Sonny turned, grabbed a handful of that black mane and with one long leap, flew up and landed on Dancer's back. For the next ten minutes, he rode Dancer at a lope, steering him only with the pressure of his knees or boots, darting across the arena, from right to left, from one end to the other, and then running him all the way back to come to a sliding halt in front of them.

Garrett sighed. "That's the fastest horse I've seen off a racetrack. He's magnificent, Sonny. I'd give a king's ransom to own him, but I'm thinking he's a one-man horse."

Sonny slid off Dancer and took an apple treat out of his pocket. Dancer took it from his palm and crunched until it was gone, then Sonny winked at Travis.

"Are we good now?"

Travis was so enamored with the man and the horse, that all he could do was nod.

"Let me get Dancer put up and then we'll go up to the house. The registration papers are there. Huey, Dewey, and Louie are welcome to come, too."

His bull-riding buddies burst out laughing. "After that remark, you better have a beer waiting," Colorado said.

Sonny grinned. "Meet you all inside. Back door's open. Go on in."

Chapter 19

HOURS LATER, A DEAL HAD BEEN STRUCK BETWEEN Garrett and Sonny, and he'd just finished filling out registration transfers to the AQHA online. The new registration papers would be mailed to Garrett, listing him as the new owner, and he'd given him a bill of sale for the four Quarter Horses.

Garrett's son, Travis, was in a corner of the living room watching TV. Thumper, Colorado, and Garza were eating through the snacks Sonny had put out earlier, and laughing as they reminisced about their rodeo days with Sonny.

Garza popped a Frito in his mouth, chewing as he talked. "Hey Sonny, remember that blond buckle bunny who kept wearing a feather in her hair in the cowboy bars after rodeo events, hoping you would notice her?"

Sonny grinned. "We all noticed her after some drunk stuck his cigarette to the feather and it went up in smoke."

"Yeah, and somebody from a nearby table grabbed their pitcher of beer and threw it in her face to put out the fire," Thumper added.

"Wonder what ever happened to her? I never saw her around the rodeos after that," Colorado said.

Sonny shrugged. "It's hard to show your face again after everyone you know saw your tailfeathers on fire."

They burst out laughing.

"Speaking of women…there's a real pretty one who waits tables down at the Yellow Rose," Colorado said. "She waited on our table when we were eating lunch. Dark hair, bluest damn eyes I ever saw, and sass to spare. I always did like a sassy woman."

"Before you comedians say anything more you might regret, that one's already spoken for. She recently gave up her place in Crossroads to come live with me, and I'm marrying her as soon as I can get a ring on her finger. Her name is Magnolia Rae Brennen, and pretty soon she'll be adding Bluejacket to all that."

Garrett laughed at the stricken looks on the men's faces. "Now look what you went and did, Sonny. You broke their hearts, destroyed their fantasies, and they'll never be the same…until the next pretty girl comes along."

They were still teasing each other when Sonny heard a car coming toward the house and looked out the window.

"Speaking of my girl, she's coming down the driveway now. She was a good friend to Emmit. Used to clean house for him on her days off, so she knew more about this place than I did when I arrived."

"Dang it. I'm always a day late and a dollar short," Colorado said.

"Be nice. All of you. I don't want her to think my friends are heathens, too. She's already had a dose of Walker. It's a miracle she even wants anything to do with me," Sonny said.

"What do you mean?" Garza asked.

Garrett already knew the story. "I'll fill you all in later. I'm sure that's the last thing she'd want to discuss, but suffice it to say, Sonny handled it like a boss. You have my sympathy and my admiration," Garrett added.

And then the back door opened, and she came in smiling.

Sonny went to meet her. "Hey, darlin'. I imagine you know Garrett Dillon, and his boy Travis. And I heard you served these three clowns at the Rose today. That's Thumper, Colorado, and Garza. They're bull riders like I was, and friends from my rodeo days. Everyone, this is Magnolia, my future wife."

"Maggie to all of you," she said, and then saw Travis in the corner. "There's my chicken-fry guy."

Travis looked up, beaming. "Yes, ma'am. I do love me some chicken-fried steak."

"And Miss Pearl makes the best, doesn't she?" Maggie said, then eyed the table full of crumbs and empties. "Did anyone happen to leave a cold Pepsi for me?"

The three bull riders jumped up at once and scrambled to the refrigerator, trying to be the first one to get one for her.

Sonny gave her a quick hug. "You have conquests."

She shrugged. "It's the pink Ropers," and then Thumper came flying toward her with a can of Pepsi.

"She likes it on ice," Sonny said.

Colorado grabbed a red Solo cup from the table and filled it from the dispenser.

"Thank you, boys, so much," Maggie said. "Now if somebody could find me a place to sit, I'd be…"

All of a sudden, every chair at the table was empty and Garza was holding out a chair.

"Right here, Miss Maggie. It's the cleanest spot," he said.

At that, everyone was laughing, including Maggie. She emptied the can of Pepsi into her cup and took that first sip. "Don't you just love it when that fizz hits your nose? Now what on earth has been going on here today?"

"Garrett bought the mares, the gray stud, and the biggest bay. We've been working on registration transfers for a while now," Sonny said.

Maggie's eyes lit up, and then she clapped her hands in delight. "Sonny! This is wonderful. Emmit would be so proud of you!"

"I'm pretty happy about it," Garrett said. "I was interested in the gray stud before Emmit got sick and then, as I told Sonny, it didn't seem like a good time to bother him after that."

Sonny glanced back at the screen on his laptop. "Okay, Garrett. That was the notification from my bank. Your money transfer went through. And we've finished the registration transfers. When do you want to pick up the horses?"

"Tomorrow morning around nine o'clock, if that time works for you."

Sonny nodded. "Then I'll stable the stud and the bay for the night. It'll save rounding them up tomorrow."

Garrett stood, then shook Sonny's hand. "Pleasure doing business with you. Next time I have a roping event at the ranch, why don't you bring that Appaloosa and show off a little for us. It would be good advertising for you to let people know you're in the area. Good trainers are hard to come by. You said you used to train for ranchers down around Henryetta?"

Sonny nodded. "Among others."

"Then I know some cowboys riding horses you likely worked with."

"Sure, why not?" Sonny said. "Just let me know the day and time and I'll load up Dancer and head your way."

"Will you ride him like you did for us?" Travis asked.

"Sure," Sonny said. "Dancer doesn't much like saddles and bridles anyway."

"How do you know?" Travis asked.

"Because he told me," Sonny said, and then winked.

A few minutes later they were gone, and Sonny was on his way to the stables to put down bedding, hay, and water in two more stalls. He let the bay in first, and latched the door, then went back for the gray stud and put him in another stall and latched that door, as well.

"This is our last night together," he said, as he gave each of them an apple treat, and went back to the house.

Maggie was pulling off her pink boots as Sonny came in the back door with the big garbage can, and began cleaning off the mess they'd made.

"I think they ate every snack item we had in the place," Sonny said.

"We can always get more, but you can't get more good friends like that. The best ones are the ones you have history with," Maggie said, then pulled her T-shirt over her head and wrinkled her nose. "I smell like french fries again."

Sonny wiped the last of the crumbs from the table, then wrapped his arms around her bare shoulders. "Do I smell like money? I should because I just sold two hundred and fifty thousand dollars' worth of horses."

Maggie's eyes widened. "You did what?"

"Four registered Quarter Horses, trained for cutting and roping. One a stud, one a competition horse, and two mares due to foal within the next month. A good cutting horse will easily sell for at least twenty-five, and competition horses can go as high as fifty thousand. The gray was Emmit's stud horse, which makes him worth more. There are the two foals yet to be born, which because of their bloodlines, are still worth a lot. Garrett wanted them, and I had them for sale," Sonny said.

"Oh my God! Sonny! I had no idea those horses were worth money like that! Congratulations! This is so exciting for you!"

"For us," Sonny said. "For us. Everything I do will be for us, and the family we raise. I'll take some of the money from the sale and buy a couple of registered Quarter Horses with good bloodlines, already broke to ride but untrained, and do it all over again. This is how it starts, darlin'. This is our future. Start small. Grow the business while you paint your masterpieces," then he unhooked her bra and tossed it on the back of a chair.

Maggie moaned as he cupped her breasts. "I need to shower."

"I already told you I like french fries," he said, then picked her up and carried her to bed.

Maggie was already aching. "You keep carrying me to bed. One day, I'm going to forget how to walk."

"We're not going for a walk. We're going for a ride," he said.

"Bareback?" Maggie asked.

"Bare all over," he said.

Moments later, they were coming out of their clothes at breakneck speed.

———

Maggie was gone before sunrise, and Sonny was already at the stables, making sure the horses were good to go.

The other horses had meandered out of the open gate at the corral and were grazing in the distance.

The blades on the windmill at the water tank were spinning like the rotors on a helicopter as he walked out into the corral. A hawk was circling the sky above him, and the sun was warm on his face. So much had happened in such a short space of time that there were moments when none of it felt real.

He'd gone from existing to life at its fullest, and all because of Emmit Cooper.

"Wherever you are, buddy, I know you can hear me. Thank you for trusting me to continue your legacy. You were a damn good bullfighter. And I was a damn good bull rider. And then life changed for both of us, and it was nobody's fault. Your Maggie is my Maggie now. I'm taking care of Sunset, and I'm taking care of Maggie. She was the unexpected bonus in all this, but I can promise, I won't let either of you down."

In the distance, he could see a big black pickup driving toward the ranch, and pulling a long silver horse trailer. Garrett Dillon's men were on the way.

Chapter 20

WALKER BLUEJACKET'S BIG TURQUOISE BELT BUCKLE was locked up somewhere with his personal posses- sions. The braids he'd worn all his life were gone, he was missing three teeth, his nose had been reset but it was sore and swollen and it still hurt to breathe. Today, he was being moved from the prison infirmary to a cell. He'd have a cellmate to cope with, and he couldn't bear to look at himself anymore. His swagger was gone. He didn't talk unless spoken to, and knew in his gut he wouldn't live long inside this place. If a prisoner didn't kill him, the loss of his freedom would.

And still, with everything he'd lost by what he'd done, he still wished his son to hell. His baby boy had grown up bigger than him. Better looking than him. Braver than him. He dared to ride the bulls. The behe- moths of the rodeo world. He became a star in that world, and with every bit of Sonny's success, Walker's jealousy and envy grew.

He'd been so focused on taking what Sonny had, that he'd lost sight of reality. But the biggest mistake of all was messing with another man's woman. He hadn't expected that girl to fight. He hadn't known about the visions. Not once had he ever been afraid of another man until his own son came close to killing him. But not with a gun. And not with a knife. With his fists. One blow after another, with a rage unlike anything Walker had ever seen.

Then he heard footsteps and looked toward the door at the end of the ward, watching as it opened, then seeing the three guards coming toward him.

They stopped at his bedside.

"Let's go, Bluejacket. It's moving day."

They uncuffed him from the bed rail, put shackles on his ankles and cuffed his hands in front of him, then stood him on his feet and lay his pillow and bedroll, two changes of clothes, a towel and washcloth and a bar of soap across his outstretched arms.

He clutched the stack against his chest like a shield as they began walking him out of the prison ward, through the halls, up the stairs, and then down the walkway to a cacophony of jeers and shouts.

His heart was heavy. His steps were slow and shuffling. He could no longer hold his head up high. He'd been shorn of his manhood. Beaten into submission he didn't know how to navigate. And had yet to see the face of the man he would share a cell with.

Then they stopped at a cell and one of the guards shouted. "Morris! Step back!"

Walker heard keys rattling, and then the cell door swung open. One guard removed his shackles and the other removed the cuffs.

"In you go," the guard said, and the moment Walker cleared the threshold, the door slammed shut behind him.

He heard the key turn in the lock, and looked up.

The man before him was mid-forties, bald, white, and tatted on nearly every inch of skin Walker could see. Then he smiled, and Walker knew he had to make a stand now, or it would be too late to set the pace.

"You smile at me like that again you ink-faced monkey, and I will peel the skin off your face with my teeth."

Morris blinked. Clearly, there was more to this man than the eye could see. He shrugged.

"Just being friendly. My bad."

"I don't want friends," Walker muttered, and threw his bedroll onto the bottom bunk, which Morris was clearly occupying.

"Hell no. That's my bunk," Morris said.

Walker glared back. "Do I look like I can climb? It's either that, or I pull the mattress off the top bunk and sleep on the floor...right next to you. Your choice."

Morris's hands fisted as he stood, eyeing the raggedy gray hair and the black eyes in the old man's bruised and battered face, and decided the farther away from him, the better off he would be.

"Ah, what the hell," he muttered. But instead of moving his bedding, he moved the whole mattress with the bedding on it, yanking it all on the floor, then he pulled the bare mattress from the top and threw it onto the bottom, then put his mattress, with his bedding on it, onto the top bunk.

The sheets were awry, the blankets in a wad, but he straightened them, then crawled up and laid down with his back to the wall, keeping an eye on the old Indian, until he heard him groan as he eased down onto the lower bunk.

At that point, Morris realized the man was in worse shape than he appeared, and let go of his anger. His new cellmate could have been a bulked up perv with anger issues. At least this one didn't have much to say.

While down below, Walker was stretched out, eyeing his gear on the shelf. And Morris, whoever the hell he was, had already backed down.

Whatever will be, will be, and if I'm lucky, someone will stick a shiv in my back, and all of this will be over.

―――――

As soon as the Dillion crew left the ranch with the horses, Sonny cleaned the stalls before going back to the house. It was nearing noon, and the visitors from yesterday had gone through the pantry like a horde of hungry grasshoppers, which meant a trip to Belker's for groceries. No way was he having Maggie do all that shopping after a long day at work at the Rose. He had some bookkeeping to update, but after he washed up and put on a clean shirt, he grabbed the truck keys and headed into town. The first stop would be to have lunch at the Rose, and get a sweet kiss from his girl.

———————

Maggie was just coming back from the kitchen when she saw the tall, heavyset woman from Darla's area get up from her seat and lay some money down on the table for her meal. But instead of walking straight to the exit, she walked to an empty table that had yet to be cleared, took the tip someone had left and slipped it in her purse, and then continued to do that at three other tables as she headed to the door.

"Pearl! Runner!" she shouted, and bolted for the door, skidding in front of the exit to block her. "I saw what you did, and you're not going anywhere until you empty your purse."

The woman gasped, and clutched her purse against her breasts. "Help! Somebody help me! This woman is trying to steal my purse!"

Maggie rolled her eyes. "Everybody in this room knows that didn't happen! I watched you take the tips off of four different tables. One of mine and three of Darla's. Now do what I said, or I'm calling the law."

"You don't have any law in this town," she snapped.

Then Pearl appeared in the dining room with her shotgun.

"We have law in the county, and then we have our version of the law," Pearl said, and lifted the shotgun.

Maggie saw the diners watching and pointed. "This woman just stole the tips off of four tables, and I saw her do it. There will be four different bills in the outer pocket of her purse. Three five-dollar bills and one ten. I saw them when I brought out my last order," Maggie said.

The woman was getting red in the face, and the sight of that shotgun was less than reassuring.

"I'll sue you," she shouted. "I'll own this café before I'm through with you."

"Oh, shut up," Maggie said, and yanked the purse out of her arms. The woman lurched at Maggie just as Pearl jabbed the barrel of the shotgun in her back.

"You lay a hand on that girl, and they'll be burying you in two pieces."

Maggie calmly pulled the bills out of the outer pocket and held them up for everyone to see.

"Three fives and a ten, just like I said. Darla, call the sheriff."

"I already did," Darla said.

"No, no, there's no need to do that," the woman said. "I just had a weak moment. I'm sorry. You've got your money and I'll be on my way."

"Not before you get a mug shot and fingerprinted for petty theft and assault," Pearl said.

The woman turned, knocked the gun out of Pearl's hands and pushed her backward, then snatched the purse out of Maggie's hands and pushed past her, rushing toward the exit.

All of a sudden, the door opened, and the silhouette

of a man blocked out all the light. The woman froze, trying to decide whether to fight or run, when the growl in his voice ended all thought.

"Lady, I don't know what the hell you've been doing, but I know it's not good, because Pearl's got her gun, and that angry woman you tried to bulldoze is mine. If you so much as lay a hand on her, I will tie you to the hood of my truck and drive you to the sheriff's office myself." Sonny walked inside and closed the door. "Do I need to call Reddick?"

"I already did," Darla said.

Sonny pointed at the woman. "Sit yourself down."

She started to back up to a chair.

"No, not there. On the floor, over in that corner," Sonny said.

"But it's hard for me to get up," she whined.

"The officers will help you up when they cuff you," he said.

She started to wail. "I don't want to go to jail."

Maggie glared. "You should have thought of that before you stole the money."

The woman flopped herself down, and began glaring at everyone who was staring at her.

"What do you think you're looking at?" she shouted.

"Floor show?" one diner said.

"More like dinner theater, and we all got to see 'who done it,'" another diner added.

Maggie immediately turned to Pearl. "Did she hurt you, honey?"

"No, but getting a two-hundred-and-fifty-pound shove made me drop my gun. Next time I'll put a little space between us, or just go ahead and shoot."

Sonny shook his head. "How am I ever going to get stuff done, if I'm worrying about you two all the time?"

"We were fine," Maggie said, "but I have to admit, I would have liked to see you take off to Silverton with that woman on the hood of your truck."

"Bloodthirsty little thing, but I sure do love you," Sonny said. "I'm going to sit right here between her and the door, and I'll take whatever the special is today."

"Coming up," Maggie said, and went to turn in the order.

Sonny sat down, put the purse she dropped on the floor between his feet, and stared at her until she looked away.

Calm returned to the diners. The orders went in, the food came out, and time passed.

Sonny was finishing up his chicken-fried steak with mashed potatoes and gravy when a car from the sheriff's office pulled into the parking lot. Two officers got out and hurried into the Rose.

Sonny put down his fork as Maggie came to meet them.

"We're pressing charges against that woman," Maggie said. "She stole tip money off four tables, and assaulted the owner, Pearl Fallon. I was the one who witnessed the thefts and stopped her before she could get out the door."

They took the purse Sonny gave them, checked her ID, and then walked over to the corner where the woman was sitting.

"Your name is Babe Elwood?"

She glared. "Yes."

"Get up, ma'am. You're coming with us."

"I can't get up on my own," she muttered. "I told him that when he made me sit in the corner," and then pointed at Sonny.

They gave Sonny a look and then both of them grinned at him. "Sonny Bluejacket. Did you just put Baby in the corner? Nobody puts Baby in the corner."

"I did suggest she take a seat there," Sonny drawled.

Reference to the *Dirty Dancing* movie turned the drama of the theft and takedown into a witty joke that eased the tension in the room, for which Pearl was grateful.

Each of the officers grabbed an arm and pulled Babe Elwood to her feet and cuffed her.

"What happens to our tip money?" Darla asked.

"We'll log it into evidence and eventually you'll get it back."

As they were walking Babe out of the Rose, Sonny heard her asking what was going to happen to her car. He knew the answer. They'd tow it to the impound yard and when they released her, it would cost her way more than the money she'd stolen to get it back.

He looked down at the food still on his plate and then took out his wallet.

"Are you leaving? Do you want a to-go box?" Maggie asked.

He turned. "No, I'm good, darlin'. Just have a couple of things to do here before I go home. Our guests yesterday pretty much cleaned out the pantry. I'm headed to Belker's. Is there anything in particular you want me to pick up for you?"

"We need eggs and milk. I was going to get them on my way home."

"I'll add them to the list. Have a good rest of the day." He kissed her on the cheek. "You are going to make one hell of a mother for our boys."

And then he was gone, leaving Maggie with a kiss and a prophecy that gave her goose bumps. *Our boys? Why does he say that with such certainty?*

She smiled to herself for even questioning that. What he knows, he knows. So, she moved into her field of expertise and began eyeing the diners who'd stayed the course with them during the takedown and the arrest, checking to see if someone was in need, when she heard Pearl call out, "Order up," and headed for the kitchen.

———

That evening, as they were closing up the Rose, Pearl locked the front door and called a meeting of the staff.

"I want to commend all of you for your behavior and your assistance during today's chaos. Also, it was a lesson for all of you. Don't leave your tips on the table.

I don't care how busy you are, you can't start one thing when you've left another undone. Carson, don't leave bussing the tables up to waitresses, especially if we have a full house. There are twenty tables and booths all along the walls, and only two waitresses to serve them. I'm getting a commercial-grade dishwasher installed next week that will make your job a little easier. Davey, you are doing a great job, but watch your drips. The floor in front of the grill is slick by the end of the day. Somebody's going to slip and fall, and I don't want it to be me."

They were all listening and nodding and agreeing with everything Pearl was pointing out, and took it to heart.

"Also," Pearl said. "Don't forget, Maggie will be off tomorrow and Sunday, so both Cheryl and Darla will be on full shifts."

"Gonna sleep in, are you, girl?" Darla said.

"No. Sonny and I are going to Amarillo to get my wedding dress and pick out rings," Maggie said.

At that point, everybody began congratulating her.

"When's the wedding?" Pearl asked.

"We'll figure that out tomorrow," Maggie said. "Hopefully within the next two weeks."

Darla shrieked. "Two weeks. It took me longer than that to decide what colors I was choosing for my wedding."

Maggie shook her head. "I don't want a big wedding. I don't want to spend money on stuff I won't wear but once. I don't have relatives. But I have Pearl, and she's the closest thing to a mother I've ever had. Sonny's brother and family will come, but we both lean toward an intimate family gathering. Besides, nothing I could buy would ever mean more to me than the man who loves me."

"Where are you going to have it, at the church?" Darla asked.

Maggie frowned. "No. At the ranch. I want to get married at sunset, with heaven painting the backdrop. I'm not walking down some aisle to meet a man I already sleep with. He's already in my heart. Saying the words together is just making it official."

"Okay, that's enough prying into Maggie's business. I think we all understand where we are with the jobs we do. Go home. Get some sleep. See you tomorrow."

As the others were leaving, Pearl caught Maggie's hand and held her back. "You just about made me cry," Pearl said. "I can't have children, but then God went and gave me one, anyway. Magnolia, you are the dearest thing on earth to me, and I could not be happier for you. You and Sonny have the best day ever and safe travels tomorrow, okay?"

Maggie kissed Pearl on the cheek. "I meant what I said. I love you, Pearl. So much. Sonny thinks the world of you, too, which is good, because one day our children will be calling you Grandma. You will be the only grandparent in their lives. Stuff is happening for Sonny and me. Stuff I never dreamed of, part of which will change my world, but it won't change what you've become to me. And don't get that look on your face again. We're not leaving Crossroads."

Pearl's eyes welled. "Anything that will make your lives better will make me proud, girl. Now go home and hug that pretty man of yours."

Maggie smiled. "I will."

Pearl stood at the back door to the Rose, watching until Maggie was in her car and driving out of the parking lot before going back inside and locking up.

She wiped her eyes, blew her nose, and headed for the phone. She had to make a new order for the wholesaler and pay some bills before her day ended.

———

Maggie's heart was so full of joy it felt like it could just pop at any moment. Expectations were something other people had, and she was a novice at accepting them. But this wasn't just a dream. This was really happening. It was real.

She drove until she reached the entrance to the ranch, and drove beneath the sign. SUNSET RANCH. Their home.

She could see the herd, smaller now by four horses, but that would change. As she drove closer, she saw Sonny sitting on the top rail of the corral. Her heart skipped at the sight. He was minus a shirt, his hair was loose, and he looked deep in thought. Was he seeing visions, or just imagining the ranch's future—their future? She knew when he heard her car, because he jumped down and came to meet her with that ever-present devilish grin, and haste in every step.

He was at the door by the time she parked.

"Hey, darlin', I was sitting out in the sun to let my hair dry and missing you, and I look up and see your face."

She put her hand over the butterfly tattoo.

"You make it beat faster," he said, then slid his arms around her waist and pulled her close. "You ready for that trip to Amarillo tomorrow?"

"More than ready."

"You still want to get married here on the ranch?" he asked.

She nodded. "At sunset. I can't think of a better blessing to start our lives together. Anytime within the next two weeks?"

"Can't be too soon for me," Sonny said. "We can check the calendar, pick a day and time, and I'll give Charlie a call so he can make plans for the trip out."

"I already told Pearl she's invited, since she's the only mother figure I've ever had. So, we have the guests. We have the location. All we need is a preacher."

"I know a cowboy preacher. Maybe I'll give him a call," Sonny said.

"Oh Sonny, that would be perfect. The only place around here to get a marriage license is at Silverton, which is the county seat of Briscoe County."

"We'll do that one day next week, but not Monday. That's when Max Andros is coming to get your paintings," Sonny said. "I'll whisk you away from work for a couple of hours on Tuesday and we'll get it done. There's a seventy-two-hour wait between getting the license and getting married, so we don't want to delay anything. Let's go inside. After all the excitement you had at the Rose, you must be exhausted."

He took her hand, listening to her chatter as they entered the house, and thinking how her eyes flashed when she was excited, and how she could turn him on with nothing more than a smile.

"Supper is warming in the oven," Sonny said. "A frozen version of a mac and cheese casserole and some brisket from Belker's Deli."

"That sounds so good," Maggie said. "Give me a few to get out of these clothes."

"How about I help you with that…just to speed things along?"

She smiled.

He didn't wait for an answer.

━━━━━━━━━━

Long after the sun was gone and the dishes were done and the stars were out, they lay sleeping, wrapped in each other's arms, and the next morning, Sonny woke to the sound of running water. Maggie was already in the shower. He got up, put on a pair of jeans, and headed to the kitchen to make coffee, then went out to the back porch to look for the horses. They were all eating from the round bale in the hay ring. Satisfied that they would be fine while he was gone, he went back inside to finish dressing.

Maggie was out of the shower and standing in front of the closet in her underwear.

"Good morning, Magnolia. You are a beautiful sight to wake up to," Sonny said, and kissed the back of her neck.

She turned to face him. "I saw you first. You were talking in your sleep."

He frowned. "What did I say?"

She shrugged. "You weren't speaking English, so I couldn't begin to tell you."

He grinned. "Sorry. I didn't know I did that."

"And I don't know what to wear. Do I dress up, or dress like me?"

"Dress how you want. We're going to Westgate Mall because I know where it is and the stores they have, including several jewelry stores. Then we're going to a place called David's Bridal, and after that, I'm taking you to the Red River Steakhouse at noon. It's where the locals eat, and I've been there plenty of times in my rodeo days."

Maggie was so excited she almost clapped her hands. "I rarely go to Amarillo, and when I do, it's just a quick trip to the art supply store and home. I can't wait to see it with you."

"Go cowgirl if you want. You sure won't be alone."

"I can wear jeans and my old pink Ropers?" she asked.

"Yes, ma'am. Now get some clothes on, or I'm going to want to take off what you already have on."

She began grabbing clothes, while Sonny picked out a shirt and his best boots, then the belt with one of his Bull Riding Championship buckles.

When he went into the bathroom to brush his hair, Maggie followed, took the brush from his hands, and did it for him.

"Braid or loose?" she asked.

"Loose."

"Then you, my handsome man, are good to go, and so am I."

"Coffee is ready. Make us some toast, okay? I just need to brush the dust off my hat."

"Coming up," she said, and grabbed her purse as she went.

He brushed the black Stetson and then took it with him to the kitchen.

They ate toast and downed a cup of coffee apiece, and then they were gone.

They turned west on Highway 86 that ran through Crossroads and drove to Tulia to get the I-27 north into Amarillo. As they drove, Sonny reached for her hand.

"That cowboy preacher I was telling you about… he lives somewhere around Amarillo. I'm going to give him a call later today, so while we're still on the road, it would be good if you could check the calendar and pick a date. I'll need to know all that before I call."

Maggie dug her phone out of her purse, pulled up the calendar for the month of May.

"Today is the 4th. Two weeks from today would be the 18th. Both Saturdays. Sunset is around 8:00 p.m., so if we began at 7:30, the sky will be gorgeous."

"Then 7:30 p.m. on the 18th of May. Just our immediate families—my brother and family, and Pearl. If you want a little flower girl, Julia Bluejacket would be over the moon to do it for us."

Maggie's eyes lit up. "Oh yes! That would be perfect. And tell her to wear the pretty dress she wore at the daddy-daughter dance. She looked like a little princess."

"She needs to feel special," Sonny said. "She's still traumatized by what happened at the creek."

"How could she not be? I still have dreams of Walker stuffing napkins down my mouth and choking me unconscious. I thought I would never see you again. I came to as we were driving away, but I kept my eyes closed. I didn't want him to know. I just laid there without moving, knowing that you would find me. Julia has her mommy and daddy for backup. I have you."

"And I have you."

"How far away are we from Amarillo?" Maggie asked.

"Fifteen, maybe twenty more minutes. Why?"

"Because getting there is opening another door into the business of becoming your wife, and I can't wait for the day I get to be that woman."

"You already are in my heart. We're just tying up the loose ends with a license and a ceremony. White-man stuff," he said, and then winked.

She laughed.

He grinned and kept talking. "In the old days, I would have had to give horses to your father to ask for you."

"Well, I just saved you a butt load of horseflesh. I've been on a clearance rack since birth. I come free to the man who loves me."

He frowned. "In my eyes, you were the wild horse used to making your own decisions and your own rules. That, I honor. That, I admire. You see you on a clearance rack. I see you standing on a mountain, unwilling to come down. You are a strong woman, Magnolia. I am honored that you chose me."

"I chose you the same way Dancer chose you. It was already meant to happen. All we had to do was find each other first. Why else would I be marrying a man I have known less than three months?"

"And here I thought it was because I was irresistible," he drawled.

Maggie laughed. "Just shut it, cowboy. You already knew that."

They relaxed into an easy silence until Sonny pointed. "Amarillo. Dead ahead."

Chapter 21

AFTER THAT, SONNY BECAME THE TOUR GUIDE AND Maggie the tourist, turning to look at everything he pointed out, and listening to the stories he was telling. The further they drove, the more entranced she became, and then he pointed to a huge mall she could see up ahead.

"Westgate Mall. Our first destination!"

They parked and got out. Sonny settled the Stetson on his head and Maggie picked up her little purse and slipped the strap over her shoulder.

They looked at each other and smiled.

"Let's do this, Maggie Rae."

Maggie took his hand.

They walked across the parking lot and into the mall—the tall good-looking cowboy and the pretty girl at his side, unaware of the second looks they were getting.

They walked the mall, pausing to point out things in the window displays, laughing, talking, telling stories about crazy diners in the Rose, and crazier cowboys, the ones like Sonny, who challenged wild bulls, and rode horses yet to be broken.

"Here we are," he said, as they approached one of the jewelry stores. "First stop, ring shopping."

"I don't want a big, expensive one, Sonny. I don't lunch with the girls. I serve lunches to them. I don't need big diamonds to feel loved."

He paused, looking down into those big blue eyes, and then to the three freckles on her nose. "I see you, Magnolia, all the way to your soul."

She shivered. "Okay then," and they walked in together.

A man was walking out of the jewelry store as they were going in. He glanced at Sonny, and then did a double-take and stopped.

"Sonny Bluejacket?"

Sonny paused. "Yes."

"Oh my God, man! Oh my God. I didn't know you were still in the world. I'm a fan. I saw you ride countless times. I saw your last ride. I did not know you survived it." Then he glanced at Maggie and began apologizing. "I'm sorry. I'm sorry for intruding. It was just such a surprise."

Sonny smiled. "It's okay. I didn't get your name."

"Benny. Benny Wilson. My brother is not going to believe this. Could I get a picture with you?"

"Sure," Sonny said.

"I'll take it," Maggie said, and took the man's phone and snapped several shots before handing it back.

"Thank you, man. Are you still riding?"

"I don't rodeo anymore. I have a ranch outside of

Crossroads training horses. Nice to meet you," he said, then slipped his arm across Maggie's shoulder and moved into the store.

A clerk approached, and minutes later, they were at a jewelry counter. The clerk sized Maggie's ring finger, then began pulling out trays of wedding ring sets.

Maggie eyed them all before ever trying one on, then announced, "I like the oval-shaped stones. Square cut is like a box. There are no corners in an oval. No beginning. No end. Just eternity."

Sonny pointed. "Like that one?"

She eyed the bands on both the engagement ring and the wedding band. They looked as if they'd been braided, and the oval diamond looked beautiful on it. She pointed. "I'd like to try that one on."

The jeweler handed it to her, but she handed it to Sonny instead. "You do it."

"It would be my honor," he said. It was a perfect fit and looked beautiful lying along the length of her finger.

"This is the one. I don't need to look at any others," she said.

"Good choice," the clerk said. "You'll want to try the wedding band for size as well, before you leave the store."

So, she did, and it fit, too, then they watched the clerk put the band in a little box and write up the ticket.

Sonny pulled out a credit card. Minutes later, Maggie had an engagement ring on her finger——the wedding

ring in its little box in her purse—and they were walking out the door.

"You didn't get the down-on-one-knee," he
whispered.

Her eyes were swimming in happy tears. She kept
looking at the ring on her finger and then up at him.

"Doesn't matter. Like I said before, you had me at
ant hill."

He laughed, then swung her into his arms and
danced her down the mall with a two-step to the music
coming from the sound system.

People passing laughed and clapped. One couple
joined them for a moment, dancing a few steps behind
them, and two young teens grabbed their phones and
started filming, and then someone else recognized him
and shouted, "That's Sonny Bluejacket!"

Back home, he might as well have been a stranger.
For the past five years he was a rodeo has-been for
some. A walking miracle in the eyes of God for others.
But in the rodeo world, he was an unforgettable face.

He absorbed the attention for what it was, and kept
on dancing. Until he finally spun them to a stop.

"Where's a good country band when you need one?"
he said. "Come on, woman. Let's go find that wedding
dress."

They left the mall hand in hand and then drove to
David's Bridal.

Sonny stayed in the truck, accepting the banishment
from the bridal shop. He'd expected it. While Maggie

was inside picking out her dress, he was in the truck calling Wes Dugan, the cowboy preacher, and hoping he was still around. But when he made the call, he got voicemail instead, and so he left him a message.

"Wes, this is Sonny Bluejacket. If you're still in the marrying business, I have a job for you. It would be on my ranch south of Crossroads, just off Highway 86. May 18th at 7:30 p.m. Give me a call back at this number to let me know, and thanks for all the prayers you said on my behalf. My brother, Charlie, told me about them. Since I'm still here, it appears they worked."

Satisfied that he made first contact, all he could do was await an answer. He glanced at the time. She'd been in the shop less than an hour, and he'd missed a lot of sleep last night. So, he leaned his seat back into a reclining position, upped the air conditioning, pulled his hat down over his face, and closed his eyes.

———

The stylist greeted Maggie warmly. "Hello, I'm Jennifer. Are we shopping for a wedding gown?"

Maggie nodded. "Yes. I'm Magnolia Brennen."

"What a beautiful name," Jennifer said, then looked around to see where her family members were. "Are we waiting for family to arrive before we begin?"

"I don't have family. I'm one of those throwaway babies who grew up on her own. So, let's get to it."

Jennifer was taken aback by the woman's candor, and

felt an instant empathy for the young woman shopping on her own.

But Maggie had already decided that the floor length gowns wouldn't work. No need even trying to drag all that skirt across the yard at the ranch, and shifted focus.

"This is an outdoor wedding on a ranch. A very simple, intimate family wedding. There won't be a dozen people there, and none of these long dresses will work. I also don't want a sheath style, or strapless. Think white and knee-length, with a gathered waistline and tiered skirt, a fitted bodice with a square or round neckline, and some kind of sleeve, preferably a loose one."

The stylist blinked.

Maggie laughed. "Yes, I know. But I also want those white boots in your front window. The ones with the colorful embroidery running from the top of the shaft to the vamp. I looked. They're my size and style, and I'm not hiding them under a dress."

Jennifer nodded. "Understood. I'll get the boots, and I have some dresses to show you. Follow me to the dressing room."

Ten minutes later, Maggie was sitting in her underwear, admiring the fancy boots on her feet when Jennifer came back with a half-dozen dresses, all in the style Maggie wanted, but with different necklines and sleeve lengths.

Maggie pointed to the one with a square neckline and long puffy sleeves. "That one," she said.

Jennifer took it from the garment bag, unzipped it and slipped it over Maggie's head, then helped her into the sleeves and zipped it up.

Maggie turned around, saw herself. All the years of secondhand clothes and Walmart specials ran through her mind as she started crying, and Jennifer immediately misunderstood.

"Oh honey! Oh no! Don't cry! We have others. Here, let me—"

"No, I don't hate it. I love it. It's perfect, and Sonny will love me in it."

Maggie kept turning one way and then another, loving the way the tiered skirt flared as she turned, and the length of bare leg showing between the hem and the top of the boot shaft.

"Do you want to try on another dress, just in case?" Jennifer asked.

"No, thank you. This is perfect! I'll take the boots and the dress with me. Just make sure they're in bags you can't see through. Sonny is sitting out in the truck waiting for me."

"Sonny is your fiancé, I take it."

Maggie got her phone, pulled up the picture of them together taken in the front yard at the ranch, and then showed her.

Jennifer looked, and then looked again, staring intently. "Is that Sonny Bluejacket? The rodeo guy?"

"Yes, that's him. Do you know him?" Maggie asked.

Jennifer sighed. "I know *who* he is, but I never met

him. I hear rumors that he died. Clearly, he did not. Girl, every buckle bunny I knew wanted that man, but he didn't play."

Maggie had heard the phrase before but didn't really know what it meant. "What's a buckle bunny?"

Jennifer sniffed. "Oh, they're pretty young things who hang around rodeos hoping to sleep with the cowboys with winning buckles. They run in packs, or in pairs and compare notes afterward," Jennifer said, and then blushed. "I wasn't one of them. I just know that about them. Did you meet at a rodeo?"

"Nope. He walked into the diner where I work. I didn't know him from Adam, and even after I heard his name and his story, it still didn't mean anything to me."

Jennifer handed the phone back to Maggie. "Well, congratulations, anyway. I heard he was a really nice guy."

"The best," Maggie said. "And he's still waiting for me, so let's get this done."

A short while later, Maggie exited the bridal shop loaded down with a big sack and an even bigger garment bag. She wasn't even off the curb before Sonny came running.

"Looks like you scored. Let me help you, darlin'," and took the packages out of her arms as they walked back to the truck, unaware that Jennifer, the salesclerk, was standing at the window watching them go.

Jennifer's envy was laced with empathy for Magnolia. "Lord, I hope you're proud of that one, because he sure turned out fine. That face. Those shoulders. Those sexy long legs…and all that long black hair. I need a cold shower."

But Jennifer's moment of regret had nothing to do with Sonny and Maggie's joy. As soon as they got everything loaded into the back seat of the truck, they were back on the road.

"Where to now?" Maggie asked.

"The Red River Steakhouse. Be hungry because I'd hate to have to eat your leftovers."

She burst out laughing. "I'll do my best because I wouldn't want to put you through that."

He was still grinning when his cell phone rang. He glanced down at caller ID. "Maggie, honey, answer that and put it on Speaker, will you?"

She reached for the phone, swiped, and then hit Speaker.

"Hello, Wes. This is Sonny. Thanks for getting back to me this quick."

"It was good to hear your voice," Wes said. "You weren't talking last time I saw you, and how did you wind up on a ranch in Texas?"

"Remember Emmit Cooper?" Sonny said.

"Yes, I do. I was at his funeral."

"He named me his heir. I live at the ranch now. I was training horses for ranchers in Oklahoma, and now I'll be training horses for myself."

"Do I know your lady?" Wes asked.

Sonny glanced at Maggie and winked. "I don't know. Ever been to the Yellow Rose Café in Crossroads?"

"Yes."

"Do you remember the pretty dark-haired woman with the sky eyes?"

"Miss Maggie? You're marrying Maggie?"

"Yes, I am. She's sitting here in the truck beside me. We're in Amarillo buying wedding stuff. So, are you free for the date I sent?"

Wes chuckled. "Yes, I am, but if I wasn't I would already be adjusting my schedule to make it happen. It will be my honor. And hello to you, Maggie. Pearl calls me Preacher. Maybe you remember me. Short. Bow-legged and bald?"

Maggie giggled. "Oh, that Preacher. I sure do. Biscuits and sausage gravy and two eggs over easy, and you carry your own Tabasco Sauce."

Wes laughed. "You *do* remember me, and yes, I'm honored to be asked. It will be my joy to marry you and Sonny. I have already put it on my calendar, and I'll see you at the ranch on the eighteenth of the month. God bless you both."

"Thank you, Wes. This means a lot. See you soon," Sonny said.

The call ended.

Maggie shivered and looked down at her ring again. "Every little step," she whispered.

"Gets us where we need to go," Sonny added.

A few minutes later, he was pulling into the parking lot at the Red River Steakhouse. The sprawling red building looked a little like a barn that had been added

on to from both ends, and a parking lot to accommodate the any number of diners.

"This brings back memories," he said.

"How so?" Maggie asked.

"This was our go-to steakhouse after competing."

"Did you stay in hotels or motels around here?" she
asked.

"No. I pulled a little Airstream...my home away
from home. Sold it afterward to help pay medical bills.
Cowboys are always pulling something...usually a
horse trailer with their horse, or a little camper to have
a place to sleep."

He reached for her hand, kissed the ring on her
finger, then kissed her.

"I can't wait to show you off. Let's go eat."

Sonny walked with his hand on her back all the way
inside to the Red River restaurant décor. Old wood,
used bricks, the red Naugahyde on the booth backs and
seats, rural memorabilia hanging on the walls, an old
lantern on a post. A small bar to one side, booths along
the walls, and wooden topped tables and chairs.

"I love this," Maggie whispered. "It's not fancy, and
look at that old buggy!"

"You're right, it's not fancy, but it's cowboy," he said.

A hostess approached. "Two for lunch?" she asked.

"Yes."

"Booth or table?" she asked.

Sonny looked at Maggie.

"Table. He needs leg room," she said.

Sonny felt seen. A woman who took his side.

"Follow me," the hostess said, and started through the busy dining area and seated them at a table. "Your waitress will be here soon. Enjoy your meal," and left their menus.

Sonny sat with his back to a wall and Maggie on his right, out of the line of traffic. The undercurrent of voices was like a low rumble across the room until Sonny saw a man in a dirty gray Stetson suddenly stand up and point.

"That's, by God, Sonny Bluejacket, sittin' at that table."

Once again, Maggie was startled by people's reactions. She glanced at Sonny, and when she saw he was grinning, she relaxed. More rodeo friends. It had to be.

But that man's loud shout made a dozen other heads turn, and then the buzz in the room got even louder.

Sonny sighed. "I'm sorry. It's been over five years. I didn't think they would remember. Do you want to go somewhere else?"

"Is there a somewhere else in this town where they may not know your face?"

He shrugged. "Jail maybe."

She grinned. "So, you're saying you never got into trouble."

"I left that up to Walker."

"Then say hello to your friends. Half of them look like they've seen a ghost," she said.

The man who'd yelled was already up and heading

their way. Sonny stood, just as the man threw his arms around Sonny's shoulders and thumped him on the back.

"Man, you are a sight for sore eyes. What are you doing here? Are you back on the circuit?"

"Marvin, this is my fiancée, Magnolia Brennen. Magnolia, this is Marvin Carver. Another bull rider from my past."

Marvin yanked off his hat and all but curtsied. "Miss Brennen, it is a pleasure to meet you," he said, then he shifted back to Sonny. "Well? Are you ridin' again?"

"Not in this lifetime," Sonny said. "I have a small ranch south of Crossroads with a few horses on it. I inherited it from Emmit."

Marvin's eyes widened. "Emmit gave you Sunset! I'll be damned. He never did get over what happened. So, no more bulls."

"Just training horses," Sonny said. "What I have right now is what's left of Emmit's herd. I'm not going to breed horses like he did. I plan to buy good three- or four-year-olds, and train them to cut, rein, and rope."

"Well, it's damn good to see you." He nodded at Maggie. "Ma'am," and then walked off.

Sonny sat back down and opened his menu. "Let's try this again. What looks good to you?"

"You. You look good to me," Maggie said. "And I'm going to order fried catfish and hush puppies. I can't remember the last time I had that, and I love it."

The waitress showed up, took their drink orders,

and when she came back, they ordered their food. And despite Sonny's best efforts, their celebration lunch turned into a whole other thing.

———————

Sonny was cutting off another bite of steak when Maggie looked up, then tapped his arm.

"Honey...incoming. Chew fast or wait."

He put down the knife and fork and looked up just as a young boy in a cowboy hat a size too big for his head approached their table carrying a piece of paper and a pen.

Sonny grinned. "Hey buddy. Nice hat."

"It's Daddy's. He said I could wear it for a minute. My name is Warren Klingman. My daddy's name is Joe. Do you reckon if I could have your autograph?"

Maggie saw the adoration on the little boy's face and immediately understood, then wondered if that was how she looked when she saw Sonny for the first time.

Sonny took the paper and pen. "Do you know who I am?"

"The best durn bull rider ever?" Warren said.

Sonny grinned. "Did your daddy tell you that?"

"Yes sir. He's got a poster of you ridin' one of them wild bulls up on the wall in his den. I wanna be you when I grow up," Warren said.

Sonny signed the autograph. "Go tell your daddy to

come over to my table. We'll all take a picture together, okay?"

The little boy's eyes widened, and without bothering to go back, he just shouted, "Hey Daddy! C'mere!"

Maggie laughed.

Sonny grinned.

And the tall, lanky man who'd been watching Warren's every move bolted out of his chair like he'd been ejected, and came running.

"Sorry, Sonny. I shouldn't have said he could bother you. I didn't mean to..."

Sonny stood and shook his hand. "Joe Klingman, nice to meet you. Warren's wearing your hat. Do you want it back for the picture?"

"You done wearing it, boy?" Joe asked.

The little boy nodded. "Yes, sir. I got my autograph."

Joe lifted it off his son's head, settled it back on his own, and handed Sonny his phone.

Maggie stood up. "I'll do the honors," she said, waited until the trio had organized themselves, then took several pictures before handing it back.

"Thank you, ma'am, thank you. And thank you, Sonny. Are you ever going to ride again?"

"Only well-mannered horses," Sonny said. "And the pretty lady who just took our pictures will soon be my wife. Her name is Magnolia, just like the flower."

Joe tipped his hat to her. "It's a pleasure. Your man is one of a kind. I been around rodeo all my life, but I never saw the likes of him before or since. Sorry to have interrupted your meal," and off they went hand in hand.

Sonny and Maggie sat back down. "Does all this upset you?" he asked.

"No. I'm just realizing that I'm not the only one who thinks you hung the moon. It's all good."

He stole a quick kiss before they resumed their meal.

After that, it was a continuing stream of requests for pictures, requests for autographs, and shocked responses to the fact that he was still alive in the world.

Finally, Sonny waved their waitress down. "We're going to need a couple of to-go boxes. I didn't expect all this. Hope it hasn't interfered with serving your tables."

At that point, the young woman giggled. "Not at all. I'll be right back with your check and your boxes. And before you go, could I get a picture with you?"

"Sure," Sonny said, and then looked at Maggie. "I've been a hermit for too long. This was nice, but seriously unexpected."

"Well, now you know what's going to happen when you show up at Garrett Dillion's roping competition and ride Dancer. You had better start training some more horses fast. Everyone's going to want a piece of Sonny Bluejacket, even if it's just a horse you trained."

He just shook his head. "I did not see this coming."

"It's a way for you to stay in the rodeo world without getting yourself killed. Again. And I would never expect you to change who you are."

He nodded. His truth was in her words. "What I do will always be for us, not just for me. Understood?"

She nodded. "Understood."

Within a few minutes they were gone, taking the revelation of this day home with them.

———————

Maggie took her wedding dress and the bag with the new boots down to Emmit's vault.

"Emmit, honey, I'm just going to leave this here for safekeeping," she said. "Don't let Sonny peek. And thank you for sending him my way. Between Pearl, you, and now Sonny, you have given me something I never had…a future and a family. Miss you. Hope you have a pretty horse to ride where you are."

And then she ran back up the stairs, changed into old clothes to do chores with Sonny. Today had been a revelation for her. To keep their lives moving in the same direction, she wanted to educate herself in the world of horses and rodeos, because he was already on board with her and the art.

Before Sonny, she waited tables and painted pictures as a hobby. But he had given her the courage to do more, and look what happened.

Chapter 22

THEY WERE LYING IN BED, FLOATING ON THE AFTER-glow of making love, but too wired to sleep. Her head was on Sonny's chest, and she had her hand cupped over the butterfly tattoo, as if trying to keep it from flying away.

"Did you call Charlie about the wedding date?" she asked.

"Yes, he's all excited. Said he was going to bring Auntie. It made me happy. She's seventy and doesn't go far from home these days. But it will ease her heart to see us, and where we live."

"I have an idea," Maggie said. "Tomorrow, before Max Andros comes to get the paintings on Monday, I want you to help me pick out two sunset paintings to keep back, and one with Pearl in the diner. I've been painting for more than four years straight. There are so many others it won't matter if I keep back some, and I want those for the people we love. Then your Auntie and your brother will see the same sky you see every night, and they will know where you are. And Pearl will always have me in the diner, even after I'm not working there anymore."

Sonny stilled. "That is the most thoughtful, loving thing you can give them. It's perfect. Yes, I'll go with you."

She snuggled a little closer to him. "This makes me happy."

He pulled the sheet up over her shoulders. "You make me happy. Good night, love."

"Night, Sonny. Love you."

———————

The next morning after chores and breakfast, they headed into town to her old house. She was relieved to know there was going to be a place for her paintings now, instead of stacked against a wall in a spare room. She still had to bring the easel and her paints and brushes home, along with a few unpainted canvases, and was going to put them in the vault and out of the way until the studio was built. And, until then, she was going to keep working at the Rose. There was no need to quit only to go home and do nothing, but she was excited for what was yet to come.

Sonny pulled up at the house and then they went inside.

"It's a little stuffy in here," Maggie said. "I think I'll turn the air conditioning up as if I was still here, so it will be comfortable for them when they come to get the canvases."

"It will take a while," Sonny said. "He has to

photograph and tag every piece, so he can catalog your work before he leaves with it."

"Oh, I didn't think of that. Maybe I better call Pearl and have her keep Darla and Cheryl on full schedule for Monday and Tuesday, so we can do the paintings and then the marriage license."

Sonny nodded. "Good idea. In the meantime, let's go look at some sunsets."

"I want you to pick Charlie and Auntie's paintings for me. I'll find the one with Pearl. There are several, but I know which one I want. I might save a sunset for her, too. Lord knows she put up with me dawdling on the porch at the Rose every evening, watching it happen."

"Sure thing, darlin'. Point me in the right direction and I'll get at it."

"All of the sunsets are on the west wall. You know... sun sets in the west."

He grinned. "Of course," then headed for the west wall, while Maggie moved to another section of the room for paintings of the Rose.

After much searching and debating, Maggie finally chose the one with Pearl at the register, the three old cowboys in the corner of the room, a couple having an argument, a lovesick couple holding hands while they tried to eat, and a table full of cowboys with their heads bowed, saying grace before their meal. She carried it over to where Sonny was at.

"Hey honey, what do you think about giving this one to Pearl?"

He turned around, stared, and then took a deep breath. "I know you can do this, but I don't understand how. Andros said something about Wyeth, but this has the heart of Norman Rockwell stuff, only yours comes to life. They look so real. Not caricatures of people, but living, breathing ones."

"I think that's why he said Wyeth," Maggie said. "There's a Wyeth painting called *Christina's World*. It's haunting. There's a really moving story behind the painting, and it's of a person who actually lived it."

Sonny smiled. "You may teach me something besides horses and rodeo yet," then picked up the two sunset paintings he'd chosen. One was shades of purple and pink, with a rim of gold just above the horizon, and the other was all shades of yellow and orange, with one burst of white just as the sun disappeared.

"Perfect," Maggie said, then dug through the others until she found one that was shades of orange and yellow. "I want to get my easel and paints before we leave. I thought I could store them in the vault until the studio is built. Would that be okay?"

He nodded. "A perfect place to keep them safe until they have a place of their own. I'll carry the paintings to the truck. You start gathering your stuff and I'll come back for that."

She handed him her paintings, and then turned to look for a box as he headed for the truck. She soon had the easel folded up, the brushes and paints boxed, the bag of frames she had yet to use, and the blank canvases in a stack.

She locked the door behind them as Sonny carried the last load to the truck and then headed home.

Sonny carried her art supplies and the paintings she'd kept down to the vault, while Maggie went to separate laundry and started washing a load. Days off weren't for lounging. They were for getting the things done that you didn't have time for on the job.

Sonny came looking for her. "If you don't need me for a while, I'm going to take the truck and some fencing, and drive the fence line to check for sags or breaks."

"No, I'm good," she said. "Just keep the phone in your pocket. A thousand acres is a big place to get lost in. I don't want to have to look in every prairie dog hole to find you."

He laughed. "Yes, ma'am. Call if you need me."

"I will. Just take care of your pretty self. Love you."

"Love you more," Sonny said, and left her reeling from the goodbye kiss.

Chapter 23

VONNIE SUTTON'S LIFE WAS IN FULL BLOSSOM. Getting home to her parents and having a safe place to be had become the turning point in her and her son's lives, and she had Sonny Bluejacket to thank for it.

The quiet generosity of handing her five hundred dollars to get her and Randy to a safe place was something she'd never forget. One day she hoped to be able to pay that gesture forward. But for now, she had a new job in the wings. A place to live, and grandparents begging to take care of her boy while she worked.

One day she and Randy would move out on their own again, but for now, they were sheltered in place, and it was their blessing to be there.

———————

Heather Kincaid had gone home, as well. Back to Houston, and into the world in which she'd been raised. If it hadn't been for the presence of her baby, Carlie, she could almost believe she'd never left. Her parents were supportive and loving and laying no blame, but they all knew where it was—on the shoulders of the man who'd betrayed her trust.

Some days Heather felt hopeless of ever getting over what Del had done. She had loved him so much, but on other days, she had to admit that she hadn't known him at all. All she'd known was the face he presented to the world. The dark, secret side of him willing to steal had been a complete unknown.

She stayed in contact with Delroy, her father-in-law, because she'd promised, and because he would always be Carlie's other grandpa. Delroy didn't deserve to bear his son's shame, but she knew he would, because he was an honorable man.

She sent pictures of Carlie and had taught him long distance how to make video calls, and Carlie was beginning to recognize his face and voice every time, which elated Delroy to no end.

She called him PopPop. He called her Toot.

And every time she and Carlie waved goodbye, even when he was smiling, she saw the sadness in his eyes.

She had no idea what was happening to Del. She didn't know his high-powered lawyer had been worth the money, after all, or that the judge in Del's case had given him probation and a hefty fine instead of jail time. But she wouldn't have cared to know. His crime was not hers to bear.

———

Nubby Zane was counting down the days to his release and knowing what he was facing when he went home. He could ignore it. He could lie and pretend it never happened. But the truth was the target on his back. Everybody he knew, was aware that he'd left town with Walker. And they now knew where Walker was, and how he'd got there. Retha told him that their people no longer spoke Walker's name. It was the same thing as a death. He no longer existed to them.

It was the single reason he knew he wouldn't go home. When he got out, he wasn't going any further than Tulsa. He knew people there who didn't care about honor or good names. And neither did he.

———————

Walker cursed every day he woke up, and went to bed every night in the hopes that would be the end. But the evil within him was stronger than his desire to quit. He'd spent his life full of envy and rage, and now, even that had been taken away.

His right to make his own decisions had been stripped.

His desire for revenge had turned into the desire to be left alone, which was impossible in a prison full of angry men.

Morris, the tattooed guy Walker shared a cell with, gave him a wide berth. All Walker had to do to freak him out was get in his face and start speaking his native language.

It never failed to scare the hell out of Morris, and he'd made it known within their free time in the yard that the old Indian cast spells, and to leave him alone if they didn't want to be cursed. But it was also stirring up a contingent on the grounds that viewed his power as a threat.

Walker was marking time and knew it.

———

While Sonny was working on the ranch, Maggie had framed the paintings for Pearl, attached the wires for hanging, had them loaded in her car, ready to take to work. Her work schedule with Pearl was set, and she was ready for tomorrow.

She knew Pearl was up and in the shower by four thirty, so she was going to come in early and hang them before Pearl came downstairs. She needed to show Pearl what she'd been doing in secret, and explain how Sonny finding them had changed her life.

———

After making and baking a chicken pot pie for their supper, Maggie left it in the warmer and went out to the back porch with a glass of ice water—the cubes tinkling against the sides of the glass as she sat.

The day was like most other days, hot in the sun, hawks and buzzards in the air, and horses on the ground. Somewhere in all that was the man who'd changed her life, and she was waiting for the sight of his face.

Her glass was nearly empty when she thought she heard his truck, and then she stood and walked to the edge of the porch. When she saw the horses in the pasture turn and look to the south, she knew it was him. And then the truck came into view and there was that moment of relief. She knew he would stop and tend to the horses before he came to the house, so she picked up her glass and went back inside.

Like water, life had found its level again.

Sonny didn't know she'd been watching for him, but he'd been thinking about her. When he finally drove to the house and got out with the bouquet of wildflowers he'd picked on the way home, all the cares of the world fell away.

He checked the bouquet one last time before opening the door and saw a persistent little bee that had been crawling inside a fold of petals.

"You're done here," he said, and blew gently on the flower to make sure the bee flew away, then walked inside.

Maggie met him as he crossed the threshold into the kitchen and welcomed him with a kiss. "I missed you," she said.

He handed her the flowers. "I missed you, too."

"Oh Sonny, thank you. I love them."

"Wild and beautiful, like you," he said, then went to fill Emmit's recycle jar with water to put them in. "Something smells good."

"I made chicken pot pie. It's in the warmer."

He hugged her. "Sounds wonderful. How about I go clean up now and then we can eat? I'm plenty hungry."

"Do your thing, and I think you made the evening news. I saw an early trailer on Channel 10 News in Amarillo. Apparently, you have risen from the dead," she said.

He shook his head and walked off.

She didn't know if he was pleased with the revelations, or just wondering what the fallout was going to be, but time would tell. The way she looked at it, a second chance at life was a gift, and the wrappings it came in didn't matter.

———

Maggie left the TV turned up on purpose when they sat down to eat, knowing the evening news was about to air.

Sonny glanced at her as he sat down and caught her watching him. He winked.

"No, I don't mind being on the news. I'd rather not be thought of as dead until I am."

She nodded. "Okay then. Just making sure."

They dipped out a spoonful of the chicken pot pie on their plates, added servings of salad, and dug in.

"Magnolia, you are a really good cook. Thank you for this."

"Welcome, honey, oh…they just mentioned your name," and she upped the volume with the remote.

Sonny listened as he ate, but didn't comment. Clearly, they'd garnered their information from someone at the restaurant because the pictures they were showing were of the ones people had taken with them there. They also mentioned his horse training business on a ranch south of Crossroads, and Magnolia Brennen as his fiancée, and ended the piece by rejoicing at his return to the public eye.

"You made the news, too," Sonny said. "But your name is really going to blow up after Max gets your stuff ready to hang."

"Do they always frame pictures for clients?" she asked.

He shrugged. "I don't know. You'll have to ask him, but I'm guessing he's doing it because he's anxious to hang your work. He'll get his cut of a sale. Don't worry about that."

"Anything I get is icing on the cake considering how long they've been stacked up in the spare room."

———

They were getting ready for bed when they heard a coyote howl, and then an answering yip.

Sonny got the rifle and went outside, listening. The yips sounded again, but further off and fading. They were moving away from the ranch, which was fine with him.

He came back inside, put up the rifle, and went back to Maggie.

The only thing she was wearing was the ring he'd put on her finger, and a smile.

"Have mercy," he whispered.

She smiled and patted the bed next to where she was lying.

"Don't mind if I do," he said.

———————

Maggie left for town in the dark. She'd dressed for the day in one of her favorite summer dresses and her pink Ropers, and couldn't wait to get to the Rose and hang the paintings. When she pulled into the back parking lot and saw that the only lights on were in the upstairs apartment, that meant Pearl had yet to come down. She grabbed her purse and the two paintings, and headed for the door. Once inside, she disarmed the security system, then relocked the back door and slipped through the kitchen to the dining area. She already knew exactly where to hang them, and quickly turned on enough light in the dining room to see.

She could hear the water still running in the upstairs shower, so she grabbed the hangers and the little hammer she'd brought with her, and put the first hanger in the center of the east wall, and one on the center of the west wall. Then she hung the paintings and stepped back.

One was tilted a little off center, so she ran to read-just it, and then nodded in satisfaction. It was the first time seeing her work hanging on a wall, and she was a little anxious about how they would be viewed, but that was something she couldn't control.

She heard the water go off and glanced at the time. It was twenty minutes to five. She took a deep breath, turned on all of the downstairs lights, and sat down at a table to wait.

Within minutes, Pearl called out. "Who's downstairs?"

"It's just me, Pearl!" Maggie shouted.

"Then start the coffee, please. I need a cup."

"Yes, ma'am," Maggie said, and put her purse away, tied on an apron before getting to work, all the while listening for the sound of Pearl's footsteps on the stairs. And the minute she heard them, she went back into the dining room to meet her.

Pearl was looking at Maggie when she caught sight of the sunset painting over her shoulder. She gasped, then pointed.

"Where did that come from?"

"From me," Maggie said. "It's a gift for you."

"Well, it's just gorgeous, baby, and I love it. Where did you get such a thing?"

"I painted it, Pearl. It's kinda been my hobby. I always loved to draw, but I didn't start painting until after I moved into your house."

Pearl looked like she was seeing a ghost. "You can do this, and you never said?"

"I didn't think they were any good. I was just doing them for me," Maggie said, and then pointed to the other wall. "I brought you one more."

Pearl turned and started toward the other end of the dining room, with Maggie at her side. By the time Pearl reached the painting, she was crying.

"Sweet baby Jesus, girl. It looks like if I spoke to them, they would turn around and talk." She took a deep breath, and then reached for Maggie's hand. "You made me pretty."

Maggie frowned. "Honey, you are pretty. That's how you look to all of us."

Pearl covered her face and started to weep, slow, quiet tears she'd long ago buried.

Maggie put her arms around her and just held her. "This was the news I was going to tell you about. Sonny found them when he was helping me pack clothes to come stay with him after Walker's attack. He nearly lost his mind. I didn't believe him when he said they were good. He begged me to let him contact an art dealer he knows in Santa Fe, so I did, but told him it was going to be his embarrassment to deal with when they told him no. But it was just the reverse. The art dealer had a bigger fit than Sonny. Long story short, the dealer is

on his way from Santa Fe today. He's coming to catalog them, and take them to his gallery, and have this
big show of my work to introduce me to the art world.
Sonny knows him personally. And this is not a joke.
If all of their carrying on about my paintings is real, I
might be about to get rich and famous."

Pearl wiped her eyes and started smiling, and then
she started to laugh.

"This is the best news I've ever had in my life, and
you know what the first thing I thought of when you
said rich and famous?"

Maggie smiled. "I can't imagine."

"Jerry Lee, one day finding out that the girl he
dumped on the steps of the Yellow Rose Café has gone
and turned herself into a star."

Maggie laughed. "That would kinda chafe his butt,
wouldn't it?"

"All the way to the bone," Pearl said, and then looked
back at the painting again. "I can't get over it. It's almost
like looking at a photograph instead of a painting. You
are so blessed, so very blessed by this gift. Thank you
from the bottom of my heart. Two Brennen originals
hanging on the walls of my little café."

"It's just me, making sure a piece of me is always at
the Rose with you," she said. "Now enough crying. Let's
make biscuits and get this show rolling. The others will
be coming in soon, and I'll have to leave when the dealer
arrives. His name is Max Andros. As soon as all of the
paintings are out of your little house, I promise to clean

it up good for the next renter. Then tomorrow, Sonny and I have to make a flying trip to Silverton to get a marriage license; after that, I'm back on regular schedule with you until I'm not. Are you okay with that?"

"I'll keep you as long as I can, then celebrate your new journey," Pearl said, and headed to the kitchen.

———

Max Andros and his driver landed in Amarillo on the early morning flight, picked up their vans at the rental agency at the airport, then Max sent Sonny a text.

> We're at the airport in Amarillo and just about to head out. See you in an hour or so at the Yellow Rose.

Then he signaled to the other driver to follow, and headed for the exit that would get them to the access road for I-27 south. He was as anxious as a kid at Christmas to meet Magnolia Brennen, and see what she'd amassed in four years of paintings. He'd enlarged the pictures Sonny sent to the point that he could see the brush strokes on the canvas and was still in awe of her work.

He had staff already at the gallery gathering frames from storage, and he would get his framers on the job as soon as they returned. He hadn't had an opening for a new artist in ages, and could not wait to coordinate this event.

Sonny was in the pasture on the John Deere with a big, round bale on the hay spike. He'd already moved the feeder ring a few yards from where it had been so the horses could get to what was left on the ground, and was about to drop the new one into the ring when his phone signaled a text. He dropped in the bale, then stopped to check his phone.

Max Andros was on the ground and headed to Crossroads, which meant he needed to get cleaned up and meet him there. He'd gotten Maggie into this, and he wasn't going to leave her dangling, trying to figure all this out on her own. A short while later, he was on his way into town, and upon arrival, parked at the Rose and headed inside.

Maggie and both of the other waitresses were waiting tables when he walked in. He took off his hat and headed for one of the smaller tables, noting the paintings she'd hung on the wall. Even as he was sitting down, one of the old cowboys in the corner called out, "Hey, Sonny. Did you see what your girl did? She's gonna make us famous."

He grinned. "Well heck, Duroy, I thought you already were."

His answer had them slapping their knees and

agreeing and then they went off into their own little world about the old days on the circuit.

Maggie walked up behind him and kissed the back of his neck. "Hey, good-looking. Want something to drink or are you just waiting for Max?"

"I'm just waiting, darlin', but I'll take a Coke anyway."

She flipped away, with her skirt swinging with the sway of her hips and those pink boots tapping out a rhythm all their own, then came back within moments with his drink.

"Pearl was over the moon. She cried. We cried. We're good," she said. "Gotta pickup. Talk to you later."

So, he sat, watching how deftly she handled fussy patrons, messy children, and fielded the young male diners with their date invitations and marriage proposals. Whatever she said left them laughing. He smiled, knowing all too well how some cowboys worked, proposing to someone at least once a week, and trying to bed the ones who refused.

About a half hour later, Sonny saw two long white vans pulling into the parking lot. He laid some money on the table for his drink, gave Maggie a nod, and pointed outside.

"Be right there," she said, and took off for the kitchen. "Pearl, they're here. I have to go now. I'll see you Wednesday, okay?"

"Very okay. Go meet your future, little girl. So proud of you." Pearl said.

Davey turned around. "Where's she going?" he asked.

"You weren't paying attention this morning, were you?" she asked.

He grinned. "I reckon not."

"We'll talk about it later," Pearl said, and slapped a burger on a bun and began building it.

Maggie traded her apron for her purse, and went back through the dining room and out the front door.

Sonny saw her coming. "There she comes now, Max."

Max Andros turned just as the pretty dark-haired girl exited the Rose. Her hair was flying. Her skirt tail billowing in the breeze, and the smile on her face would have stopped a weaker man's heart.

"Holy shit, Sonny. She's stunning."

"She's also full of sass," he said, then put his arm around her shoulders as she slipped up beside him.

"I probably smell like french fries, but I'm ready to go when you are."

Max blinked, and then burst out laughing and held out his hand. "I'm Max Andros, and I have a feeling we're going to become great friends."

Maggie's gaze was fixed on the stranger's face, and she wasn't smiling.

"Sonny gave you a glowing recommendation. But I can see through a snow job when I hear it, so kindly don't let me down. This is a dream I don't want to end."

"Understood, and duly put on alert," he said. "You two lead the way, and we'll follow, okay?"

Maggie gave Sonny the side-eye. "You did tell him

not to make fun of Pearl's Christmas lights, didn't you?"

Sonny turned. "Max. Don't make fun of Pearl's Christmas lights."

Max looked confused. "I wouldn't dream of it," he said, without knowing what they were even talking about.

"Okay Magnolia, he has been warned," Sonny said.

She nodded, then circled his truck and let herself in.

Sonny saw the bemused look on Max's face. His driver had a similar one.

"She's as real as it gets, so let's do this," he said, then got in his truck, gave Maggie's hand a quick squeeze, then started it up and drove away.

Maggie had the house key in her hands when they got out, and all but danced up the steps and into the house, with the men right behind her.

"This house belongs to Pearl. I've been living here for a little over five years. It's kept me safe, and it's kept me warm, and when I didn't know what to do with my free time, this is what I chose," she said, and led them into the spare bedroom, and stepped back.

Sonny knew she was anxious, but he also saw Max's reaction. She was already in.

"Sweet bird of youth," Max muttered. "I feel like Indiana Jones discovering an unknown treasure. My heart is beating so hard I'm losing my breath. Let me look. Just let me look. We'll start cataloging soon. Is there an order to this?"

"The sunset paintings are all on the west wall because suns set in the west. The paintings of the Rose and the people who stop there are over there. The random ones are inside that closet. The portrait of Sonny is on the easel, under the cloth. I'm going to go sit down in the living room now so you can't see me cry from the joy I am feeling."

Max removed the cloth from the painting of Sonny. He'd seen the picture of it, but it didn't come close to the actual thing.

"Jesus, Sonny… I keep expecting you to talk."

Sonny nodded. "I'm going to go check on Maggie. You look your fill, and then we'll help you catalog and number."

"Are these paintings titled?" he asked.

"Look on the back."

Max found faint writing in pencil. "Excellent," he muttered, and started combing through the sunsets, then the paintings from the Rose, and slowly sorted them into his own system of filing. After that, the four of them began the job. The driver was taking photos with his fancy camera, while Max recorded the number and the title to coordinate with the order in which they would be on the memory card.

Hours passed. Sonny called in a to-go order of brisket sandwiches and cold drinks from Belker's Deli, and Maggie volunteered to pick them up. She needed space to breathe.

When she came back, they paused long enough to

go to the little kitchen to eat. As they sat down, Maggie glanced around the little table.

"In all the years I lived here, this is the first time I've ever had guests at this table, and now it will also be the last." Then she took a drink of her Pepsi, unaware of how much she'd revealed about herself.

"First and last. I am honored to be present," Max said.

As soon as they finished, they went back to work, and two more hours passed, while she sat on the sofa in the quiet of the little house, listening to the three men in the other room until she finally heard Max say, "I think we're done here." At that point, she felt a tug of anxiety again, and then let it go. What would be, would be.

After that, and at Max's direction, they began carrying out certain paintings in groups, and loading them accordingly, until the little room was bare, and there was nothing left but a little dust and the faint scent of acrylic paint lingering in the air.

Maggie watched them driving away, and wondered if this was anything like what a parent would feel, putting their babies on a school bus for the first time, knowing something so precious was now in the care of others.

Sonny walked up beside her, and slipped his hand under her hair and gave her neck a slight squeeze.

"Hard day, honey?"

She made herself smile. "Just tired. Now we wait."

"Now we wait," he said. "Let's go home."

Chapter 24

THE NEXT DAY WAS A WHIRLWIND TRIP TO THE County Courthouse in Silverton. They walked in with their drivers' licenses and social security cards, and walked out with a marriage license.

"This place isn't any bigger than Crossroads," Maggie said.

"No, but it's the county seat of Briscoe County," Sonny said, as he backed away from the curb.

He'd ridden through here on the bus, but he'd never been in the town where Matt Reddick worked before. They got back on the highway and headed home, and as they were driving, Maggie got a text from Max Andros.

Arrived in Santa Fe after midnight. Your precious works are all safe and sound at the gallery under lock and key, with a security guard on night duty. We will be in touch soon.—Max

She looked at Sonny and smiled. "Max letting me know they arrived safe. The paintings are locked up. He has a security guard. He'll be in touch."

"Awesome. You just took another step onto your new path. Now all we have to do is have a wedding and find a builder for our addition."

"Grow old along with me. The best is yet to be, the last of life, for which the first was made," Maggie said, then reached for his hand. "Robert Browning. I've always loved that line, and now it's coming true for us."

———————

The next day Maggie was back at work, and Sonny was overseeing a crew digging footing, and building a frame for the concrete pour that would be the base of the gazebo he had ordered. It was after three the same day before they finished, but it was done, and Sonny had concrete coming from a concrete company out of Tulia, and two locals from Crossroads were coming to work the pour and set the big pins that would anchor the gazebo poles.

After that, it was a matter of waiting a couple more days for the concrete to cure and then hoping the prefab gazebo made its delivery date. After two hectic days, and another two days to wait, the gazebo arrived, bungeed down on a big flatbed trailer, already primed and painted with white, weatherproof paint, and in sections designed to reassemble.

It was the weekend by the time it was all done, but it was perfect. Where there had been no shade under which to rest, now there was.

That evening, he and Maggie watched their first sunset from the built-in benches, and sheltered by the ornate cupola above their heads.

They sat long after the sun was gone and the stars were out, listening to the far-off howl of a coyote, and the screech of an owl on the hunt. The horses knew they were there, and had gathered at the nearby fence to bed down.

Maggie was tired from the day and fell asleep on his shoulder. Reluctant to wake her, he picked her up. She mumbled something, and he shushed her, whispering love words to her she didn't understand as he carried her inside and put her to bed, then went through the house, locking doors and turning out lights before he returned.

She'd awakened long enough to strip, leaving her clothes in the floor right where she'd walked out of them, and was already under the covers.

He heard the words, *All woman and still the child,* and undressed and slipped in beside her. Whatever she was, she was his to love.

He slipped his arm around her waist and closed his eyes.

The ensuing days passed fast, until all of a sudden it was the day before the wedding, and Sonny knew Charlie and the family would be arriving sometime today. He felt like a kid at Christmas, excited about what was yet to come.

Maggie had taken off work today, and for the next five days. She'd cleaned the house so many times Sonny was afraid to dirty a glass for a drink of water, but he understood her need to do her best. His family would be her family, too. Something she'd never had, and she was desperate for them to like her.

It was a little after 2:00 p.m. when Sonny got a text.

We just checked in at the Lodge. Everybody but me is peeing. Again. I will get a turn later. Nobody wants to wait to come see you. Are you ready for this onslaught?

"Maggie, where are you?" he shouted, then heard the screen door on the back porch slam, and she came running.

"I was taking out trash. What's wrong?"

He handed her his phone.

She read the text, laughing. "Tell him yes, and we have food, and a place to pee."

He grinned, and repeated her words in his text, got back a big LOL from Charlie, and then sighed.

Maggie hugged him. "You have so missed them, haven't you?"

He nodded. "If it hadn't been for you, I would have been lost. I predict Julia is going to have a few moments of jealousy."

"Then give her all your attention. I know where I stand with you. Never shortchange the child for the elder."

He nodded. "Your wisdom is far beyond your age."

"I just remember being the little girl wanting someone special to love me. I have a little present for Julia, too. I found it in the dirt they dug up when they were doing the gazebo. I know she likes rocks, because she gave you her special one, so I'll give her one back from the land where her Uncle Sonny lives now."

"Show me," Sonny said.

Maggie went to their bedroom and came back holding a cloth wrapped object. She laid it on their dining table and unwrapped it, revealing a small, oblong piece of rock with the most perfect leaf fossil Sonny had ever seen.

"That is amazing. It has to be thousands of years old, because there are no plants or trees around here anymore with that kind of leaf. Where did you say you found it?"

"In the pile of dirt from where they dug the footing before they poured concrete. I thought of her and put it away so it wouldn't get broken."

Sonny looked at her and smiled. "You always think of others before you do yourself. That is a rare and wonderful trait, Magnolia. She will love it."

Maggie wrapped it back up and then took it back to the bedroom. "I'll wait for the right moment," she said. "I have their paintings framed and waiting, too. I just brought them up from the vault and put them in our closet."

"Say the word, and I'll get them for you when you're ready," he said.

She shrugged. "They don't know any of this painting story."

"Then I will brag on you, and you can answer all their questions, okay?"

Then they both heard a big truck shifting gears and went to the window.

"It's them," Sonny said, and grabbed her hand as they ran out to meet them.

———

Auntie was sitting in the back seat with Julia, taking in all the land that she was seeing, knowing that Sonny's land began somewhere around the two-mile mark from Crossroads, and then it was everything they could see to the west as they drove. Compared to the acres of wooded lands and abundant creeks where she lived, this was closer looking to desert landscape than she'd expected. But a thousand acres of this was a gift. And then they saw the horses. Eight of them running south, their heads up, manes and tails flying, and when she saw the Appaloosa, she grunted. *Warrior horse.*

As Charlie drove beneath the big metal sign over the entrance to the ranch, he could see Sonny had come into his own. A big roping arena, a long building he guessed were the stables, the huge barn attached to an even larger corral—it all left him speechless.

"There they are," Frannie said, pointing to the couple coming out of the house. "Oh, Charlie, look at Sonny's face. He is so happy, and look at that beautiful gazebo. I would love one like that."

"You wanted a chicken house," he said. "A fancy place for sitting outside will have to wait."

And then they were out of the truck, and much hugging and talking ensued, and trying to introduce Maggie to everyone amidst the noise, with little Julia getting lost in the shuffle until Maggie gave Sonny a nudge.

"Somebody's feeling left out," she whispered.

He turned around, saw Julia holding on to her mother's skirt, and let out a whoop.

"There she is! There's my best girl. Don't you hide from me. I've been missing you," he said, and swooped her up in his arms.

Then she was all giggles and hugs, and talking a mile a minute as they all walked into the house.

Auntie was walking behind, and when she got to the porch where Maggie was holding the door open, she looked into Maggie's eyes. "I saw what you did. You have a kind heart, Magnolia. Thank you for including the child."

Maggie was trying to decide whether to laugh or cry when she realized everyone was inside except her. She stepped across the threshold and closed the door, and let the sound of happy voices wash over her.

Charlie was a stockier version of Sonny and wore his hair in two braids. Frannie was beautiful in her pink slacks and pink-and-white shirt. She wore her long hair down and fastened at the back of her neck with an ornate beaded clip.

Auntie's mien and demeanor, and her status as family elder gave her a cachet she didn't really need. She was obviously the matriarch, and had come wearing a loose-fitting denim dress and sandals, hand-beaded earrings, and her thick gray hair in one long braid, hanging down her back.

Julia was wearing pink shorts and a pink-and-white top—a tiny version of her mother.

What Maggie didn't know was how anxious and embarrassed Auntie was feeling, facing the woman who'd been a victim of her brother's actions.

Charlie saw Maggie watching them all. Her sky eyes were sparkling, her lips slightly parted in a smile waiting to happen. When she looked his way, he winked and grinned. "Have we scared you off yet?" he asked.

Sonny looked up, suddenly worried that he'd missed something, but Maggie just shook her head.

"I don't scare easy. Sonny will attest to that. The second time he saw me, I was going after a man with a baseball bat."

The room got quiet, and then Sonny chuckled.

"It's true, and it was the most magnificent thing I'd ever seen. Took a minute for me to figure out that it was the same man who abandoned her nineteen-year-old

433

self on the steps of the Rose six years earlier, and drove off without her. He never imagined she'd still be there, and I'm entering the café and I see this guy on his hands and knees, blood dripping from his mouth and nose, trying to get out of this puddle of water on the floor, but he kept slipping and falling."

Maggie sniffed in disgust. "I didn't bloody his nose or his mouth. He did it to himself when he slipped, but I did dump a pitcher of water on his head and tell him to get out. It was Pearl coming out of the kitchen with her shotgun that scared him. She thought I was being killed. Guess I was screaming a little loud. Sonny already knew the pitiful story, put two and two together, and without saying a word, picked the man up by the back of his jacket and dragged him out of the Rose, and dumped him in the dirt. We saw them exchange a few words, but couldn't hear anything, and then all of a sudden that guy was running for his car. He got in, and then it wouldn't start, and we could see him bawling like a baby while the starter just ground and ground, and then it finally it fired, he took off like a scalded cat."

By now, the whole family was in stitches, laughing at the story, and Sonny was watching their faces and seeing Maggie come alive.

"What happened after?" Frannie asked.

"Oh, Cool Dude over there comes sauntering back in, promises that he's seen enough to never want to make me mad, and then Conrad, our dishwasher, asks Sonny, 'What did you say to him?'"

Maggie looked at Sonny. "You tell them what you said?"

Sonny put his hands over Julia's ears. "I told him if he ever showed his face in Crossroads again, or bothered Magnolia in any way, I would strip him naked and stake him on an ant hill. He took one look at my indigenous self, and seemed to take it seriously. Like I told Maggie… I didn't think people actually believed that. I thought it was something Hollywood made up. Anyway, I made it my business after that to stay on her good side."

"And it worked," Maggie said.

They were still laughing, and she was no longer anxious that they didn't like her. What she didn't know was that, by standing up for herself and for the way Sonny had defended her, they'd already taken her as one of their own.

After that, the food and drinks came out. The women sat at the table to eat and talk, and left the men on the sofa, holding their plates in their laps. And so it went, until Sonny changed the subject.

"I recently found out this woman had been keeping a secret from me, but a very good one. The deal is, Maggie is an amazing artist. She draws. She paints, and she just considered it her hobby. Never talked about it, never showed what she did to anybody, because she didn't want to be made fun of, and I understood why. She's never known her family. She was dumped at a fire station when she was about two weeks old, right honey?"

Maggie nodded. "Somebody threw me away. I don't even know who named me. I don't know squat about my birth other than they didn't want me, and nobody ever came looking. I grew up in foster care and was always in trouble for wasting paper with my drawings. But after I aged out and wound up in Crossroads, I taught myself how to paint what I was drawing. Then Sonny found them all in the spare room when he took me home after...after my abduction, and I thought he was going to pass out. Then I wanted to pass out, taking his silence for disgust."

Sonny laughed. "To the contrary. I begged her to let me send some photos to Max Andros."

"Isn't that the guy who has the bull-riding photos of you on display in his gallery?" Charlie said.

"The same. I sent a bunch of pictures and Max called me, and the rest is history. As of this past Monday, her paintings are at his gallery being framed. He's organizing a big event for her work. She'll be on-site at the opening, and he swears she's going to be famous. He can't talk about her paintings without tearing up."

"That's wonderful," Charlie said. "I wish we could have seen them."

"Maggie, show them the picture you took of the painting you did of me. I'll be right back."

Maggie pulled it up from her phone, then handed it to Charlie. The look on his face went from shock to awe.

He handed it to Auntie, who looked, then stared at it for a long time, and then looked up at Maggie. "You don't just see a face as you paint. You see the soul. This is the gift you were given for all the sadness within you."

Maggie's eyes welled, as a look passed between them.

Frannie took the phone, looked at the painting and then at Maggie.

"You have been given a most remarkable gift. This doesn't look like a painting. It looks like a photo of the real man. Did he sit for this?"

At that moment, Sonny walked in with the paintings. "No, I didn't sit for that," he said. "I didn't even know she'd done it until I saw the whole room full of treasures. And speaking of treasures. One of Maggie's things is watching the sunsets. They're magnificent here. She wanted to give one to Auntie, and one to Charlie and Frances so that you would all see what I see every evening as the sun goes down. That's why I built the gazebo…to watch the sunsets with her, and then the stars with her. Maggie, you do the honors. They're your gifts to give."

She took the first one. It was the one to give to Auntie. "I asked Sonny to pick them out for me, because he knew you all best."

Auntie gasped and then touched the light hovering over the horizon, half expecting it to burn. "You have given me a piece of the sky."

Maggie took the other one and gave it to Charlie and Frances. "It's different, but then all of the sunsets every night are different. Charlie said you would like this best."

Frannie's fingers trembled as she held one side of the frame as Charlie held on to the other.

"This is beautiful," Charlie said. "It will be a great honor to hang this in our house."

Maggie saw the wistful look on Julia's face and knew it was time.

"And you, my little flower girl, I have something different for you, but it is very special. Wait a moment and I'll go get it," she said.

Julia's dark eyes sparkled as she flashed a shy grin. "Something for me, Mama."

"I know," Frannie said.

Maggie came back holding the little cloth-wrapped package, and then she got down on her knees in front of Julia and laid it in her lap, then carefully unwrapped the cloth. "Uncle Sonny told me how much you like rocks, and I found this on his land. Do you know what it is?"

Julia's eyes grew big, as she traced the embedded shape. "Is it a real leaf in the rock?"

Maggie smiled. "It's called a fossil. It is many thousands of years old, and all that's left of the leaf is the imprint of it."

"Like when there were dinosaurs old?" Julia asked.

"Very likely," Maggie said. "See that leaf? Those kinds of trees and bushes don't grow here anymore. It is from the time before."

"It's kind of like an X-ray," Charlie said. "Remember when the doctor took pictures of your arm to see if the bone was broken but it wasn't?"

Julia nodded.

"So, the leaf fell in the mud and when time passed the mud got hard, and the leaf crumbled to dust, this is what was left behind. It's very special, and very valuable, and very old. Are you old enough to take care of something this rare?" Charlie asked.

"Yes, Daddy, I am. I won't play with it, and you can make me a box with a window, so I can see it. And we can hang it on my wall like you hang Maggie's painting."

"We can do that," Charlie said. "Now what do you say to Maggie for such a fine gift?"

Julia wrapped it back up, handed it to her mother for safekeeping, and then threw her arms around Maggie's neck. "Thank you, and I am happy you are going to be Uncle Sonny's wife. That means you will be my Auntie Maggie, won't it?"

"You're so welcome, and yes, I will be your Auntie. Thank you for making me feel welcome," Maggie said.

Julia beamed. She liked Maggie Brennen a lot.

———

They all stayed for the sunset, watching from their seats in the gazebo as the sky turned into a melting pot of color upon color, but it was the sunburst at the last second before it disappeared that made them gasp.

Auntie was stunned. "I have lived my seventy years watching the sun fall below the treetops, but this is the first time I've seen it take its last breath. I will never forget this, and now I have a painting to remember it by. I am ready for bed now, Charlie. I am old, and it has been a long day."

After that, they quickly loaded up with their gifts and were getting into the truck to leave when Maggie spoke.

"Breakfast at the Rose is the best. I have two more paintings hanging there. You might like to see them, too. Come back to the ranch to spend the day. Bring your clothes for the wedding. We'll spend the wedding day together. And if somebody wants to teach me how to make fry bread, I will be eternally grateful. Sonny bemoans the loss of Auntie's fry bread at least every other day."

The old woman beamed, and Frannie smiled. "It would be our pleasure. We'll bring the ingredients when we come."

"Hot damn!" Sonny said. "A belly full of fry bread, and a wife by sundown. My life is perfect."

"And the Appaloosa," Charlie said. "I want to see you ride it bareback with no halter like you did in the video."

"I can do that," Sonny said, and then Sonny and Maggie were standing in the yard, watching as they drove away.

"That couldn't have been any better," Sonny said.

She leaned against him. "I think they like me."

"Magnolia Rae Brennen, they love you and you know it. Now come to bed. I'll be sleeping with a married woman tomorrow night. Gotta make this one last."

She laughed all the way into the house, then happily obliged.

———————

They woke the next morning, rolled over in bed, and looked at each other and smiled.

"This is go-day," Sonny said. "No backing out now."

"As if," she said, kissed him hard, and got up and beat him to the bathroom.

Sonny groaned. "Definitely need another bathroom," he muttered, and lay there waiting his turn. His phone dinged a text. Thinking it was Charlie, he swiped to read it and saw it was from Garrett Dillon, instead.

Roping event at the ranch two weeks from today. The offer is still open for you to do some fancy riding on the Appaloosa. Are you game?

Sonny thought of the TV story mentioning his horse training business, and decided it was the best opportunity to start making connections through the rodeo world again.

Send me directions and a timeline. I'll be there.

A few moments later, he got a thumbs-up.

The water came on in the bathroom. He smiled. "No need wasting water," he said, and threw back the covers.

The family arrived before 10:00 a.m. with two sacks of groceries.

Maggie had dug through her art stuff, pulling out colored pencils and drawing paper, and had cleared off the coffee table in the living room, making a play area for Julia, and the moment they came through the door, it was the first thing Julia saw.

She stopped, her eyes wide with expectation. "Auntie Maggie, is that for me?"

Maggie grinned. "Why yes, it is. How smart of you to know that. Make me a pretty picture. I will hang it on the refrigerator for everyone to see."

"Make me one, too," Sonny said. "I need to hang one in the barn for the horses to see."

Frannie was unloading groceries at the counter. "Thank you for thinking of her, Maggie, but I warn you, you might have created your own little monster. She will use up every piece of paper in the house."

Maggie immediately flashed on being in trouble for wasting paper, and shook her head. "Then I will find her some more," she said, and the day began.

Sonny and Charlie left the house together, while the women settled in for coffee and a chat, leaving Julia to create. But it wasn't long before Charlie came back.

"Sonny said he'll ride the Appaloosa for me now, before the day gets too hot. Who wants to watch the show with me?"

"We all do," Auntie said.

"Then follow me," Charlie said, and pointed at Julia. "You, too, short stuff. Wanna see Uncle Sonny ride the pretty horse?"

She nodded and ran to hold his hand.

They were walking toward the arena when they heard a shrill whistle, and then a second, and then soon, the sound of running horses. Watching those big animals crowding around Sonny for attention was one thing, but seeing them follow him like puppies was eye-opening.

"He wasn't always like this," Charlie said. "When did this happen?"

Maggie shrugged. "Maybe after he survived. That's when the visions came. Maybe this came with it."

They all looked at Maggie, and then at each other. She knew his secrets, which meant he trusted her with his life. Then they headed for the arena. As soon as they settled on the seats, Sonny came walking in with Dancer beside him. They saw Sonny speaking to the horse, and then gave him a thump on the rear, and the moment Dancer started to move, Sonny grabbed a handful of mane and swung up on the run.

Maggie heard Auntie's quick intake of breath, and then her eyes never left the man and the horse. Sonny let Dancer run free as he circled the arena at a full gallop, and then turned him one way, and then another, and backed him up, and then at the last when Dancer was flying, Sonny turned loose of the mane, threw his arms out to the wind. His head was back, his eyes were closed, and man and horse had become one.

Dancer skidded to a stop on his own. Sonny threw his leg over and slid off, then hugged the horse before walking him to the rails.

"Everyone, this is Fancy Dancer, but you can call him Dancer. He loves apple treats and me. Now who wants to give him his treat for such a good show?"

Auntie stood. "I want to honor the warrior horse," she said, and held out her hand. Sonny laid the little biscuit treat in her palm as she leaned over the rail.

Dancer snorted, then sniffed, then picked up the treat with those soft, velvety lips. Sonny heard his Auntie speaking to the horse and said nothing. The message was personal, between her and the horse. She'd called him warrior horse in the language of their people, and the walk back to the house was silent as they all absorbed the man Sonny had become.

When he came back inside shortly after and saw the women elbow deep in flour, he let out a whoop. "Fry bread is happening."

Maggie laughed. "See, I told you. He's been having withdrawals. Don't worry, Sonny. I am going to be proficient in this before the day is over."

"Go sit down," Auntie told him. "Men get in the way."

They all laughed, especially Sonny. Men knew where they stood in the family, and they knew where they stood in the kitchen, and rarely did the two ever meet.

As soon as they began to take fry bread out of the

deep fryer and put it on the racks to cool, Auntie made the announcement.

"Maggie gets the first piece. She helped make them and she's never had it before. We have Maggie's beef vegetable soup to eat with it, but the first taste ever needs to be sweet to get the full effect. We eat it plain with butter or a dusting of powdered sugar, or a little jelly or a drizzle of honey. Maggie picks."

"Butter and honey," Maggie said.

"Let me make it for you, baby," Sonny said, and grabbed a little plate, made it like he would like it, and handed it to her. "Fingers only. Expect it to be messy. Licking fingers afterward will work."

She took the plate, picked up the fry bread, and took a bite. The crunch of the outer layer, the buttery, sweet topping, and the soft interior as she chewed.

"Ohmygod," she mumbled, talking around the bite she was chewing and rolling her eyes in ecstasy.

"I think she likes it," Sonny said. "Do you like it, Magnolia?"

She nodded as she swallowed. "I could eat this every day for the rest of my life and waddle into old age."

Once again, laughter filled the house and as it did, Maggie kept thinking, *If only Emmit could see this…his house…alive with laughter.*

They ate fry bread with the sweet stuff, and with the pot of beef vegetable soup Maggie had made special for their visit, and then once the kitchen was cleaned, they sent Auntie and Julia to their bedroom for a much-needed rest, while the brothers and their women took over the sofa and the recliners in the living room and continued the visit.

When suppertime came, they made Indian tacos out of the leftover fry bread, but Maggie was too excited to eat. All she could think about was saying "I do" at sunset, and becoming Sonny's wife.

———————

It had taken some doing with one bathroom and one bedroom for privacy, but by 7:00 p.m. the whole wedding party was dressed and sitting in the living room. Julia was wearing her dress from the daddy-daughter dance—a lacey yellow party dress that fell just below her knees and with a big yellow bow at the back of her hair.

Then Pearl arrived, all decked out in a short-sleeved blue sheath, with her silver-gray hair shining, carrying two bouquets of flowers and a little basket of dried sage leaves. And the smile on her face as Sonny introduced her as Maggie's stand-in Mama was electric.

"Where's Maggie?" Pearl asked.

"Getting dressed," Sonny said. "Why don't you go through to the bedroom. She might like a little motherly help," and he pointed the way.

Pearl had never been in Emmit's house, and was surprised by the modern appliances and the way he'd remodeled it. She knocked on the bedroom door. "Maggie, it's me. Can I come in?"

Maggie opened the door. Her eyes were a little teary. "What's wrong, honey?" Pearl asked.

"Absolutely nothing, and you just fixed it. Every bride I've ever known has had a mother or a grandmother, or a best friend to help her dress, and here I was, with everything wonderful happening and still feeling the stigma of the throwaway baby. Will you zip me up?"

"I'd be honored," Pearl said. "And just so you know, Sonny is the one who suggested you might need me. He sees all. Knows all. You'll never be able to keep a secret from him. Not that you'd want to," she added.

By that time, she had Maggie smiling again and wiping away tears. "You look so beautiful, and those boots! Girl! When you go to that first art event, you better be wearing them."

"Yes, ma'am," Maggie said, and then they were ready.

"Who's walking you down the aisle?" Pearl asked.

"We're walking down the aisle together. Charlie is Sonny's best man. Julia is our little flower girl. You're my matron of honor, and Frannie and Auntie are the audience."

Sonny's phone signaled a text. "Preacher is in Crossroads, heading this way now," he said. "As Charlie would say, if anybody needs to pee again before the ceremony starts, now's your chance."

Julia raised her hand, and Auntie stood up and went with her. They knocked on the bedroom door and Pearl opened it.

"We need to use the bathroom, please," Julia said.

Maggie was standing behind the open door of the closet so they couldn't see her, and as soon as they left, Pearl went with them. Maggie knew when they left the house for the gazebo, Sonny would let her know.

Wes Dugan arrived in a cloud of dust. The photographer he'd brought with him quickly began setting up. The sun was already preparing for its final curtain, ablaze in all shades of yellow and orange.

"Wes, I'm ready when you are, and we're losing light."

Wes sent Sonny a text. "We're set up and ready. Seat the audience, then start the procession."

Sonny got the text.

"It's go time, people. Charlie, you walk your ladies to the gazebo and get them seated, then wait with the preacher. Pearl will come next, and then Julia will be last, right before us. Are you ready, girl?" he asked.

Julia was big-eyed and smiling with her little basket of dried sage leaves ready to scatter.

And so it began, as the first three left the house and stepped onto the paver walkway leading to the gazebo. Auntie and Frannie took their seats, Charlie moved next to the preacher, as Pearl came toward the gazebo carrying a small bouquet of white daisies.

Julia was a few steps behind her, diligently scattering sage leaves for the bride and groom to walk on. They walked into the gazebo and took their places. And then they all turned toward the house, watching for the bride and groom.

The moment Julia was out the door, Sonny grabbed the last bouquet from the kitchen table and headed for the bedroom, opened the door, and then froze.

"My beautiful bride, everything about you is perfect. You walk in light," and he handed her the bouquet as she came toward him. Her eyes were shiny with unshed tears, but she was smiling as he handed her the flowers.

"Magnolias!" she said.

"Pearl brought them. I thought you knew."

"I just told her white flowers," Maggie said.

Maggie clutched them to her waist and took his hand. They walked out of the house into the glow of evening. She glanced at the western horizon and knew one day she would paint that sunset and call it *The Beginning*. It was the end of a day, but the beginning of their lives.

The walk to the gazebo felt like a dream. Sonny in his dark starched Wranglers, and a snow-white shirt. The turquoise setting in his bolo tie at the collar. His hair hanging loose and long down his back, and as black as Dancer's mane. Then standing before the preacher, saying the words as the sky exploded behind him. And then the words that now bound them as legally as they were already bound by love.

"I now pronounce you husband and wife. Sonny Bluejacket, you may kiss your bride."

Sonny turned, cupped her face in his hands and

kissed her, then they turned to the west. The sound of drumming and the singing that had been with him during the day was fading with the sun.

The security lights were already on, and the motion detector lights at the gazebo lit up when they began moving back to the house. The marriage certificate was signed in their kitchen while the photographer was loading up his gear.

And after all the details were finished and the preacher paid and gone, out came the little wedding cake and more celebration, until it was time for goodbyes.

Pearl left first, promising to let them know when she got home.

Charlie's hug with his brother was a little tighter, a little longer, because they didn't know when they might see each other again.

Frannie had Maggie's number and email as they hugged goodbye, promising to stay in touch.

Maggie hadn't been hugged this much in one day in her entire life, and she loved it. And when she told Auntie goodbye, she whispered in her ear.

"Every time I make fry bread, I will feel you with me."

"And you with me," the old woman said.

Julia was asleep and still wearing her party dress when Charlie carried her to the truck, and then they were gone.

After all the energy of the day, it felt like the house had just exhaled.

"Say my name," Sonny said.

Maggie's heart skipped. She remembered this from her naming day. "Sonny Bluejacket."

"Now say your name," he said.

"Magnolia Bluejacket."

"Who do I love?" he asked.

"You love me…Magnolia Bluejacket."

"And who do you love?" he asked.

"I love Sonny Bluejacket."

He nodded with satisfaction. "Now you know who you are. Tonight, I make love with my wife," and held out his hand.

Epilogue

THE BLEACHER SEATING AT GARRETT DILLON'S roping arena was packed. The noise in the crowd was at its usual rumble as they waited for the next round of events.

And then the announcer's voice…speaking the name of a man they once thought dead. Shouting with excitement as he walked into the arena alone and then watched as he turned and whistled.

Within seconds, a big black-and-white Appaloosa came running, heading straight for Sonny as the announcer was shouting another name above the roar of the crowd. "Ladies and gentlemen…Fancy Dancer!"

And as Dancer ran past, Sonny grabbed on to his mane and in two long steps, swung himself up onto the back of the horse and let him run.

No saddle. No bridle. Not even a rope around his neck.

The crowd went wild, watching Sonny as he put him through the paces of a show horse, letting him run like the wind with nothing but the pressure of his knees or the touch of his boots, staying seated with only the strength of his own legs and the beautiful balance between horse and man.

And then Sonny rode him to a sliding halt into the middle of the arena and swung his leg over the side and slid off. He took a bow, and then stood there while Dancer nosed every pocket Sonny had. Finally, Sonny pulled out the apple treat in front of the crowd, held it up for them to see, and then gave it to Dancer, waved at the crowd again, and walked out of the arena with Dancer right beside him.

Sonny thought it was over until he walked into a wall of reporters and photographers and realized Garrett Dillion had really hyped up his appearance.

He posed with Dancer for pictures and answered questions until he and the horse had both had enough, and ended it.

"Dancer is ready to go home, and so am I. Been good visiting with you," he said.

"Are you going to take him on the circuit?" a reporter asked.

"No, Dancer likes to run, but he doesn't like to ride. I train horses now. Thanks for coming."

And he slipped a rope around Dancer's neck as they left the arena, then loaded him up and drove away.

But it was the advertisement he'd needed. Within days, he was getting calls, wanting him to train horses, or wanting to know what he had to sell, and as the work came in, so did his need for help, but it had to be people he could trust. So, he gave his request to the ancestors, and let it go.

Then one day while Maggie was at work, he had a vision. He saw a cowboy filling up his truck with gas at the station at Crossroads, and saw him paying with cash inside the store, and looking to see if there was enough money to buy a cold drink and a snack, then putting the wallet back in his pocket. Then he saw Maggie pull into the station and park at the pump on the other side of the man's truck, and the vision faded.

Sonny immediately called Maggie, and she answered just as fast.

"Hi, honey. I'm just about to gas up and head home."

"Is there a thirty-something cowboy parked beside you? Driving an old green truck?"

"Yes, why?"

"He needs a job. Tell him I've got one for him."

"What…wait…what if he doesn't…"

"Then hand him your phone. Tell him your husband wants to talk to him. Hurry."

Maggie sighed, then turned around and spoke. "Excuse me, but my husband is on the phone and wants to talk to you about a job."

The man blinked. "Say what?"

Maggie laughed. "I know…and I live with him. Just talk to him please," and handed him her phone.

"Hello? This is Chris Jackson. I think you have the wrong—"

"Hello, Chris. My name is Sonny Bluejacket. That woman you were talking to is my wife. I'm told you cowboy up. Do you want a job? I need a hired hand."

"THE Sonny Bluejacket…bull-rider Bluejacket?"

"Yes. Our place is only three miles south of Crossroads. If you are interested, follow Maggie home. But be polite. I put the last man who laid his hands on her in a hospital. He is residing in a Texas state prison as we speak."

Chris turned and stared at Maggie. "Is he for real?"

"Just as real as the Yellow Rose where I work."

He handed back her phone. "Tell him yes I will follow you home, and yes, I am interested in a job but I don't have the money to pay rent, and if that's a deal-breaker then that's where we stand."

Maggie's eyes widened, as she put the phone to her ear. "Did you hear what he said?"

Sonny chuckled. "Every word. Tell him we'll figure it out. Just come talk to me. See you soon."

Maggie put the phone in her pocket. "Mr. Jackson, if you'll give me a few minutes to refuel, then we'll be heading home."

"Yes, ma'am," Chris said, and got in his truck in disbelief. This couldn't be happening, and yet it was. If ever there was a time to believe in angels, this might be it. A few minutes later, he was following the pretty woman out of town, and when she took a turn off the road and drove under the big metal sign that said Sunset Ranch, he followed.

It wasn't until he saw the big man standing in the front yard that he knew this was really happening. He knew that man's face by heart. He'd watched him ride, and he thought he'd watched him die.

Clearly, he'd been mistaken.

And that's how Sonny got his first hired hand.

Now Chris Jackson was living in Pearl's rent house under orders not to tear shit up, and working the ranch with Sonny every day.

———

Four months after Max Andros left Crossroads with the Magnolia Brennen collection, he had a date set for the opening show, advertising in every art venue that mattered, and a suite reserved at one of the best hotels in town. Maggie would work and sell under her maiden name.

The renovations were finished at the ranch, and Maggie had moved into her studio and given notice at the Rose. She was preparing herself for a whole new world, and gone shopping twice in Amarillo for clothes in the styles Max suggested for the events, and brown embroidered boots like the white ones she'd been married in. She was as ready as she was ever going to be to do this.

Sonny took her to the Amarillo airport and told her to trust Max to take care of her, and he'd fly out for the opening, to be with her.

"This moment, Magnolia, is where you spread your wings. Max will be waiting for you at the place where you will collect your luggage. You will know how to get there by following the signs and by asking for help. And if he's not there in person, he will have sent someone special who will be holding up a sign with your name on it."

She blinked. "Just like in the movies?"

He hugged her. "Yes, darlin', just like in the movies. The flight is short. Less than an hour. You'll be there before you know it. Happy first flight. Within a year, you're going to be a pro."

He kissed her soundly and kept the smile on his face until she disappeared beyond the security checkpoint, and then groaned beneath his breath and left the terminal.

"I expect you guys to have her back," he muttered, then got in the truck and drove away.

Maggie spent the next two days in a whirlwind. An on-air interview at a local television station. Photos for publicity packets. Lunches with reporters, and always with Max at her side. She longed for Sonny, but this was her world to conquer, just as he'd conquered the rodeo world.

Maggie woke up with a text from Sonny.

Arriving in Santa Fe around 4:00 p.m. Going straight to the hotel. Be sure to let them know I'm coming so they'll let me in your room. Can't wait to see you. I miss your face. Love you forever.—Sonny

She started typing a reply.

> I've coped without you for too long. Missed you
> more. I have all my fancy duds ready for tonight,
> but I can't wait for you to take them off after it's
> over.

She hit Send, then threw back the covers and went to take a shower. Max was sending a car for her at 10:00 a.m. She was getting a full spa treatment today. Sauna. Massage. Hair and nails, and none of this had yet to feel real.

She had rolled her eyes at Max yesterday, when he told her what was next on the agenda, then shook her head and shrugged.

"Max, honey, I'll go, but I'm just warning you, no amount of hot oil and seasonings are going to turn a pork chop into a steak."

He frowned. "Magnolia, I have no idea what you're talking about."

"Just that there's not enough hairspray or nail polish to change who I am. I don't play games with snobs or leeches, and I will not kiss up to anyone."

He laughed. "Oh, we all already know that, dear. That's part of your charm. The pretty part is for me wanting you to be admired. I don't want to change a hair on your head, but a little spritz won't hurt."

She nodded. "But we're doing all this for you, not for me."

"Deal," he said.

And that deal was why Maggie was about to have breakfast in bed. She was peopled out and saving herself for tonight. Maybe time at a spa was a good idea after all. No talking required there, either.

Lord. Sonny couldn't get here too soon.

———————

Sonny boarded his flight carrying a garment bag and a carry-on, wearing Wranglers, a blue long-sleeved shirt, his best boots, and a new gray Stetson. His hair was tied back at the nape of his neck, and when he boarded the flight, every eye was on him. He stopped in first class to stow his stuff, then sat down. Folding himself up in coach wasn't happening. Then he ignored the looks of the boarding passengers and set his hat in his lap.

And of course, someone recognized him and then the hour-long flight became a circus.

By the time they landed, and he got to the hotel, he'd lost his desire to smile. But the moment he got inside Maggie's suite, and saw her things, and smelled her perfume, and the hairbrush she used when she brushed and braided his hair, he began to relax.

And then he found her note.

We're having room service snacks in the room before we leave for the gallery, and dinner afterward with Max. I'm exhausted. I'm all smiled out. I miss you so much. This is hard, but I am also learning to be proud of what I can do, and I have you to thank for all of this. Without your belief in me, I would still be serving chicken-fries at the Rose. See you soon. Love you more.

She hadn't signed her name, but she'd drawn a little flower. It took him a second to realize it was a magnolia. She had signed it after all.

He hung up his dress clothes, laid his hat on the table, and kicked off his boots before stretching out on the bed. He was excited for her. Anxious for people to love her. He already knew they would appreciate her skill. But he wished so much for her to feel the emotions of their delight.

And then he heard a click at the door and knew someone had just swiped their key card. That someone had to be her. He bolted toward the door just as she walked in.

"Now I can breathe," he said, and kissed her, then kept kissing her—on her neck, on her chin, the tip of her nose, until she was laughing.

"These were the hardest three days of my life without you," she said.

"Come sit, baby. You look beautiful, by the way. Where have you been?"

She sat and kicked off her shoes. "At a spa. Max's request. Sauna. Massage. Facial. Hair and nails. I did it because he said I had to."

"But now you are rested and relaxed and you will enjoy tonight. I will make sure of it. Consider me your bodyguard."

"I want you there as my husband. The beautiful man from the painting, which, by the way, is the first thing you see when you enter the gallery. Prepare yourself."

"I'm still trying to get over the flight out," he said. "They had me cornered. I had no place to hide."

She laughed. "Well, we'll soon be back to the ranch and our real lives, so I guess enjoy it while we can."

Then there was a knock at the door. "That will be room service."

"I'll get it," Sonny said.

The man wheeled a food-laden cart into the room, then set the food trays out. Maggie signed the ticket, added a tip, and then he was gone.

"I haven't eaten since breakfast," Maggie said, and popped a cold shrimp in her mouth.

"What time does the event begin?" Sonny asked.

"At 7:00 and ends at 9:00 p.m., but he said sometimes it goes over. He's sending a limo to pick us up at 7:00, after which we will make a late grand entrance after patrons are already there. At least that's his plan. Lord, I hope all of this works. He's invested so much time and money."

"I wouldn't worry about Max. He knows what he's doing, and he has people who will come to make up the numbers if he's worried. Kind of like baiting prospective buyers. If they think others want something, then they want it first."

She frowned. "How do you know all this?"

He shrugged. "Lots of personal appearances and signing poster events."

She smiled. "In a way, I am following in your footsteps. I like knowing that."

He laughed. "Darlin', you are already so far out of my realm, and you don't even know it, but I have a feeling you will before this night is over."

They grazed through the appetizers, talking as they ate, with an eye on the time they needed to get dressed.

Maggie glanced at the time, then made herself get up and went to wash up.

Sonny put the trays back on the cart and pushed it out into the hall. As soon as Maggie came out and started to get dressed, he confiscated the bathroom.

They were ready and waiting when Maggie got a text that their driver was waiting downstairs. Sonny grabbed his hat and pocketed the key card, and they headed to the elevator.

"It's ninety degrees outside and I'm wearing denim and suede. I hope Max is happy," Maggie said.

"But you look stunning, and you do realize he's dressed you to fit the theme of your work and the Santa Fe vibe."

They crossed the lobby and were soon in the limo and on their way to the Andros Gallery.

Everything Max had hoped for was happening so fast that even he couldn't believe it. The oohs and aahs, the gasps, the tears, and SOLD tags already going up on the frames was surprising even him. But it was the crowd standing around Sonny's portrait that had congested the flow of people coming in. She had named the portrait *Bluejacket,* and they couldn't get enough.

The myriad choices of sunsets and the varied colors of the sky were viewer favorites, until they came to the room called Diners at the Yellow Rose. That's where the gasps of disbelief began. Pointing out the tears on a little girl's face. The ketchup on a little boy's shirt and chin. Sad people. Happy people. People you could tell were there—in that place—in that moment—because they had nowhere else to go.

And then there was a flurry at the door.

Max turned. They were here! His heart thumped as they walked in. The first thought that went through his head was Western Royalty. Lord in heaven, what a couple they made. Bluejacket from the painting, alive and walking inside, and Magnolia Brennen—the young beauty who painted humanity into every face she put on canvas.

Max saw the crowd parting like Moses parting the Red Sea as they headed toward him. He opened his arms in a dramatic fashion.

"Magnolia! It's time to be introduced to the world. Sonny! I'm so glad you could be here for her!"

"Wouldn't be anywhere else," Sonny said.

Max moved them to the portrait. "You two stand here. I'll be on the other side."

The media on-site were already taking pictures, and two photographers from local TV stations were there with video cams.

Max picked up a mic, tapped it to see if it was live, and then cleared his throat.

"Welcome to all of you. It is a thrill to be introducing this amazing new artist to the world. And I must confess that never in my lifetime did I believe raw talent at this level of perfection existed until I saw it for myself. And it happened because this man, Sonny Bluejacket, rodeo royalty in his own right, believed in the woman he loved, and he knew of me and my gallery. When he first saw her work, he begged her to let him show them to me. Magnolia isn't fond of the limelight, but she has graciously agreed to let me have my moment in the sun. Tonight, I am honored to share her and her talent with all of you. Miss Brennen, could you tell us what this night means to you?"

Maggie glanced at Sonny, felt his hand touch her back for assurance, then clasped the mic and took a breath.

"It means many things, but most of all, it means I am no longer hiding. I no longer care that I don't know where I came from, or know the names of the people who threw me away. These paintings are me pouring out my heart in a way I could never voice. I didn't think they would ever matter because I didn't think I mattered."

Sonny heard a muffled sob from somewhere in the crowd and knew she had them. She'd revealed her soul and they'd seen past the beauty of her face to her God-given gift of capturing priceless moments that would otherwise have been lost in time.

Maggie continued. "This man beside me is my husband. His name is Sonny Bluejacket, the man of the beautiful face in this portrait, and I will say, he has a heart to match. He has given me the courage to face rejection or success with the same level of belief in myself. We first met at the Yellow Rose. It's where I was abandoned for a second time by a good-for-nothing boyfriend. The white-haired woman in those paintings is a real woman named Pearl. Pearl picked me up off the steps of the Rose and gave me a job, and a place to live. She became the mother I never had. And every evening when the sun began going down, I would go out onto the front steps of the Rose, and watch the magic and beauty of the sunsets, and tell myself that it was God's apology for every bad, sad thing I'd ever endured."

Half the room was now in tears, including Max.

"Nobody knew that when I went home every evening, I painted. Nobody...until Sonny Bluejacket came into my life. A man of the rodeo world. A star. With championship buckles for bull riding, until the night one stomped him into the ground. He died twice that night, but he says the ancestors weren't through with him. Knowing a man who refused to quit was my blessing. That he promised to never quit me, was all it took. And so, here we are. I am honored you have come to see my work, and Sonny and I are most honored to meet you."

She handed the mic back to Max, and reporters swarmed, shouting questions at them from every direction until Max called a halt. "Please. She's said what she felt needed saying, so enjoy the exhibits. Magnolia and Sonny will be moving among the rooms. Feel free to visit."

———

Max had been right. Closing at nine became a joke. And the longer they were there, the more SOLD stickers went up on paintings. Maggie had seen the prices he put on them and was immediately certain it would be a deterrent. She'd been wrong. And the NOT FOR SALE sticker on the Bluejacket portrait elicited many a groan. She couldn't begin to imagine the financial boon this was making in her life.

And the best part for Max were the dozens and dozens of other paintings yet to be framed and hung. Selling tonight was only going to make space for the others in the weeks to come. And once Magnolia's beautiful face and tragic story hit the late-night news, there would be even more art lovers wanting in on the ground floor to collect this brilliant new artist's work.

When the last buyer was escorted out the door, Max threw his arms around Maggie and shouted.

"You did it, girl! You did it. I did so turn your pork chop into a steak."

She laughed, and then saw Sonny's frown. "It was just me being negative. I'll explain it later."

"I'm done," Max said. "Night security is already on duty and we're turning out the lights and locking up. I'm starving, and there's food awaiting at my penthouse and my driver is outside. Let's eat, Cinderella. I can still get you and the prince home before midnight."

And he did.

———

Long after they were back in their hotel, and way after the afterglow of making love had come and gone, Maggie was asleep in Sonny's arms.

But he wasn't sleeping. He was locked into a vision that wouldn't let him go, watching Walker Bluejacket's death.

He didn't know when it would happen, but he knew it would be out in the rec yard, in the bright light of day, because he could see it. The killer, surrounded by a gang of inmates, stabbing him over and over without a sound being uttered. It was only after the inmates were being moved back into the prison that his body was found on the ground, with a river of blood pooling beneath him. Then the voice in Sonny's ear.

It is done.

In the vision, he had no feeling of remorse for the end of life.

Someone from the prison would call Charlie since he was listed as next of kin. Charlie would call him, and then Walker Bluejacket's name would be spoken no more.

Maggie jerked in her sleep.

He pulled her closer.

Held her tighter.

And felt lighter, as if a terrible burden had been lifted from his heart.

Like the ancestors said.

It is done.

About the Author

New York Times and *USA Today* bestselling author Sharon Sala has 145+ books in print, published in eight different genres—romance, young adult, Western, general fiction, mystery, women's fiction, children's books, and nonfiction. First published in 1991, her industry awards include the Janet Dailey Award, five-time Career Achievement winner, five-time winner of the National Readers' Choice Award, five-time winner of the Colorado Romance Writers' Award of Excellence, the Heart of Excellence award, the Booksellers Best Award, the Nora Roberts Lifetime Achievement Award, the Will Rogers Gold Medallion, and the Centennial Award in recognition of her 100th published novel. She lives in Oklahoma, the state where she was born.

Website: sharonsalaauthor.com
Facebook: sharonsala
Instagram: @sharonkaysala_

WELCOME TO JUBILEE, KENTUCKY

Riveting and pulse-pounding small town romantic suspense
New York Times bestselling author Sharon Sala

Don't Back Down

Army veteran Cameron Pope arrives back in Jubilee, Kentucky, for the first time in years when he becomes embroiled in a deadly hunt for the human traffickers who are destroying the peace of his mountain town. When he's reunited with Rusty Caldwell—a woman from his past he's never stopped thinking about—he wants to believe they can finally be together. Cameron and Rusty will have to find a way to end the feuding between the locals and take down the human trafficking ring if they're to have any chance at happiness.

Last Rites

Eldest brother Aaron Pope returns to his life as a police officer, and is settling in just fine. Then Aaron's investigation into an attempted murder leads him right to Dani Owens. She may hold the key to a long-lost part of the Pope family's past, and more importantly, she may hold the key to Aaron's heart.

Heartbeat

Amalie Lincoln moved to Jubilee, Kentucky, to start fresh, build her business, and heal the scars of her past. Little did she know she'd run into Sean Pope, a beloved childhood friend she hasn't seen in decades. On the day she moves to town, a helicopter explodes under suspicious circumstances, wreaking havoc on the families of Pope Mountain. But as the investigators uncover the truth and the crooks behind the attack set Amalie in their sights, Sean must face the danger or risk losing Amalie forever.

Left Behind

Jubilee PD Officer Wiley Pope thinks he's ruined things with Linette Elgin. But when Wiley walks in on a bank robbery with Linette as one of the hostages, his training and protective instincts kick into full gear. As he and Linette begin anew, Wiley finds himself in over his head with a murder investigation linked to Pope Mountain and an attempted money scheme that results in a seven-year-old girl abandoned at the police station. But the minute the woman signs over her parental rights, Wiley and Linette welcome the wary little girl into their family and show her what real love looks like.

Bad Seed

It's love at first sight when head pastry chef Brendan Pope meets private investigator Harley Banks at the Serenity Inn in Jubilee, KY. Harley is staying there for her latest investigation. But unknown to them both, Harley has a hit man after her, courtesy of the wrong-doer she put behind bars on her last case. The FBI gets involved to clean up the loose ends so Harley can continue the investigation at the inn. But after nearly losing her, Brendan will stop at nothing to make sure Harley is safe and the criminals get their comeuppance.

For more info about Sourcebooks's books and authors, visit:
sourcebooks.com

Also by Sharon Sala